ACADEMY ARCANIST

ASTRA ACADEMY BOOK I

SHAMI STOVALL

Contents

Published by
CS BOOKS, LLC

ACADEMY ARCANIST
Copyright © 2022 Capital Station Books
All rights reserved.
https://sastovallauthor.com/

Cover Design: Darko Paganus

Editors: Amy McNulty, Nia Quinn, Justin Barnett

IF YOU WANT TO BE NOTIFIED WHEN SHAMI STOVALL'S NEXT BOOK RELEASES, PLEASE VISIT HER WEBSITE OR CONTACT HER DIRECTLY AT

s.adelle.s@gmail.com

ISBN: 978-1-957613-16-1

To John, my soulmate.
To Justin Barnett, who is way too good to me and helped so much.
To Gail and Big John, my surrogate parents.
To Henry Copeland, for the beautiful leather map and book covers.
To Mary, Emily, James, Ryan & Dana, for all the jokes and input.
To my patrons over on Patreon, for naming the Academy.
To my Facebook group, for all the memes.
And finally, to everyone unnamed, thank you for everything.

CHAPTER 1

IN MY DREAMS

"I don't want to sleep," I said. "The monsters will return. They'll…"

My father lingered by the door, half inside my bedroom and half in the hall. He turned down the light of my oil lamp, though he didn't snuff it out. The shadows in the corners of my room grew darker. I dared not stare at them.

"The monsters aren't real, boy." My father offered a gentle smile. "Those were just nightmares. Everyone has them occasionally."

I sat on the edge of my bed, my posture stiff as I tried to act twice my age. With my throat tight, I lifted my left arm. An injury ran from the crux of my elbow all the way to the edge of my palm, scabbed over and red. It was a straight and shallow cut, but it stung worse than a normal wound.

"The monsters are real," I said, defiant. "I told you—they attacked me."

"*Gray*, we talked about this," my father said, sighing.

His shoulders sagged and his eyes were heavy lidded. He *looked* tired. Probably because he was. Every day, he worked from sunup until sundown, mixing waxes and perfecting wicks. He was our island's only tallow chandler—a person who made candles with oil, wax, and animal fat.

My father wore an apron marked with his profession, stained by the hot wax. He rubbed his blistered hands down his sides, no doubt trying to think of what to say. I already knew what he would eventually settle on.

He would say, *"You just fell out of bed."*

"You just fell out of bed," my father muttered.

And then he would say, *"I know your arm hurts, but it was an accident. Just go to sleep."*

"I know your arm hurts." My father half closed the door as he spoke. "But it was an accident. Just go to sleep."

All those long hours working meant my father didn't like dealing with problems. He was rather predictable. His most common advice was to just ignore my problems. *"They'll go away eventually,"* he often muttered. *"Keep your head down and do your work."*

That was easier for him, I supposed.

And although I knew he cared about me and my brother, I sometimes feared he didn't listen. The monsters in my dreams? They were real. One had attacked me, and if I hadn't woken up, it would've ripped me apart.

"I didn't fall out of bed," I said.

"Gray. Please. It's late."

Two nights ago, when the monsters had attacked, I had awoken wrapped in blankets stained with smears of my blood. That was when I had panicked and shouted, stumbling toward the door, unable to free myself from the bedding.

My stepmother had rushed into my bedroom. She had calmed me down by spinning a tale of how I must've fallen off my mattress and cut myself on the corner of the nightstand. Now my father wouldn't believe anything I told him. He repeated the same things over and over again, claiming it had all been in my mind.

Again, I knew why. It was easier to think that my fears were just childish imaginings.

"What if it's a mystical creature attacking me?" I whispered.

My father crossed his arms and then propped them up on the top of his protruding gut. His arms were muscular, but the rest of his body hadn't kept up. He resembled a pear, and his stomach hung so far out it sometimes looked as though he were hiding a second person under his massive apron.

"The only mystical creatures who live on our island are hippogriffs and a couple of unicorns," my father said matter-of-factly. "They don't have the types of magic to peek into your dreams. You need to stop making up tall tales, Gray. It's embarrassing for a boy your age."

I glared at the floor, uncertain of what to say to him.

The world was filled with all kinds of mystical creatures—some that could invade the dreams of others. But my father was right. Our Isle of Haylin only had two mystical species. The unicorns who roamed the southern field were beautiful when they trotted across the green grass, their ivory coats glittering in the island sunshine. They were immune to poison and known for their speed.

But unicorns didn't have any magical abilities to walk through dreams.

And the hippogriffs—who were half horse, half eagle—roosted on the peak of Haylin Mountain, watching over our small port city. Their golden feathers and sharp talons were the pride of the island. Hippogriffs could manipulate the wind and were sturdy beasts who navigated the skies with magically enhanced senses.

But just like unicorns, hippogriffs weren't the type of creatures who entered the dreams of others.

"What if the beasts in my dreams are mystical creatures who came to the island?" I asked, scooting to the edge of my rickety bed. "Maybe they're dream creatures who're walking into my dreams because they want to hurt me specifically."

My father narrowed his eyes, the dark rings under them noticeable even in the dim lantern light.

"You're saying *powerful mystical creatures* came to the island to hunt the son of the local candlemaker?" He spoke every word with a healthy amount of sarcasm. "Thirteen-year-old boys must be in short supply on the mainland."

"I'm being serious."

"Oh, wait. I just remembered something..." All emotion drained from my father as he stared at me. "An ancient prophecy about our island said a young boy with the name of a color would be destined for greatness and hunted by great evil."

I held my breath for a long moment. Then I whispered, "*Really?*"

All his sarcasm returned as he frowned. "Don't be ridiculous. Of course not. The Isle of Haylin has no prophecies. We're lucky if we get anything other than storms."

With a huff, I turned away from him. Again, my father wasn't listening. I could shout about my problem until I ran out of breath, and he'd still rather ignore it in favor of sleep. Or dismiss it with a quick joke.

I didn't want to depend on him to solve this. I didn't want to depend on anyone. But what *could* a thirteen-year-old do? I would have given anything to have the power to solve this myself.

"Good night, Gray," my father said as he closed the door all the way, leaving me alone in the room with the darkness.

I hadn't slept since the night of the attack.

Probably a mistake.

The beasts in my dreams... Could they really be dream-manipulating creatures who wanted to hurt me? The ability to walk into someone's dream was rare. Very rare. And my father was right. Why would anyone want the random son of a tallow chandler? There was nothing to gain from my death.

Nothing.

I pulled my legs up onto my bed and held my knees close to my chest. What was I supposed to do now? In my dreams, the monsters had been hideous beasts made of shadow. I never got a good look at them. It had been a dream, after all—everything had felt nebulous and abstract. Once the monsters had appeared, it had turned into a hunt. They had chased me... And when they had caught me, I had felt their bloodlust.

Maybe the monsters weren't mystical creatures? Maybe they were something else.

Mystical creatures were usually intelligent. They could speak, reason, and concoct plans. A thunderbird had once come to town to warn us about a nearby hurricane, and the hippogriffs had flown into town to talk to the mayor about the problems at the docks.

The unicorns didn't particularly like being here, though. They had arrived on our island four months ago when a ship had wrecked on our shores. The hold of the ship had been filled with unicorn foals—seven in total—and since then, the goat ranchers on the island had looked after them. But every rancher complained about how needy the unicorns were.

Spoiled. That was the word everyone used to describe them. The unicorn foals always wanted the freshest fruits and the most bizarre flowers.

The monsters in my dreams had never said a word.

They hadn't even growled. The monsters had come at me as silent as a grave, and with the cold malice of murderers.

Fortunately, my brother wasn't having any nightmares. Just me.

Good ol' *lucky* me.

I dwelled on the problem, fatigue settling over me like dust across the furniture. My eyelids grew heavy as I glanced at the window. The moon shone through the cracks in the curtains. My bed, nightstand, dresser, and wardrobe were the only things in my bedroom. Well, them and the ten candles scattered around, ready to be lit in case I wanted more light.

The benefits of having a tallow chandler for a father.

Then I closed my eyes, exhaustion jumbling my thoughts. What was I thinking about? My stepmother always said I was the smart one of the family—she sometimes said I was *too* clever for my age. I tried to tell her the word was *precocious*, but that just resulted in anger.

Whenever I got tired, though, my mind got fuzzy, and my thoughts drifted off into tangents.

I smacked my cheeks, trying to stay focused. Time crawled by, the moon my only companion as I stood and walked around my bedroom. Unfortunately, it didn't take long for my legs to hurt. I sat back down on my bed.

The creak of door hinges caught my attention. I glanced up, suspecting I'd find my father. Instead, my brother crept into my room, tiptoeing with all the grace of a drunken ox. He stumbled into my wardrobe as he closed the door behind him. The clatter of the wooden furniture was no doubt heard throughout our small house.

My father and stepmother would likely ignore it.

My brother, Sorin, smiled as he made his way over to my bed. The room was too small for the both of us. Well, probably just for him. Sorin was so large, most people thought he was ten years older than he was.

"Here I am," Sorin said, holding his arms out. "Your big brother is here to protect you."

"We were born on the same day," I muttered. "And I was technically born first."

"Yeah, but I'm *physically* bigger, so my statement is still accurate." Sorin placed a giant hand on my head and tousled my black hair so much it puffed outward the moment he stopped.

Sorin was a mix of muscle and meat, somehow fluffy while still retaining considerable strength, just like our father. I didn't know where they got it, though. It wasn't like we ate well. The universe itself seemed to feed into them.

When we had been ten years old, Sorin had already been six feet tall—twice the height of any other ten-year-old on the island —and no one had any explanation for it.

He just *grew*.

Now, at age thirteen, he had the sturdiness of three men.

It made me jealous. I was barely five feet and clearly hadn't finished growing yet. At least, I *hoped* I hadn't finished.

That was the problem with being twins. I was dubbed "the weak one" no matter where we went, just because I wasn't as large as Sorin.

I moved over so that my brother could sit next to me on the bed. The bedframe groaned as Sorin sat down, like it was complaining about the weight. Despite that, I appreciated my brother's company. He was one of the few people in the world whom I never minded being around.

And Sorin and I weren't *that* different.

Sure, I was a little shorter. And I wasn't large, but I wasn't puny, either. The shepherd girl who lived near our school liked to call me *tree-like*, but I didn't agree with her. She needed glasses, anyway.

Sorin and I both had black hair, dark-tanned skin, and blue eyes so pale, they were practically gray. People often said we were exotic. The light coloration of our eyes contrasted harshly with our dark complexion and hair.

That was how I had gotten my name.

My mother—my birth mother—had only held me in her arms for a few minutes after my birth. Then she had passed away.

During those few precious moments, when I had first opened my eyes, my mother had whispered, "What lovely gray."

Her last words.

My father had thought it appropriate that she name me, so... *Gray* it was.

My birth mother had had brown eyes, and so did my father. No one knew where Sorin and I had gotten the pale-eyed trait. Little hometown mysteries with no answers, it seemed.

Sorin moved across my mattress until his back was against the wall. Then he yawned and pulled some of my blankets over his legs. He wore a pair of sleeping trousers and a tunic—as did I —but Sorin always cocooned himself when he slept.

"Okay," he said. "Here's my idea. I'll sleep next to you. That way, we'll be in the same dream together."

"That's not how it works."

"Really? Even with dream magic?"

I opened my mouth to offer a retort, but I didn't actually know. Obviously, I didn't have any dream magic. I had just heard about it in books we had read at school.

"How about I just try to keep you awake?" Sorin asked. "I'll slap you around if your eyes start to shut."

"What a great protector you are." I couldn't help the sardonic tone.

"It'll keep you awake, Gray. Trust me."

I glanced down at the wound on my left arm. Staying awake was what I had done the last few nights, but I couldn't do that forever. At some point, I'd have to figure out a solution.

"Maybe the monsters went away," Sorin said.

I turned my attention to him. "You think so?"

"Well, uh, I don't know. But maybe? Or maybe you'll always wake up when they hurt you because, it, uh, startles you. Or something."

With a sigh, I returned my attention to my arm. In the dream, the monsters had been relentless. How had I woken up? It hadn't been from the injury. I had just realized it was a dream, and only then had I woken.

If I could do that again, perhaps I could save myself.

But it seemed like a big risk to take, considering that it was only a theory.

Sorin placed a hand on my shoulder. "Stop lookin' so worried. I don't like that. You can be happy—I'm here for you."

I smiled as I glanced over. Fatigue ate at my resolve. "Thank you, Sorin."

"The dream monsters are probably long gone."

"I hope..."

"Don't worry about anything. I promise, I'll be here." Sorin held up a finger. "*I know you fear your time of sleep,*" he said in poetic rhythm. "*Where wicked monsters sometimes creep.*"

"Sorin, I don't—"

"*They fill your mind with hate and dread, dark-hearted schemes, and perhaps undead. But you needn't worry, cuz we're a team—I'll be here, so you can finally dream.*"

With half a smile, I asked, "Did you just make that up right now?"

"Well, I've been thinking about it for a few days now. Ever since you told me about your nightmare. And the schoolmaster helped with me the rhyming."

My brother had the spirit of an artist trapped in him. Not literally, of course, but that was what I told people whenever he painted something wonderful or shot off a poem. Just like our bizarre eyes—no one knew where his artistic trait had come from.

I scooted next to him. "You're really talented, ya know that? Don't let anyone tell you otherwise."

Sorin pulled me close and then wrapped some of the blankets around me as well. "Nah. You're the one with all the brains." He tucked everything tight, so that we barely had any room to move. "I'm sure you'll figure out what's going on and put an end to it."

"I'd like that. Or maybe we can figure the mystery out together."

"Well, *you* figure out the mystery. *I'll* deal with all the shadow monsters." He mock punched the air. "I'll get 'em right in the mush. Or maybe they just need a strongly scented candle to put their minds at ease." He shrugged. "Either or."

"Sounds like a plan," I said with a smirk.

His optimism never failed to make me smile. The gentle moonlight acted as our blanket as I closed my eyes, thankful for the rest.

My brother had never let me down before.

Perhaps tonight...

The monsters would be gone...

But when I opened my eyes, I caught my breath.

I was no longer in my bedroom. It wasn't even on my home island. With my teeth gritted, I stood and glanced around, unable to stop myself from trembling.

I was in the middle of a rocky field, marked with crags and boulders. The dead landscape went in all directions—no trees or shrubs to be seen, not even the ocean on the distant horizon.

This was the same barren location I had been in right before the shadow beasts had attacked me.

CHAPTER 2

ARCANIST PROTECTION

The black rocks beneath my feet glistened, obviously wet. The sky above me roiled with storm clouds, casting everything in darkness. Somehow, my sight wasn't impaired. The distant horizon, dominated by jagged boulders, was clearly visible. Dream logic, I supposed. It was dark, but somehow, I could see.

This was a place crafted from terror. My rising panic caused my knees to go weak and I stumbled backward and almost fell onto the rocks. Without my boots, I feared for my feet. What if I stepped on something sharp? What if I tried to run, but I tripped just as the monsters were about to catch me?

"Hello?" I asked.

My voice carried across the desolate landscape.

This dream was different from last time. I was more aware of my surroundings, and aware of my actions. I knew I was dreaming. That hadn't been the case last time—until I had managed to wake up.

"I want to wake up now." Again, my voice drifted in every direction. "I don't want to be here anymore."

But nothing happened. I wasn't waking.

I wished Sorin were with me. Although I hated admitting that I needed him, his constant optimism and reassurances always helped give me strength when I needed it. But where was he now? I rubbed at my arms, cold both from the weather and loneliness. Icy winds slipped across the rocks, silent as they chilled everything they touched.

Then the sound of clicking rose from between distant boulders. It was the clack and tap of wood on rock.

"I'm just a candlemaker's son," I called out, louder than before. "I don't have anything to give you. And I'm probably covered in wax. That stuff tastes terrible." With a nervous chuckle, I added, "Don't ask me how I know that. Just trust me."

I wondered if I could *logic* the monsters out of my dreamscape. Was that even possible? I hoped it was. I hoped with everything I had.

Something emerged from a crack between two black boulders. Wooden hands. The hands of a puppet or marionette. Then came the body—a clicking, clacking spider made of wood and held by invisible strings. Eight hands were attached to the ends of the long legs, freakish human additions to the spider-body form.

Not a normal spider, the size of a toenail, but a gigantic monster spider the size of a horse. It moved with jerking steps, each of its eight legs clicking on the rocks as it walked toward me.

It didn't have a spider face, either. Instead, it had a face mask —a blank, emotionless mask, like a stage actor, complete with two eyes and straight-line mouth.

In my last dream, it had been a beast made of shadow. Now it was some sort of nightmarish puppet? My heart crawled up into my throat. Although childish, I wished Sorin would just *sense* I was in danger and then wake me from this nightmare. Twins could do that, right? Maybe? Hopefully?

I didn't have much time to react. The marionette scuttled toward me, clicking faster as it ran, its mask face "staring" at me. Again, I stumbled backward, my feet slipping on the wet rocks. I gasped as I turned to run.

But just like a dream, I moved at the pace of molasses while the monster clicked across the rocks faster and faster, the sounds becoming louder as it drew near.

At some point, the beating of my heart drowned out all other sounds. I ran forward, the creature gaining on me. I didn't even glance over my shoulder—I just felt the monster's intense malice getting closer with each breath.

Agony shot through my back. I grunted as I stumbled forward, hot blood weeping down my spine.

Knives had cut through my tunic, and my flesh. I tried to run again, but I slipped and fell. I hit the black rocks chin-first. My teeth rattled together, and while I was dazed, the spider-puppet moved close. The fingers of its eight human hands had become knives at some point. One hand glistened with my blood.

Panicked, I staggered to my feet. When the puppet-spider swiped with a hand, I ducked underneath the attack and then ran in the opposite direction. I kept my balance over the wet rocks, gulping down ragged breaths as I went.

The spider scuttled after me, never speaking, never demanding.

It just wanted me dead.

That terrible thought ran through my mind over and over. How could I get away? Where would I go? What was going on?

"I don't want to fight you!" I shouted.

It didn't reply.

I ran between black boulders, weaving through the dismal terrain, trying to calm the frantic beat of my heart. The spider relentlessly pursued. It didn't breathe, it didn't pant, it didn't wheeze—the puppet moved along as though carried on strings, its stamina infinite, and its bloodlust eternal.

Why wasn't I waking up?

But then I started to pull ahead, running faster than the monster could keep up.

Maybe I could escape!

And then, as in any good nightmare, two more marionette spiders appeared from between the boulders in front of me, their combined sixteen legs clicking on the rocks as they scurried forward. Their face masks were identical, as were the knives that made up their human-like fingers at the end of their long spider-like legs.

I couldn't dodge around them. With my jaw clenched, I stopped and held my ground.

My hand shook as I knelt and grabbed a black rock from between my bare feet. If I couldn't outrun them, I would fight. Determined to live, I threw the rock as hard as I could.

The stone bounced off the wooden body of the puppet, barely scratching the beast.

One marionette swiped with its knife claws. I dodged backward, tripping in the process. The sting of the fall was nothing—I barely felt it in my panic.

"Help!" I yelled out, unsure of what else to do. "*Sorin!* Anyone!"

Then... the storm clouds parted.

Not slowly or leisurely, the clouds broke apart in an instant as though cleaved in half by a giant from above.

The spiders stopped and turned, each gazing at the beautiful night sky that had appeared above us. Thousands of stars twinkled overhead. More than would normally be seen at night —this was a cluster of stars from a hundred nights all combined into a single sky.

I held my breath as the stars glittered and twinkled.

And then they grew larger and larger as they headed towards

the rocks below. They were shooting stars, raining to the ground and shattering the black rocks with the destructive power of meteorites. And through dream logic, I somehow knew they wouldn't harm me.

The stars struck the puppet spiders and smashed them apart in an instant. They splintered and broke, like the side of a sailing ship hit with a heavy cannon. My eyes remained wide as I watched a dozen more stars striking the splinters of wood, annihilating the puppets.

And then the stars stopped falling, leaving the night sky pristine and beautiful once again.

I wanted to stand, to get a better view of what was happening, but agony flared across my back.

Fortunately, I didn't need to stand. A woman descended from the night sky. She wore a dress that glowed with the light of the moon and trailed behind her like mist. Her inky hair fluttered as if caught on the wind, so elegant and wondrous I couldn't look away.

With the poise of a dancer, she touched down on the black rocks, her bare feet barely making contact. She made no noise as she came to stand on the tip of a broken boulder, weightless and graceful. Then the woman glanced down and spotted me, her eyes a brilliant shade of lavender.

"Was it you who called for help?" she asked with a slight smile.

The woman descended from the broken boulder, moving through the air like a feather, and landed next to me. Her lithe and slender form made me think she was made of air. She wore a silver bracelet on her left ankle that softly jingled each time she stepped down with her left foot.

Then she knelt, her delicate fingers grazing my shoulder. "Poor thing."

That was when I saw it. The mark on her forehead.

She was an *arcanist*.

The seven-pointed star on her forehead was proof.

Mystical creatures roamed the land, filled with magic and power. But they never grew older unless they bonded with a mortal—any person without magic, basically. Once bonded, the human became an *arcanist* and the mystical creature became their *eldrin*. Together, they formed a mutual partnership.

Eldrin grew older, and more powerful.

And in exchange, arcanists gained the magic of their eldrin.

Phoenix arcanists could heal and summon fire. Thunderbird arcanists could fly and create lightning. Each arcanist's magic was completely dependent on the creature they had bonded with.

The mark on the arcanist's forehead reflected the arcanist's eldrin as well. This woman... Her seven-pointed star was laced with a spiral shell.

What mystical creature had a spiral shell?

"Can you stand?" the woman asked, her voice clear and singsong.

She sounded just as beautiful as she appeared.

I shook my head.

"Don't worry."

A gentle pulse spread from her fingertips through my body. The pain subsided, leaving me numb, but strong enough to stand. Slowly, and carefully, I got to my feet. The woman stepped back and held her hands together in front of her.

"Unfortunately," she said, "I cannot heal your injuries. This is a dream, and in this realm of slumber, I can only alter your perceptions. You won't feel the pain anymore. At least, not until you awaken."

With shaky hands, I dusted off my sleeping tunic and trousers. "But the monsters can hurt me? Why?"

"I don't know what magics those puppets were using, but mine only affects your dreams."

"What if I bleed out while I'm sleeping?"

"You needn't fret. Time passes differently here. Hours passed here are but mere seconds."

Her white dress had no sleeves, revealing the blue and pink swirling tattoos flowing across the skin of her shoulders. They were in the shape of storm clouds, stylized and glittering with some sort of magical power.

I had never seen anything like it.

"I'm Gray Lexly," I said. "Thank you for, uh, saving me."

"Gray?"

"Yeah. Like the color."

"I see." She smiled as she said, "My name is Rylee Helmith, but most refer to me as *Professor Helmith*. I don't mind which you choose."

"You're a professor?" Then I shook my head, my attention landing on the cracked rocks all around us. "Wait, no. I need to ask... What just happened? Why were the spiders attacking me?"

Professor Helmith glanced down at the ruined black stone, and then to the starry night sky overhead. Her gaze seemed rather pensive, though I couldn't guess why. "For the last few months, people have been reporting attacks—attacks that only occur in their dreams." She sighed as she turned back to me. "I don't know why this is happening or who is behind it, I apologize."

"O-Oh, no. Don't apologize. It's fine."

"I'm currently investigating these attacks. Unfortunately, your dream only contains more monsters. Just like all the other dreams I've visited." Professor Helmith carefully tucked some of her silky black hair behind one of her ears. "Several people have died from monsters attacking them in their dreams."

"They have?" I blurted out.

Professor Helmith held up a hand. "Don't fret. I've dedicated myself to bringing the attackers to justice."

I tensed as I shoved my hands into my armpits, the hot

sensation of my own blood on my back still present. "You think you can find whoever is doing this?"

"Someone thinks they're clever enough to get away with murder, but I won't allow them to use magic for their heinous schemes." She stared at the barren wasteland.

I thought Professor Helmith was about to leave, so I held out a hand as I stepped forward. "Wait! You said you were a professor. Where do you teach?"

She smiled. "Astra Academy for Arcanists."

I had never met anyone like this professor. Sure, arcanists came to our island, and one even lived in town, but every single arcanist I had ever met had been dismissive and distant, barely offering me a second glance as though I were beneath them. And they certainly weren't overflowing with magic and power, like Professor Helmith.

No other arcanist came close to her eldritch presence.

The magic radiating from her called to me. It called to me like nothing I had ever experienced. Perhaps our meeting was destiny.

I desperately wanted to become an arcanist.

It was far better than becoming like my father. My greatest nightmare—worse than the monsters attacking me—was making candles for the rest of my life. What if I could become more like Professor Helmith? What if she could teach me all sorts of magics?

Then I would have the power to protect myself.

I wouldn't need to depend on others or live on a forgotten island in the middle of nowhere.

"Can I attend Astra Academy?" I blurted out. "I mean, my tiny island home only has the one schoolhouse, but I've read every book there. Everyone says that I'm—"

"It's an academy *only* for arcanists," Professor Helmith interjected. "You must be bonded with a mystical creature to enroll as a student."

"Well, o-okay. That's not a problem. Some unicorns shipwrecked on my island. When I wake, I'll go bond with one immediately. Then I'll enroll."

The professor raised an eyebrow. "Aren't you a little young to become an arcanist?"

"I..."

She was right. Every island I knew had a law about bonding with mystical creatures—only those who had reached the age of fifteen would be given the opportunity. The Isle of Haylin was the same way. I hadn't spoken to the unicorns because the goat ranchers stopped anyone who wasn't of age.

"People say I'm mature for my age," I lamely concluded. With a quick slide of my hand over my hair, I smoothed the locks out. "Very mature."

Professor Helmith chuckled, her voice almost a giggle. "Is that so?"

"Absolutely."

"You know that mystical creatures have a Trial of Worth you must pass before they'll bond with you, right? Most creatures won't even consider you unless you're an adult."

My shoulders bunched at the base of my neck as I slowly nodded.

The Trial of Worth...

Of course. How had I forgotten about that?

Every mystical creature had a *Trial of Worth*. It was a test to see if a person was deserving of bonding. If a mortal passed the test, the mystical creature would be willing to become their eldrin, but every species of creature had their own trial.

Some Trials of Worth were easier than others, or so I had read.

And the reason children couldn't participate in the trials was because, once bonded, an arcanist's soul fed their eldrin—it was what gave the mystical creature power to grow. So, a person's soul affected the creature, and children hadn't yet developed into who they would be as a person. A child's personality was often unpredictable. The creature could be affected negatively.

"Unicorns prize physical prowess," Professor Helmith said matter-of-factly. "Their Trial of Worth will no doubt involve showing off your athleticism."

"I can do it." With a hesitant smile, I added, "I'm not the type to give up so easily."

Professor Helmith mulled over my statement. Then she shook her head and said, "You should wait until you're older. Then you can apply to Astra Academy when the time is right and proper. Don't fret over becoming an arcanist just yet."

I held my breath, trying to resist the urge to argue. Professor Helmith seemed so knowledgeable and magically talented—who wouldn't want to go to the academy she taught at?

And *everyone* wanted to become an arcanist, so of course Sorin and I had discussed it. We had always talked about the hippogriffs' Trial of Worth, which was more about tradition and family. The mayor organized a series of tests, and the hippogriffs watched over the new hopefuls every year.

The unicorns...

They weren't like that. They were new to the island. No one presided over their Trial of Worth, because nothing had been set up yet.

"I'm concerned your dream monsters might return," Professor Helmith said, drawing me back to the present. "With your permission, I'd like to visit your dreams for the next few nights. I'll protect you from anything, or anyone, who tries to harm you."

"Of course. *Yes*. Definitely come visit me."

Professor Helmith waved her hand in a wide arc. The creepy and lifeless environment of my dream shifted all at once. The black rocks melted into emerald grass. The night sky shattered like glass, the pieces raining down like a gentle rain, twinkling as they fell. The broken pieces revealed a clear blue sky, bright and filled with sunshine.

A river of liquid sapphires sparkled into existence, and a tree of silver leaves sprouted next to it.

The wondrous environment was everything a dream was *supposed* to be—beautiful and over the top, in a way that reality could never compare to.

"You *control* dreams?" I whispered.

"That's right." Professor Helmith motioned to her forehead. "I bonded with an *ethereal whelk*. It's a special kind of mystical creature made of light and dreams."

"I've never heard of an ethereal whelk before."

Wasn't a *whelk* a type of sea snail? It didn't sound that impressive, but it explained the spiral shell design of Professor Helmith's arcanist mark. She had bonded with a dream snail? I wondered what kind of Trial of Worth *they* had.

When she turned to me, she wore a playful smile. "When you come to Astra Academy, perhaps I'll show you my eldrin in person."

"I'd like that," I said.

"Until then, why don't we have a picnic? You can tell me all about when the monster attacks started. Perhaps there are clues hidden within tiny details that will help me solve this mystery."

"Of course! There's not much to talk about, but I'll tell you all the details."

With another wave of her hand, Professor Helmith created a blanket and two plates of pastries topped with sugar and berries. My thoughts immediately went to raspberry tarts—those were my favorite. Professor Helmith set the blanket on the ground, and we sat down together, the summer winds warm.

Luckily for me, Professor Helmith did have raspberry tarts. A whole stack of them.

"I love these pastries," I said, picking one up and examining the sugary goodness up close. "How'd you know?"

Professor Helmith placed a finger on her lips. "Magic," she playfully whispered.

I couldn't help but smile. Perhaps she had spoken with Sorin ahead of time? How else would she have known? Some sort of magical ability that allowed her to see my inner desires?

"Raspberries are my favorite fruit," I muttered as I took a bite.

"Mine as well."

After I swallowed a bit of pastry, I shook away my nostalgic thoughts and focused on the here and now. The bizarre dream monsters needed to be stopped.

So I explained my previous dream to her—and also my father's dismissal. She listened the entire time, occasionally commenting, never getting bored or distracted.

I was disappointed when I was suddenly jerked awake.

CHAPTER 3

A FOOLPROOF PLAN

"**G**ray! *Gray*! Wake up!"

My brother jostled me until my eyes fluttered open. The sheets of my bed were spotted with my blood, and Sorin propped me up and tore the bedding away. I stared at my brother, his light gray-blue eyes the same as mine. It took me several minutes to process everything—to realize I wasn't speaking with the professor anymore—and shake my head.

"I've got you," Sorin muttered.

He effortlessly lifted me into his massive arms. Then Sorin lumbered out of my bedroom, carried me down the hall, and entered our home's only washroom. We had a brass bathtub and a water pump, along with a stove heater. It was an advanced system for our island. My father had made a deal with the carpenters—they would get all the candles they needed in exchange for helping my father fix and alter our home.

My brother knelt and gently set me next to the tub. Then he grabbed towels and extra blankets from the cabinet. He practically buried me in fabric in his frantic rush to gather everything.

SHAMI STOVALL

"You're bleeding," Sorin said as he patted my back. He was so rough, I sucked in air through my teeth. "G-Gray? What's wrong?"

"Not so hard," I said, my jaw clenched.

"Right. Right! I'll be gentle."

With slow motions, he rubbed the injuries on my back. Once cleaned, he wrapped me in fresh towels. Our stepmother would be angry. She hated it whenever the towels got stained, and once she saw the blood, she'd be irritated.

Sorin lit a lantern. Then he pumped some water and started the stove. The whole washroom warmed within a couple of minutes.

Sorin heated the water and then dumped it into the tub, filling it halfway. He helped me up, tugged me out of my sleepwear, and then eased me into the tub.

"You're going to be okay," my brother said. "I'm right here."

"Thank you," I muttered.

Sorin knelt next to the tub, his elbows on the edge as he leaned over me. "Do you need anything? A washrag? Some soap?"

"I... I met someone."

My brother obviously couldn't comprehend my tangential statement. He stared for a long moment, blinking slowly. "You *met someone*? That's a weird thing to say. When did you meet someone?"

"While I was sleeping. But first, the monsters returned."

"What happened?"

I smiled. "I was saved. Professor Helmith rescued me, so I don't have to worry anymore."

I knew I sounded insane. Without any context or explanation, no one could grasp the situation, but here I was, struggling through the description like Sorin should just know what I was talking about.

"A *professor* saved you?" Sorin asked.

"Yeah. She came to me in my dreams." I exhaled, my back flaring with agony, especially when I leaned back on the metal of the tub. "She was so beautiful, and her magic so amazing..."

"The professor was a girl?"

"A woman." I rested my head on the edge of the tub. The brass was hard and uncomfortable. I just wanted to relax. "She's an arcanist, Sorin. An actual *arcanist* came to me in my dreams and defeated all the monsters."

Sorin stared at me, his eyebrows heading for his hairline. I almost laughed. He *really* didn't believe me.

"She teaches magic at Astra Academy," I muttered.

"Did the monsters hurt you?" Sorin motioned to my back. Then he stared at the water. "You're bleeding."

The water was pink with my blood. Despite that, I knew I would be okay. The cuts were shallow, even if they hurt more than any other injury I'd had in my life. Soon, the bleeding would stop, and I would be fine. Maybe I'd have some scars, but that didn't matter.

"Professor Helmith is trying to figure out what's happening. She's going to protect me while she investigates."

"Really?" Sorin leaned heavier on the side of the tub. "She sounds nice."

"She's kind and... amazing."

"I should go get Dad and Mum," Sorin said as he got to one foot.

I grabbed his sleeping tunic, keeping him close to the tub. "Wait. Sorin—I need to talk to you." My brother knelt again, and I lowered my voice to a whisper. "You know the unicorns in the southern field?"

"Yeah."

"We need to bond with them, Sorin. You and me. We need to become arcanists."

Sorin stared at me. The soft orange glow of the washroom

lantern kept the darkness away, but the corners of the room were still filled with shadows.

I tried not to dwell on that.

The unicorns were perfect. I'd just tell them I was fifteen, pass their Trial of Worth, and head straight to Astra Academy to learn magic from Professor Helmith. Nothing had ever sounded more exciting to me in my life.

And while the professor had said to wait, that seemed silly. Nothing sounded more exciting than flying off on an adventure to solve a mystery that had originated in my dreams. Perhaps other people had the restraint to sit and listen, but I wasn't one of them.

"We're too young," Sorin finally said. "We still have a year and a half before we can participate in a Trial of Worth."

"The unicorns don't know that."

My brother slowly realized what I was suggesting. I saw the moment he grasped the concept. His expression changed from bewilderment to amused shock.

"Oh, I see... We're going to tell the unicorns we're fifteen." He rubbed his temple. "But will they believe us?"

"You look old enough, Sorin. You could be my father."

"I don't look *that* old."

"Old enough. And if you say I'm your twin, they'll probably believe us. I hope."

Sorin glanced at my shoulder. He touched the side of my neck, and I leaned forward so he could get a better view of my injuries. My brother got up, grabbed a washrag, and then returned so he could gently pat around my wounds.

"Why do we have to become arcanists right now?" he asked. "So we can fight dream monsters?"

"Well, *yes*. If I had some magic, maybe I could protect myself." I met his gaze. "But also so that we can go to Astra Academy."

"But why? You've never mentioned going to an academy before."

"Sorin, you know I don't want to stay on this island. We've never left. Not once. This is our chance. Aren't you excited to leave? To see the Academy? To see the world and learn magic? Doesn't that sound amazing?"

"I thought Dad wanted one of us to become the next tallow chandler? We told him if we became arcanists, we'd still live around here, so we can train someone new, or help Dad ourselves."

With a huff, I turned away from Sorin. I didn't want to be shackled to this island just because our father was the only one who made candles. They weren't even useful anymore! Most people had lanterns, and the wealthier merchant families had *glowstones*—rocks embedded with magic that glowed forever.

If our father died tomorrow, and the Isle of Haylin had no tallow chandler, there wouldn't be pandemonium—people would just go to bed earlier until more lanterns were shipped to the island.

I didn't want my father's life.

Sorin must have sensed my frustrations. He set a hand on my bare shoulder. "Hey, Gray, if it means that much to you, we'll definitely go to the Academy, okay? Dad can always take on an apprentice. We can find a solution—there's always a way."

I slowly glanced back over at him, the sting of my wounds fading from my mind. "Thank you, Sorin." I splashed some of the warm water onto my face. "You don't mind bonding with a unicorn?"

"Well, I had always dreamed of becoming a griffin arcanist, but riding a unicorn sounds fun. Have you seen how fast they are?" Sorin slapped his knees, creating mock galloping sounds. "I'd zip through town after town, impressing everyone with my trusty eldrin steed."

"Yeah... That would be brilliant."

Sorin frowned. He stopped his galloping. "But what rhymes with *unicorn*? Not much. *Uniform*? Maybe. *Stillborn*? That's awfully gloomy."

"Don't say that word around our father."

"Oh! Shouldn't we tell Dad and Mum about your injuries?"

With a scoff, I said, "Just tell our father I fell out of bed, rolled down the road, and landed on the blacksmith's sword rack."

"Gray, I don't like lying to Dad. I don't think we should do that."

"It was a joke. Let's just not say anything. I'm not *that* injured. Everything will be okay."

"What if you get an infection?"

"Fine—we'll tell him *if* something happens." I rolled my eyes. "Will that make you happy?"

Someone stomped into the hall and then banged on my bedroom door. "Gray? Is that you? Are you makin' noise again?"

"We're in the washroom," Sorin called out before I could say anything. "Gray's taking a bath. He, uh, woke up."

"I don't wanna hear about those nightmares anymore, boys." Our father went back to his own room, the stomp of his steps betraying his anger. "You're too old for this nonsense. Get these weird fantasies out of your heads. *Go to sleep.*"

"Okay, Dad."

Our father slammed his bedroom door shut.

We waited a few moments in utter silence. Once we were sure our father had gone back to bed, Sorin's smile returned in full force. Then he slapped some of the water out of the tub, clearly filled with so much excess energy he didn't know what to do with it. "So, tomorrow we'll go talk to the unicorn foals? And we'll bond? And then we'll be unicorn arcanists and head to the mainland?"

"Exactly."

ACADEMY ARCANIST

"But what if we get caught? We'll be punished. Maybe even..." Sorin poked at the pinkish bathwater. "Maybe even kicked off the island," he whispered.

"They wouldn't do that. Not to us. We'll be fine."

"But thieves and murderers get sent away."

Sorin was right, but I didn't want to think about the consequences if we failed. Besides, if other people could become arcanists, Sorin and I could do it, too. And once we were arcanists, things would be different.

I reached my hand out of the tub and tapped the side of Sorin's arm. "We'll definitely bond. Then it'll just be you and me on an adventure. Studying at an academy to become great arcanists."

Sorin glanced over and half-smiled. "Yeah. Nothing will stop the two of us. We can do whatever we set our minds to."

CHAPTER 4

A Unicorn's Trial Of Worth

We crept around the backside of Old Man Finn's barn, hiding in the tall weeds. Sorin stayed close to me, crunching through the vegetation, completely incapable of stealth. Fortunately, Old Man Finn always went to the market in the morning—his routine as regular as the sunrise—and he wouldn't be back for a few hours. Sneaking through the farm probably wasn't necessary, but I didn't want any chance of someone seeing us.

Everyone on the Isle of Haylin knew Sorin and I shouldn't have been anywhere near the unicorn foals, and if they spotted us heading to the southern field, they would stop us.

Glorious morning sunshine flooded the island, tall trees and island grass swaying in the salty breeze. I stood to get a better look at the southern field. The seven unicorn foals were easy to spot.

Their white coats shone like the scales of wet fish, and their ivory manes and tails fluttered behind them as they ran. Each one of them had a spiral horn made of pristine bone, but because they were young, the horns were only a few inches in length. Their hooves gleamed as if cast from silver, stunning and magnificent. The unicorns giggled as they played some sort of game of tag.

"It's your turn," one called out, his voice childish but harsh.

"No," another answered, her tone authoritative. "It's Windsweep's turn! I went last time."

"But Windsweep is no fun. He gets tired too fast!"

One of the unicorns stopped and bucked his back legs into the air. With a snort and a stomp, he said, "*That's not true.* You're just being mean, Starling."

Before any of them glanced in my direction, I ducked back into the weeds.

"It's time," I muttered.

Sorin slowly parted some of the plants to stare at me. "You sure? I mean, we could just sit here and watch them for a bit."

"Old Man Finn won't be gone forever. We need to act now."

"All right. I'm ready."

After a deep breath, I stood from the weeds and entered the field, my stride confident. My brother lumbered behind me, an intimidating shadow even if *I* knew he had a gentle soul and wouldn't lash out unless provoked.

The seven unicorns all stopped and turned, their ears tall and their eyes wide. They had the lanky bodies of baby horses—all legs and neck, barely any torso. Riding on them would be impossible for a year or so once they were bonded, but after that, they'd be faster than any normal steed.

"Hello," I said, waving as I approached. "My name is Gray Lexly, and this is my brother, Sorin Lexly."

My brother also waved. "Hello, honored unicorns."

The seven mystical creatures all exchanged quick glances. Six of them had bright blue eyes, the same shade as the cloudless sky, but one of them had dark eyes. That was the unicorn who stepped forward.

"My name is Starling," the unicorn said. He held his head

high, his nose turned upward. "And we were told that no one would come to visit us."

"Oh, is that right? Does that mean none of you want an arcanist? I was under the impression that all mystical creatures wanted to find someone worthy to bond with."

I stroked my chin as I spoke, feigning ignorance. Probably too much, to be honest, but these were foals. They once again glanced between each other, their long tails swishing back and forth. One of the unicorns pranced around the group.

"We want to find arcanists," Starling finally said. "Do you know of anyone wanting to brave our Trial of Worth? We prefer knights, and nobles, and royalty. Those are the types of people worthy of our magics."

Sorin frowned. "Nobles? Are you saying lowborn people aren't good enough?"

"We unicorns prefer individuals of higher standing, that's all." Starling flipped his mane from one side of his neck to the other, a few ivory strands catching the morning light just right. They glittered like white gold.

"You just so happen to be in luck," I said, imposing myself between them. "My brother and I want to prove ourselves to you. And we're definitely knight material. We might even have royalty in our blood. I bet we have a cousin who used to be a duke or something."

Starling snorted, his whole muzzle wrinkling in disgust. "I doubt either of *you* are royalty. Plus, you're too young." He swished his tail and then turned around, facing his rump toward me. "I think you two peasants should go."

"What?" I motioned to Sorin, and all his considerable height. "Do you see this guy? He's old enough. And he has enough muscles for three knights. Certainly not a peasant."

I was surprised by how small the unicorn foals were. They stood three feet at the shoulder, and all of them were as thin as beanstalks. Their white coats were magnificent, though. I wanted to touch one so badly, but I didn't want to risk upsetting them.

How had they remained so clean and beautiful while playing out in the field? It was a mystery.

Starling turned back around, his nostrils flaring. "*He's* old enough. But not you, surely."

"What? We're twins. Obviously. Tell them, Sorin."

My brother nodded vigorously. "That's right. We're twins."

One of the unicorns whinnied—cute and childish—and another snorted. When they exchanged glances this time, they all eventually whispered agreement.

Starling returned his attention to me, his head once again held high, his nose even higher. "Very well, *Lexly Twins*. You may attempt our Trial of Worth, but it won't be an easy undertaking. We're majestic mystical creatures capable of *great magic*, and we demand *the best* from our arcanists."

I smacked Sorin with the back of my hand, square in his chest. "We're ready."

Starling stomped his hooves. "Then we will have a race! That's the best way to determine if you're worthy."

"A race?" I balked. "Between me and Sorin?"

"Not between you two—you have to race *us*."

I held my breath for a moment, my thoughts buzzing. Normally, a mystical creature's Trial of Worth didn't involve the creatures themselves. They tested *people* against other *people*. Solving puzzles, climbing mountains, acquiring a specific hidden object the creature had hidden previously...

Why were the unicorns making us race them? Was it because we couldn't win?

"If you beat us at a race, you may bond with a unicorn of your choosing," Starling said.

I slowly glanced at Sorin. He met my gaze with a deep frown. My brother was anything but fast, and I wasn't really the *running type*. The unicorns had definitely chosen this to mess with us. How was I going to get us through this?

"Where are we racing to?" I asked, crossing my arms, trying to think of a plan while I spoke.

Starling pointed with his horn to the other side of the field. "We'll start here, and then run across the grass, stopping by that distant fence."

The edge of Old Man Finn's property. I suspected the unicorns had been told not to leave the fenced areas.

"That's only a few hundred feet," I said, pointing at the fence. "That's *barely* a race."

"Hmpf!" Starling snorted and stomped his hooves again. "How dare you! I'm a majestic unicorn, and I get to set the terms of the race!"

"I thought you only wanted the best individual to bond with? A *peasant's race* is just across one field."

"Insults! I don't hear *you* coming up with anything better."

"Oh, I have something better. What if we raced from here, the southern field, all the way to the *northern-most field*?"

"Honeysuckle Meadow?" Sorin asked, his eyebrows rising toward his dark hair. "You want to race *all the way* to Honeysuckle Meadow?"

I offered a casual shrug. "I mean, that's more of a proper race, wouldn't you agree, brother? And a unicorn's Trial of Worth deserves a proper race."

It took Sorin several seconds to grasp my words. He just stared, until it finally clicked. Then he smiled wide and nodded once. "Yeah. *Yeah*. Racing to Honeysuckle Meadow would be a great idea."

The unicorn foals huddled together, shoulder-to-shoulder, whispering among themselves. Their tails swished angrily back and forth, and a couple of them shot me glares, but I didn't react. I just smiled and waved whenever I caught one looking my way.

Starling stepped away from the group of foals. "We're not supposed to leave this field."

"Because no one wants to see you in any danger," I said, holding up a finger. "But we'll be racing through town. There's no danger there. And Honeysuckle Meadow is the most beautiful—and peaceful—location on the whole island. Trust me. You'll be perfectly safe."

"Well..."

"And isn't finding someone to bond with the most important thing for a young mystical creature? Surely, everyone will understand why you needed to leave the field for just a short while."

The unicorns all nodded at my statement, their adorable eyes wide. Then they pranced around, whispering excitedly about finally growing into adult unicorns and escaping the island. I understood the sentiment—I wanted to be an adult and leave the Isle of Haylin as well.

"Very well," Starling said. "We will start here—" He dug his hoof into the dirt and drew a short line. "—and we will race to Honeysuckle Meadow." Then he glanced up, his ears twitching. "How do we get there?"

I pointed to the road past Old Man Finn's barn. "The main road leads straight through town, and curves with the island all the way to Honeysuckle Meadow. There are signs, and everyone in town will tell you it's the fastest way there."

"I see." Starling pranced around the starting line, lifting his gangly legs high with each step. "Then prepare yourselves for a grand race, Lexly Twins. Although, I doubt either of you can triumph. Unicorns were born to run with the wind and challenge the horizon."

"Sounds excellent," I said with a smile.

But right as I was about to step to the line, Sorin grabbed my shoulder and yanked me back. He pulled me close and whispered, "Gray, are you insane? We can't race the unicorns across the island! We'll definitely lose."

I slid an arm over his shoulder and behind his neck. "It's okay," I whispered. "Besides, we can't give up before even trying, right? We have to give this our all."

"But it's impossible."

"Never say something is impossible. It only becomes *impossible* when you decide it is. Just trust me. I've got an idea."

Sorin reluctantly remained quiet. I could tell he wanted to argue, to say something about how this would never work, but he held back. I let my arm fall to my side and then walked over to the starting line, pleased that the unicorns had taken my suggestion.

I hadn't lied to them—the fastest road to Honeysuckle Meadow *was* the main road straight through town. Unfortunately for them, the morning market was currently underway, and there would be hundreds of people milling about.

Sorin and I didn't need to take the main road. There were smaller paths—less filled with people—that were sure to help us succeed.

The seven unicorn foals lined up on either side of me. My brother also positioned himself behind the line, though he was hesitant to do so. With a smirk, I readied myself for the initial run. I had to make it look good.

"Are you prepared, Lexly Twins?" Starling asked.

I snapped my fingers. "You know it."

"I guess I'm prepared," Sorin replied.

Starling nickered. "Then here we go—the race has begun!"

We didn't have a pistol or a bell to ring, but Starling's shout was good enough. Everyone bolted from the line and headed straight for the road beyond Old Man Finn's barn. The unicorns lived up to their reputation—each one flew like a bird on the wind, their hooves barely touching the ground as they galloped away. Sorin and I were obviously slower, but that didn't bother me.

The road from the southern field to Honeysuckle Meadow was several miles in length. The unicorns would be plenty winded long before they reached their destination.

The unicorn foals laughed as they reached the dirt road. They kicked up dust as they went, and one of them even shouted, "Eat that, peasants!"

Once Sorin and I reached the beginning of the road, I grabbed my brother by his tunic and yanked him toward one of the goat trails.

"Where are you going, Gray?" Sorin asked. He motioned to the distant unicorns as they hurried off into town. "We're *definitely* going to lose at this pace. We can't afford to take the scenic route."

"Don't be ridiculous," I said as I dragged him down the path. It led straight to Old Man Finn's house—and to his stables. "I have an idea. C'mon. We don't have much time."

"Are you sure?"

"Of course. We'll be to the meadow in no time. Just follow me. And stay quiet. We need to borrow a couple of Finn's animals."

Chapter 5

A Race To Honeysuckle Meadow

"Gray," my brother said. "I think the unicorns meant *we* had to beat them at a race. On foot. Without any help."

"It'll be okay. Trust me."

Old Man Finn kept his two horses close to home most of the time. He treated them like family. His two donkeys, on the other hand, were the ones who pulled his carts to the market.

"Come here," I said as I coaxed the sorrel-colored steed away from his stall.

The large horse stopped munching on his oats and slowly clopped over to me. He was probably bored, because he seemed eager to trot right out and greet me.

Then I opened the stall of the second horse. "Good morning, you majestic beast."

This horse also wandered over, confirming my theory.

I backed away, not the most comfortable with horses. Which was ironic, considering I was about to bond with a unicorn. Fortunately, Sorin didn't share my hesitation. Both the beasts wandered over to him, their large muzzles tickling his ears as they play-nibbled his hair. He laughed and stroked their long necks.

"Look! I think they like me, Gray!"

"I think so, too," I said.

"*Horses may be beasts of burden, but they're friendly, and, er...*" Sorin patted the horses again, smiling. "What rhymes with *burden*? Uh... *unburden*?"

"Never mind that. We don't have time. We'll use these two horses to run around the outside of town, then we'll hop off, get back on the main road ahead of the foals, and head over to Honeysuckle Meadow."

Sorin didn't say anything. He lowered his gaze, his expression melting into something neutral. He didn't have to voice his opinion—I already knew. Sorin didn't like this.

"The unicorns didn't say we couldn't use horses," I said, trying to brighten his spirits. "And most mystical creatures don't compete against the hopefuls in their Trials of Worth."

"Really?"

"Yeah. Usually, the mystical creatures give people a test, and then they watch from afar. The unicorns racing against us... They're obviously not taking this seriously. You heard what they said about lowborn people. I think they just wanted to show off."

"But—"

"Unicorns have four legs. Horses have four legs. We're just evening the odds."

Despite my rationalizations, Sorin just kept stroking the manes of the horses, no change in his attitude. That was fine. I would show him. Once he was an arcanist, he would thank me.

With the help of the stall door, I pulled myself up onto one of the horses. Bareback riding wasn't my favorite, but I could do it. The horse didn't seem to mind, either. I patted his brown coat, muttering pleasant words.

Sorin stepped onto a portion of the nearby fence and flung his leg over the back of his horse. His steed seemed happy with him, even though he was bigger. He whispered kind nonsense as he scratched around the horse's ear.

I tapped the side of the horse and clicked my tongue. "Let's go."

The horse seemed to understand. He walked forward—but that wasn't fast enough. I pressed my heels into his sides, and my horse picked up his pace. I clung to his mane for support, my thighs hugging his body as we quickly broke into a fast trot. I prayed to the good stars that I wouldn't fall off.

There was a small road that went around the town, mostly used by the shepherds. I urged my steed down that narrow dirt path, behind most of the larger buildings on the Isle of Haylin. We wouldn't be seen by the foals, whom I hoped would be slowed by the market area.

Brilliant sunshine fell from the clear sky, setting the world alight with vivid color and filling the air with warmth. The grass was bright green, the distant ocean a radiant blue, and my heart pounded hard against my ribs as my horse picked up his pace once again.

Sorin motioned for his mount to follow mine, and the two brother horses obviously knew what was expected of them. Together, we rode around the stone buildings, never faltering. Most of the homes and businesses on the island were made of a gray stone that had been brought in from the neighboring isle. It reminded me of volcanic stone, but I wasn't sure of its proper name.

With the wind whipping through my black hair, I grinned. Sorin and I raced around the town. We found no other people on the narrow roads behind most buildings. The cuts on my back stung a bit, reminding me of my bizarre nightmare, but I managed to ignore them as we continued across the island.

In the distance, I heard the chatter of the market, occasionally punctuated by a shout or a laugh. The foals had to be running through the crowd. In my mind's eye, I pictured the citizens of the isle delighting in their beautiful galloping.

I urged my horse to go faster.

A fully grown horse could outrun a unicorn foal, right? And the market square would slow them. I had to stick with the plan and not question everything now.

My horse huffed as he ran harder. This was a familiar road, and the animal ran it with confidence.

Sorin didn't push his mount as hard as I did. He kept his head down and whispered things to his animal, eventually falling behind. For some reason, that angered me. Why didn't Sorin want this as much as I did? Wasn't he thrilled to become an arcanist? We were going to do it!

It wasn't long before the excited chatter of the market faded into the distance. The northern edge of the town was made up of smaller houses, some with giant chimneys that gushed smoke at all hours of the day. Bakeries, mostly. Some of them made charcoal and coke, to help with the other fires around town.

Once I had passed a couple of homes, I leaned back. The horse knew I wanted to slow, and he did so without me saying a word. The horse trotted and then came to a stop behind a house with a short chimney that bellowed thick clouds of dark smoke and ash. I slid off my horse and then hurried into the low-hanging smoke. The heavy ash was common for charcoal. I rubbed some of it on my tunic and pants.

Then Sorin and his steed finally caught up. He leapt off his horse, and I patted him a couple of times, smearing the gray-black ash across his clothes as well. Then we smacked the horses, and they ran back the way we came. I was certain they were well trained enough to return to their stable, but there wasn't time to consider it further.

I yanked Sorin toward the road. Once our feet hit the dirt, we ran straight for the far fence.

There it was. A few hundred feet ahead of us.

Honeysuckle Meadow.

And the honeysuckles were in bloom. The beautiful tube-like flowers came in a huge range of colors. Red. Yellow. Pink. White. Blue. They were mixed together in such great masses that sometimes the colors blended. Red and yellow flowers became waves of orange. Pink and blue became a rolling hill of gentle purple.

Nothing on the island compared to Honeysuckle Meadow.

I could smell it from half a mile away. Sweet, ripe, like honey and citrus.

And few knew that honeysuckles grew as large bushes. The field was deeper than it looked, the bushes a good three feet tall, but so scrunched together that you couldn't see the ground anymore. Stepping on the bushes would result in someone sinking up to their waist in flowers.

Someone shouted. I glanced over my shoulder. The people in town were pointing and yelling. The unicorn foals exited the crowds of the market, running as fast as their slender legs could carry them. Their silver hooves sparkled as they ran, their magic giving them a light and quick step, enhancing their speed.

I shoved Sorin and sprinted toward the fence. This was the last little bit! We had to beat the unicorns to the fence or we'd lose.

Sorin ran with me, gasping like forge bellows. He was strong, like our father, but he had the stamina of an elderly dog. We hadn't been running very long, but sweat already poured from Sorin's armpits like he had hidden pitchers of water under his tunic and the contents were sloshing out everywhere.

The foals rushed toward the fence, but Sorin and I were *so close*.

I scrunched my eyes shut and pushed that last little bit. The huff of the unicorns grew louder and louder, as did the beating of my heart and the slam of my footfalls. Then I opened my eyes and reached out my hand.

I grabbed the fence, practically slamming into it, but that didn't matter because I had won. Then Sorin crashed into the fence, clearly swept up in his own running. He tumbled over the fence and landed in the honeysuckle bushes. The unicorns reached the fence two seconds later.

Two seconds too late.

They had lost—Sorin and I had won.

I turned around, my arms up. Although I was out of breath, and my legs were burning, I still managed a weak shout of triumph. The unicorns gulped down air as they paced around the area, their tails swishing.

Only six of them were here. I counted them twice, a little confused.

To my surprise, the last unicorn—the seventh white foal—trotted out of the crowds of the market. The citizens of Haylin shouted and gathered in the market square. It wouldn't be long until they came to the meadow, demanding an explanation. They were probably waiting for an arcanist, though. Old Man Finn would get involved... It was a good thing Sorin and I were about to bond.

Arcanists were always treated differently. Since they had magical powers—and some could do marvelous things, like alter the weather—they were given elevated status in every society I knew of. No one in town would yell at Sorin or me once we had bonded with our eldrin.

While I caught my breath, the last unicorn hurried down the road and finally reached us a good thirty seconds later.

"*Windsweep*," Starling said, rolling his eyes. "You didn't even try!"

Windsweep wheezed and then laid down next to the fence of Honeysuckle Meadow, his four legs tucked under his body. "How... How dare you... I tried. I tried... so hard." He coughed and snorted, and then rested his head on the dirt.

My brother pulled himself out of the flowers and hopped

back over the fence. He brushed off the golden pollen and stood by my side. While Sorin was a poor runner, he always recovered from exertion faster than me. It took me another minute before I felt capable of speaking normally.

"We won," I said, holding out a hand. With my breath caught, I stood confident. "That means two of you get to bond with me and my brother."

Starling stepped forward, his head held high, his horn pointed skyward. "I, obviously, will be the first to bond."

The other unicorns bickered among themselves, arguing over who would be the second, some of them whispering harsh words. While they discussed the situation, Sorin grabbed my arm. I turned to him, and he leaned in close to my ear.

"Gray, we shouldn't do this."

His throat sounded twisted, like he could barely get the words out.

"It'll be fine," I whispered back. "Don't worry."

"But once we bond, we'll be partners for life, right? Eldrin can't *unbond* with their arcanists. What if they find out, and they resent us forever for starting our life together with a lie?"

Sorin was right. Mystical creatures couldn't unbond from a mortal human. Once they were bonded, the only way to end the relationship of *eldrin-and-arcanist* was through death. Either the arcanist or the eldrin had to die... Only then could they find someone else to bond with.

"We'll treat them nicely," I said, keeping my voice low. "We aren't going to lie to them about everything. One little bluff isn't going to hurt anything."

Sorin slowly released my shoulder. He kept his gaze on the dirt, his gray-blue eyes never focusing. His depression irritated me further. What was wrong with him? Couldn't he see how amazing this was?

"Well," Sorin finally murmured, "if you think this is for the best..."

"I will be the second unicorn," one of the foals said, her voice proud. "My name is Equinox." She bowed her head until her small horn touched the dirt. "It's a pleasure to finally meet my arcanist." Then she quickly glanced between me and my brother. "Er... Whichever one I bond with."

Starling trotted to Sorin's side. "I will take the strong one."

The strong one?

No matter how many times I heard it, the phrase still bothered me.

"You can have the weaker one," Starling finished, taking my annoyance to a whole new level. "Since I was the fastest unicorn, I get the first choice."

Sorin didn't argue. He just sighed and held out his hand, his palm up.

I hadn't realized how tense I was until I thought about his gesture. My hands were clenched into tight fists, my nails digging into my palms. Why? After a short exhale, I forced myself to relax. Was I upset over what the unicorn had said?

No.

It was because of Sorin.

He said nothing, even as the foal moved over to his palm. That wasn't like him at all. He wasn't rhyming or dancing or whistling some tune. He was just stiff and dour, going along with the plan because I had told him to.

Technically, I was the "big brother."

I had been born first. Our mother had held me, and Sorin had come just as she had taken her last breath.

And as the big brother, it was my responsibility to look after my younger sibling.

What would our mother think if she saw what I was doing now?

Before Sorin touched the unicorn, I grabbed his wrist. That action startled everyone. Sorin stared at me with wide eyes, and Starling leapt away, reminding me of a deer.

"I know you're *jealous* because I'm the best unicorn," Starling said, a sneer in his tone. "But you cannot force yourself between an eldrin and his arcanist!"

"What're you doing, Gray?" my brother asked.

I jerked his arm away, and then motioned for him to stand back. When I faced the unicorns, my chest felt tight, and it was difficult to swallow.

"*Get out of here*," I said, practically shouting. It was the only way to get the words out. If I spoke normally, the words would've just died in my throat. "You've all been fooled. My brother and I aren't fifteen. We're thirteen. And we didn't run to the fence—we rode horses."

The unicorn foals nickered and exchanged quick glances. Windsweep stood from the ground, his ears twitching. "What're you saying?"

"Are you *deaf*? I said *you've been duped*. My brother and I tricked you. We're not worthy of bonding. *Go home*."

Starling stomped his hooves and kicked up dust. "I knew it!" He turned, swishing his tail. Then he leapt over to the other unicorns and pushed them back toward the market by poking them with his snout. "They're both scum. These liars made us look like fools!"

"They did," Equinox said, her tone one more of distress than disgust.

Starling snorted as he turned to glare at me. "You're worse than peasants! You're dirty rats. How dare you try to make *us*, beautiful unicorns, look like chumps. We're special and precious, and you're just filth!"

The other unicorns nodded along with Starling's statements, all of them glaring.

"I knew the moment I saw the two of you! You're not worthy of a unicorn. You're not worthy of *any* mystical creature. I'll tell everyone of your deceit! You'll never bond with anything!"

Those were some big words for a little unicorn. Obviously, he was just frustrated and shouting things. He didn't have the authority, or even the connections, to speak with any other mystical creatures, not even the hippogriffs on the island.

I would just find other creatures to bond with. Sorin and I would be fine.

We just... wouldn't ever bond with these unicorns. They clearly wouldn't forgive us.

The foals galloped toward the market. The people of the island were hurrying out to greet them. I wondered if Old Man Finn was among them.

"We're gonna get in to so much trouble," Sorin muttered.

I grabbed his arm and dragged him into Honeysuckle Meadow. The deep bushes were the perfect hiding spot. We could "swim" through the sea of flowers and exit on another trail that led back around the other side of the island. It'd take us several hours, but we'd eventually get home—and we'd smell nice.

Once in the field, Sorin and I ducked beneath the canopy of flowers. Hidden in the shade of the overgrown honeysuckle bushes, we'd be able to sneak away undetected. It wouldn't stop us from being punished, but perhaps once everyone saw that the unicorns were unharmed—and unbonded—they wouldn't be so concerned about Sorin and me. Perhaps they'd even go easy on us.

I hoped.

My brother jerked me to a halt and then wrapped his arms around my neck for a tight embrace. "Gray!"

I could barely breathe. With a strangled gasp, I managed to murmur, "S-Sorin!"

"Why did you do that?"

I pushed his arm away, freeing myself enough to gulp down air. "You know why."

"Thank you, Gray. That was amazing."

I shoved myself away from him, frowning. "We might never get another chance to bond again." I patted at my tunic and huffed. "That could've been our only chance to become arcanists. You know that, right?"

Sorin just smiled like an idiot. His grin reached both ears as he shoved the flowers to the side and crouch-walked forward. "Ah, you don't mean that." He whistled for a bit, his melody on par with any songbird's. Once we had walked for a few minutes, he stopped and said, "I think that was the right decision, Gray. I really do."

I waded through the flowers of Honeysuckle Meadow, their sweet scent almost overpowering. "Let's never mention this again."

"Everyone in town is gonna be upset. Dad'll be so angry."

After a long sigh, I said, "I know. But the two of us... We never need to discuss it again."

"My brother, the martyr," Sorin said, placing a dramatic hand on his chest. "And I, the poet, will never speak of this again."

His over-the-top statements got me smiling again, even though I hated him for it. I wanted to be mad. Why was he ruining my anger? Couldn't he let me have at least *one* thing?

CHAPTER 6

EQUAL OPPORTUNITY

"You deliberately disobeyed everyone." My father had never been so red. His arms, his neck, his face—his anger bubbled beneath the surface of his skin, changing his complexion. "You knew what you were doing was wrong! You made our whole family look like criminals. I have a business to run, boy. You're lucky they didn't banish us all from the Isle of Haylin for your stunt today."

He paced around my tiny room, taking three steps and then turning on his heel. He ground his teeth as he walked, the grating sound giving me goosebumps. The oil lamp flickered as my father shook the house with his stomping.

In my mind, I couldn't help but fill in the rest of the argument. My father would yell, *"What do you have to say for yourself?"*

"What do you have to say for yourself?" my father bellowed.

Then he'd say, *"Don't you dare be silent with me."*

Right on cue, my father came to an abrupt stop. He turned to me, his complexion darkening to an angry purple I hadn't realized humans could achieve. "Don't you dare be silent with me."

He hated it when I didn't say anything. I had learned that years ago. If I remained quiet, my father spiraled into anger faster than if he had burned himself with hot wax. But I was just taking his advice, after all. This was easier. *Keep your head down.* That was what I did. I stared at the floor, waiting for him to issue some sort of punishment.

"*Gray.*"

I said nothing.

"Curse the abyssal hells, boy—if you stay quiet, I'll tan your hide."

I still refused to engage. The angrier he got with me, the more he would forget that Sorin had even been involved in the situation. It wasn't my brother's fault—he didn't deserve to be punished. Everything had been my idea, so it didn't bother me to receive the punishment. I'd just keep my father's anger focused on me, and everything would turn out all right.

Perhaps my father sensed my plan.

He didn't say anything for a long time.

The door opened, startling the both of us. My stepmother poked her head in, her chestnut hair tied back in a neat bun. She had a kind face, but her dark eyes were always watery.

"Chester," she whispered. "Please. It's late. You've been yelling for hours."

She was shorter than most—some called her *itty bitty.* Sneezing too close to her might cause her to break. My father could probably carry her on his protruding gut, like a reverse kangaroo, if he wanted.

My father paced one more lap. He grabbed at his apron, obviously unsure what to do with his hands. Then he stomped over to the door and shut the hatch on the lantern, killing the light.

"You stay in your room," my father stated. "You don't leave, not for any reason, you hear me! Not until I say you can leave."

Then he slammed the door so hard that the lantern fell off

the hook, its decorative glass window shattering across the wood floorboards.

Feeling numb, and frustrated, I rested back on my bed, my muscles as stiff as the wood frame. Sorin wouldn't dare leave his room—not on a night like tonight—so I closed my eyes and just allowed my fatigue to take me. At least, while I slept, I could finally relax.

It didn't take long to drift away.

When I opened my eyes, the first things I noticed were the purple clouds and sparks of lightning. Bolts of power flashed in the sky. Then they shot to the ground, cracking and thundering for the few seconds it took them to travel downward. The wondrous atmosphere felt both primeval and exciting, like standing on a continent while it was forming.

I stood on the edge of a cliff with a waterfall. The mist from the falls wafted into the air, glittering whenever the lightning flashed through the sky. This waterfall made no sound, which was rather strange. Every waterfall I had ever seen rumbled from the constant crash of the river flowing to lower ground.

But this was a dream.

Somehow, I knew.

With short breaths, I glanced around, afraid that I would see more puppet-monsters.

And I did find them. Or what was left of them. Splintered wood was strewn across the rocks, the white face masks still partially whole. They had been here, in the corners of my mind, waiting for the dreams to begin.

But why?

Then I spotted Professor Helmith. She stood near the river that fed the waterfall, her inky hair fluttering in the warm winds.

Her white dress twisted around her, dancing with the weather. Again, she was barefoot, a single silver anklet shining on her left ankle.

The blue and pink spiraling tattoos on her shoulders seemed to glitter with the same kind of power radiating from the lightning. I rubbed at my own shoulders, wondering if I could ever get similar mystic tattoos.

She had killed the monsters. She must have.

"Professor?" I called out.

When she turned to face me, she smiled. The seven-pointed star on her forehead, along with the spiral shell, were just as intriguing as the tattoos. I wanted to be an arcanist—I'd do anything for a similar mark.

"Gray," the professor said. "There you are. Don't worry. I've dealt with the threat."

I jogged over, wearing my sleeping tunic and pants. I stopped once I reached her, but despite the fact that I was elated to see her, I didn't know what to say. Embarrassment stole my words. Somehow, it had never occurred to me that I would fail the unicorn's Trial of Worth. What if Professor Helmith found out?

What if she found out I had lied?

Would she deny me entrance into Astra Academy?

Why hadn't I thought about this before?

I shook my head, trying to dispel the thoughts. As long as Professor Helmith didn't discover my shameful acts, I would be fine.

Professor Helmith's eyes were as violet as the clouds. When she met my gaze, I couldn't stare for long. I just remained quiet, hoping she would have something to report about the spider-puppet monsters. Maybe she would give me an update, and then leave. That would probably be for the best.

"Gray," Professor Helmith whispered.

My shoulders bunched around the base of my neck. "Yes?"

"You tried to bond with the unicorns."

I glanced up, my eyes wide. How did she know? Had my father spoken to her? No. That was preposterous. My father never left our island. But then who had told the professor about the unicorns?

"W-Well," I began, trying to think of a way to describe what had happened without it sounding too terrible. "Sorin and I did approach the unicorns, but..." I stepped back, rubbing the tops of my arms. I couldn't maintain eye contact with her. "But we failed the unicorns' Trial of Worth. So, you know. No harm done. We were just practicing."

Maybe she didn't know I had lied to the unicorns. I feared what she would say if she discovered the truth.

Professor Helmith lifted her delicate hand and waved it through the air. The wind stopped, the lightning ceased, and the mists from the waterfall dried in an instant. It left us on the edge of a cliff, the purple sky swirling with agitated storm clouds.

The world was quiet.

My heart beat in my ears. The tension in the air thickened.

"You didn't need to approach the unicorns to attend the Academy," Professor Helmith said.

"Well... I was afraid they would leave the island soon. It was now or never. And the hippogriffs only bond with—"

She lifted a hand. I stopped talking immediately.

"Gray—the headmaster of the Academy knows that sometimes people are born into less favorable circumstances."

Words still failed me. I didn't know how to respond.

Professor Helmith laced her fingers together in front of her. "Some people are born into wealth. Some people are born into poverty. Some are born on islands without mystical creatures— far from anyone else. Some people just never have an opportunity to become an arcanist. That isn't fair, wouldn't you agree?"

It took me a moment, but I eventually nodded.

"Headmaster Venrover came up with a solution," the

professor said. "He created a menagerie within Astra Academy—a place for mystical creatures to live in harmony. Every year, we pay ship captains to offer young people passage to the Academy. We allow individuals to wander the Menagerie—to find a creature they think would find them suitable—and give them a chance to pass that creature's Trial of Worth."

I caught my breath. Once the shock wore off, I hesitantly stepped closer to her again. "The headmaster does this?"

"He wants to give everyone a chance to bond, no matter their starting position in life. The headmaster is very passionate about giving people a chance to prove themselves. He gathers all kinds of mystical creatures. Pixies, phoenixes, griffins—sometimes we even have dragons in the Menagerie."

"He lets anyone into the Menagerie?"

Professor Helmith shook her head. "Not *anyone*. For obvious reasons, we don't allow criminals. The soul of a person influences their eldrin, and we don't want negative forces in the world."

"B-But just, like, murderers, right? Not people who—"

"Who lied to a group of unicorns?"

My eyes widened.

She knew.

I kept my arms tightly crossed against my chest. What was I supposed to say now? There was nothing to add. I had lied to the unicorns—I had lied to her when I said we failed their Trial of Worth.

Professor Helmith tilted her head to the side. "If you had bonded with the unicorns through deception, I would've been forced to deny your entrance to the Academy. Headmaster Venrover takes issue with crimes of moral turpitude more than any other. But I'm glad you came to your senses and listened to your brother."

"How do you know *everything*?" I blurted out.

I hadn't told anyone about what had truly happened with

the unicorns. My father didn't know I had lied—and he didn't know I had denied the foals at the last minute, either.

Had the professor spoken to Sorin?

Professor Helmith giggled, and shook her head. "In the realm of dreams, your thoughts are as visible to me as the distant lightning, Gray. *You* told me about the unicorns and their Trial of Worth the moment you dwelled on the experience."

I...

I didn't know what to say.

"Your arcanist magic allows you to see my thoughts?" I whispered. "That's how you knew my favorite dessert." I should've realized in the last dream...

"That's right. As an ethereal whelk arcanist, I have that ability. Something I'm sure you'll learn in detail once you make it to the Academy."

"You... You still think I should attend? Even though I lied?"

The professor stepped close enough to place a hand on my shoulder. Her gentle touch eased some of my fears. "Deception is a tool. Just like a pistol or a sword. And tools aren't inherently evil—it depends on how you use them. A pistol can protect you from a pirate. A sword can cut through the netting of a trap. Deception can trick a blackheart into revealing his wicked plans."

I listened intently, unable to think of anything to add.

"As a professor, it's my duty to help people to learn how to use all the tools and talents they have at their disposal. And to ensure they use what I teach them for the betterment of all." She turned her attention to the distance. "And I think you'll do great things, once you're pointed in the right direction."

I glanced over, wondering if she was staring at anything specific. The clouds swirled over the dreamscape horizon, but I didn't spot anything of note.

Then Professor Helmith returned her attention to me.

"*However*, you must promise me you won't lie to any more mystical creatures to undertake their Trial of Worth."

I grimaced and then forced a quick laugh. "Oh, yes. Of course. I swear to you that I'll never do that again. I'll wait until I'm fifteen."

"Good."

With a spring in her step, Professor Helmith leapt back. The skies parted above us, revealing the glitter of stars.

She held up a finger. "The Astra Academy Menagerie is filled with all types of mystical creatures. I'm sure you'll find *something* there that matches your unique personality."

"Sorin, too, right?" I asked. "My brother is also welcome?"

"Of course. Although I've never met your brother, I've heard what you think of him. I'm certain Sorin will enjoy the Academy."

Thank the good stars. If she hadn't allowed Sorin...

I wouldn't have wanted to attend.

"Don't you have anyone to help you investigate all these dreams?" I asked. "I mean, I don't want you to leave, but... It seems like a lot of work for just one person."

"The other professors at the Academy help in any way they can. And the headmaster provides resources and safety, but the ability to dreamwalk is very rare. Not many mystical creatures can do it. So... Yes. I must do this alone."

I hated to hear her say that.

"Perhaps I'll bond with something that can help you," I whispered, trying not to sound too hopeful.

Professor Helmith offered me a small smile. "Perhaps you will." Then she held up a finger. "But in the meantime, *if* those monsters do return, I want to be here to catch them. I'm hoping to glean some sort of valuable information. Or better yet, discover who's sending them. If I'm lucky, this whole mess will be solved before you bond with anything."

Although I still felt a little awkward, I relaxed a bit. The professor seemed eldritch and mystical in a way I hadn't really considered before. If she was going to be spending time in my dreams, I was going to use that opportunity to learn all I could from her.

Professor Helmith put a hand over her mouth and giggled. "You want to learn all you can from me, huh?"

My face grew hot, and I almost smacked myself. I had already forgotten she could hear my thoughts in this dream.

"Well, if you're going to be here anyway," I said sheepishly.

Professor Helmith laughed, her purple eyes alight with genuine amusement. "I have many dreams to travel... but when their currents carry me to you, I will be happy to teach you everything I can."

I almost clapped my hands and shouted, but I held back. Instead, I just imagined all the different creatures I knew about. Phoenixes, unicorns, mermaids, hippogriffs, griffins, kappas, hydras, dryads—and there were so many more I didn't know about! What would I find in the Astra Academy Menagerie?

I couldn't wait to find out.

CHAPTER 7

TWO YEARS LATER—AGE FIFTEEN

Finally.

Three weeks ago, I had finally turned fifteen years old.

Today was the day I left the island.

My bedroom seemed smaller than ever. I practically stumbled into every piece of furniture as I shoved clothing into my backpack. They were my best clothes, but that didn't mean much, unfortunately. The pants were too short. I had grown a few inches since last I had visited the tailor.

I still wasn't as tall or large as Sorin, but at least I was catching up in terms of height.

With my things packed, I flew out the door and hurried down the hall. My father and stepmother waited in the front room. Late morning sunshine lit up our home, the light bright enough to rival my high spirits. With a smile, I grabbed a handful of raspberries from a bowl sitting in the middle of the table.

"The ship should be leaving soon," I said, trying not to sound too cheerful.

My father grunted some sort of acknowledgement.

The *Sapphire Dune* had taken all morning sailing around the nearby islands to gather Academy hopefuls. The Isle of Haylin was the last stop. Once it was finished boarding, we'd be on our way.

"Sorin already headed to the docks," my stepmother said.

He already left? That miffed me. Why hadn't he waited?

My stepmother's watery eyes fixed on me, and then they grew glassier with barely restrained tears. "I hope you'll have safe travels."

I really didn't want my departure to be tainted with bittersweet emotions. I ignored most of her statement as I made my way to the front door. After popping a few berries into my mouth and swallowing, I said, "Astra Academy is one of the most incredible places in the world. Sorin and I will be fine."

When I tried to exit the house, my father posted his arm across the doorway, blocking my path. I turned to him, tense and uncertain of what would happen next.

"Listen, Gray," he said. "All important days in your life start with either a good or a bad omen."

"Oh?"

"That's right. You need to pay attention to the details. Good weather, good sounds, even the good scents—you need to pay attention. You're a clever boy. Sometimes you get too cocky. You miss the little things."

My father used that *bad omen* stuff as an excuse to avoid a lot of island drama. If the weather was poor, or his breakfast was sour, he would say today wasn't a day to go to the market. He liked staying home.

He wanted me to do that? Seemed childish.

"I'll keep a look out," I said.

My father reluctantly lowered his arm, allowing me out. "There's magic all around us, boy. Just... keep that in mind, when you think you see signs. I'll be rooting for you two boys to succeed at this academy. I'll be a proud father if I can say you and Sorin became arcanists."

His words threatened to break my composure. I tried not to dwell on them. "Thanks. I'm certain Sorin and I will do okay." We had a secret advantage, after all. Professor Helmith had told me all about the Academy.

My stepmother held her arms open for a hug. Again, I didn't want to get mired in emotions, so I gave her a quick embrace before exiting the house. My father watched me go, his face stuck in a slight frown.

I ate a couple more raspberries as I hurried down the road. What was my father worried about? Today was a good day. That was what I had thought, until I caught a whiff of rotting fish. Every so often, the fish sat on the pier a little too long. That stench covered the whole island.

Was that my omen? Perhaps. Some people might see a rotting fish as a bad omen for leaving, but I saw it as further proof that I needed to leave. I didn't want to rot like those fish.

My father was content to stay here doing the same thing forever, but not me.

I shrugged off the thought as I headed into town and straight for the port. The morning mists rolled in from the bay, creating an ominous atmosphere the closer I got to the ships. The chill seemed to seep into everyone's spirits.

Despite that, I kept my head high. No number of ill signs would sway me from my path. I held my tiny backpack over my shoulder.

Others would be joining us on the trek to Astra Academy. Would we all become arcanists? That was unlikely. Some mystical creatures had difficult Trials of Worth.

The stronger the creature, the more difficult the trial, at least according to Professor Helmith.

My brother waited for me near the gangplank. I recognized his silhouette in the morning fog long before I saw any details.

His broad shoulders and barrel chest were difficult to miss, even among the sailors. I jogged over to greet him, smiling wide.

"*Sorin*," I called out. "You left the house without me."

"I couldn't sleep," he said as I got close. His voice had definitely deepened in the last year and a half. He sounded like a man in his thirties. He even had the stubble on his chin to match. "I was just too excited."

I glanced around. None of the dockhands or sailors seemed to share that sentiment. They grumbled to one another as they loaded the ship with all the supplies we would need for the trek.

I ate my last raspberry, prepared for anything.

"Did Father give you a speech about good and bad omens this morning?" I asked.

Sorin nodded twice. "Oh, yeah. He said I needed to keep a look out for the signs of magic. He said, uh, something like, *Magic is the breath of the world. When it's tired or stressed, you'll see it groan.*"

"He didn't say it like that."

"But that's how I remember it." Sorin grabbed my shoulder, his hand larger than most. "Are you worried? You shouldn't be. So many good omens today—our trip will be excellent."

I stared at the sad sailors, then the gloomy mist, and I even wrinkled my nose when the stench of the fish washed over us with the wind. "So many good omens," I muttered sarcastically.

"Yeah. Did you see the sunshine this morning? No clouds on the distant horizon. And Mum went out and picked all those raspberries, just for you. She must've done it while it was still dark out. She loves you, Gray. What's a better omen than that?"

My throat tightened. With a shaky hand, I swept back my black hair. "I hadn't thought of it like that."

"Seemed obvious to me."

Then Sorin pulled on my shoulder and practically dragged me up the gangplank. When we reached the deck of the boat, he smiled wide and motioned to everything with a dramatic wave of his arm.

This was a frigate. Three masts, raised quarterdeck, and twenty-four guns. Most people considered them warships, but frigates also transported people. They were the terrors of the seas, unless up against an airship. Few pirates ever dared to face a frigate in one-on-one sea battles.

A modern vessel that every nation hoped to fill their fleets with.

The figurehead on the bow of the ship was a griffin. Its lion-head was open in a roar with its talon-like claws flexed outward. I appreciated the craftsmanship.

A couple dozen individuals stood around on the deck, each with their own backpacks and bags. If I had to guess, I would say all of them were the age of fifteen, same as Sorin and me. A few were a little older—I would guess twenty-something—but for the most part, all young hopefuls.

These were the other passengers from nearby islands.

"Look there, Gray," my brother said, his eyes wide. "The captain."

I turned to see a man in an ankle-length swashbuckler coat. He walked down a set of stairs from the quarterdeck. His clothing was the kind meant to keep a person protected even in the thickest of storms.

He wore boots up to his knees—just like me and Sorin—and a button-up shirt with a few stains on the belly. The man's protruding gut moonlit as a table. It reminded me too much of my father. My chest twisted with regret when I realized I hadn't hugged him goodbye.

I shook away the thought. I would see him again.

The captain poked at the rim of his tricorn cap, exposing his forehead. I caught my breath. His forehead had a mark on it—an etching in his skin.

An arcanist mark, just like Professor Helmith.

Well, not *exactly* the same.

His seven-pointed star was laced with the image of a griffin. The mystical creature had eagle wings, as well as the body and head of a lion. I loved the look of it and stared more than polite society considered reasonable.

Would I bond with a griffin? They were similar to hippogriffs, which reminded me too much of home, so probably not.

"I wonder what the star represents," Sorin whispered as the captain strode onto the deck of the ship.

"According to Professor Helmith, the seven-pointed star is the symbol of magic. The creature on the star determines what kind of abilities the arcanist has."

"Wow. Your kooky classroom dreams are amazing."

"They're not *kooky*," I said under my breath.

"*Welcome, ladies and gents and all those in between,*" the captain shouted, his voice boisterous enough to reach the mountains on the other side of the island. "My name is Captain Minnis. Once my crew finish loadin' everything aboard, we'll get everyone into their cabins. You'll be sleepin' four to a room—cramped quarters, I'm afraid."

A few people on the deck of the ship groaned.

"The *Sapphire Dune* is my baby," Captain Minnis said. He grunted and stroked at his beard. It was a small thing, barely covering his entire chin, but it was striped—black and gray hairs grew in solid lines. "You'll treat my ship like she's your lover, you understand me? Gently and graciously."

A single person on the deck of the ship laughed.

Captain Minnis's eyes twitched. "Oscar!" he shouted.

A guttural growl emanated from the quarterdeck.

My brother punched my shoulder, causing me to stumble. I rubbed at the soreness on my upper arm, but Sorin didn't seem to notice.

He pointed. "Here it comes, Gray! Look. A griffin."

I glanced up. That was when I saw it.

A majestic and wondrous griffin stood proudly on the edge of the *Sapphire Dune*'s quarterdeck, its golden fur and dark mane rippling in the morning breeze. The lion-headed creature scanned over the people on the crowded pier, its amber eyes bright.

"That's a male griffin," my brother said. "You can tell because he has the head of a lion. A female griffin has the head of an eagle."

"I know. Professor Helmith told me."

Sorin glanced over with a slight frown. "Did she tell you all about the rare types of griffins, too? I mean, I love your kooky professor, but I was hoping I could be the griffin expert, and tell you all about them."

The professor *had* told me about rare griffin varieties, but I decided to humor my brother.

"What about this griffin makes it rare?" I asked.

Sorin smiled and then pointed. "This griffin is a spotted griffin. See those markings on his flank, right there? Those spots that look like a jaguar's?"

The captain's griffin swished his majestic tail. Although he had a lion's head, he had a jaguar's tail, without the tuft on the end like a lion's. Black spots covered the creature's flank.

"I see them," I said.

"Spotted griffins only come from way down south, and even then, most people never see them. So, this is a very rare griffin. We're lucky to see it."

My brother loved griffins. He wanted to bond with one more than any other mystical creature. He loved their noble bearing, but no matter how I tried, I couldn't see the appeal.

They just weren't for me.

The griffin spread his wings and leapt down to the main deck. He landed hard, shaking the entire ship with his 600-pound body.

"This is my eldrin, Oscar," Captain Minnis said with a half-smile. "If any of you so much as breaks a splinter off my beautiful boat, I'll have Oscar handle you. Understand?"

The griffin, Oscar, snorted as he folded his wings close to his body. "You all are guests on this vessel," he said, his voice deep and regal. It sent a shiver down my spine. "The journey will only last a day. It shouldn't be difficult to keep everything tidy."

The silence of the crowd was the only answer Captain Minnis needed. Once the crew had loaded the last of the supplies, he motioned to the sails as they unfurled. "Now that everyone has boarded..." He reached into the pocket of his long coat and withdrew a piece of parchment. "I assigned everyone to cabins."

Oscar spread his wings, flapped them a few times, and then leapt back onto the *Sapphire Dune's* quarterdeck. With all the disinterest of a housecat, the griffin walked in a circle several times, and then laid down with a *whump.*

The sailors had to work around him.

The bustle of the crowd became all-consuming. I could barely hear myself think. My brother—who got excited over every little thing, including funerals—hurried toward the captain with earnest enthusiasm. He stopped mid-step and then turned back around for me.

"C'mon, Gray!"

Sorin dragged me through the crowd on the deck, yanking my arm. I almost lost my backpack, but I managed to hang on to the strap with all my wiry might.

We were practically the first ones in front of Captain Minnis. No one bothered to yell at my brother, likely for fear of being pushed into the water. Not that Sorin would do that—but most people didn't know Sorin like I did. He was just so large...

"You two here for the Academy?" the captain asked as we approached.

"That's right," my brother said. Then he pulled me forward.

"This is my twin brother. We're gonna become arcanists together."

"Yar twin?" Captain Minnis snorted and then gave us both the once-over. "Was there a triplet you ate, boy? That's the only way I can reason out the size differences here." Then he glared at our faces. "Look at yer eyes. Those are... almost unnatural. Can you two see all right?"

I frowned. "Yeah. We're fine. Do we have a room or not?"

The captain glanced down at the paper. When he brought up his second hand, I caught my breath. I hadn't noticed until then, but Captain Minnis didn't have a second hand. He had a wooden prosthetic, carved from some fine oak, and half-wrapped in leather.

"I have Sorin Lexly here," the captain muttered. Then he poked the paper with his fake hand. "And here is *Gray* Lexly." He glared at me again. "You named after a color, boy?"

With a sigh, I replied, "That's right. My name is Gray. Not *White*. Not *Black*. Just *Gray*."

"Heh. Strange. You're a little thin, too. And you only have a backpack? No weapons? Extra gear?"

Everything about us was strange to this man, apparently.

"We'll be fine," I said.

"Uh-huh. Welp, I've seen plenty of kids attempt to bond at Astra Academy, and ones who make it look a little more prepared than you two. Maybe you want to change your minds? Go back home while you still can?"

"I think we'll end up surprising you," I muttered, trying to keep my disdain out of my voice. Who was this guy to judge us?

"I doubt it. And if I gotta sail you back to your home island within the week, you owe me a drink."

Sorin patted my shoulder. "My brother and I have been waiting for this for nearly two years now, sir. Gray even speaks with one of the professors of the Academy all the time. I'm sure we'll get in."

The captain rubbed at his chin with his fake hand. "Oh. You have an insider pullin' some strings for you. All makes sense now."

I gritted my teeth and refused to say anything. Professor Helmith wouldn't cheat to get me into the Academy. I knew her well enough to know that. It angered me that he'd even think I would need that.

"You Lexly Twins will be stayin' in the cabin marked with the number four, got that?" Captain Minnis pointed to a door under the quarterdeck. "You'll find hammocks within. I'll send you your cabinmates in just a moment. Now git."

With that unceremonious blessing, Sorin and I walked over to the cabin door. My brother shot me a sidelong glance. "Don't be upset."

"I'm not upset," I stated.

"We'll just prove to him that he's wrong, is all."

I forced myself to smile. "You always have a way of seeing the bright side."

"C'mon! I'll race you to the room. Whoever wins gets to pick their hammock first!"

He shot off toward the door, lumbering as fast as he could. I just jogged behind him, trying to dispel the anger I felt. Sorin was right. Soon, I'd prove them wrong.

We just needed to get to Astra Academy.

CHAPTER 8

TRAVELING TO THE ACADEMY

Our tiny cabin came equipped with four hammocks, one in each corner. A single porthole allowed light to stream in, but the fog did its best to keep us blanketed in darkness. We had a lantern by the door, nailed in place so it couldn't fall if the ship hit rough waters.

"I won, so I get to pick my hammock first," Sorin said as he hurried over to the far corner. He sat on the hammock closest to the porthole. "This one." He swung back and forth, treating his new bed like a swing. "The rope is brand new."

I went over to the hammock opposite his. Just as my brother had said, the woven rope of the hammock was new. I sat on mine, wondering if the captain had prepared for the many passengers who wanted to attend Astra Academy.

Before we could get too settled, the door opened, and a small girl slipped inside. She shut the door without making any noise and then turned her attention to Sorin and me.

Was this girl here for the Academy? She was so short I would've sworn she was eleven years old. And potentially stunted. She was barely five feet, which meant she was a good foot shorter than I was—and a foot and half shorter than Sorin.

Her hair, as dark red as regal wood, was cut to the length of her shoulders, and her heart-shaped face was adorned with thin glasses. She pushed the glasses up her nose a bit as she shuffled over to an empty hammock. Despite her small frame, she carried a backpack on her shoulders, a sack dangled from one hand, and she wore a belt covered in pouches.

How many things had she packed? She had enough supplies to last for weeks.

"Hello," the girl whispered.

Sorin slid off his hammock and smiled wide. "Hey, there. Nice to meet you."

She cringed away from my brother, a slight frown on her face. He was... so much larger than her. His head almost touched the ceiling of our cabin.

"Don't worry about him," I said. "My brother's harmless. His name is Sorin, and I'm Gray." With a sigh, I added, "*Yes*, like the color. *No*, it's not short for anything."

"I'm Nini Wanderlin." She set her bag on the hammock and then pulled her backpack off her small shoulders and placed it on the floor. "I'm here to visit the Astra Academy Menagerie and bond with a mystical creature."

"You're fifteen?" Sorin gawked at her. "*You*?"

Nini's face instantly went pink. She wore a long, black coat and long, brown pants, both of which seemed too large for her. She practically sank beneath the collar of her coat, hiding herself from the conversation. She even buttoned it up, like a turtle hiding itself from a predator.

"I'm *sixteen*," Nini murmured into her clothing. "No one ever believes me when I tell them my age, but... it's the truth."

Sorin ran a hand through his hair. "Oh. Well. You're, uh, youthful. Child-like, even. Wait! *Pixie-like*. That's a better way to describe it. It rolls off the tongue. Nini—pixie—you hear it?"

"Um."

"Pixies are so small. Some of the smallest mystical creatures.

And you're the smallest sixteen-year-old I've seen, so you're similar."

"R-Right."

"What island do you hail from?" I asked, trying desperately to claw out of this awkward conversation.

"The Isle of Leen," Nini said, leaning away from my brother, her eyebrows knitted.

"Where all the leviathans are?" I almost hopped off my hammock, excitement flowing through me. "I heard they nest by the rocks near the southern beach of the isle."

Nini slowly exited her giant coat and smiled. It was only then that I noticed the many freckles that covered her nose and cheeks. "That's right. The leviathans are so majestic when they're swimming in the waves. They're giant sea serpents with glorious fins, and their colors remind me of lapis lazuli."

"Did you try to bond with one?" Sorin interjected.

Nini flinched at his voice and then retreated a bit back into her oversized coat. She shook her head. "Oh, you probably didn't hear. The leviathans left the island a year ago."

"What?" Sorin and I asked at the same time.

"There was no bonding ceremony, even though that was when I turned fifteen." Nini sighed. "I thought I'd get to participate in the leviathan's Trial of Worth, but I'm not very lucky."

I hadn't ever heard of something like that happening. Normally, the people of the islands went out of their way to take special care of mystical creatures. The Isle of Haylin did everything it could to care for the hippogriffs, and we had tended to the unicorns until they had eventually been taken from the isle, even though they weren't native.

The Isle of Ruma had phoenixes.

And the Isle of Landin had griffins.

The mystical creatures were always the pride and joy of all the isle citizens. Why would the leviathans leave?

"Some of the leviathans were having trouble sleeping." Nini patted her hammock and then carefully sat on it, right next to her bag. She sank a bit, almost swallowed whole by her new bed. "Um. They kept complaining to our doctor about nightmares. A few died one night. No one knew why... It looked like they had been attacked, but the leviathans said no one had been in the waters."

"They died?" I asked, my voice low. "From unknown injuries that just appeared at night?"

Nini nodded.

I found it difficult to breathe.

"And then the leviathans said they needed to leave for a while," she said.

Although Nini hadn't specifically said the dreams had been the cause of the deaths—I knew the truth. The leviathans had been visited by the same puppet-monsters that haunted my nightmares. They had been attacked and killed.

My thoughts buzzed, filled with all sorts of theories. Professor Helmith *still* hadn't discovered the source of the dream-monsters.

But they had shown up in my dreams less and less frequently over the months...

She had said she couldn't seem to detect who was sending them, no matter how many times she destroyed the monsters in my dreams.

"Did you say the leviathans were having strange *dreams?*" Sorin stepped close and grabbed my shoulder. "I've got good news. Gray knows all about dreams! His honeysuckle comes to visit him every night while he's sleeping."

I almost choked on my own breath as I whipped my head around to glare at my brother.

"His honeysuckle?" Nini asked, one eyebrow up.

"Yeah. You know. The person he swoons over."

I grabbed Sorin's shirt and jerked him over to my hammock,

so angry I couldn't find the right words without sounding like a blackheart. *Honeysuckle* was the term we used on the Isle of Haylin to refer to someone's romantic flame. Obviously, the term came from our northern meadow. People would sneak wild honeysuckles off the bushes and give them to their potential significant others.

"*Professor Helmith isn't my honeysuckle*," I growled through gritted teeth, hoping I kept my voice low enough so that Nini couldn't hear. "Helmith is an *arcanist*. Arcanists can live for hundreds of years. Remember? When a mystical creature bonds with them, it's like they're stealing a person's ability to age. That's how an eldrin grows older."

"So, your professor is an old woman?" Sorin asked, his brow furrowed.

"W-Well, I don't know her actual age."

"She *could* be a grandma or something?"

Nini slid off her hammock and stepped a bit closer to us. "Wait, did you just say Gray's honeysuckle is a grandma?"

I shoved Sorin to the side and forced out a quick sigh. "Professor Helmith isn't a grandma." I didn't know that, but that was the story I was sticking to until I knew otherwise. "She's a powerful arcanist who visits my dreams. *That's it*. She's not my *honeysuckle*. She's just—"

"Someone who teaches at the Academy." Nini smiled wide again and then pushed her glasses up higher on her nose. "I've heard about her. They say she's descended from royalty. It's so amazing you know her personally."

Descended from royalty?

"Gray sees the professor all the time," my brother said.

I shook my head. "I haven't seen her for the last few weeks. She's busy."

No dream-monsters had attacked me in a while. I thought, at the very least, Professor Helmith would've said goodbye, but she just hadn't shown up in my dreams since I had turned fifteen about three weeks ago. It felt strange. Like something was wrong. But I kept that thought from my mind.

I'd speak to her in person soon enough.

Then I could put this fear to rest.

"If you know the professor, you two must be part of a merchant family?" Nini raised an eyebrow. "Or maybe you're part of the nobility? Or recordkeepers?"

"Actually, we're the sons of tallow chandler," Sorin said before I could answer.

Nini's eyes went wide. "What is *that*? I don't think I've ever heard of that profession."

"It's someone who makes candles," I said.

"Oh." She stared for a long moment before continuing with, "I, uh, didn't know there were still candlemakers around. I thought everyone used lanterns or glowstones. Candles seem..."

"*Antiquated*?" Sorin asked. Then he smiled and laughed. "I like to think of them as *romantic*. They're from a time when everything was handmade and woven from the rawest of materials."

For the first time since she arrived, Nini seemed to relax. Whatever Sorin had said, it had resonated with her.

Before we could continue the conversation, the door opened again. A young man, probably the same age as Sorin and me, stepped into the cabin. He wore a black cloak over his shoulders, and a large cap on his head, hiding most of his features like he was out in the desert sun, and he didn't want to get burned. He walked to the last hammock and took a seat without giving us so much as a glance.

"Hello," Sorin said with a half-wave. "I'm Sorin Lexly. And this is my brother, Gray."

The fellow regarded my brother with a slight glance. For a short moment, the man said nothing, and then he went about organizing his bags around his hammock.

Was he ignoring Sorin? Seemed so. That didn't bother me

that much. If this guy didn't want to speak, that worked out for everyone involved.

But my brother couldn't leave well enough alone. "I said, *hello.*" Sorin strode halfway over to the other man's hammock. "Just in case you didn't hear me. Some people don't hear as well as others. I learned that a few years back when the baker would always just wave whenever I said anything, because he just assumed—"

"I heard you," the man said, cutting Sorin off.

"Oh. Then... you just didn't want to speak to us?"

The unpleasant fellow lifted his cap a bit and glared at my brother with dark eyes. He *was* suntanned, way more than I originally thought.

He also had scars on his cheek and chin—the type from an animal. Claw marks.

"I'm not here to make friends," the scarred man said.

"Obviously," I quipped.

Sorin frowned. "But we're all going to Astra Academy together."

"We're not *all* going to attend." The man pointed to my brother's forehead. "You're not an arcanist yet, right? Neither am I. Some of us won't impress a mystical creature at the Academy—and if you can't pass a Trial of Worth, they'll send you right back home on the boat you sailed over on. So... it's better if we save our introductions until *after* we know we'll have a place at Astra Academy, don't you think?"

Pragmatic.

Not the way I would've handled things, but I couldn't fault his logic.

Nini frowned and hid in her coat. "Hmm."

My brother shifted his weight from one foot to the other, like he wanted to say something, but couldn't find the right words. In my mind, this new guy wasn't worth speaking to. If the man thought it was useless to speak to us—because we hadn't proven ourselves to be important enough yet—that was his business. Who cared if he liked us or not?

Sorin eventually shuffled over to his hammock and sat down.

I turned my attention to the porthole, wondering just how long I would have to wait to see the Academy with my own eyes. The vessel rocked as it left port. The *Sapphire Dune* would reach the Academy in one day...

It felt like forever.

I only slept for a few hours during our travels.

No dreams. No Professor Helmith.

Another night, and she still hadn't visited. Thankfully, there had been no puppet-monsters either, but that didn't puzzle me as much as her disappearance. Perhaps someone else needed her help? Was that why she was gone? That made sense. Or perhaps she had finally discovered the individual behind the attacks.

When I woke, I sat up on my hammock and watched the porthole, keeping track of the time through the shifting of the colors in the distant sky. The darkness gave way to dark purple and blue and then finally to orange and yellow. The dawn reminded me of an amateur painter who couldn't decide on a color.

Sorin barely fit in his hammock. He took deep breaths, never snoring, but getting dangerously close.

The unfriendly man slept with his cap over his face. He had clearly ridden on boats hundreds of times before. No matter how much the ship rocked and swayed, the man never stirred.

Nini wasn't as fortunate. She tossed and turned, rolling in her hammock, clearly uncomfortable. Any time waves crashed against the hull, she sat up for a moment and glanced around. Her glasses were tied to her backpack on the floor. She squinted at everything, even the porthole, staring for several seconds before determining everything was okay and going back to sleep.

Once the sun had risen into the sky, clearing away the last of the night, I slid off my hammock and went straight to Sorin. With a few shakes, he eventually opened his eyes. I held a finger to my lips and then pointed to the porthole to show him the light.

Sorin offered a groggy smile as he slid off the hammock and stretched. He smelled weird. He always smelled weird when he woke up, but today it seemed worse. He scratched at his wrinkled shirt and rubbed at his eyes.

Then I quietly motioned him out of the cabin.

Restless and eager to see new sights, I walked out onto the main deck of the *Sapphire Dune*, my brother close behind me.

The ship's crew hurried about, their energy high. A couple grabbed ropes and tied down barrels, while a few others secured hatches in place so the doors wouldn't swing open. When I turned my attention to the waves, I saw no islands or landmasses. There were no clouds, either. No storms, no other ships. Why were the sailors so excited?

"*We're approaching the Gates of Crossing!*" a man shouted from the crow's nest.

Captain Minnis leapt onto the railing of the quarterdeck. "All right, ya lazy bones! Prep the ship. Take down the sails! Bring up the star shards! Git!"

His spotted griffin, Oscar, walked along the railing of the quarterdeck, watching the sailors comply with the captain's orders. Then the lion-headed griffin turned his attention to me, his eyes bright.

The captain's eldrin stared at Sorin and me for a long moment. I simply slipped my hands into my trouser pockets and stared back, unsure what the beast wanted. Were we allowed on the deck? The captain hadn't said otherwise.

The sailors lowered most of the sails, but kept the main ones in place. It slowed our travel, and my heart raced a bit.

"What's going on?" Sorin asked, glancing around. "What're the *Gates of Crossing*?"

"Professor Helmith told me all about them." I grabbed my brother's arm and guided him over to the starboard side of the ship. "That's why I woke you up. I can't wait to see your reaction."

"I see something." Sorin pointed to the far horizon, in the direction the ship was heading.

I leaned most of my weight on the side of the ship and stared. There was a ring of metal in the ocean, half submerged in the water. It was a giant, metal ring—large enough that the *Sapphire Dune* could easily sail through.

We were heading straight for it.

Although Professor Helmith had told me about the gates, I hadn't realized they would be *that* large. I smiled to myself, still eager to see them in action for myself.

The sailors shot up from the hold, some of them hauling sacks, but one of them carried a small wooden box. I turned around and watched as the sailor carefully opened the wooden container and held up a single crystal.

The crystal was no larger than his thumb, and it glittered with inner power.

"What's that?" Sorin asked. "Is it a star shard?"

"Yeah. Definitely."

Professor Helmith had told me about star shards. They were magical crystals that had fallen from the sky like shooting stars. They were bits of raw magic, solid and tangible. And most importantly, they were used to create magical items. Sorin's confusion didn't surprise me. Our school didn't teach us much about star shards other than we needed to report them to the mayor if we ever found one.

Our teacher had said that star shards were rare and valuable, and that only arcanists should have them. A single shard was worth more money than I had ever seen. Probably.

The sailor placed the single star shard in the middle of the deck. It sparkled in the daylight, glinting with power. No one approached it after that. All the sailors kept their distance.

"What's going on?" Sorin whispered to me.

Although I knew the answer, I just smiled. "You'll see. Don't worry—you'll love it."

"You're really not gonna tell me?" Sorin punched my upper arm.

I half-stumbled away and rubbed at my shoulder. With a smirk, I said, "Nope."

"It's not fair that you got a professor to tell you all the amazing things that'll happen. I'm just in the dark."

"Trust me. It'll be more exciting if you just *experience it*. I wish I didn't know."

Sorin grumbled something else under his breath, but I didn't quite hear. Then he stared down at me. "Is the gate a magical item?"

"Yeah. Well, technically, they're *artifacts*. Which basically means they're powerful magical items. Professor Helmith said the Gates of Crossing were made by talented rizzel arcanists."

My brother's eyebrows lifted. "Rizzel arcanists? I've never heard of a *rizzel*. What kind of mystical creature is that?"

"You'll see."

Sorin didn't like that answer. He tensed like he was about to punch me again, and I flinched in anticipation. He just chuckled and playfully shoved me.

"Everyone prepare yourselves," the captain shouted. "We'll be travelin' soon."

The *Sapphire Dune* sailed a bit slower than before, but we made steady progress toward the gate. It wouldn't take long before we sailed right through the ring.

The sailors grabbed the railings, and a few actually tied ropes to themselves, and then to the masts. It felt odd not to have some sort of safety measure. I grabbed the nearest bit of railing and hoped I was strong enough to weather what was about to happen. Sorin did the same.

"Here it comes," Captain Minnis said.

I held my breath, my eyes fixed on the ring. It grew larger as we got closer.

And then the single star shard on the deck of the ship glowed with a radiant inner light.

CHAPTER 9

THE GATES OF CROSSING

O nce the *Sapphire Dune* drew close to the Gates of Crossing, I realized the metal ring was engraved with images of ferrets. The cute little weasel-like pictures circled around the ring as though frolicking. Those were the *rizzel*. Professor Helmith had said they were creatures of great mobility and freedom.

The metal ring itself, though?

When I squinted my eyes, it appeared to be an ouroboros—a serpent eating its own tail. According to Professor Helmith, the ouroboros was the symbol of eternity, or sometimes infinity. A mythical symbol used by powerful arcanists to sometimes represent their influence.

The etchings of the rizzel glowed as our ship neared.

Sorin pointed. "Look at that, Gray! What's going on? What are those things?"

"Those are the rizzel."

"They're so cute." He turned to me, his jaw clenched. "Are those the creatures that made the gate? Why are they there?"

I nodded once and then motioned back to the gate. "Just keep watching."

Professor Helmith had already told me all about the amazing powers of the rizzel. Now it was time to see them in action. I held my breath as the bow of the *Sapphire Dune* went through the Gates of Crossing—the whole ring glowing with such intensity, I had to shield my eyes.

The single star shard melted into the deck of the ship.

My body twisted. It felt as though I were being jerked through a wind tunnel. I coughed and hacked and stumbled across the ship. Then a gust of chilly air washed over us, sweeping across the deck in one frightening blast. When I managed to open my eyes again, I couldn't help but laugh.

The *Sapphire Dune* wasn't in the ocean anymore.

The ship had sailed through the gate and teleported to a whole new location.

We were now on a giant mountain lake. The clear waters reflected the blue sky above. Small rivers fed into the lake in the distance, but the ocean was nowhere to be found. Our giant frigate—a terror of the ocean waves—floated across the lake as though it had fallen out of a storm.

The Gates of Crossing stopped glowing. The little rizzel etchings returned to their dormant state. The *Sapphire Dune* slowly floated across the calm waters.

It was harder to breathe here. My head hurt, and I had to rub at my temples.

Sorin grabbed my arm and shook me. He pointed to our surroundings, smiling widely. Then he took a few deep breaths, obviously struggling to get air.

"Where are we?" Sorin asked.

Eager to see the Academy, I glanced around. Cannons built into the mountain rocks were the first things to catch my attention. They were heavy guns—the types used to destroy ships, not injure them. They were pointed at the gate, at least six of them.

Would they have fired on us if we weren't permitted here?

Professor Helmith had said the Academy had its own defenses. Perhaps this was what she meant.

I turned my gaze to the peak of the nearby mountain. Pine trees surrounded the base—a massive evergreen forest of pointed tops and prickly leaves. Then the slate-gray mountainside rose up out of the forest, jutting high into the sky. At the plateau was a massive castle-like building made of black bricks and steel. White ivory accented the roofs, pillars, and balconies, all of it glittering with pristine beauty.

Astra Academy.

The black bricks reminded me of the night sky. And the building was so high—like it was reaching for the stars themselves.

Distant mountains dotted the landscape all around us. We were in a mountain range of summits, far from civilization, yet somehow close, thanks to the Gates of Crossing. Other black buildings sat perched on distant mountaintops. Were they parts of the Academy as well? Was the Academy spread throughout this whole area?

I counted at least five buildings, and that wasn't including the main castle.

A long road up the mountain led to the massive front gates of the Academy.

"There it is, Sorin," I whispered, pointing to the castle facility. "Astra Academy."

My brother shook me again, harder than before. The pain in my head intensified, but I managed to grin through it all. The elegant—yet haunting—Academy was unlike anything I had pictured. It was more mysterious and beautiful than even Professor Helmith had described it to me.

"Where do you think the Menagerie is?" Sorin asked.

"Underneath."

"In the mountain?"

"That's what Professor Helmith said."

When I glanced around a second time, I realized there were other Gates of Crossing around the edges of the lake. Four others. They glowed white as I stared at them, each shining in the center and revealing a different—and distant—place. Four other ships sailed through, each crashing into the peaceful waters and then slowly rocking into a casual pace. The Gates of Crossing stopped glowing afterward.

The new ships were the size of our frigate, though each flew the flag of a different nation. One I didn't even recognize. That boat was thin and flat, longer than most. The sails were stiff triangles. Where did it hail from?

Captain Minnis waved his arm. "Wake the passengers! Tell them we've reached Astra Academy. We'll be weighing anchor shortly."

"I'll get our things." Sorin rushed across the deck and slammed through a door under the quarterdeck. It only took him a few moments to return with our backpacks. He jogged to my side, dropped the bag at my feet, and then pointed to the port. "We're almost there."

With a grin, I said, "Excited yet? Think they'll have a whole pride of griffins in there?"

"*Finding this amazing castle, I thought it would be more of a hassle. Bathed in beautiful light, a simple answer to our plight.*" Sorin cracked his knuckles. "You think that was good? I need to practice more."

I grabbed his sleeve and pulled him close. In a low voice, I said, "You might want to cut down on that."

"Why?"

"You don't want to be alone forever, right? I think arcanist women aren't going to find random rhyming or poems to be endearing. It's kinda weird." I released his sleeve as the *Sapphire Dune* leisurely drifted to the port. "I'm just lookin' out for my little brother."

Sorin sarcastically glanced at me, and then at himself, and then back to me, one eyebrow raised. "I think I'll be fine."

My brother never listened, no matter how many times I told him it was embarrassing to spout off random artsy language. I'd just have to keep a close eye on him while we attended the Academy. If anyone started hassling Sorin, I'd put them in their place.

The *Sapphire Dune* docked at the lake port, the sailors running to tie down the ship and secure the last of the sails. Sorin and I prepared to disembark. I had my bag on my shoulder and my heart in my throat.

Once the sailors had the gangplank in place, I leapt down the wooden board and jogged toward the road connected to the pier. Sorin was a little slower. He lingered back, waved to the captain's griffin, and then hurried to catch up with me.

I slowed my run as I made it to the road. A single sign—wooden and warped with water—was the only thing waiting for me. The sign read:

FUTURE ARCANISTS
PLEASE WAIT HERE

The road was faded and overgrown with weeds. Had it been used any time recently? The entire pathway was in desperate need of repair. I stared at the road as I made my way over to the sign.

The path went far up the side of the mountain and led to a set of stone stairs. The stairs went even higher. When I reached the sign, I stopped and glanced around.

No one was here. It was... somewhat disappointing.

The other ships secured themselves to the docks. A flood of individuals poured out onto the piers, each carrying their belongings. The majority of people had more than one bag.

Some people had pistols or swords blatantly hanging from their waist.

There were at least thirty people here, most of them wearing island attire. Long coats. Boots. Caps. They were all around my age, and they stared at Astra Academy with the same wide-eyed wonder.

Nini shuffled her way through the crowds, her dark-red hair shiny under the rays of the sun. She kept half her face buried beneath the collar of her oversized coat, her glasses barely poking up above the fabric.

Some of the other hopeful students called to form a line. Nini tapped the tips of her fingers together, her brow furrowed.

I waved her over to us, hoping we could stick together.

To my delight, she poked her head up a bit, a slight smile at the corner of her lips. She attempted to walk around some of the others, but a man grabbed her shoulder. Nini whirled around, her eyes wide.

The man—some circus act with a pointed hat and a long, white cape—shoved Nini back into the crowd. "We're forming a line," he said matter-of-factly. "Pay attention."

He was tall, and lean with muscle, I could tell, even through his fancy velvet fabrics. He also wore a black vest, tight-fitting pants, and a shirt with sleeves that ended in ruffles. It seemed ostentatious, but perhaps he wanted to stand out. He was the only weirdo with a pointed cap. It was the clothing equivalent of a slanted chimney.

Sorin stormed over to the man, which took me by surprise. I hadn't seen that coming.

Before I could get any words out, Sorin stepped in front of Nini, coming between her and the pointed-hat man.

"*Hey*," my brother barked. "What's your problem? Didn't your mother ever teach you manners?"

"O-Oh, please don't argue," Nini said, her voice so quiet it was immediately drowned out by the shouting from the nearby crowd.

The moment Sorin stepped closer to Pointed-Hat, a few of the men clapped their hands and whooped. They were clearly waiting for something interesting to happen.

Pointed-Hat wasn't as large as my brother, though. He was at least half a foot shorter. The difference obviously chipped away at Pointed-Hat's confidence. He gave my brother the once over and then forced a smile.

"You know what? You're right. That was rude of me." Pointed-Hat turned to Nini. "I should've used my words before reaching out like I did."

Nini's face was as red as her hair. She half-hid in her coat. "It's fine." Her words practically evaporated into the mountain winds.

Pointed-Hat grabbed the brim of his hat with two fingers and tipped it slightly. "I'm Knovak Gentz, from the Isle of Ruma. And we're forming a line. I would be ever so appreciative if you paid attention and followed suit. We'd like to maintain order."

Gentz?

I half-huffed and half-laughed. The Gentz family was made up of a bunch of overachieving merchants. They sailed from island to island, exchanging all sorts of goods. And there were *hundreds* of Gentz. They were everywhere. Their whole family tree had grown so large, it was circling back around itself and becoming a wreath.

"I-I'll try to pay more attention," Nini muttered, her gaze on her feet.

Sorin shuffled his feet for a moment, clearly torn. He glanced over to me, and I motioned him to speak. This Knovak fellow had taken the diplomatic route, so Sorin would have to do the same.

"I'm Sorin Lexly, from the Isle of Haylin," my brother said.

He bowed his head slightly, which was custom for everyone from the islands whenever meeting someone in a formal manner. Then he motioned to Nini. "And this is Nini Wanderlin. She's from—"

"You fight her battles, *and* you speak for her?" Knovak said with a sneer. "What a hero."

Sorin gritted his teeth, his whole body tense. "I didn't mean to—"

"Maybe if you also paid attention, you'd see that the girl was speaking just fine without your assistance."

"Well, I was taught that..." Sorin stepped closer to Knovak. I suspected he was trying to being intimidating, but I wasn't positive. "I shouldn't sit by and do nothing when I see this kind of rude behavior."

"Me? *Rude?*" Knovak forced a single laugh. "You're the one who lumbered over here, prepared to use your *lummox strength* to handle a perceived problem. You're not needed, brute. Get back in line."

A few people in the crowd laughed and encouraged more escalation.

"Teach him a lesson, Knovak! C'mon."

Another person added, "This guy was lookin' for a fight!"

"I don't want this," Nini whispered, but I was probably the only person who heard her as the wind carried her quiet words straight to me.

Knovak was one of the few people here with a sword. It wasn't anything impressive—a basic short sword in a scabbard hanging from his belt. It was a straight edge, which meant it couldn't be too long. Curved swords meant long blades—they were easier to pull from scabbards, even with their considerable length.

With his confidence obviously bolstered by the crowd, Knovak placed his hand on the hilt of his weapon. "Did you hear me? *We're forming a line.* Bumpkins should head to the back—before they get hurt."

I had seen enough.

"Oh, look!" I shouted as I smacked the wooden sign. "It's one of the Academy professors coming down the path!" Then I waved my hand upward, motioning to the shabby road.

The crowd collectively flinched and then hurried to form their supposed line. They ran around the pier, their boots stomping on the wood boards, everyone hushing each other in an attempt to seem civil. Even Knovak straightened himself, taking special care to smooth his cape.

Sorin returned to my side, his hands shaky.

But Nini just opted to go all the way to the back of the line, practically disappearing into the sea of people.

Silence descended over the group of hopefuls. I leaned on the sign, unable to stop myself from chuckling. They were all so desperate to impress the Academy arcanists—it was an easily exploitable weakness.

"Sorin, you need to watch yourself," I said to him under my breath.

"Sorry, Gray. That wasn't how I imagined that going in my head..."

"Hey, where's the professor?" someone called out from the middle of the line.

"Keep looking." I pointed to a grouping of bushes. "I could've sworn they were right around there... with an eldrin and everything."

Silence again. This time with squinted eyes and deep concentration.

What a bunch of rubes.

"He's lying, *you bumpkins,*" Knovak said through gritted teeth. He stepped out of the line, breaking formation. He grabbed the brim of his pointed hat and headed forward, anger alight in his eyes.

Before we could discuss the situation or devolve into a fight, a pop of air caught my attention. I turned on my heel, thinking I'd see something small. Instead, two people had *appeared* out of thin air. They had blinked into existence right next to the wooden sign in a flash of white glitter and magic.

Were these people our professors?

CHAPTER 10

ASTRA ACADEMY MENAGERIE

A man and a woman had appeared.

And then two creatures appeared shortly afterward, one large, one small. Those interested me a bit more than the people. My eyes went wide, and I caught my breath. Professor Helmith had told me about the eldrin of the arcanists who taught here, but I didn't think I'd see some of them so soon.

A three-headed dog had appeared—a *cerberus*. It was giant. Muscled. And its short fur rippled with every movement. The beast reminded me of a black-and-rust-colored hound, its six ears floppy and its tail sleek and long. The cerberus had a barrel chest and lean legs, its paws and claws massive.

It was practically the size of a horse.

The other creature was a tiny white ferret with silver stripes. *A rizzel*. Just like on the Gates of Crossing. It was so small—and so fast—that it disappeared from my sight as it scurried to a spot behind the two people.

The cerberus snorted and stood tall. Two of the canine heads stared at us with glowers, but the third head panted and smiled, observing everyone with wide eyes. When it caught sight of me, it smiled a bit wider, its white fangs apparent.

The man who had appeared had an arcanist mark on his forehead.

The seven-pointed star was intertwined with a three-headed dog.

He was the cerberus arcanist.

And he looked like it, too. It was hard to explain, but the man had the grizzled—and weathered—appearance of a dog who had lived a long and difficult life outside. His leathery skin, dark tan, colored by the unforgiving sun, contrasted nicely with his white hair.

White hair...

It wasn't from age. Although the man was grizzled, the cerberus arcanist appeared to be thirty. Arcanists typically retained their youth, since they lived so long, never really aging. Which meant his white hair was probably natural. There were no gray locks, or any other color for that matter.

Even his eyebrows were white.

It made him seem a bit ridiculous, like his facial features were trying to disappear. Although his darker-colored skin made his beard more visible, which was helpful.

He wore white trousers, black boots to his knees, and plate armor over his shoulders and upper legs. His tunic, marked with dirt and paw prints, had seen better days.

"*Quiet down, fellows,*" the man shouted, his gruff voice practically blasting to the other side of the lake. He waved a gauntleted hand forward. "We have important information to cover before we take you to the Astra Academy Menagerie. I am Guardian Captain Leon Slinn. You may refer to me as *Captain Leon.*"

The man placed his hands behind his back and straightened his posture. Then he narrowed his dark eyes and examined the crowd, his square jaw practically jutting out further than his upper lip.

The woman who had appeared with him was less formal.

"Not so loud," she said, her voice scratchy. She rubbed at her temples. "Just... don't yell as much, all right, Leo?"

I had almost forgotten about her. She was the exact opposite of the cerberus arcanist—in every way. A woman. Slender. Shorter. Supple and beautiful—nothing about her was grizzled. If the man was a dog, this woman was a cat.

Her black hair, long enough to reach her waist, shimmered like oil.

She had the youthful appearance of someone in their early twenties, except for the dark rings under her eyes. Those she had stolen from someone in their forties.

Captain Leon frowned, his white beard practically twisting with his deep disapproval. "*Piper*," he hissed, trying to keep his voice low, but that was impossible. "Get your act together. This is an important step to the acceptance ceremony."

This woman—Piper, I supposed—wore a tasteful dress, but it was wrinkled near her ankles and smudged with dirt, like she had dragged it on the ground. When she threw back some of her hair, I finally caught sight of her forehead.

She, too, was an arcanist.

Her star was laced with the ferret-like rizzel.

She, obviously, was the rizzel arcanist.

"Just get on with it," Piper muttered, pinching the bridge of her small nose. "This speech doesn't need to be too long, does it?"

Captain Leon frowned harder, if that was even possible. He turned, his chest puffed out, and then he glared at the crowd.

"Listen up! None of you are students of Astra Academy. Not yet, anyway." Leon held up a large, armored hand. "Our institution is one of the best—an elite school where we produce skilled arcanists. We have a reputation for excellence, which means *a lot* of people want to attend."

Piper sighed, her eyes squinted.

Ignoring her, Captain Leon continued, "Thousands of people would love to attend, and some of them are already arcanists or they offer this institution piles of gold coins for the privilege of walking our halls. We turn away hundreds of individuals every year."

Soft whispers wafted through the crowd. My brother and I stayed close to the wooden sign, slightly separate from the others, and I wondered if we should join them.

"*However*," Captain Leon said, stressing the word, "Headmaster Venrover believes that everyone deserves a chance at greatness. It was *his* coin that brought you here today, not the Academy's. He paid for the ships, paid for the star shards to activate the Gates of Crossing, and personally maintains the Menagerie. You should keep that mind before you enter the school and be thankful that you were given this opportunity."

"Okay," Piper said with another sigh. "You don't have to browbeat all the potential students." She wobbled a bit. It was then that I realized she was wearing boots with tall heels. She was clearly struggling to maintain her balance.

Captain Leon quickly faced her. "*Piper*," he hissed again, his voice a little lower, but still audible. "Your. Behavior. Is. *Inappropriate.* You shouldn't be—" he lowered his voice to a soft growl, "—*drunk* during these introductory ceremonies."

Sorin and I were the closest, and probably the only ones who heard the last bit.

Piper narrowed her eyes. "I'm not *drunk*," she whispered. Then her expression softened, and she held up a finger. "I'm *hungover*. There's a big difference."

"*There isn't a difference.*"

"No, ya see, one affects my *ability* to perform, and the other just affects my *desire* to perform." She waggled her finger and smirked like she had given irrefutable answer.

Their hushed conversation wasn't sitting well with the other hopeful students. Collective sighs and frowns passed between them.

With his restraint visibly waning, Captain Leon grabbed his beard and tugged downward slightly. He kept his jaw clenched, his face reddening. "Piper. Please. You're on thin ice. You remember what the headmaster said. *These are future students.*"

"It's fine." Piper waved away the comment. "Most of these kids aren't going to bond. After today, we'll never see them again."

The whispered conversations of the crowd grew louder. People didn't know what was going on, just that something was wrong. I, on the other hand, wanted to laugh. *This* was the state of Astra Academy? Professor Helmith hadn't mentioned any of this kind of behavior. The captain was right. It *was* embarrassing.

As if sensing the agitation in the group, the cerberus stepped forward. The massive three-headed dog flashed its fangs and growled.

Everyone went quiet.

Then the rizzel ran out from around Piper's legs, seemingly appearing out of nowhere. He scurried over to the cerberus and then teleported to the beast's back. The rizzel didn't move with the boundless energy of a weasel, though. The little rizzel was sluggish, and his eyes half-shut as though squinting against the light.

The captain and the hungover professor continued their quiet argument, but the cerberus moved between them and the crowd, blocking most people's view of the situation.

"*Enough,*" one of the cerberus's heads growled. It was the middle head, the one that was lifted highest in the air. "Listen here. My name is Sticks, and I'll be—"

"*Sticks*?" someone half-said, half-snorted. "*That's* your name? Really?"

The other two heads of the cerberus inhaled, and then exhaled with such force, it took everyone by surprise. Red and orange flames flowed from their mouths, pouring onto the road, pier, and nearby lakefront. The heat was so intense, I had to close my eyes. The fire licked at my boots, and I hopped backward, stumbling into Sorin.

Shouts and cries of surprise rang out through the group.

"He's gonna kill us!"

But the panic was unnecessary.

Once the flames stopped, I opened my eyes and noticed that the fire hadn't actually hurt anyone. The flames had just scorched the ground and surrounding area. The other hopeful students were huddled close together, none of them making comments anymore, some of them shaking so hard, I thought they were shivering.

Sorin held on to my shoulder with a tight grip. I patted his knuckles, trying to let him know it was okay.

The dog just wanted to scare us into compliance.

The display of flames didn't stop Captain Leon and Piper from arguing. They muttered dark words to each other, bickering like old lovers.

"Yeah, that'll teach you *ingrates*," the rizzel said with a snort and chuckle.

His cute little ferret voice almost made me smile. He dragged himself to the top of the tallest cerberus head, his own eyes ringed with darkness, like he hadn't slept. Or he was part raccoon.

The rizzel stood on his back paws. "Listen up, *punks*. Sticks will be enforcing the rules, and I'll be filling you in on the rest of the presentation." He placed a paw on his little white chest. "My name is Reevy." He glared at the group. "Anyone have a problem with that?"

Sticks snorted a few more embers from all three heads.

Everyone shook their heads and muttered a few quick platitudes. Even my brother remained stiff.

"I love the name," someone said from the group. "I'm gonna name my first kid that name, that's how much I love it."

Reevy clapped his little paws together. "*Quiet.* There are, like, thirty of you here, right? Well, listen really hard. There are only *twelve* mystical creatures in the Menagerie. I assume you planks of wood can do the math?"

Tension replaced fear as the individuals in the crowd glanced around, quickly making eye contact with their fellow competitors. I hadn't realized there were so few mystical creatures. That meant even if *all* of them found someone to bond to, at least eighteen people would still be sent home.

Reevy huffed, his little voice practically a squeak. "That's right. Some of you will be going home. Especially since three of those twelve creatures have been here for years. They refuse to bond with anyone unless they're the best of the best. You chumps are gonna have a hard time finding yourself an eldrin."

If three of them wouldn't bond, that only left nine creatures...

"So pay attention," Reevy continued. "In a few moments, I'll take you all to the Menagerie. You'll have until nightfall to compete in the Trials of Worth. The Menagerie isn't a maze—all the creatures have their own little areas where they're the most comfortable, and it's all laid out in a neat and organized manner. There's no excuse for not finding a creature and attempting to prove yourself."

Sticks wagged his tail. One of the heads turned up to look at Reevy. "I like the area with the pond and rocks."

Reevy sighed, his exhale practically a groan. "*You* won't be going, Sticks. Just the kiddos."

One of the cerberus's heads frowned as his tail stopped wagging.

Knovak stepped forward, his pointed hat making him taller than everyone here, including the cerberus. He grabbed the brim and tipped it forward in a short bow of his head. "Pardon me, but may I ask a question?"

Reevy crossed his little arms. "What is it?"

"Can you tell us what twelve creatures are in the Menagerie? So that we can mentally prepare for the Trials ahead?"

"No," the rizzel snapped, his voice practically a squeak. "It's a surprise." Then he coughed and muttered, "Mostly because I don't go to the Menagerie often, and I forgot all of what we have there this year." He clapped his paws together. "Any other questions before we go? Or are you sandbags ready?"

"I think it's inappropriate, and frankly *rude*, that you address us that way," Knovak continued, clearly never satisfied unless he had the last word on a manner. "We're all adults here."

"*We're all adults here*," Reevy said, mimicking Knovak in a pompous tone. Then Reevy glared. "There are some things in life that, if you have to say it, everyone knows it's untrue."

Knovak's face brightened to a glowing crimson.

The rizzel glanced around. "Any *other* questions?"

I stepped forward, eager to ask something.

The rizzel turned to me, his dark eyes squinting. "Hmm?"

"Will Professor Helmith be there?" I asked. "At the Menagerie, I mean."

The question got everyone's attention, even all three heads of the cerberus. No one had been expecting me to ask about a specific professor, apparently.

"Professor Helmith?" The rizzel stroked his chin. "What does it matter if she's there or not? She's not involved with admitting new students."

"Well... I'm just worried about her. I haven't seen in her in a while, and—"

Reevy snorted and laughed at the same time. "*You*? A friend of Rylee?" He waved a paw. "What a farce. She'd never associate with someone like you. She's royalty. And talented. And she doesn't mingle on tiny islands in the middle of nowhere."

The crowd of hopeful students stared at me. A few pointed and exchanged whispered comments. I ignored them—their chattering wouldn't stop my line of questioning.

Before I could add anything, my brother stepped forward. "Actually, Gray has seen Professor Helmith in his dreams. They talk all the time."

A few people in the crowd laughed. The whispered conversations multiplied.

Sticks glanced over with two of his heads. One chuckled, exposing his canine fangs. "Yeah, I *bet* a teenage boy would see Professor Helmith in his dreams."

"*Ha!* Good one." Reevy smiled. "But seriously—calm your horses, kiddo."

"Is she okay?" I demanded. I didn't care if they believed me —I didn't care if they all made jokes—I just wanted to know if something had happened. "I haven't seen Professor Helmith in three weeks. Has she gone somewhere in that time?"

Reevy huffed and didn't answer.

But Sticks was different. One of his heads frowned. "Rylee is here at the Academy, doing her research. She keeps to herself. Nothing is wrong."

His answer...

"Has anyone checked on her recently?" I asked.

I wanted to know more, but the laughing from the crowd intensified.

Someone said, "He just wants to search her room."

"What a creep," another person muttered.

"I can't believe he admitted to dreaming about one of the professors."

The rizzel clapped his paws together. "Enough! *Enough*. It's time for me to teleport you to the Menagerie, got it?"

"Wait, I'll do it," Piper said as she stepped around Captain

Leon. She walked with a stiff and slow gait. Like she was trying to avoid tripping. "That's my job. I'll be taking the potential students to the Menagerie."

She moved closer to everyone and held out a slender hand. Then she motioned for the crowd to come over.

Sorin and I were the first to step close. I raised an eyebrow, wondering what she would do. Rizzel arcanists could teleport people, obviously, but how would it work? I didn't see another Gate of Crossing.

"Everyone, hold hands," Piper said. "And then we'll go together."

The many people gathered around did as they were instructed. I held Sorin's hand, and somebody else's, prepared for the transport. Once it seemed as though everyone was together, Piper smiled.

"Here we go. Don't let go. That's the most important thing."

And then there was another sensation of being jerked around, like my insides were trying to escape my body. With a pop of air and puff of glitter, we all disappeared.

CHAPTER 11

BAD OMEN

We appeared in an underground sanctuary. I stumbled forward, my attention on the black bricks beneath my feet. It was a beautiful pathway, made with care and dedication—each brick perfectly placed to create an intricate pattern.

Then I glanced up, my heart racing.

At first, I thought we weren't actually underground. A beautiful summer sky shimmered overhead. White clouds tumbled across a bright blue backdrop. It was only when I stared that I saw the stone ceiling behind everything else. Was the sky an illusion? Or some sort of magical painting hanging in midair?

The walls of the underground cavern were clearly visible. They, too, were black stone.

They appeared shiny as though wet.

I stared at the walls. They had been worked and smoothed and made beautiful through massive amounts of effort, *and I recognized them*. They were the stones that appeared in my dreams whenever the puppets appeared. I knew for certain. The images of the monsters, and their terrible world, were etched in my mind.

But... what did it mean?

Sorin grabbed my shoulder, jostling me from my thoughts. "Look over there, Gray!"

I turned, my hands unsteady. Sorin pointed to the area in front of us.

The black brick pathway led to an underground grove of trees. How could they survive without sunlight? Perhaps a dryad arcanist was keeping them healthy. I wasn't certain. But then the road continued on to a lake, an actual field, a tiny hill of boulders, and to several buildings, and then beyond that to a marsh, complete with mangrove trees.

Several arcanists had to be actively maintaining this place. There was no other explanation for the beauty on display.

Everyone knew arcanists were capable of great things, like controlling the weather or helping plants grow in places they shouldn't. Leviathan arcanists protected seaside towns from storms. Phoenix arcanists healed people when they were injured. Every civilization treated arcanists with respect and reverence for their ability to alter nature and keep people safe.

The Menagerie was a testament to that fact. This place was living proof that arcanists were everything the legends said they were.

It was difficult to see everything from my current location, but the Menagerie wasn't constructed on a flat surface. The whole cavern had hills, for lack of a better term. The buildings, three in total, were higher up than the trees and the marsh. The boulder pile was large enough to be seen anywhere in the Menagerie. A mini mountain inside the cavern.

The three buildings themselves seemed old and a bit ominous. Pillars surrounded the outside of each, and all were made of white and gray marble. Were they tombs? The buildings had all the welcoming warmth of a graveyard.

The "sunshine" from overhead clashed with the shiny black of the walls. Everything was well lit, but it was as if we stood in a void—a pocket of space surrounded by darkness. The Menagerie itself was beautiful, but anytime I glanced at the walls, I remembered how cramped this area was.

It felt like a beautiful cage.

Piper smoothed her dress and then glanced around at the group. She rubbed at her eyes as she silently counted each of us. "Curse the abyssal hells," she mumbled. "I forgot four of them..."

With a heavy sigh, Piper disappeared with a pop and a puff of glitter.

She reappeared a moment later with four others from the boats, their eyes wide, and one stumbling around until he fell onto the brick pathway.

Once we were all gathered around, Piper motioned us close. Then she placed a finger to her lips, quieting us even though most of us weren't even speaking.

"Okay, pay attention." Piper gestured to the Menagerie. It was probably supposed to be an elegant motion, but she did it with such speed and halfhearted effort that I almost missed it. "Welcome to the Astra Academy Menagerie. Mystical creatures live here, some fierce, others wise."

Her voice was louder than before, but not a shout, and Piper's words drifted around the cavern, like a soft echo or the flap of distant wings. When the echoes reached the walls, glimmers of color shone across the wet rocks, lighting them up in flashes of rainbow-iridescent glow.

Was the cavern alive?

I admired the colors, my attention on my surroundings, rather than the instructor.

Piper continued, "You may approach any creature you find. They're aware of your arrival and have prepared Trials of Worth to test your resolve."

"Can we go now?" someone from the crowd asked, eagerness in their voice.

Even their words added to the rainbows that briefly lit the wall.

Piper waved away the comment. "Wait. First, you have to be aware that the Academy has a policy not to interfere with the Trials of Worth. Some creatures test their future arcanist through extreme means. We're not gonna help you or get you out of any trouble you put yourself in. Do I make myself clear?"

Most everyone nodded, including myself, but a couple people grimaced. They hesitated, lingering behind.

"I'm gonna leave you all here and return at midnight. And then I'm taking everyone who hasn't bonded, and I'm putting them on the ships back to their home islands."

The last statement really struck me. I returned my attention to Piper, no longer fascinated by the walls.

I wasn't going to go home.

I wasn't going to become another candlemaker, stuck on an island doing nothing, incapable of saving myself from the monsters.

No matter what, I was going to find a creature here and become an arcanist.

"Don't get cold feet now," Piper said, eyeing the cowardly individuals near the back. With a sigh, she added, "You'll be fine. If something *does* happen, just run back to *this* spot. I won't help in a Trial of Worth, but I will make sure no harm comes to anyone." She half-smiled. "Just don't tell the headmaster I said that. I'm not supposed to admit I keep an eye on the Trials."

Her statements seemed to ease the worries of the others.

"Understand?" Piper asked again.

"Yes," came the crowd's response.

"Good. And remember…" She pointed at us, her eyes narrowed. "You're all considered adults. Act like it. The mystical creatures will take note of individuals who conduct themselves like children."

Her extra warning sank into the group like a rock hitting a pond.

We nodded, but even I was bursting with anxious energy. I got it. We wouldn't get any help. The Trials of Worth could be dangerous. I didn't need any more information.

"Good luck," Piper said. She wobbled a bit as she stepped back. "Astra Academy will welcome you with open arms once you succeed."

Then she disappeared in a flash of glitter and a pop.

Rizzel magic...

I wondered if there was a rizzel here. The ability to teleport seemed thrilling, but would it help me in a dreamscape? Teleporting was useful to move around—to never be *physically* trapped—but I could still be trapped in my mind, couldn't I?

"Let's go, Gray!" Sorin grabbed my arm and dragged me forward.

The others rushed around, all twenty-eight of them. Nobody bothered to give Sorin and me a second glance. Well, that wasn't entirely true. Nini waved to us as she hurried into the Menagerie. She, too, came with us to the trees.

The grove was perfectly arranged, the trees an equal distance from each other. A few trees had pink blossoms, their canopies light and mystical. Another few had white blossoms, and the petals rained around us like snow. The last few trees were willows, with branches that hung like curtains.

None of these should grow together, but that only added to the magical beauty. This grove would never exist in the wild. It had been created for this underground sanctuary.

Sorin, Nini, another girl, and I slowed our steps as we entered the grove.

A fox awaited us in the center.

Not just *any* fox. Its red coat, vibrant even underground, shimmered as it moved. And the white on the tip of its tail, as well as its feet, blazed like fire. The fox pranced around the center of the grove, its flames never burning anything—the fox didn't leave tracks.

This was a kitsune.

Professor Helmith had told me all about these mischievous foxes. Kitsune grew multiple tails as they aged. Just as hydras gained more heads, the more tails a kitsune had, the more powerful it became. They created illusions, and tricked people with their charms.

The four of us approached, and the kitsune kit stopped its prancing. The little fox sat and held its regal head high.

"Greetings," the fox said, her voice lyrical and feminine. "My name is Miko. I'm a kitsune." The flames on her paws flickered and flashed as she jumped up. "I'm a powerful mystical creature! But also mysterious." She twirled around, her puffy tail covering half her face as she spoke. "Only clever individuals should dare to face my Trial of Worth."

Nini fidgeted with her giant coat. She said nothing—she just waited as though the creature would call on her.

The other girl stepped forward. She wore a long black coat that went to her ankles, and her black hair was trimmed neatly to her shoulders. Unlike most islanders, her ears were pierced three times each, from the top of her ear down the back.

"I'm Zyn Velli," the girl said, her voice flat and basically emotionless. "I'm clever. *And* I'm ready to ace your Trial of Worth."

"I have a question," I said.

The fox perked her ears straight up. Then she wrinkled her nose. "A question for me?"

"That's right."

"Very well." Miko swished her tail. "I'll allow it."

"If I bonded with you... would the magic you grant me help in my dreams?"

The kitsune tilted her head to one side and then the other. "You mean... does my magic alter dreams?"

SHAMI STOVALL

"Yeah. In any way."

Miko shook her head. "No. I'm a creature of trickery, not dreams."

I sighed, already feeling nervous. I definitely wanted a creature that could help me in *some* way while asleep. What if Professor Helmith needed assistance? What if the monsters returned while she was away, and I had no way to defend myself? I needed a creature who could grant me magics that would help in that situation.

Then I turned to my brother. "Sorin, if you want to participate in the kitsune's Trial of Worth, you can. But I'm going to look around more."

Nini's eyes went wide. "B-But what if you can't find anything else? Or what if... you fail all the other Trials?"

"That's just a risk I'm gonna have to take."

I headed for the grassy hills in the distance, hoping none of the other potential students had gone that way yet. Nini didn't follow. She stayed with the other girl and inched closer to the kitsune. Hopefully, she'd bond with the fox. That way I could see more of her at the Academy.

Sorin didn't stay, though. He chased after me.

"Wait up, Gray!" he called out. "I want to go with you."

I shot him a smile. "We can't both bond with the same creature, genius. We'll have to split up at some point."

"I know. But I want to see what other creatures are here, too." He effortlessly kept pace. His legs were so much longer. "You want me to carry you like a backpack? Since you're so short and all."

"I'm not that short," I said through gritted teeth. "I'm taller than most of the people here."

"What was that? I can't hear you from up here."

Sorin laughed as he ran, and I couldn't stop myself from smiling. Why did he have to tease me like that? Was it because I had sarcastically called him *genius*? We couldn't do that in the

Academy! We had to be more mature—more adult. I wanted Professor Helmith's impression of me to be positive.

She already knew me from the dreams, but when we met in person... That would be different.

Sorin grabbed my shoulder, jerking me out of my thoughts. He pulled me to a halt and then pointed to the buildings.

"Gray! Look over there."

I craned my head to get a better look at the creepy tombs. At first, I saw nothing. I almost punched Sorin right in his fat shoulder, but then I spotted it. Something moving between the pillars.

It was a cloak—dark red, tattered at the bottom. A rusty scythe floated around with it, and a single chain made a faint clinking sound as it moved. I couldn't see many other details, though.

"What is that?" Sorin whispered.

"It's a reaper," I replied.

Professor Helmith had said that reapers were rare, but after the God-Arcanists War, several had appeared on the battlefield. They were a sign of bad luck and ill omens. And from what I could remember, they were mystical creatures that grew stronger through killing.

"We should go investigate," Sorin said.

I glowered at him. "You want to bond with a reaper? That doesn't sound like something you'd match with."

"I still want to talk to it."

The floating cloak disappeared into the giant building, its rattling a faint noise from within. For some reason, I got an uneasy feeling from the mystical creature, but I supposed it wouldn't hurt to go speak with it.

"All right," I said with a sigh. "Maybe there'll be other creatures in the building as well."

CHAPTER 12

MANY TRIALS OF WORTH

The three marble buildings in the Menagerie glittered under the false light and despite the architecture's beauty, my unease grew as Sorin and I approached. While the rest of the Menagerie seemed bathed in eternal afternoon sunshine, the insides of the buildings were so dark I couldn't make out their contents. There were no lanterns or candles.

I cursed under my breath.

Why was I thinking about candles at a time like this?

Sorin practically hopped with every step. When we reached the first marble pillar, he bounded over to it and placed his palm on the side.

"It's so smooth," he whispered. "Just like I imagined."

Although I didn't want to look like an islander rube who hadn't seen anything fancy in his entire life, I also ran over and touched the pillar. The cold marble had a luxurious feel to it. I couldn't stop myself from smiling.

The flapping of wings ended my amazement.

Sorin and I both glanced up.

A black pegasus foal landed on the flat roof of the marble

building, its hooves clacking against the surface as it skidded to a halt. Its inky mane and tail settled onto its beautiful black coat. The pegasus almost looked blue under the bright light, its raven wings shimmering as it tucked them close to its body.

Pegasi were fascinating. They came in every color a bird could come in, at least according to Professor Helmith. The first thing on the subject I had asked about had been regarding cardinals. They were so red—was there a pegasus with the same shade of scarlet for a coat? The professor had assured me there was.

"Hello there, hopeful arcanists," the pegasus said, her voice feminine and confident. She puffed out her chest as she play-pranced along the edge of the roof. She was only ten feet above us, but she lowered her head as far as she could as though trying to make sure we could hear her. "My name is Ramona, and I'm a powerful pegasus."

Sorin smiled and offered a small wave. "Hello. I'm Sorin, and this is my brother, Gray."

"I have useful magic!" Ramona said without acknowledging my brother. She opened her wings wide and then flapped them forward. A gust of wind shot out, swirling with noticeable intensity. Once the wind had vanished, Ramona tucked her wings back against her body. "Did you see that? *Glorious!* I'm already a master of evocation!"

"Of what?" Sorin asked, his eyebrows raised.

"Evocation. You know. *Evoking things.* All mystical creatures can create something for a short period of time." Ramona spread her wings and then leapt down. She alighted on the pathway, but she flapped her wings hard before the landing, softening her descent.

"Pegasi evoke wind?" I asked. I already knew the answer, but Sorin seemed to be enjoying himself, so I decided to play along.

"That's right," Ramona stated. She pranced around us, swishing her tail.

"Oh, that means the cerberus can evoke fire," Sorin said as he glanced at me, obviously putting everything together. "That's interesting. Do you think the kitsune can evoke fire, too? It had little flame paws..."

Ramona stopped her joyful prance. She laid back her horse-like ears. "Kitsune evoke *fox-fire*. It's like illusions."

"Wow. That would be useful." Sorin smacked me on the shoulder. "Can you imagine what kind of trouble *you* could get into if you had illusions? Maybe you should head back to the woods."

"I'm not going to bond with the kitsune," I muttered.

The pegasus stomped her way between us. She was only three feet tall, and even when she fluttered her feathers, she seemed lean.

"Um, excuse me," Ramona said. "Not to be rude, but I think pegasi are much better eldrin than kitsune. Obviously, you came here looking to bond, yes? I think it's time for my Trial of Worth."

Sorin crossed his arms. He glanced back at the marble building, his gaze narrowed. "Well..."

I knew my brother better than anybody. He wanted to see the reaper. I didn't know why, but the look of longing on his face was easy to identify. For whatever reason, he had a curious itch he just wanted to scratch. Stopping to do this pegasus's Trial of Worth would hinder that.

Ramona's ears drooped a bit. "Y-You want to bond, right? I mean, you think pegasi *are* amazing, surely? You saw the wind I evoked. Very few mystical creatures do that."

"What's your Trial of Worth?" Sorin asked.

"That's a good question!" She fluttered her wings. "You two will compete against each other. And possibly more people, since there are so many here." Ramona lifted her head. "Pegasi are creatures of freedom, flight, and loyalty to a cause! We also prize physical prowess. In order to prove you're worthy of me, you must collect ten of the special objects I've hidden around the Menagerie. They're in hard-to-reach places! Only the nimblest and most free-spirited will prevail."

"I can do that, no problem." Sorin turned to me. "Think you're up to it?"

I shrugged. "If you want to participate, that's fine."

"The special objects are small stone figurines in the shape of pegasi," Ramona said. "I've placed them all over. Whoever brings me ten first gets the honor of bonding with me."

Sorin frowned. "You're not going to try, Gray?"

I shook my head.

Ramona's wings fell a bit. She swished her tail and nervously stomped her hooves. "But..."

"They're not here to bond with you," came a voice from within the darkness of the building. It had a scratchy child-like quality to it, but was clearly masculine. "Go fly down to the ones by the trees and you'll have better luck."

The pegasus huffed, and flapped her wings once. "What do you know, *Twain*? Don't you remember what Venrover said? You're supposed to put yourself out there and *try* to bond with someone. You can't stay cooped up forever."

"Oh, yes, I can."

"You're not going to develop any magic if you don't bond!"

"I don't care."

"Look up there!" someone shouted. A small group of hopeful students stood a hundred feet down the hill. They pointed up and waved people over. A whole group of six hurried toward us. "There's a pegasus! Let's go speak with it!"

Ramona perked up. "Oh! They're excited!" She happily ran down the hill to greet the group of eager individuals. "Yes, I'm here to bond with someone. Only a worthy individual!"

I watched her go, my chest tight with anxiety. I couldn't pass up *all* the mystical creatures. I'd have to participate in *someone's* Trial of Worth. When I glanced over at Sorin, I frowned. What if we kept exploring together? I couldn't compete against him. What if he lost out on bonding? What if one of us became an arcanist and the other didn't?

What if it was my fault, because I beat him in a Trial?

"You're not going to run after the others?" the child-voice asked from the darkness of the building.

Without prompting, a small figure emerged from the shadows.

Very small.

A kitten, in fact. The pegasus had called the cat *Twain.*

He was a little orange thing with large ears that ended in tufts of fur, similar to a lynx's. He didn't have a long tail, like most cats I saw on the islands. Instead, the little kitten had a bobtail—a short nub that reminded me of a rabbit.

"Aww," Sorin said as he knelt. He held out a hand. "You're so cute."

The kitten, Twain, immediately sat down and glared. "I'm a powerful mystical creature."

"Who is *very* adorable." Sorin scooted closer, trying to get his hand near the kitten. "Can I hold you, little kitty?"

Twain swiped his paw at Sorin, his claws catching my brother's finger. Sorin jerked his hand away, blood beading from the tiny scratch.

"I'm not *a little kitty.*" Twain huffed, and arched his back. "Didn't you hear me? *I'm a powerful mystical creature!*"

Sorin turned to me. "He's so grumpy. It makes him even more adorable."

I chuckled because it was true, but that obviously angered the kitten. His ears lay flat against his skull, and he hissed.

"What's your Trial of Worth?" Sorin asked.

"You two bumpkins couldn't handle my Trial," the kitten said, his voice high-pitched with anger. "And even if you could, I wouldn't bond with idiots!" Twain flashed his tiny fangs before turning and running into the building as fast as his little legs would take him.

Sorin stood and brushed himself off. "What was that?"

I opened my mouth to respond, but stopped myself short. Domestic housecats weren't mystical creatures. So... what kind of creature was that kitten? Griffins were much larger as cubs. And so were shachi, the mythical river tigers. And sphinxes had human heads.

I couldn't think of many other feline mystical creatures.

"I don't know what it was," I said.

"Really? Maybe it really is rare."

A clatter of metal stopped our conversation short. While the others halfway down the hill were busy engaging in a Trial of Worth to win the favor of Ramona, a bizarre creature showed itself to Sorin and me.

A red cloak floated out from the building. It hovered in midair as though wore by an invisible man. The hem of the cloak, tattered and filled with holes, was a good six inches off the ground. A gold chain of two links hung out from the folds of the cloak. A rusted scythe with a wooden shaft floated around the cloak as well, circling in a perfect motion, never speeding up or slowing down.

The hood of the cloak was up, but there was no face to behold.

"I see Twain has made some new friends," a voice from within the cloak said. His tone was cold and masculine, and his words icy.

I shivered as I stepped back.

A reaper.

Just as I had suspected.

"So, you two have come hoping to become arcanists?" the reaper asked, his voice now filled with callous mirth. "Interesting selection this year."

The scythe stopped in front of the reaper. Then it spun

around and thrust forward. Sorin and I both flinched and stumbled backward, but the scythe merely pointed at my brother.

"You." The reaper floated a little closer. "What is your name?"

Sorin forced himself to smile. "I'm, uh, Sorin Lexly. What about you?"

"I am known as *Waste*." The reaper brought his scythe back to his cloak body. Then he bowed, the hood falling forward. After he straightened himself, he said, "You have come seeking a mystical creature, and fortune smiles upon you. *I* will bond with you."

My eyebrows shot to my hairline.

"Wait," I said. "Doesn't my brother have to pass your Trial of Worth?"

"He already has."

Sorin turned to me, smiled, and then glanced back at the reaper. "Really?"

Waste swung his scythe around again, twirling it slower, but still in a threatening manner. "Oh, yes. You see, reapers are creatures of death. We revel in blood. In ruin. Our Trials of Worth are all the same, and the moment you pass, you've passed for life."

"But what is the Trial?" I whispered, dreading where this was going.

"Our Trial of Worth is simple. Anyone who wishes to bond with a reaper must kill someone else. A blood relative, to be specific. That is all."

I held my breath, my thoughts whirling. That seemed harsh. And bleak.

The implications of what the creature had said hit me like a brick. My heart pounded. Sorin's grin vanished. We locked gazes and I saw confusion and dread in his gray eyes, but not guilt. The knotted feeling in my chest relaxed. Sorin didn't know what the creature was talking about. My brother wasn't a murderer.

"You can tell if someone has killed somebody else?" I asked.

Waste nodded his empty cloak head. "I can."

"Can you tell who the supposed victim is?" I motioned to Sorin. "Because my brother has never harmed a fly in his entire life. You must be mistaken."

Sorin shook his head. "Yeah, I think you've got the wrong person. I definitely haven't killed anybody. I just became an adult and left my home island for the first time."

The reaper didn't say anything. He hovered in the air, his empty hood impossible to read. Was he contemplating the situation? Was he just staring at us? Could reapers even see? I stepped forward and carefully waved my hand into the cloak, trying to feel for an invisible body.

There was nothing.

The cloak floated in midair without any real tangible inside of it.

Waste chuckled. "I thought it a deception, but you truly don't know?"

Sorin frowned. "If you know who I killed, say it. Otherwise, *you're* the deceiver."

"Very well," Waste said, his icy tone without remorse. "T'was your mother you killed. Your birth was too much. It cost your mother her life."

The vicious words cut into my heart like a frozen blade.

I hadn't been expecting something so heinous and hurtful. I turned to my brother. His face had gone as pale as death. He didn't say anything. *I* didn't say anything. And it pained me when Sorin didn't even move. It took a few moments for him to even really breathe properly again.

I turned to Waste, my heart hammering. "That's not... It's not true. Sorin isn't to blame for our mother's death."

The reaper didn't reply.

"Take it back," I demanded. Sorin didn't need that kind of guilt. "Even if our mother died, it's not like Sorin *wanted* that."

"Intent is irrelevant to reapers," Waste said. "How or why the death happened isn't my concern. All that matters is that I bond with someone who has taken the life of a blood relative. A reaper's magic grows with each subsequent kill—family or otherwise. We are one of the few mystical creatures who can even rival dragons, if we've empowered ourselves with enough death."

The reaper hovered toward my brother. A part of Waste's cloak floated forward, as if it were holding out an invisible hand.

"Come," Waste said. "I have waited here for many years, unable to bond with anyone. None of the past hopeful students could bring themselves to kill someone in their family... You are the first in a long while already stained with blood. Let us grow powerful. *Together.*"

Sorin hesitantly stepped away. His hands shook as he crossed his arms and then uncrossed them. The gravity of the situation obviously weighed on him. Crushing him. I placed a hand on his shoulder, and Sorin flinched at my touch. After a short moment, he relaxed.

"Gray?" he whispered.

"Don't listen to this thing." I tightened my grip on him. "Let's just find another mystical creature and try for another Trial of Worth."

"There aren't many left," Waste darkly muttered.

I glanced down the hill and took stock of the situation in the Menagerie. The kitsune in the woods, the pegasus close by. There was a snake-like creature in the marsh, and a frog creature in the lake. Each of the creatures had two or three people around at the bare minimum, each competing in a different Trial.

There were twelve creatures here, and I had already seen six of them. Where were the other six? Surely we could find *something* that wouldn't traumatize my brother.

"I don't want an eldrin that focuses on killing," Sorin muttered.

Waste laughed once. "Those are the words of someone who has grown up in gentle times. Sometimes power—and the ability to destroy—is all that protects you from the darkness."

Although I agreed with the reaper, I knew Sorin didn't want to hear it. My brother just wasn't someone who reveled in power. If he did, he would've used his size and strength to get what he wanted.

No.

My brother and this reaper weren't a good match. And he must've known it, too.

"C'mon, Gray," Sorin said. He motioned to the darkness of the building. "Let's go talk to that kitten again. Or maybe find something else."

The reaper hovered in the air, as silent as a corpse. He didn't attempt to stop us as we walked by. I tried not to look at Waste's crimson cloak or his vile scythe.

Once inside the building, and shrouded by the shadows, I stepped closer to my brother. Sorin said nothing about the encounter as we walked, our bootsteps echoing off the barren walls. I wanted to say something positive, but I wasn't sure what.

"I doubt Mother wants you to feel—"

"*Don't*," Sorin said, cutting me off. He clenched his hands into fists. "Let's just find another mystical creature."

Our conversation soured. I turned my attention to the surrounding building, curious as to why it had been built. Names were etched into the walls, but it was too dark to make out most of them. Was this a memorial? To honor the dead? That seemed more reasonable than a tomb, and I cursed at myself for not thinking of that. Why would they keep corpses in the middle of the Menagerie?

While we walked through the memorial, my mind on

abstract problems, sound filtered into my perception. It sounded like the clatter of wood on stone.

I held my breath and stopped dead in my tracks.

That sound...

I knew that sound.

Sorin kept going, obviously wrapped up in his own thoughts. It was also dark, and I suspected he hadn't even seen me stop.

But...

The click-clack of wood filled my mind with memories of my nightmares. That was the sound the puppet-monsters made whenever they walked across the bizarre stone terrain. They hid behind boulders and rocks, just waiting to leap out in an attempt to kill me.

The sounds grew louder and louder, filling the memorial with echoes.

My held breath burned in my lungs, but I still refused to exhale or inhale.

One of the puppets was here. In the Menagerie.

Just behind me.

And then it quickened its pace, the sound of its movement growing louder and louder with each frightening step.

It was coming for me. Here. Right now. And I couldn't even see it.

CHAPTER 13

A PUPPET

I ran.

Without looking back, I pushed myself to run full speed ahead. The memorial was dark and cold, but the light of the distant exit was plain as day. I headed straight for it, desperately seeking an exit from the shadows.

That was when I almost tripped over something. My foot caught an object, and I heard a distinct *meow-yelp* as I stumbled and flailed my arms. The click-clacking of the puppet didn't stop, though, even as I took a moment to regain my balance.

"What's going on?" a child-like voice hissed. "You kicked me!"

I bent over, waving my arms until my hand bashed against the side of the kitten. Although the little hellion scratched me, I scooped him up into my arms and ran for the exit.

"What's going on?" Twain shouted, his little kitten voice almost drowned out by the puppet's clacking movements. "Put me down!"

Sorin had already exited the memorial. I rushed out the door. Without slowing at all, I slammed into my brother. He grunted as he took a single step forward, but I practically bounced off him, losing my footing. Sorin grabbed me before I toppled over.

Twain shuddered in my arms, having no doubt felt the brunt of the collision. The dazed kitten didn't say anything.

"Gray?" my brother asked, concern in his voice.

With shaky breaths, I tried to steady myself. Before I answered, Sorin turned his attention to the false sky overhead.

"Are those dark clouds? I wonder why the Academy would change the weather." With a sigh, Sorin added, "It's like the sky wants to write a poem for my mood."

I grabbed his coat. "*They're here,*" was all I managed to choke out. The click-clack of the monsters hadn't stopped. I pointed back at the darkness inside the memorial. "We have to go!"

He glanced back at me, an eyebrow lifted. "Who's here?"

"The monsters! From my dreams. Right over there."

"Monsters?"

But we had run out of time.

The very same nightmarish creature that plagued my dreams emerged from the darkness of the memorial. A spider marionette—a wooden doll held by invisible strings—clattered its way out the door. It had hands at the end of its eight, long legs, and its face was an emotionless stage mask, complete with circle holes for eyes and a line for a mouth.

If it were the size of a spider, it wouldn't have been a concern, but the monster was slightly larger than a horse. It moved with jerking motions, its wooden hands clicking against the stone floor as it walked.

All of Twain's fur stood on end as his kitten eyes went wide.

"What is that?" Sorin shouted. He grabbed my arm and pulled me away from the puppet. "*Gray?*"

"It's a monster," I said, unable to provide more of an explanation. "We have to run!"

The marionette spider lifted one of its legs. The fingers on its hand sprouted knives—long, sharp, deadly. A phantom pain shot through my back as I recalled the agony of its attack. I was frozen for a moment, caught in my own memories and dread, trapped in the quicksand of panic.

Sorin pulled me as he ran, and I was jerked back to my senses. With a deep gulp of air, I dashed away from the puppet as it made its first swing. The blades whistled through the air, but missed both Sorin and me.

We ran around the building, my heart pounding straight up my throat. Piper had said the arcanists of the Academy wouldn't help us with the Trials of Worth, but wouldn't they help us if we were in trouble? She had made some sort of comment about returning to her, hadn't she?

Sorin must've had the same thought. He veered toward the location where we had first arrived in the Menagerie. I ran alongside him, but I was naturally faster. I pulled ahead as we ran down the hill.

The puppet chased us relentlessly, though slower than it did in my dreams. When it ran down the grassy hill, the knives of its hand slashed up the ground, leaving even the Menagerie wounded.

The illusioned sky had turned on us. Gone was the sunshine and warmth. It had all been replaced with dark clouds and an ominous chill. There was enough light by which to see, but just barely. I didn't know my way around the Menagerie. Was there a way out of here that didn't involve teleportation?

I hadn't seen a door.

With a huff, I arrived at the starting location Piper had brought us to. I glanced around, my heart racing.

"Where is everyone?" Twain asked in a tiny voice. "I don't see anybody..."

Sorin ran up to me, his breathing labored. I grabbed his arm and pulled him toward the grove of trees. Wasn't there a kitsune there? Her fox-fire could help!

"Gray?" my brother asked between gulps of air.

The puppet chased us toward the grove.

My heart sank when we reached the first grouping of trees.

No one was here. I glanced around wildly, trying to spot even a *trace* of the others' presence, but I saw nothing. No footprints. No kitsune fur. Even the grass seemed undisturbed.

"Help!" I shouted. "Anyone!"

But no one answered.

When I turned my attention to the branches overhead, it seemed as though a fog had settled over us. The Menagerie wasn't as pristine or beautiful as it had been when we had arrived —it was hazy, like a dream. Where were we? I hadn't fallen asleep. Sorin and Twain were with me. What was this?

It had to be a dream. But how had all three of us gotten here?

"Gray!"

My brother's voice almost didn't register. I turned on my heel just in time to catch sight of the marionette-spider rushing up on me. It lifted its bladed hand, and I didn't have time to leap away.

Sorin pushed me out of the way just as the puppet swung. The blades caught Sorin's shoulder, slicing through his clothing and flesh, splattering the ground with his blood. He yelled as he grabbed at his injured shoulder, his face contorted in pain.

The puppet-spider didn't seem interested in my brother, though. It turned its face mask on *me*. But I couldn't buckle, not now—not when I was so close to becoming an arcanist. I ran right toward it, and the spider tilted its head as though confused.

Twain dug his kitten claws into my arm, causing me to bleed. He, too, was probably confused.

I went for one of the puppet's legs and kicked it on a long, thin portion of the wood. I had given it my all, and the leg of the monster splintered under my boot. It didn't *break*, but it had *fractured*. The sound of wood cracking filled the grove.

My leg hurt for a moment, but the pain was forgotten as I stumbled away.

The puppet didn't cry out or flinch, but it did lift its leg and hold the broken portion in front of its mask. The thing had no eyes—the holes of the mask just showed more wood—but it "examined" the injury as though observing it like any normal creature.

"Let's go!" I shouted as I grabbed Sorin's uninjured arm.

Together, we ran out of the grove, but I was at a loss when it came to where to head next. Instead of hesitating, I ran for the underground lake. It was near the marsh. I had seen a giant frog in the water. Would it still be there?

The marionette attempted to follow us, but its leg splintered even further when it took a step. The jerking of its movements as though it were on strings, didn't mean it was weightless, apparently. The spider examined its broken limb a second time, its mannerisms almost irritated.

"What's going on?" Twain shouted. He still had his tiny claws in my arms. "Why are there monsters here? Where's the headmaster? He'll save us! He has to!"

I ignored the kitten's cries as we made our way to the lake. Sorin huffed and puffed until we came to a stop. Then he inhaled at a fierce rate, his body shaky. Blood wept from his injured shoulder. The puppet had cut him deeply.

I placed Twain down on the ground and examined my brother's injury.

"Help!" Twain shouted. He bounded to the edge of the water. "Come out here, Itachi! We need your help!" The kitten pawed at the smooth waters. A slight ripple spread out from the shore. "Itachi? Can you hear me?"

The body of water was more an ambitious pond than a lake. It was only four feet deep, even in the middle. Decorative boulders were placed at strategic places around the edges, and a single weeping willow was positioned on the far side. The

123

pristine waters were clear enough to showcase the beauty of the lake's floor. There were colorful stones embedded in the dirt—a mosaic in the shape of a feathered dragon.

But there weren't any creatures swimming in the water. Whoever "Itachi" was, they weren't here.

Sorin knelt on to one knee, his body shaking harder than before. "Gray... I feel weird..."

I grabbed under his arm, digging my hand into his armpit as I struggled to lift him. "Get up!"

The puppet was moving toward us at a slow but steady pace. It didn't want to put weight on its broken leg, and it occasionally stopped to inspect the damage as though it was a problem it didn't know how to deal with.

"I'm cold," Sorin said, his voice quiet. "Gray, just go. I'll..."

Although the puppet seemed interested in me, it had also displayed some intelligence. If I left Sorin, would the monster use my brother as bait? Would it harm Sorin until I surrendered? I couldn't take that chance. We had to stick together.

"Get up," I commanded.

"I can't. I... I feel weak." Sorin scrunched his eyes closed. "Just go, Gray. I don't... I don't want to be responsible for your death, too."

His words stabbed me, even through the sheer terror of the situation.

"The headmaster abandoned me," the kitten muttered. Twain lay on the ground and pressed his paws over his ears. "Everyone always abandons me... This is it. This is how I die."

Their despair was infectious.

For a flicker of a moment, I almost gave in and joined them —I almost wallowed in our seeming defeat. But that moment faded just as quickly as it had come.

I yanked on Sorin's arm, forcing him to his feet.

"Gray?" he asked.

"*We're not giving up,*" I shouted. "I don't care what's in our

124

way! If it's a wall, we'll go left and walk around. If that doesn't work, *we'll go right*. If that doesn't work, we'll climb or dig! I'll find a way to travel around the whole world and approach the wall from the other side if that's what's needed! So *never* give up, do you understand me? We'll think of something!"

My brother and Twain both stared at me, their eyes wide. The kitten had mismatched eyes—one pink, and the other... gray. Not as pale blue as Sorin's and mine, but an unmistakable gray that caught my attention in that brief moment.

"You'll find a way?" Twain whispered.

The puppet-spider approached us, its knife-hand lifted for an attack.

I pulled Sorin into the pond. We splashed through the water as the monster swung and missed with its knives. Twain, panicking, leapt from the shore and hooked his claws into my arm. I sucked in air through my teeth as sharp pain flared through my body.

Twain clung to me, shivering. "I... I don't want to give up."

I plunged my hand into the pond and grabbed a mosaic stone. As the spider slowly crept into the pond, its mask facing me, I asked, "Do you have magic? *Anything?*"

With a grunt, I threw the decorative stone at the monster. It clacked against its wooden body and did nothing.

"Mimics only have the power of the creature they've transformed into," Twain said, his voice warbling. "I-I don't know what to do..."

Twain was a *mimic?*

Oh, that was right! Professor Helmith had said that mimics were little *copycats*. They transformed into other mystical creatures—exactly as they were. If the creature was old, the mimic would be old. If the creature hadn't developed its magics, the mimic wouldn't have any, either. The mimic always transformed into the perfect replica.

"Transform into a mystical creature!" I shouted as I dragged

Sorin deeper into the lake. He was resting more and more of his weight on me as though he couldn't hold himself up.

"I can transform into *anything* nearby," Twain said as he closed his eyes. "There are so many! I don't know what to do!"

And all the mystical creatures around us were all so young.

The pegasus. The kitsune. All baby mystical creatures. And since they hadn't bonded yet, all their magics would be weak.

But the professors were nearby. Piper had a rizzel. Captain Leon had a cerberus...

Then the answer came to me.

The puppet-spider reached its long leg out, slashing at me in a wide arc. I splashed backward, the cold water numbing half my body.

The cerberus had said Professor Helmith was nearby—in the Academy.

"Transform into an ethereal whelk!" I commanded.

Twain's ears shot straight up. "R-Really?"

"Do it!"

Twain nodded once. Then his body contorted in my arms, his orange fur shifting and shimmering with deep power. He felt warm. And then cold.

He released his hold on my arm and floated a few feet away from me as he transformed.

Within the blink of an eye, Twain had changed forms.

Chapter 14

Becoming An Arcanist

The little kitten had transformed into... a sea snail.

A magical snail, but still a snail.

Twain had formed into a spiral shell the size of a human head, the outside sparkling with rainbow iridescence. Tentacles similar to an octopus's, hung out of the shell as he floated through the air, completely unaffected by gravity. He moved as though he were a petal hovering back and forth on a gentle breeze. The snail's eyestalks were tall, and the eyes a void-like black.

Twain had transformed into an *ethereal whelk*.

What a bizarre creature.

It was clearly magical, and I saw that it was almost transparent as though made from light itself. He was just a few feet from me, but I could see right through him.

I couldn't dwell on any of that. The puppet splashed forward and slashed with its knives. I couldn't move fast enough. The combination of the water, and my brother's weight, prevented me from sidestepping the attack. The blades cut me across the chest, the searing agony enough that I cried out. I stumbled backward, taking Sorin with me. My brother grabbed my bloody shirt, his fingers twisting the fabric.

"Twain!" I shouted. "End this!"

The mimic floated around as an ethereal whelk. "How?" he asked, his voice now singsong and soft. "I can't fight with a body like this!"

The puppet-spider swung at me again. I shoved Sorin into the water, and then I dove beneath the surface as well. The spider slashed at me and missed. When I emerged from the water, it swung again, faster than before. It nearly took a chunk of my face, but I leaned away.

"*Twain!* You can do anything! It's a dream! Just control it! That's what ethereal whelks do!" I didn't have any more specifics than that. I wasn't an arcanist—I didn't know how to use magic. But I had seen Professor Helmith alter dreams many times. I knew Twain could do it!

"This isn't a dream..." Twain whispered. "R-Right?"

"It's a dream! Trust me."

The spider grew bolder. It swiped again, and then again. I splashed through the water, half-swimming, half-standing, barely able to dodge. Sorin gasped as he surfaced, his blood blooming into a pink cloud that stained the water.

"Make anything!" I yelled. "Fire! A windstorm! A snake that specifically eats spiders, I don't care!"

The monster stopped mid-swipe.

Then it slowly circled around to Twain, its facemask emotionless and unmoving, yet somehow, the gears of its tiny mind were turning. It *was* intelligent. The puppet *knew* Twain could end this whole fight. And now the monster was going to do something about that.

"Twain! Curse the abyssal hells, *just do it!*"

He wiggled his tentacles, but nothing happened.

When the spider-puppet lifted its hand, I splashed through the pond, determined to protect Twain. The monster swung, but I lunged just in time, getting in the way of the attack. The beast caught me with its blades, but I grabbed its wooden leg at its bizarre wrist.

Blood gushed from the new gash across my ribs.

The marionette tried to yank its hand from my grasp, but I wrapped both my arms around its leg and held on.

Twain squeaked in fright. "What're you doing?"

"I'll hold it!" I shouted, my voice weaker than before. "C'mon!"

"You're bleeding…"

The monster lifted another one of its legs, and a *second* hand sprouted knives.

I was going to get cut to ribbons.

But then a pulse of power filled the air. I held my breath, familiar with the sensation. I half-expected Professor Helmith to descend from the air and blast this puppet away, but… that wasn't the case.

The water swirled and moved with a mind of its own. The puppet halted all its attacks, its facemask "glancing" around as though confused. Sorin stood in the middle of the pond, on the mosaic stones, his breathing heavy. He watched the event unfold with wide eyes.

The water congealed as it lifted and twisted together, becoming a semi-transparent serpent of ice and dread. It all happened with the speed and eerie orchestration only possible in a dream.

The water-snake was far larger than anything around us, including the trees.

I released my grip on the puppet just as the serpent lashed its tail and struck the wooden monster. The ice of its body smashed the monster into splinters, breaking apart the mask and abdomen in one fatal blow.

I stumbled backward, shaken by the powerful blow. If I had been caught up in that, I would've surely been crushed.

"Ha!" Twain yelled. He lifted his tentacles. "Take that, *vermin!*"

The icy serpent lifted its tail and then smashed it back down on the shattered wood of the puppet, splintering it further. Then the serpent did it a third time. And a fourth time. Each time breaking the marionette into fragments smaller than kindling.

Twain cackled with delight, his laughter on the edge of maniacal. "You thought you could best *me?* I'm a *mimic!* Capable of all magics! And you? You're just splinters."

But right after he had made his dramatic statement, Twain's body bubbled. His shell, his tentacles—even his eyestalks. They warped and jiggled as they slowly sprouted orange fur.

"Oh, no, I'm transforming back," Twain said in a panic. "I'm too weak..."

"Wake us up," I said. "*Hurry.*"

Twain, with the last of his ethereal whelk powers, waved his little tentacles.

The dream landscape faded away, melting all around us. My equilibrium became distorted. At first, I thought I was standing in the middle of an empty pond, but then it felt as though I were lying on my side. When I blinked my eyes, my entire surroundings had changed. Darkness surrounded me.

And my eyes felt crusty...

I blinked harder until I realized I was on a cold, stone floor in the middle of a dark room.

Had I been sleeping?

With a groan, I tried to roll over, but my injuries flared with pain. Blood pooled around my body as my heart beat furiously against my ribs. When I tried to call out, my lungs burned.

Was I back in the memorial? Yes. I was. Had I fallen asleep when I had been in the darkness? I supposed I had. But how had *that* happened?

"Let me go, fiend!" Twain called out.

Concern flooded me. I pushed myself to my feet, my injuries be damned. With a stumble, I groped around the darkness, wondering where Twain had gone. Light shone from both ends of the memorial—the entrance and the exit—but it wasn't enough to completely dispel the shadows. With the dim illumination, and my head spinning, I detected the silhouette of a person and maybe a kitten.

The person stomped on Twain.

Fueled by anger, I charged forward and threw a punch.

I wasn't really a *fighter*. My father had never taught me anything about combat. That being said, Sorin and I had wrestled a bit, as all brothers will. When I threw my punch, I managed to connect with the person's head. They grunted—feminine sounding, even through the crunch of grinding teeth. I had struck her in the side of the head. My knuckles hurt afterward.

Then I knelt and scooped Twain up into my shaky hands. "I got you," I whispered. "Just hang on."

He meowed weakly.

The person—the mysterious *someone* who had stomped Twain—threw a punch right back at me. Only instead of aiming for my head, she struck me in my bleeding ribs. I cried out as I stumbled back against the wall.

"*You're supposed to be dead,*" she hissed under their breath.

I didn't recognize her voice.

Could she see? How else would she know to strike me in an injury?

"What's going on here?" someone shouted from outside the memorial. "What're all these sounds and lights?"

My attacker cursed under her breath.

"We're in here!" I rasped.

That was too much for my attacker—she ran. The sound of her shoes... They made a *clack-clack-clack* sound that was different from the puppets'. She went straight for the exit, just as someone else appeared at the entrance.

Our savior was Piper, the rizzel arcanist. She and her eldrin stood at the door, the light shining behind both of them, like they were heroes sent from the good stars.

"Help!" Twain called out. "That lady running... she tried to kill me!"

To my surprise, the tiny little ferret leapt off of Piper's shoulder. With a puff of glitter and a pop of displaced air, Reevy the rizzel disappeared and reappeared near my attacker. After a deep inhale, Reevy exhaled a *whoosh* of white fire. It flooded the memorial—right near me, but never touching me—illuminating everything with a mystical ivory glow.

The flames...

They weren't hot. They *disintegrated* things—breaking them apart as though they were teleporting little bits at a time and displacing them around. Dust filled the air as the black rocks of the memorial were broken apart, bit by bit, by the deadly white fire.

The bright white allowed me to see a bit more.

Sorin was slumped on the ground, obviously still asleep. What had happened to us? Who had put us into a forced slumber?

My attacker...

When I glanced over to catch sight of the woman who had attacked me, I saw nothing. Just the blazing ivory flames of the rizzel. The fire disappeared a moment later, casting us back into darkness. A mist hung in the air that smelled of dirt and rock.

"Well, that was cathartic," Reevy said, his little voice echoing in the memorial. "I haven't been allowed to totally destroy a villain in quite some time."

Totally destroy?

Had Reevy dealt with her? It had appeared as though she'd gotten away.

But I wasn't sure.

Piper ran over to me. When she drew near, she asked, "Are you okay? What happened?"

But I wasn't really in a place to answer. Now that the dangers had faded, my consciousness was going with them. My head felt light, and my injuries burned more than normal. I tried to hand her Twain—so that she could help him—but I felt myself slip.

Piper tried to catch me.

Then my vision went black.

When I managed to open my eyes again, the first thing I saw was a stone ceiling.

It was night. Light shone from a lantern by my bed, and from one hanging on the far wall. With some effort, I rubbed at my neck and glanced around. Someone had placed me on a bed. The white sheets were soft and comfortable, and I almost wanted to pull them over my face and go back to sleep.

But then the memories of the Menagerie came rushing back.

"Sorin?" I croaked, my voice rusty. "*Sorin?*" I forced myself up into a sitting position.

"Ow!"

Twain tumbled off my chest and landed on the bed, right by my side. He flailed around the blankets for a moment, and then jumped to all four of his paws. His orange fur stood on end. He was so puffed, he looked like a living potato.

"Be gentle," Twain said. "I'm recovering, too, ya know!"

With my head throbbing, I took in the rest of my surroundings.

We were in a giant room filled with many similar beds. At least three dozen. They were small—meant for only one person each—and curtains hung between most. This was an infirmary. A place for the sick and wounded. My island only had one physician, and he was older than everyone on the island put together, but his clinic was not this large or clean or decorative.

Pictures of calm skies hung on the walls, and at the far end of the room, there were windows that stretched from the ceiling to the floor. The darkness of night greeted me beyond the glass, but I could still see that this infirmary overlooked the nearby mountain ranges that surrounded Astra Academy.

We were high above it all, overlooking the peaks, with a view straight into the darkness between the individual mountains.

Twain and I were alone in the infirmary. No one else slept on the beds, and I didn't spot a physician anywhere around.

"What happened?" I asked.

Twain de-puffed himself. Then he licked the back of his paw and wiped his face with it. "Apparently, we were in a dream. And then we were attacked by a gigantic child's toy." Twain sat and narrowed his little eyes. "Was it your fault? It feels like it was your fault."

"Is my brother okay?" I glanced around again, hoping to spot Sorin. "Where is he?"

"He got up a long time ago. You were way more injured. The doctor said you needed to rest more."

I rubbed my face. "How long have I been sleeping?"

"I dunno. Maybe eighteen hours?"

"*Eighteen hours?*" I balked. "Really?"

"The dream monster cut you so much... I didn't even know wounds in a dream could follow you back to the waking world."

The statement reminded me of my injuries. I threw the blanket off and glanced down. I wore a pair of flowing white pants—pristine and loose—but nothing else. The slashes across my ribs and chest were healed, but not forgotten. My skin had white scar lines everywhere the monster had attacked me. I touched the faint reminders of the fight, grazing my fingertips along the entire length of a single scar.

"What was that?" Twain asked as he tilted his head to the side. "I've never seen a monster like it."

"I don't know," I whispered.

"*And who attacked me?*" Twain huffed and then arched his back. "Someone came out of nowhere and tried to squish me after I woke up! What a dastardly tactic. If it had been a straight fight, I would've vivisected them."

"I don't know that, either."

Twain eventually calmed enough that he lowered his back and returned to his sitting position. For a quiet moment, he said nothing. Absentmindedly—because he looked so much like a normal cat—I gently petted his head.

Twain purred. I stopped, mildly surprised by his reaction. He shot me a glare, his two-colored eyes reminding me he was, in fact, a mystical creature and not a common housecat.

"Listen," Twain said as he stood, turned around, and then sat with his back to me. "The Trials of Worth in the Menagerie are all over."

"They are?"

"Yup. Everyone has bonded. Eleven new arcanists."

My heart beat hard again. I clenched my jaw, worried that I had failed my brother. Had he gotten back in time to bond with a creature? What if he had been stuck in the infirmary the whole time, and he had missed his chance?

What if *I* had missed my chance?

"I've been in the Menagerie for years," Twain stated matter-of-factly. "Headmaster Venrover said I would find someone to bond with eventually... But that day never came."

With an exhale, I leaned back on the bed and stared at the ceiling. "Why not?"

"Well..."

"Well?"

Twain sighed, and his ears drooped. "I'll tell you, but only if you promise never to repeat what I'm about to say."

With half a smile, I said, "I promise."

"It's because... I don't have a Trial of Worth."

I propped myself up on my elbows to stare at him. "What? Really?"

"Yes, really!" Twain huffed. He straightened his posture and then glanced at me. "All the other mystical creatures... They all knew the type of person they wanted to bond with. The pegasus wanted *loyalty* and *physical prowess*, and the kitsune wanted *cleverness*, and the golem wanted someone who was *reliable* and *steadfast*. But me..."

Twain didn't finish his statement.

"You went years without bonding because you didn't have a Trial?" I asked. "Why not bond with *anyone*? That's how mystical creatures grow, right? Don't you want to grow older and more powerful?"

Twain shuddered. "I can't just bond with anyone! It's a lifetime commitment. And every person I've ever met has always left me." He jumped onto my chest and then lay down. "Even my mother left me... I just..." Twain nuzzled my shirt. "I'm afraid."

I didn't know what to say. Instead, I slowly brought my hand to his head and scratched him behind the ear. The little kitten leaned into my palm. With a purr, Twain closed his eyes.

"Why didn't you just make up a Trial of Worth?" I asked. "I mean, some of the Trials seemed simple enough. A race? A scavenger hunt? Surely you could've thought of something."

Twain pulled out of my hand and then stood tall on all four legs. "But all the other creatures *knew* their Trials of Worth in their hearts. They just *knew*. That's what they told me. They never needed to think something up. It came to them through magic itself."

"Interesting."

"I never felt that. I never *knew*." Twain pawed my chest, like he was stomping in anger, but it was too cute to be considered aggressive. "What if I'm defective? What if that was why my mother left me? Why everyone eventually *leaves...*"

I said nothing. The quiet of the infirmary was almost oppressive. What was I supposed to say?

Twain took a breath and then stared at me. "But... when I saw you fighting the dream-puppet, I just had this *feeling*. You... How do I put this...? You just didn't stop. You thought of new tactics. Tried different things. That was when I *knew*, in my heart."

"Knew what?" I asked.

"That you were worthy of being my arcanist," Twain whispered.

I held my breath, mulling over everything he had said. With a mimic eldrin, I could use ethereal whelk magic, just like Professor Helmith. Actually, I could use *any* magic, so long as a creature was nearby for Twain to transform into.

It would be the perfect fit.

"I agree," I said. "Does that mean... I've passed your Trial of Worth?"

"I just told you I don't have one!" Twain shook his head. "It's so embarrassing."

"Nobody has to know that." With a sarcastic sweep of my hand, I motioned to the empty infirmary. "I'll just tell everyone that you have an epic Trial of Worth that I passed after I woke up."

Twain tilted his head to the other side. "Do you think people will believe you? They won't think I'm just defective?"

"Oh, trust me. People will believe. I'll spin a tale so enthralling, they'll all wish they had been here to witness our glorious Trial."

Twain chuckled. Then he pawed at his whiskers. "Yes. I like this plan. I want everyone to think I had a challenging Trial. *So difficult.*" He widened his eyes. "The more powerful the mystical creature, the more dangerous and deadly the Trial of Worth. Did you know dragons almost always have a Trial that claims lives? What a bunch of goons!"

"Dragons sound like try-hards," I quipped. Then I petted Twain a third time. "But don't worry. Everyone will think your Trial of Worth was just as epic."

With a purr, Twain said, "Excellent." Then he stopped and stared me dead in the eyes. "Very well. Gray—I deem you worthy of becoming a mimic arcanist." He glared at me as he finished. "You better not think of ever abandoning me, too."

I was about to reply, but a twist in my chest caught my breath. There was an unasked question in my mind and heart. A question of bonding. I accepted with no hesitation, and a powerful sensation—a change within me, altering everything—rippled through my whole body. My forehead hurt, but only for a split second.

A seven-pointed star etched itself into my skin, marking me as an arcanist.

I rubbed at my forehead, expecting another image to lace itself into the star. But no other image appeared—I didn't get a little kitten or a large cat. Piper had a rizzel, and Captain Leon had the cerberus, and Professor Helmith had her snail, but my arcanist star...

It was blank.

Nothing happened to Twain. He was the same orange kitten with lynx ears and a bobtail. But when he met my gaze this time, his eyes sparkled brighter than before.

However, I couldn't celebrate yet.

"What happened to Sorin?" I blurted out, my thoughts returning to my brother as soon as I realized I was definitely an arcanist. "Tell me... Did he bond with anything from the Menagerie?"

CHAPTER 15

HEALING UP

" **I** don't know if your brother bonded," Twain replied. "I wasn't there. I've been with you the whole time."

That bothered me. If Sorin wasn't an arcanist, I couldn't stay here at Astra Academy. I'd travel with him to locate other mystical creatures so that he could attempt another Trial of Worth. Anything until he became an arcanist as well. Then I could return to the Academy, and we could both attend.

Before I voiced my plan to Twain, the far door to the infirmary opened.

An elderly man hobbled into the room, followed closely by an ancient golden stag. I sat up on my bed, my eyes wide as the man and the deer strode through the infirmary, straight to my side.

The man was odd. He wore a long, brown robe, but his body seemed lumpy and lopsided. He had the physique of a potato sack and a beard that resembled a long rat's nest. His face was etched with laugh lines and creased with age. The arcanist mark on his forehead was a seven-pointed star with a deer wrapped around the points.

The golden stag seemed just as old as the man. His shimmery

fur was long on his neck and near his hooves, and the antlers carried scars. Despite that, the stag was still impressive. His horns were made of the purest metallic gold, and his hooves were a mix of brass and copper. Each step on the stone floor resulted in a loud *clack* that echoed throughout the room.

His eyes were blue, but glazed over, almost blind.

According to Professor Helmith, the golden stag was a creature of harmony, healing, and nature. I believed her. The moment the stag drew near, a gentle wave of stillness came over my body and mind. I was more content and at peace than I had been in months.

The sounds of babbling river water entered my thoughts. I knew there were no brooks or streams nearby, but I still delighted in the tranquil melody of the outdoors.

"Good evening." The elderly man smiled. "I'm Physician Tomas Dravon, a golden stag arcanist. You can call me *Doc Tomas*. All the students do, after all." He chuckled at his own comment, and his whole body got in on the mirth. He practically jiggled.

"My name is Petrichor," the deer said, his voice ancient and rumbly. It reminded me of storm clouds just before the rain. "I'm Doc Tomas's eldrin and assistant."

"Why are you two so old?" Twain asked, his ears back. He glanced between them. "Arcanists don't grow old."

"I bonded with Petrichor when I was already in my twilight years." Doc Tomas patted his stag on the shoulder. His hands shook, either from arthritis or old age. "And becoming an arcanist doesn't de-age you, much to my disappointment, ha ha!" Again, he laughed at his own comment for some time, even though no one else joined in.

Twain glanced over at me with a look that said, "*Are you seeing this?*"

I replied with a shrug.

Finally, Doc Tomas calmed himself. "You see, golden stags

are one of the few mystical creatures who *only* bond to those advanced in age, like myself. Their Trial of Worth requires the knowledge of a life well lived."

His statement added to my growing understanding of mystical creatures. They all seemed to have preferences that complemented their magics or nature at a deeper level than I first expected. The golden stag only bonded with elderly individuals? It made me wonder what drove the creatures to seek these traits and virtues.

Perhaps Professor Helmith would know.

I needed to speak with her.

The elderly physician stepped close to my bed. He leaned in close, squinting at me. His eyes were a dark green, and his hair as gray as dirty seafoam. The scent of lilacs wafted around him. I said nothing as he examined the scar lines on my chest. He didn't touch me—he just stared intently.

Then he glanced up to meet my gaze.

"You have unusual eyes," Doc Tomas muttered.

I rubbed the side of my face. "Yeah. I get that a lot."

Doc Tomas leaned away. "I have good news, and even better news."

"No bad news, huh?"

"I never said that," Doc Tomas said with a chuckle. "But for right now, I think you just need to hear all the good things."

I lifted an eyebrow. "Okay. What news do you have?"

Doc Tomas lifted a single trembling finger. "You're going to make a full recovery." Then he raised a second finger. "And it'll be just in time for the Astra Academy orientation. Very fortunate, I'll say."

"Gray was sleeping for eighteen hours." Twain curled up on my lap like any good cat. "Did everyone just wait to have orientation until he was better?"

"Apparently, the Menagerie needed to be thoroughly investigated after that heinous assault." Doc Tomas frowned, his whole face sagging with the effort. He looked dramatically sad with all the folds and wrinkles around his mouth. "That took most of yesterday to accomplish. The Academy decided to hold the orientation in the morning in order to allow everyone to recover."

"Did they find anything?" I asked.

Doc Tomas shook his head. His stag eldrin walked around to the other side of my bed, his gait slow, and his metallic hooves sounded as hard as I suspected they were.

"You are stressed," Petrichor said, his regal tone melodic. I'd love to listen to him read a book or give a speech. "Please, relax. The arcanists of the Academy will handle the matter."

For some reason, my anxieties bled away. I leaned back on the bed and gently patted Twain. He purred under my touch, his whole kitten body vibrating.

Then Petrichor bowed his head until his antlers came down to my chest. The tip of one prong touched my skin. I almost knocked his head away, but the tranquility in the air calmed my aggressions. Why fight the deer? What would be gained from that?

The thoughts in my head almost didn't feel like my own.

A burst of warmth flowed through my body, starting from the antler. The golden stag flooded me with magic, and I took a deep breath afterward, all pain gone from my body.

"Did you just heal me?" I asked, breathless.

"As best I can," Petrichor said as he lifted his head. "My arcanist and I have healed you several times. For some reason, the scars on your body won't entirely fade. I apologize. No injury has ever withstood our magic."

I glanced down and touched the thin, white lines where the dream-puppets had cut me. They were still there.

"I'm looking into the matter," Doc Tomas said. He raised his finger again and smiled—he looked so much more joyous and full of life when he grinned. "And I'll have you know that I've never failed to solve a medical mystery. There's a reason I'm here at Astra Academy."

"Many reasons," Petrichor said as he trotted around the bed and returned to his arcanist's side.

Doc Tomas grabbed the blankets I had thrown off the bed. He slowly tugged them over my legs but stopped once he had reached Twain. As though he were tucking in the kitten, Doc Tomas carefully set the blanket down on Twain's body and patted it into place.

"There, there," Doc Tomas said. "All comfy. You two should rest up. At dawn, you'll be guided to the main hall, given a tour of Astra Academy, and then served breakfast. After that, you'll be given your schedules and semester goals, then introduced to your class professors."

Twain nestled himself under the blanket.

But I wanted to push it all away. The golden stag's calming presence was all just a mind trick—I had important matters to deal with.

"I have to go," I said.

The deer stared at me with his milky, blue eyes. "You must find peace of mind. You will not recover without it."

"No, I need to find my brother." I threw off the blanket, disturbing Twain. "And then I need to find Professor Helmith."

Doc Tomas frowned once again. It almost made me empathetically sad to look upon him. Like he was a sad clown mirror, and I was unable to glance away.

"You are filled with anxiety, young man," Doc Tomas said. "It isn't anxiety that kills us—but the way we choose to react to it. You are doing no one any favors by rushing from the infirmary. I can assure you that your brother and the professor are okay."

His words carried with them a sense of gravity. I was in control. Even if I feared, fretted, and worried, I was still capable of choosing how to react to those emotions. Would I cave into

SHAMI STOVALL

them? Or would I follow the recommendation of Astra Academy's physician?

The old man and his ancient deer didn't stand in my way. It wouldn't take much to run from the infirmary.

Twain clawed at the blankets with grumpy huffs. I grabbed them from him and tucked us both back in. He stared at me for a long time and then returned to purring.

"All right," I finally said. "I'll stay here."

Doc Tomas nodded once. "Excellent, excellent. You've made a wise choice, young man. Sleep well until morning." With shaky movements, he headed for the door, his deer eldrin trotting beside him. After a few steps, I caught my breath and held up a hand.

"W-Wait," I called out.

They both turned to face me, their eyes wide.

"What if something attacks me in my dreams tonight?" I asked.

Doc Tomas and Petrichor glanced at each other. Then they turned their gazes in my direction. "We will inform the other professors that you need additional protection. No need to create more worries for yourself."

I almost protested, but I decided against it. A woman had attacked me and Twain in the Menagerie. Had she been killed by Reevy? I hoped so. Perhaps the nightmares would stop now.

Before Doc Tomas left the infirmary, he rubbed his wizened hands together. "Ooh, and I look forward to having you in class with me next year. You seem like a bright young man. Full of potential."

Next year?

I wondered why, but Doc Tomas didn't elaborate. He hobbled off, leaving just me and Twain inside the infirmary.

He seemed like a pleasant physician.

"I like him," Twain mumbled into the blanket as though he were reading my thoughts. "And his deer. They're both nice."

The tranquil feeling had disappeared, but my anxieties had faded. Somehow, reaffirming that I could control my actions, despite my worries, made me feel more confident. Everything would be okay.

I was finally at Astra Academy.

I was finally an arcanist.

What could possibly go wrong?

Then I closed my eyes and allowed myself to fall asleep.

I woke up with a start, my heart pounding.

"Where am I?" I blurted out.

Soaked in sweat and panting, I glanced around. My heart settled back into place as everything came back to me. I was in an infirmary. Twain was rolled in my blankets so tightly, he resembled a fish wrap—a special delicacy on my home island. He woke up, blinking back the morning light. The mountains just beyond the window shielded us from the worst of the sun's rays, but they were still bright enough to illuminate everything.

Twain attempted to leap from the bed but instead threw himself to the floor, still caught in all the blankets. "We're going to be late!" he yelled as he sailed through the air. He hit the tile floor with a *huff* and then attempted to barrel roll his way out of everything.

It wasn't working.

Twain hissed and spat and hissed some more.

"Calm down," I said as I slid off the bed. "I'll—"

But then the arcanist mark on my forehead burned. I gritted my teeth and grabbed the mark, confused by the sudden shift in power. The etching on my forehead changed shape. Instead of an empty star, I now had a golden stag wrapped around the points!

Twain shimmered and grew in size. He *became* Petrichor, the elderly golden stag. He became so big, in fact, that he ripped through the blanket as though it were a brittle leaf. Once freed from the bedding, Twain trotted around for a few moments—practically dancing with delight—and then transformed back into his normal kitten form.

It had all happened within a few seconds.

The moment Twain was a cat again, the mark on my head burned. I rubbed at my forehead. It was a blank star.

Interesting.

"Are you okay?" I asked.

Twain turned to me, his ears perked up. "Hm? Of course. Didn't you see me *burst out of those blankets?* They didn't stand a chance." Twain's fur stood on end as he growled at the pieces of shredded cloth. "That's what they get for trying to trap *me*, the great Twain!"

I chuckled as I walked over and scooped Twain into my arms. Then I patted his head. "Yeah, you sure showed that inanimate object. I'm very proud of you."

"You're mocking me, aren't you?" Twain muttered, his eyes squinted.

I strode for the door out of the infirmary, but at a slow pace. No one was here. It was an empty room—no clothes for me, no map of the Academy. No guide.

Why hadn't anyone come to find me?

"Did you notice anyone come into the infirmary this morning?" I asked.

Twain shook his head. "No. I was sleeping. Catnaps are deep, I'll have you know."

I placed my hand on the handle to the exit. It was morning. Doc Tomas had said orientation would be starting. Although I was only wearing a pair of flowing, white pants, I figured I had to find *someone* who could help me.

"Let's go, Twain," I said. "We have an Academy to attend."

CHAPTER 16

TO ORIENTATION

I cracked open the infirmary door and glanced outside.

The door led to a wide hallway. The dark stone walls were imposing at first, but then I caught sight of the many framed pictures. Paintings of dazzling landscapes, famous mystical creatures, and regal palaces were everywhere. I didn't recognize most of the images, but I didn't need to. Silver plaques hung underneath each painting, providing the name of the artist, and a little something about its significance.

I was too far away to see them all, but the closest painting was plenty interesting all on its own. The image was the sun and moon hanging in the sky at the same time. Underneath them, the land and ocean were lit by a mix of sunlight and moonlight.

It was surreal. Like a dream.

The details on the plaque read:

ARTIST: DANIVIN KAL

A DEPICTION OF THE WORLD BEFORE THE GATES TO
THE ABYSSAL HELLS WERE CLOSED. THE SUN AND THE
MOON TOGETHER IN THE SAME SKY IS AN OMEN OF
DEATH AND PASSING.

An omen?

My father would've *loved* this painting.

"What're you waiting for?" Twain whispered. He squirmed in my arms. "I thought you said we were in a hurry?"

Embarrassment filled me as I stepped out into the hallway. I had pants. Nothing else. I wasn't *indecent*, but it seemed pathetic and unprofessional to wander around the Academy like a vagabond.

Where were my belongings? I assumed the Academy staff had done something with them, but I wasn't sure what. Before I ventured anywhere else, I took a moment to glance up and down the hallway.

The lush, blue carpets complemented the silver silk drapes that hung between the paintings. Vases filled with blue and silver flowers were also present next to each door. A plaque that read: "Astra Academy Infirmary" hung on the wall next to me, its metal practically sparkling in the midmorning light streaming in through the narrow windows.

I hated to think this, but it reminded me of my home.

I gritted my teeth and frowned. Why did everything always remind me of things I wanted to move beyond? My father, my rinky-dink island... I was in an amazing academy, finally free of my old life, yet here I was reminiscing.

What was wrong with me?

"What's wrong with you?" Twain hissed, his ears back. "We're just standing around in a hallway! We look like weirdos."

"Gray?"

The feminine voice caught me off guard. I straightened my posture as I whipped around. Twain also froze, his fur on end. I held him close, trying to hide the fact that I was barely dressed, but it wasn't really working.

Piper came storming down the hallway. She wore an ivory dress that was fancy enough for a coronation celebration. It was layered with delicate feathers on the shoulders and near the hem. She practically fluttered as she rushed to my side.

Her rizzel—his white-and-silver fur matching her outfit—had wrapped himself behind her neck, like a scarf. He just hung there, limper than I would've expected from such a creature. He was channeling the attitude of clothing, for certain.

Piper's black hair was tied up in a beautiful, braided bun.

She was *much* more composed than when I had seen her in the Menagerie. Perhaps she wasn't hungover today.

"Good stars, give me strength," her rizzel, Reevy, said with a groan. "The boy isn't even *dressed*. This is gonna be a long day."

Piper ran a hand down her face. Then she gently slapped her cheek. "I can't believe this. The orientation will start any minute." She grabbed my upper arm, turned me around, and led me down the corridor. "We need to get you dressed, and then we need to head to the central courtyard."

I glanced over my shoulder at her, my brow furrowed. "Is everyone in the courtyard?"

"Yes. The headmaster will be delivering a speech to all the first-years."

"Where're you taking me?"

I hoped it wasn't the courtyard. I couldn't go out there like this.

"To the laundry room," Piper said as she picked up her pace, pushing me forward. "Faster, faster."

She wore heels, but that didn't stop the woman from hustling like a sailor prepping for a storm. She practically shoved me down the hall, her fingers digging into my bare back, panic fueling her actions.

When I glanced back, I caught Reevy staring at me, his little blue eyes narrowed. His ferret-like face was adorable, but his glare didn't put me at ease.

Piper hustled me to the end of the hallway and then pushed me left. There were more doors, and several other hallways, but we didn't take any of those. We hurried to the far spiral staircase. Then we took the steps down, but Piper couldn't hurry through this. Her heels made the stairs difficult. When she tried to take the steps two at a time, she wobbled.

"Oh, never mind," she said with a sigh. She grabbed my bicep. "We're close enough. Hold your breath."

"What?"

Her rizzel magic caused us to teleport. It was the same jarring sensation I had experienced when she brought us to the Menagerie, like my insides were being messed with. I stumbled out of her grip a moment later, in a completely different area of the Academy.

I had no clue where we were.

Silver sparkles and glitter wafted in the air around us.

"My stomach," Twain muttered.

We stood in front of a massive set of wooden double doors. Behind me, there was another long hall, but this one had no windows. Were we underground? The paintings on the wall were of fairies this time around. Small fairies, pixies, some fairies the size of an adult...

Piper shook my shoulder and pointed to the door. "This way."

She pushed open one side of the double doors and then led me into a massive laundry room. There were wooden bins filled with clothing, and pipes protruded from the walls. They gushed water into the bins, filling them to the top. Then soap was added —beautiful lye soap, colored a bright purple.

Then the bins twisted and shook.

There were no *people* doing any of this. It was as if all the objects in the room had minds of their own.

The soap threw itself into the bins. The clothing rolled around the water, rubbing up against the wood on the edges, cleaning itself with the bubbly water. When the bins shook and spun around, they were floating in the air—no part of them touched the stone floors.

And the room was *massive.* Twenty bins, each large enough to fit four cows, all whirled around without touching one another.

The pipes...

They were made of iron? Perhaps steel?

Water gushed out of them until the bins were full, and then the pipes stopped all on their own. No more water flow.

My island didn't have these kinds of pipes, but I had heard of them. Plumbing pipes? Wasn't that what they were called? It made for easier baths and restrooms. Normally, I had to go outside to collect water for bathing or eating or washing up, but Astra Academy wasn't as antiquated as my hometown.

It was modern and sophisticated.

I loved it.

"Gray?" Twain asked. "Are you paying attention?" He extended his claws and dug them into my arm.

I sucked in air through my teeth and shot him a glare. "What was that for?"

"You're just *staring!* Pay attention."

Piper hurried into the laundry room and frantically glanced around. Her rizzel lifted his head and joined her. What were they looking for? Dry clothes?

"Oh! Visitors!"

The shocked declaration echoed throughout the room, even while the bins sloshed about.

A woman walked out from between two piles of soap and laundry. She wore overalls and a puffy, white shirt so voluminous that it threatened to break the straps of the overalls. It was amusing, only because of how short and thin the woman was— her clothing made up fifty percent of her volume.

She made her way over to us, her dazzling, golden hair in a ponytail. It made it easy to catch sight of her forehead.

This woman was an arcanist!

And the creature twisted among the seven points of the star was humanoid. A fairy? No. It was an *engkanto*. They were elves.

And just as I had that thought, an elf walked out from behind the pile of laundry as well. Although the elf was a mystical creature, it had the appearance of a gorgeous human woman, about five feet tall. The elf's skin was golden—just as vibrant as her arcanist's hair—and her ears were pointed enough to be seen from across a gigantic field. And the engkanto wore a simple dress of white lace, so elegant, it was almost enchanting.

The engkanto's hair...

It was just as silver as the metal plaques in the hallway.

Some people thought humanoid eldrin were a little odd, but I always found them fascinating. They were otherworldly—no one would mistake one for a human. And they never grew old without bonding, just like all other mystical creatures, so they weren't just odd-shaped humans.

"Hello! I'm Maryanne Beets, Engkanto Arcanist and Head of Housekeeping." The woman with the overalls bowed once she reached us. When she stood, she couldn't contain her smile. "Let me give you a tour of the facilities. It's been *so* long since someone came to visit. We have—"

Piper stepped between me and Maryanne. "We're busy, Mary. I just need some clothing."

"But—"

"Orientation is about to begin, and this first-year needs some clothing. We don't have time."

Maryanne frowned. Then she fidgeted with her ponytail, twisting the golden strands of hair around one finger. Although she was dressed for cleaning, it didn't detract from her youthful beauty and happiness. From what Professor Helmith had said, engkanto only bonded with those who were vivacious.

"But I don't get many visitors," Maryanne muttered. "And I have a whole speech prepared..."

Piper sighed. So did her rizzel. The two were so in sync, they could probably finish each other's sentences while sleeping.

"Fine," Piper said. "But please keep it short. *No. Tour.*" She glared at me. "Stay right here and listen to the speech. I'm going to grab you an outfit."

I wanted to object, but she gave me no time.

Piper hurried into the laundry room to gather clothes, leaving me with Maryanne and her wondrous elf eldrin.

Maryanne fluttered her hands around with excitement. Then she took a deep breath, calmed herself, and smiled widely. Her eldrin did the same, though it didn't speak or try to butt into the conversation.

"Let's try this again," she said. "I'm Maryanne Beets, Engkanto Arcanist and Head of Housekeeping!" She spoke in a grandiose manner, her volume much louder than necessary, given we were a mere three feet apart. "Welcome to the unseen world of administration! I manage the staff responsible for all manner of daily necessities. You might not realize it, but a tidy environment is *crucial for learning!*"

"Crucial for learning," the engkanto dramatically whispered, creating an artificial echo.

"I've always wanted to guide a tour of the Academy, but since we can't, I'll just regale you with information!"

"With information," the engkanto whispered again.

"It'll be so exciting!"

Twain twitched his whiskers. "Can you lower your voice just a little bit? You're hurting my ears."

"Oh. Sorry." Maryanne tugged at the collar of her puffy shirt before whispering, "My magic, and my staff, focus on keeping everything running smoothly so that you don't have to. Engkanto are elves with *powerful* telekinesis." She waved her hands around as if trying to demonstrate something, but I failed to see the purpose. "I won't even be touching your belongings!" Her volume went straight back to where it had been before. "I will simply clean them and return them to you while you sleep."

"Thank you?" I said, my voice hiking up at the end in a confused question.

But her comment about telekinesis made me realize what was happening in the laundry room. The soap and bins weren't moving on their own. It was Maryanne's magic. She and her eldrin were washing everything from afar.

Maryanne opened her mouth to continue, but then her gaze landed on my arcanist mark. She caught her breath and stared. A few seconds passed in silence. Even her eldrin turned to her, confused.

"Are you a *mimic arcanist*?" Maryanne finally asked.

Twain proudly lifted his head.

I scratched him behind his large ear. "Yeah. I am."

"I've never met a mimic arcanist before." Maryanne crossed her arms. "I don't think we've ever had one at Astra Academy. They're so rare."

"I *am* super special, yes," Twain said as he licked his paw and smoothed the fur on his head. "It's okay if you want our autographs. Since you're one of the staff, it'll only be a small fee."

With a nervous chuckle, I covered Twain's face with my hand. "Never mind him. He's incorrigible." Twain wormed his way out from under my hand and just glowered up at me.

Maryanne beamed as though I had scored top of my class on a difficult test. "Oh, you remind me of Professor Zahn. Which is great—don't let anyone tell you otherwise. He's so bright! And clever! I think you're going to do amazingly in his classes."

Piper popped back into existence next to me. Silvery glitter puffed out from where she had appeared. She waved it away and then shook her head at Maryanne.

"Leave the teaching to me, Mary. I'll make sure he learns enough." Piper turned her attention to me. With her tongue held between her lips, she threw a shirt over my head and then wrapped a leather belt around my waist.

I barely had time to straighten everything before she shoved a pair of shoes against my chest.

"Perfect," Piper said as she stepped back to examine me. "No one will be able to tell we did this last minute."

I examined my outfit, surprised by the quality of the fabric. The silky shirt matched my flowing pants. It *did* seem like they were a coordinated outfit. And the belt and shoes shared the same brown color—I wasn't half-bad-looking.

Twain shook his head. "I prefer orange things over white. You're too dull. More color. Don't you see what peacocks do? You need more of that."

"There are white peacocks, ya know," I said.

"What? No. Impossible." Twain squinted at me. "Right?"

"We don't have time to change," Piper said matter-of-factly. "Actually, we don't even have time for this conversation." She halfheartedly waved to Maryanne. "Thank you. We'll speak later."

Before anyone could mutter goodbyes or even protest the series of events, Piper grabbed me and teleported. There was a half second where her magic tugged on me, and I felt as though I could resist. It was fleeting, and I acquiesced to her ability, but if I had *wanted* to, I could've fought against her, and stayed in the laundry room.

Instead, I was ripped from my current location and jerked through space until I stumbled forward into a courtyard.

And not just *any* courtyard.

It was a courtyard fit for a palace.

The gargantuan square yard was positioned smack dab in the middle of the main castle-like building of Astra Academy. There were stone walls on all four sides, with windows and balconies overlooking the greenery and decorations. A brook ran through the courtyard, with several footbridges over the running water. Small fields of white sand were positioned throughout, each one with colorful rocks laid out like small mosaics.

In one corner of the courtyard stood a gold-and-silver globe the size of a small shed. It showed all of Vardin, our world as we knew it.

In another corner, there was a sundial equal in size to the globe. It was an old-fashioned clock, but it was beautifully crafted out of brass and marble.

In the third corner, there was a statue of a seven-pointed star, equal to the other two in terms of prominence. The star was the symbol for magic, as every arcanist carried one on their forehead.

And in the last corner, probably the most glorious of all, was a statue of twisted gates. They were upside down, which meant they were the gates to the abyssal hells, the place all souls went after people died.

Sunlight drifted into the courtyard at an angle. The sun had yet to fully travel into the sky. It offered enough light to enjoy the beautiful flowers and vibrant greens of the shrubs, though.

I would've loved to walk around, but there were *hundreds* of individuals on the many paths and standing on the footbridges.

Piper and I stood at the edge of the courtyard. Everyone was facing away from us. They stared at a balcony across the way. The doors to the balcony were open, but no one was there.

The whispered irritations of the crowd were the first thing I noticed. I thought these were all students of Astra Academy, but it quickly became apparent that most people here were much older than me.

An arcanist's eldrin aged once bonded, after all. That was why you could *actually* tell the age of the arcanist. They could appear twenty, but if their eldrin seemed ancient, large, and powerful, the arcanist was likely older. There were exceptions, but only a few. It was typically a good indicator.

And there were several older eldrin around. A large yeti, a snow beast I had never seen, only heard of. And a fat pixie fluttering through the air with dragonfly wings. She was the size of my fist, but her flowing hair was the length of my arm.

"What's going on?" I whispered.

Piper grabbed my shoulder and kept me close. "Orientation. Just wait for the headmaster to give his speech. Then you're coming with me."

"Why?"

"Headmaster Venrover wishes to speak with you about what happened in the Menagerie."

Ah. I understood.

I wanted to tell him everything. Especially about Professor Helmith and whoever had been trying to hurt me during the bonding process.

"I like the headmaster," Twain said as he snuggled into my arms. "You'll like him, too."

"Hm."

I barely heard Twain. I stood on my tiptoes in an attempt to look for Sorin. My brother was tall. Shouldn't he be visible? If he had bonded with a mystical creature, wouldn't he be here? If he wasn't here... that meant he had failed to find an eldrin.

My heart beat wildly as I scanned the tops of everyone's heads. Some wore hats, other bandanas. It was irritating.

But then I caught my breath.

I spotted Sorin!

It had to be him. He was taller than everyone around him, and his dark hair fluttered in the morning breeze. He stood with his back to me, so I couldn't see his arcanist mark, but if he was here, that meant he had bonded!

"We did it," I whispered to myself. My whole body relaxed after I had finished saying the last word. "Excellent."

Twain twitched one ear to face me. "Excellent? Huh. Yes. Definitely."

I wanted to wade through the crowd and speak to my

brother, but the moment I stepped forward, Piper gripped my shoulder hard and held me back.

"*Stay here*," she hissed under her breath. "I need to bring you to the headmaster afterward."

Before I managed to protest, Captain Leon marched through the crowd to our position. I recognized him because of his distinctive white hair. No one else around us had that color of hair—not even the old man, Doc Tomas, had hair as glistening ivory as Leon's.

His cerberus eldrin was also so large, and so fearsome, that most people leapt out of the way. Two of the three dog heads flashed their fangs or narrowed their eyes, but the last head...

The last head had its tongue hanging out to the side, panting as though it had gone for a pleasant run and now it was time for a gallon of water. That head had enough cheer for a whole schoolhouse of children with bouncy balls.

Captain Leon went straight to Piper. "Where have you been?" he asked the instant he was close enough to whisper his demand. "You were supposed to have the boy ready and here ages ago!"

"We've been here for a while," Piper replied in a calm tone. "Just waiting for the headmaster."

"No, you haven't. Given your performance lately, I suspect you nearly lost the boy and barely made it here."

"Piper wasn't lying," I chimed in, wanting to help her out. "When is the headmaster arriving? We've been waiting for a while."

Both Piper and Leon glanced over at me. Piper offered a coy smile. Captain Leon's frown deepened into something uncomfortable. I thought he would yell, but then his anger bled away.

"You've been here a while?" Leon muttered in an apologetic tone. "I didn't see you."

"She woke me up and provided me fine clothes for the

orientation." I motioned to my outfit. "I'm really impressed with the dedication of the Academy's faculty. Top notch."

Piper dug her fingernails into my shoulder. Through gritted teeth, she whispered, "*Stop hammin' it up.*"

Sticks, the cerberus eldrin, stepped close to me. All three of his heads crowded in close and sniffed my face, hair, and shoulders. One head poked me in the face with his cold, wet nose. Twain puffed up in my arms and then hissed loudly enough that several people nearby turned around to face us, their eyes wide.

I shielded Twain from the drooling heads of the massive cerberus. "Okay. Back up. I'm not hiding treats in my pockets, fellas."

Leon motioned once, and his cerberus instantly leapt away from me. Then Sticks happily bounded over to his arcanist and took a seat by Leon's side. His long, slender tail wagged a million miles a minute.

Then the crowd went silent all at once, as though they had collectively held their breath.

Leon whirled on his heel and stared at the prominent balcony. Piper did the same. So did Reevy and Sticks.

I lifted my arm off Twain's head and then motioned to the balcony. We both glanced up to catch sight of an elegant individual. I assumed, given his official robes and striking demeanor, that it was, in fact, Headmaster Venrover.

CHAPTER 17

HEADMASTER VENROVER

The headmaster wore an expression as interesting as his clothing.

He smiled down at the crowd, his lips strained as though he were forcing a cheerful demeanor. The man's long hair, as black as midnight, was tied back in a mass of locks that flared in every direction. It reminded me of an inky sun.

And his features were so smooth and slender, he had an almost otherworldly presence. They were a mix of feminine and masculine.

Headmaster Venrover had on a black vest, a white shirt, and a long blue-and-silver robe he wore over everything else. A sash hung around his neck and down his side. It was marked with four symbols: a globe, a sundial, a star, and upside-down gates.

A mystical creature walked out onto the balcony with him.

A sphinx.

They were elegant creatures—a lioness's body, the wings of an eagle, and the head of a woman. Her golden fur had the hue of honey, and the feathers on her wings glistened with inner health. Her hair was brown, like a lion's mane, and her eyes...

She had two human eyes, and a third eye on her forehead. It was closed.

The arcanist mark on Headmaster Venrover's forehead was too small for me to see. Was *he* the sphinx arcanist? He had to be.

"Greetings, first-years," the headmaster said, his voice articulate and loud enough to hear from across the courtyard. Yet it was calm, almost reassuring.

Headmaster Venrover stepped close to the balcony railing. He grazed his fingers along the top, his robes fluttering a bit when the morning winds flowed into the courtyard. They were colder than before.

"Welcome to Astra Academy." The headmaster motioned to our surroundings. "It gives me great pleasure to see so many of you here. This will be your home for the next five years, so think of all your fellow students as your extended family."

I glanced around, one eyebrow raised. I didn't have a great relationship with my real family—except for Sorin—so the headmaster's statement almost sounded depressing.

So many people were here, obvious relatives to the new arcanists. They wore matching coats or hats, and some people even had little signs or capes that had the words *congratulations* written across them. They were here to celebrate a new arcanist in the family.

That explained the huge crowd.

Too bad my father and stepmother couldn't afford to be here.

"I have one piece of advice for you all. The future you'll create is paid for by your actions today. Use your newfound abilities wisely, and you'll go on to do great things."

The many arcanists, and their families, applauded the statement. I joined the rest of them, wondering if the headmaster gave the same speech at every first-year orientation.

The headmaster's sphinx stepped close to the balcony.

Everyone ended their clapping. Silence blanketed the courtyard.

The sphinx stared down at us with dark eyes. "This year, we have twenty-seven new arcanists," she said, her voice deep and regal. "Twelve became arcanists in our very own Menagerie, while fifteen were already arcanists before they traveled here through the Gates of Crossing. These twenty-seven arcanists have been evenly divided into three classes, completely at random."

Nine arcanists per class.

Hushed murmurs rose from the crowd. The older arcanists muttered statements of disapproval.

A woman close to me said, "They shouldn't mix the students."

"Aren't the arcanists from the Menagerie just islander children?" a man whispered, his voice loud enough to be heard by many. "What kind of education did they even have before coming here? Counting fish with their fingers and toes?"

"My daughter better not be harassed by some boorish islanders."

A man huffed and then said in a haughty tone, "*I am a duke*. To think my child will mingle with riffraff is quite irritating."

It occurred to me then, while everyone muttered and whispered, that most of the crowd wore fine clothing. Capes, knickers, vests, cuff links, shiny leather shoes—an obvious display of wealth if I ever saw one. These were the people who had come to the Academy on their own. The ones who had bonded without help. The ones who paid for their own boats and passage.

Headmaster Venrover held up a hand.

Again, silence spread between everyone, ending their complaining.

"Astra Academy has no control over where individuals

started in life," the headmaster said, his smile gone. "And while the students are here, it won't matter."

The sphinx spread her eagle wings. They were so large, I suspected she had a ten-foot wingspan.

"Everyone," she said, "please head to the dining hall for your welcoming feast. From there, we will tour the facilities, and end the tour at your dorms for the evening."

The applause that followed was weaker than before. I clapped harder, though—I even accidentally jostled Twain a bit. I just wanted to show my appreciation for the headmaster's decision. Despite my life as a candlemaker's son, I'd show everyone here that I belonged just as much as the *child of some random duke.*

The headmaster and his sphinx eldrin left the balcony.

My attention went straight to Sorin. He followed the crowd of arcanists and their families to the main dining hall. They all funneled into a grand double doorway, entering a northern hall that was as large as a sailing ship.

I stepped forward, but Piper grabbed my shoulder and jerked me back.

"Hey," I muttered.

"Did you forget?" She shot me a frown. "We're going to speak with the headmaster."

Ah. Right.

With Twain held tightly in my arms, I just waited for her to teleport us. Piper took a moment to whisper something in Captain Leon's ear. Her rizzel glowered at me the entire time, like he was watching to make sure I didn't sneak off. He even brought his paw up to his eyes, pointed at them, and then pointed at me.

I almost asked Twain to transform into a rizzel just so we could teleport off and speak to my brother while we waited. But there was no longer any urgency. Sorin was safe. We were both arcanists. I'd see him soon.

Once Piper was finished, she placed her hand back on my shoulder and activated her magic. We were jerked out of the courtyard, my insides knotting in the split second it took to stumble into a well-furnished room.

There was a desk, and multiple bookshelves, a couch the size of a small pier, a low table for refreshments, and a tower of trays adorned with tiny cakes. He even had a clock built into the wall, which was interesting to see. Light streamed in through an open door that led to a balcony.

So this was the room the headmaster had disappeared into after his speech.

It was so cold.

I rubbed at my stomach as I grappled with my thoughts, trying to visualize everything in my mind's eye. Piper had teleported us to the second story of the main Academy building in the blink of an eye. What was her distance limitation? I knew she had one, but this was impressive. We had been on the other side of the courtyard, after all.

Piper fixed her white dress, even fluffing the feathers on the sleeves.

Headmaster Venrover and his sphinx stood next to the gigantic desk, despite the fact that there were several seats all around us.

Up close, the headmaster was much thinner than he had appeared to be from afar. His robes practically wore him.

On the other hand, his sphinx must've weighed over three hundred pounds. She had all the muscle and grace of a lioness, and her human face, though a little disturbing, was regal and held high.

The sphinx said nothing. She just watched our conversation unfold.

When the headmaster turned his attention to me, it was his sharp eyes that took me by surprise. Headmaster Venrover stared for a half second, at the most, but it was like he understood so much more about me than even some members of my family.

His arcanist mark had the sphinx wrapped around the seven points. There were odd lines underneath the mark, though. Like a fading tattoo.

When the headmaster smiled this time, it was genuine.

"Gray Lexly," he said. "*Gray...* like your eyes."

Not many people put my name together with my eyes. Since heading to Astra Academy, it had happened twice. Maybe that was a good omen. But I shook the thought away and replied, "Y-Yeah. Exactly."

"It's nice to finally meet you." Then the headmaster glanced down at my eldrin. "And Twain. I told you that your arcanist would arrive someday, didn't I?"

Twain *huffed* and then turned his head to face the wall. I held him close to my chest, hoping he understood that I wouldn't let anyone bother him.

Piper smoothed her hair and then motioned to me. "Doc Tomas said he's all healed and able to attend class. And I got him ready for the orientation. Everything was taken care of." She had an almost breathlessness to her speech. Was she anxious?

"I do have two functioning eyes," Headmaster Venrover said, a slight chuckle at the end of his words. "But I appreciate your report nonetheless." When he returned his attention to me, he said, "Gray, let me be the first to apologize on behalf of the Academy. I was unaware there was anyone in the Menagerie besides Piper and the hopeful arcanists."

His statement caused me to think back to my time in the Menagerie. There had been a woman stomping on Twain. And she had said I was supposed to be dead. Was she the source of the nightmares?

"Professor Jenkins has assured me that whoever attacked you was killed in the Menagerie," the headmaster said.

My attacker was dead? Did they really know that for sure? I never saw a body... Or even her death.

Wait.

I lifted an eyebrow. "Who is *Professor Jenkins*? How does Professor Jenkins know anything about what happened in the Menagerie?"

Headmaster Venrover pointed to Piper. "Piper Jenkins is a professor of imbuing and history. Did she not introduce herself?"

"Oh. Captain Leon just kept calling her *Piper*."

Piper's face grew red as she frowned. "Well, now you know. I'm *officially* known as Professor Jenkins."

Before I could make any sort of quip about Piper's casual demeanor, the headmaster said, "In the forty-five years I've been headmaster, there has never been an attack in the Menagerie. I was unprepared for such a circumstance, and for that, I want to personally apologize."

There wasn't much for me to say, so I remained quiet. What would the headmaster think if I told him that someone had been trying to kill me for years? Would he blame me for the mysterious woman's presence and then pin all the damage on me? I didn't want to risk it.

That woman had clearly been after me. I didn't know why, but perhaps she had been the one creating all my nightmares, even the ones I'd had back on my home island.

She was dead now? The headmaster seemed to think so.

I wanted to speak to Professor Helmith about the matter. She would figure out the woman's identity and motives. And whether she was dead or not.

Hopefully.

The chill in the room intensified. How was it colder in here than outside? It baffled me.

"Astra Academy is a fortified structure," Headmaster Venrover said, refocusing my scattered thoughts. With a half-smile, he added, "And we have dozens of talented arcanists all around us. You can rest easy—we'll protect you from those who would do you harm."

"Thank you," I said.

Twain finally glanced back at the headmaster. "Well, I can vouch for the Academy. They've taken care of me for a long time." He purred in my arms. "And they have tasty chickens they feed us from time to time."

"Good to know." I patted his head. "I wasn't worried about the attack, though. You don't need to apologize. I'd rather just get back to—"

The door to the headmaster's office burst inward.

A large man stormed into the room, his long robes billowing behind him. His hair was coppery and thin—except for his tangled mass of a beard. The man could hide a fist in that beard.

And he also had an arcanist symbol on his forehead. The seven-pointed star was laced with a fat cyclops. The one-eyed monster was supposedly related to trolls. They were physically strong but magically weak, according to Professor Helmith.

And cyclops were so large, they typically couldn't fit into buildings. The man's eldrin was probably out by the docks.

The cyclops arcanist stomped straight over to Headmaster Venrover.

The headmaster's sphinx stepped close to her arcanist, her golden fur raised between her shoulder blades. When the cyclops arcanist drew close, she growled with the fierceness of a lion. The man hesitated, his lip turned down in a sneer.

Then he glared at the headmaster. "You listen here! My son said there was *an attack* in the Menagerie. He said a boy was sent to the infirmary. You knew this, didn't you? You're the headmaster! But you didn't say anything during your speech!"

"Everyone involved in the incident, or related to the incident, has been tended to," Headmaster Venrover stated, no emotion in his tone. "And everyone who entered the Menagerie —adults, I'll remind you—knew there were risks."

"*That's* your answer?"

The room grew colder in an instant. Twain shivered in my arms, his two-colored eyes wide as though he were searching for the source of the frigid temperature. Was this the work of magic?

"Someone's nearby," Twain whispered. "I can sense their magic."

I wanted to ask him for more details, but the cyclops arcanist stepped close to the headmaster.

"*My boy* is clever, and I won't leave him here if you're just gonna throw him to the abyssal hells!" The cyclops arcanist grabbed the headmaster's robes, and with superhuman strength, jerked Venrover forward. "What kinda protections are you—"

A man appeared out of thin air.

He just... *appeared*.

Had he been invisible? There hadn't been a pop of air or rizzel glitter.

This new man—dressed in black from head to toe, including a hood that obstructed my view of his face—grabbed the cyclops arcanist by the wrist. Ice formed over the man's arm. Then the floor. Then the walls. Then the furniture.

Rime as thick as my fingernails coated *everything* but the people. I nearly slipped and fell when I tried to move away.

The sphinx roared and spread her wings.

Even Piper and her rizzel leapt to the side of the headmaster. Piper had ditched her heels at some point—I hadn't seen when —which was smart. Reevy's little ferret body was twice the size it was before, his fur puffed, his dark eyes glaring.

The cyclops arcanist gasped. He yanked his hand away and stumbled back, his gaze flicking between each of the Academy arcanists.

"That's enough," Headmaster Venrover said as he patted

down his wrinkled robes. He didn't even seem bothered. Which was bizarre. He wasn't upset? I would've been furious.

Venrover straightened himself. "Piper, Reevy—please."

The two moved away.

"Nubia," the headmaster said as he eyed his sphinx.

Nubia eased up a bit. She folded her wings close to her lioness body and then took a seat. She flinched—the ice on the floor was a shock—but then she circled once and took a seat again, this time prepared for the chill. Her lion-like tail swished back and forth in blatant irritation.

At least his eldrin showed some sort of emotion.

Headmaster Venrover glanced at his once-invisible bodyguard. "Fain. You, too. I'm fine."

The man dressed in black—*Fain*, I supposed—said nothing.

Then he shrouded himself in invisibility and disappeared from sight. The ice in the room—both the chill on the air, and the rime on the floor—slowly dissipated. Had that been *his* magics? I wished I had seen his arcanist mark. What kind of mystical creature had he bonded with?

Could Twain transform into it?

The possibility of sneaking around with invisibility intrigued me.

As a mimic arcanist, I could have *any* magical ability, so long as I could mimic an arcanist's eldrin. In theory, anyway.

"There's nothing to worry about," Venrover said to the cyclops arcanist. He smiled as he added, "As you can see, we have plenty of talented arcanists in the Academy. No one will get far attacking this place."

The man stroked his giant beard with a shaky hand. Then he nodded once. "I-I see. Yes, well, my boy will probably be safe here. I didn't realize... you had so many *defenses*."

"Captain Leon and his knights are also more than capable of fighting off any threats."

SHAMI STOVALL

Reevy waggled his paw back and forth as though it was a fifty-fifty chance Leon could handle anything.

"Were there any *other* concerns you had?" Venrover asked as though this were a casual conversation and none of the animosity of a few seconds ago had ever occurred. "Otherwise, you're missing the feast in the dining hall. This will be the last time you can see your son for some time."

"Yes. You're right, of course." The man inched his way over to the door of the headmaster's office. "Have a nice stay. Er, I mean *day*. Have a nice day."

He opened the door and left in one quick motion.

Once he was gone, everyone seemingly held their breath. No one said anything. The stillness bothered me.

"Can *I* go to the feast?" I finally asked.

Piper flinched. She whirled on her heel and stared at me as if she had forgotten I was even in the room. "Oh. Right. *Yes*. I'll take you there." She stepped close and put a hand on my shoulder. Before we teleported, she turned back to the headmaster. "Unless there's anything else you wanted to say to Gray?"

Headmaster Venrover slowly shook his head. "Oh, no. I think I've made my point. The safety of everyone in the Academy is my top priority. Please enjoy your time here, Gray Lexly." With a smile, he added, "And you, too, Twain."

Chapter 18

The New Reaper Arcanist

Piper teleported us to another set of double doors. I caught myself this time before I stumbled. The sensation of teleporting wasn't bothering me as much as it had. Instead, I held my breath, remained calm, and reassessed my surroundings as soon as we arrived.

The stone walls and floors of Astra Academy were imposing, but warm. The many paintings—of cheerful landscapes and wondrous mystical creatures—livened the place up. Without the images, the whole Academy would've felt like a crypt.

The soft, blue rugs, and many vases, also added a bit of much needed color.

"This is the dining hall," Piper said with an exhale. She motioned to the door with a quick flick of her hand.

"You know he has no idea where he is, right?" Reevy asked. He sarcastically whispered in her ear, "We teleported him here. The boy will still get lost if he just walks around."

"Shh."

Piper patted her eldrin and then shoved one of the double doors open.

The inside of the dining hall was massive. It was oval in

shape—long, and with curved walls—which allowed for one central table loaded with food, and a bunch of tables around the walls for people to sit at. It was a *serve yourself* style of buffet. The moment I glanced at the food, my stomach approved of the situation.

When was the last time I had eaten?

Twain must've felt the same way. He squirmed in my arms and made grabby paws for the meat dishes.

"What a beautiful sight!" Twain purred.

But his voice was drowned out by the sea of conversations swirling all around us.

Not only were all the first-years here, but so were many of their arcanist families and some important figures. Additionally, the second-, third-, fourth-, and fifth-year students were also in attendance. The dining hall was packed.

Each wooden table was circular, with a small stone firepit in the middle. The stones of the pit glowed with inner magic, and I wondered if they were holding the flames in place so that no embers could leap out and catch the table on fire.

I wasn't sure, though. I wasn't an expert on magical items. Professor Helmith hadn't told me much about them.

"Grab your food and take a seat right here," Piper whispered as she led me to the nearest table with a single open chair. "Eat up, and then there's the tour. I'll see you then."

I wanted to protest. Where was Sorin? Shouldn't we have been sitting together?

An odd thought struck me.

What if we weren't in the same class?

We would be. I hoped. But I wasn't certain. Would they split up twins? That seemed cruel. Although I wouldn't quit the Academy if we were separated, I would be disappointed. Maybe even depressed. Sorin and I had traveled here together—I didn't want *class assignments* to be the thing that pulled us apart.

Piper disappeared with a *pop*.

Leaving me and Twain all alone.

The nearby table had ten seats. Nine of them were filled with individuals who clearly knew each other. They talked among themselves at loud volumes. By necessity. It was difficult even *thinking* with all the noise inside the dining hall.

I followed Piper's instructions and headed to the mountain of food in the middle of the room. Twain wiggled around, happily pointing and bouncing as though energized by simply smelling the various cooked meats.

The serving table had stacks of empty plates around the sides. People walked up, grabbed empty plates, and then shoveled food onto the plates until they were satisfied. Then they returned to their seats.

I grabbed a plate and then approached the food.

The plate was made of fine earthenware. They all had the same designs—a globe, a sundial, a star, and the upside-down gates.

My father had once told me that if I saw a symbol once, it was random. If I saw the same symbol a second time, it was just a coincidence. But if I saw the same symbol three times, it was a pattern. A *definite* omen.

These four symbols had to be the iconography for the Academy.

"What're you doing?" Twain hissed. "You can't eat the plate! Get the food. Right there." He pointed with his little kitten paw.

With a nod, I grabbed a few things at random. The meat selection included smoked fish, glazed ham, sautéed beef, braised lamb, and grilled shrimp. The vegetables, stacked *higher* than the meat, included corn, cabbage, peas, beans, and sprouts. The many sauces were in large bowls, and a selection of grains were on the far side.

Once my plate was full, I headed back to the one empty seat.

I glanced around the dining hall.

Sorin eluded me.

It was beginning to cause me anxiety. I was tempted to get up and look for him, but my hunger demanded I stay seated and eat. I barely tasted anything as I shoved some beef and shrimp into my mouth and swallowed.

Twain ate right off my plate. I thought it would garner me strange glances, but no one seemed to mind. All the arcanists in the room, from the pixie arcanist to a griffin arcanist a few tables over, seemed to share everything with their eldrin.

Most people had grabbed two plates, though. One for them, and one specifically for their eldrin. Obviously, I hadn't learned my lesson. I didn't instinctively take Twain's needs into account yet. I should've made him a plate of fish.

Twain wolfed down the last of my beef and then inhaled some of my beans. He gagged and hacked, spitting them up onto the plate.

That garnered some strange looks.

One woman, dressed in a dark-blue robe and wearing a matching ribbon through her hair, glowered at Twain, and then at me. "What're you? A *domestic housecat* arcanist?"

She laughed at her own joke.

What a charmer.

But it dawned on me—mimics really *were* rare. Even the head of housekeeping had been surprised by my eldrin.

"That's right," I replied to the woman. "My powers include the ability to hack up hairballs and fall asleep in any beam of sunlight."

"*Hey*," Twain hissed.

"It's all right. I didn't tell her about our best abilities."

Twain twitched his long ears and gave me a coy smile. "That we have nine lives?"

"That's exactly right."

The woman stared at me as though my brain were flying out my ears. She clearly wasn't a fan of our humor. With a sneer, she returned to her plate of food.

"We should get more shrimp!" Twain said, pawing at my silky shirt. "Please?"

"Yeah, of course."

As soon as we were fed, I'd search for Sorin. It wouldn't be too hard to find him. I hoped.

Halfway through my third plate of food, the first-year students and their chaperones stood from their tables. I recognized a few of them from the courtyard. A couple of them had even complained about the headmaster's rules on classes and dorms.

They gathered near a far door. I got up from my seat and joined them, constantly on the lookout for my brother. We all headed out into a hallway that overlooked the courtyard. Captain Leon was already there, calling for everyone's attention.

"And now for the tour," he said.

Sticks, his enthusiastic cerberus, bounded around his arcanist, one head happy and barking, his tongue flopping out to the side. The other two heads sniffed the air and kept an eye on the large group of individuals.

"Please keep up," Leon called out, his voice booming. "Our first stop is the library. An important location! All students are encouraged to use the library regularly for their betterment."

The crowd followed after Leon and his cerberus. I stayed with them, lingering in the far back, trying to keep track of everyone by examining the backs of their heads. Twain stayed in my arms, content to have me carry him everywhere.

Most arcanists had their eldrin walk alongside them.

I caught sight of a stone golem walking alongside the group. It was a child—what was a baby stone golem called?—and barely three feet tall, but its boulder shoulders and rock body were hard to mistake. The creature looked as though it was comprised of several tan rocks held together with faint magical threads.

I knew next to nothing about stone golems. What kind of magics did *it* have?

A *coatl* was also in the crowd!

Coatls were large snakes with feather wings. This coatl was a corn snake—its scales orange and white—and its wings resembled a colorful parrot's. It had a rainbow design, and I assumed, once it was fully grown, it would be *gigantic*. Right now, it was five feet long, and its wings were the size of a raven's.

Captain Leon led our group into the Astra Academy's library.

The two-story library had a balcony for the upper level. The shelves of books went on forever, stretching up from the first floor, all the way to the ceiling of the second floor. Attached ladders were fixed to most shelves, and several decks and cushioned chairs were scattered around.

Twain snorted. "What's so great about this place? Who even reads books?"

I patted his head and said nothing. The books I had read as a kid had broadened my view of the world. And they had fueled my imagination. If I *hadn't* read, I probably would've become a candlemaker, just like my father, because what else would I have done?

Captain Leon led us through the library. He shouted facts and gestured to things, but I ignored most of his statements.

I paid attention to the librarians.

They weren't arcanists. They were mortals. They organized the books, dusted the shelves, and a few of them were taking notes on book damage. When we walked by, they nodded and waved, and a few even greeted us on behalf of Astra Academy.

I had been hoping Professor Helmith would've been among them.

That wasn't the case.

"Next we will see our training field," Captain Leon said in a showman's voice.

When the crowd exited the library, we entered another hallway with tall windows. Everyone gathered near the sills, glancing outside. The hall overlooked an impressive field covered in various training grounds.

There was a track for running, a pool for swimming, a circular sparring ring, and weights for throwing or lifting. A tall series of stands was positioned on the opposite side of the field, and it made me wonder if Astra Academy held competitions from time to time.

Someone else had the same thought.

"Are there tournaments held at the Academy?" a man asked.

"We have several clubs that organize tournaments," Leon replied matter-of-factly. "We're very proud of our arcanists here, and they're dedicated to becoming the best they can be. Competition helps them stay at the top of their game."

"The field is also where we test out powerful destructive abilities," Sticks said, his voice a deep rumble, almost a growl. "It's a lot of fun," his happy head added.

Captain Leon motioned for us to continue.

I glanced at the training field. No one was there.

And I doubted Professor Helmith would be out there, anyway. She seemed more academic and intellectual than someone interested in playing *hoop-n-stick*. Or whatever sports they played here. I didn't know.

I hurried to catch up with the crowd. We walked the length of the hallway, and then turned down another until we came to a large ballroom. Captain Leon gestured to the high ceilings and grand chandeliers.

"This is our dance hall," he said. "It's decorated for all holidays, and occasionally used to house larger visiting eldrin."

The hall was large enough to house a dragon, that was certain.

Twain tilted his head back to get a better look as we walked across the massive wooden floors. The murmuring of everyone else swirled together into an incomprehensible echo that filled the room.

Captain Leon led us out a door and down one more hallway. He pointed to the windows—to a tunnel in the mountains. Other parts of Astra Academy were far from us.

"Astra Academy uses a locomotive to keep all of its campuses connected," Leon said. "The locomotive is one of the headmaster's favorite new features. It uses steam technology developed all the way across the western ocean to move at great speeds."

A locomotive?

I had never seen that.

Or even heard of it.

Captain Leon straightened his belt and then pointed onward. "Those other buildings are for specific training. Long-term training, or nature-related training. We don't need to visit them. Come. This way."

Everyone followed the captain and his cerberus until we reached the front of a grand, spiral staircase. Leon turned, stopped, and held up a hand.

"The lower levels are used for research," he said. "We have several artificers and imbuing students working on magnificent trinkets and artifacts *as we speak*."

A few people clapped.

Then Captain Leon motioned to the upper floors. "The first-year dorms are this way. All new arcanists share their dorms upstairs. There's space for their eldrin in the neighboring treehouse."

"*Treehouse?*" someone shouted with a gasp.

"Y-Yes," Leon said, obviously flustered by the outburst. "There is a treehouse attached outside. The treehouse has been designed for a variety of eldrin. Large, open spaces, beds to accommodate their unique shapes, and plenty of grooming facilities so that they don't need to join any arcanists in the showers or baths."

I glanced down at Twain just as he turned to stare up at me.

He was so small.

Did Twain *have* to go to the treehouse?

Surely not.

I'd rather he stayed close to me. And Twain silently nodded, as if he knew exactly what I was thinking, and agreed.

"Where do the second-year students stay?" someone asked.

Captain Leon smiled as he smoothed back his white hair. "Ah. Good question. You see, once students complete their first year, they must choose a specialization. The students then head to the dorm of their specialization so that they may spend their free time with like-minded arcanists."

The whispering in the crowd grew louder.

"What kind of specializations?" someone asked.

"You'll learn more about it from your professors." Leon cleared his throat. "Now, if you'll follow me upstairs, I'll show you the dorms, and we can conclude the tour."

He took the stairs two at a time. Sticks bounded up after him, huffing the entire time. Small flames flew from all three mouths of the cerberus, heating the staircase with his excitement.

Since I was at the back of the group, I waited for my turn to climb the staircase.

The rattle of a chain caught my attention. I straightened my posture, and Twain tensed in my arms. A floating cloak, tattered at the ends, *also* lingered near the back of the group. It carried a scythe with a wooden handle—old and rusted, and rather weak looking.

It was Waste. The reaper I had met in the Menagerie.

I held my breath as the creepy mystical creature floated over to me.

Everyone else pushed their way onto the steps, trying to get upstairs as fast as possible, but I didn't mind waiting if it meant I got to speak with the reaper. Had it bonded with Sorin? Was he now a reaper arcanist?

"We meet again," Waste said as he floated over to me.

His hood hung forward, but he still had no face or anything to stare at, so I just turned my attention to the inside of his cloak. "You bonded with someone?" I asked, not bothering with pleasantries.

"I'm surprised you found someone," Twain muttered, his ears back. "You made it sound as though you'd *never* bond if you stayed in the Menagerie."

Waste's cloak fluttered in nonexistent wind. "I was pleasantly mistaken. Two individuals were worthy of my magic this year."

Two?

"*Waste*? Where did you go?"

The small, feminine voice emerged from the crowd of people. Nini, the girl from the boat ride to the Academy, forced her way between two individuals and then hurried over to Waste's side.

Nini fussed with her dark-red hair. She smoothed it out, making sure the strands went straight down to her shoulders. Then she glanced over at me, her eyes wide, her glasses smudged with fingerprints.

"Oh, Gray," Nini said. "We were worried about you. A-Are you okay? Your brother was the most concerned…"

"I almost died, but I got better," I said as I shrugged.

Her eyes went straight to my arcanist mark. "You… Your star is empty?"

"He's a mimic arcanist," Waste said, his voice hollow and dark.

"Oh, wow! That's so amazing."

My attention went to her forehead in turn.

Nini was, in fact, an arcanist. Her seven-pointed star was

laced together with... a cloak and a scythe. There was no mistaking it.

She was a *reaper* arcanist.

Nini must've seen my realization, because she practically sank into her clothing until the collar was up over her chin. Before I could ask her any questions, she blurted out, "I bonded with Waste."

But Waste's Trial of Worth...

My mouth went dry.

Nini fidgeted with her coat sleeve. "I passed his Trial of Worth. It was difficult. Because... Because it involved killing an animal! I, uh, had to find something in the Menagerie and kill it myself. And I did."

Nini recounted the bonding with the speed and shakiness of a convict cobbling together a terrible alibi. I knew she was lying —Waste had already told me the *real* Trial of Worth that reapers had—but I would've guessed Nini was spinning a lie simply from her demeanor and speech.

She was a bad liar.

"So what animal did you end up killing?" I asked, feigning interest and playing along with her farce.

Twain whipped his head back to glance up at me. He glared, like he knew she was lying, too. But he didn't say anything.

"A bunny," Nini said as she fixed her glasses. "But I don't want to talk about it."

Silence settled between us. Waste didn't correct her or offer any extra details. He just floated there with a menacing aura.

Nini had killed someone related to her.

And she didn't want to admit it.

Those facts shocked me. Nini was so small. And unassuming. She had barely spoken to me and Sorin on the ride over here, and even now, she seemed frightened to speak to me. What was she hiding?

If her mother had died in childbirth, like with Sorin, why

wouldn't she just tell me? It made me think, whatever Nini had done, it was worse than Sorin's circumstance.

"Did any of your family show up for the orientation?" I asked, wondering if I could speak to them before they left. Maybe they would tell me whom Nini had harmed.

Nini quickly shook her head. "N-No. They're busy. You know how it is."

"Yeah. Of course."

My family wasn't here. My father wouldn't want to leave our island, and I doubted he had the coin to pay a ship captain to make the trek. I'd write to him about my bonding—he'd know what had taken place—but he would never visit. I'd bet my life on it.

And I supposed I'd never be able to ask Nini's family about what had happened in her past. If I wanted to find out, I'd have to ask her.

Now didn't seem like a good time.

"We should join everyone else," Nini muttered.

Waste floated close to her. "As you wish, my arcanist."

Nini turned to me. Then she pointed to the grand, spiral staircase. "I don't want to fall behind."

"Let's go," I said with a forced smile.

I'd figure everything out after I spoke with Sorin.

CHAPTER 19

THE DORMS

N ini and I rejoined the group. We hung a few feet behind, allowing everyone else to travel up the stairs first. A few people glanced back at Waste, their eyes narrowed in suspicion.

My father would've hated Waste. He hated *anything* that was considered bad luck. Reapers were some of the worst. They were mystical creatures of death and gloom. Who wouldn't consider them a bad omen?

But Nini didn't seem to mind.

Waste floated close to her, and when I snuck a glance, I noticed she was holding a part of his tattered robes, as if to keep him nearby. Waste's scythe floated around him, held by some invisible and incorporeal force.

He really was just an empty cloak and a weapon. And a small chain.

Mystical creatures grew older the longer they were bonded. As a creature aged, their appearance changed. How would Waste change? Would he gain more... clothing? More weapons? Would he get bigger?

I was tempted to ask, but I opted to remain silent. The people glancing back at us had judgmental expressions, and the way Nini kept her gaze on the stairs made me think she wasn't in the mood to talk.

Instead, I petted Twain as we climbed the stairs. He purred the entire way.

When we reached the top, it was a glorious sight to behold.

There was a large common room that seemingly connected a myriad of dorm rooms. The common room had a wall completely made of windows that went from the floor to the ceiling, just like in the infirmary. The sight of the distant mountaintops was breathtaking. The snow, the wind, the glittering blue sky—it was an oil painting come to life.

Everyone pointed and murmured their amazement. A few people walked over to the gigantic windows to get a better view of our surroundings.

There was a fireplace, several tables, a few desks, a small bookshelf of essential tomes, and a couple of massive couches.

"This is the common room for first-year students," Captain Leon stated. He pointed to the doors. "You'll find there are two dorm rooms for the boys, and two dorm rooms for the girls. Each dormitory has ten beds, ten dressers, and a large washroom."

"With running water?" someone asked.

Leon puffed his chest and nodded. "That's right. Astra Academy is proud to say that *all* our rooms have water that comes *straight to them*. Heated. It truly is a marvel."

There were more delighted whispers that circled through the crowd.

"I've never seen water piped into a place before," Nini said to me, her voice so low, I almost missed it. "Have you?"

I shook my head. "We had a water pump for our house, but not pipes, like they have here."

"A-Are you excited to stay here?"

"Definitely."

It felt like a vast improvement over my old home. Our island probably wouldn't get indoor piping and heated water for another hundred years—maybe more. Everyone there was backward. We still had a candlemaker, after all.

With a sigh, I ran a hand down my face. It was frustrating even thinking about it.

"There are no set sleeping arrangements," Captain Leon stated. "That will happen once you become second-year students and pick your specialty. Then you'll join the dorms of your fellow students and get your own room."

That all sounded amazing.

Sorin and I'd had separate rooms back home, but they had been tiny. I could only imagine what the Astra Academy rooms would be like.

"That concludes our tour," Sticks announced. "For the rest of the evening, you're to relax, unpack, and prepare yourself for classes in the morning."

"Where are our belongings?" someone in the crowd asked.

"They're in the dorm rooms, safe and sound."

The crowd of people quickly broke off into smaller groups. Some went to the fireplace, some gathered at the tables—but I didn't care about any of that. I went straight for one of the boys' dorms. Before I left Nini, I gave her a quick wave.

"I'll see you in a bit," I said. "After I unpack."

"O-Oh. Okay. See you."

She and Waste headed for the girls' side. She glanced over her shoulder twice before committing to leaving, though. I wondered if she would be all right on her own. She seemed nervous. Was she afraid someone would figure out the reaper's true Trial of Worth? The thought crossed my mind, but I shook it away.

Then I opened the dorm room and stepped inside.

It was a long, rectangular room with ten beds, just as Leon

had described. Blue and white rugs covered the stone floor, and large dressers were positioned next to each bed, clearly creating a small personal space for everyone.

My bag was by the door, along with everyone else's.

I picked it up, went to the back of the room, and threw it down on the last bed in the row. I was the first one to claim anything.

Twain leapt out of my arms and landed on the soft mattress. He walked around in a single circle before rolling himself into a little orange croissant and purring.

"Like it?" I asked.

"Soft beds are the best." Twain kneaded his claws across the white blanket, immediately scratching it up and pulling out threads.

I snatched him off the bed—his claws still hooked into the blanket, which I dragged off the mattress by accident. He hissed at me as I untangled him from the bedding.

"What's wrong with you?" I demanded.

"I was getting comfortable!"

"Where's that treehouse?" I joked.

But then I saw it.

There was a window at the back of the room, right next to my bed, that had a walkway built into the outside sill. The walkway was the branch of a tree that had been twisted and molded into a five-foot-wide path. The branch led back to a massive redwood tree that grew next to the Academy. The tree itself was hollowed out in several areas, creating rooms and walkways.

Some of the treehouse rooms were as large as the entire dorm.

I opened the glass panel of the window and leaned out to get a better look. Twain leapt over to join me, his orange fur fluttering in the afternoon winds.

One of the treehouse rooms had hay beds. Others had

mattresses. A rare few had rocks or nests. A small waterfall spilled off the roof of Astra Academy and poured into a pool in the tree. That pool had its own small waterfall that traveled all the way down to the roots of the tree. The cascading waterfalls left some mist hanging in the air, which in turn created rainbows.

The whole area was...

A paradise.

"Wow," Twain said, his eyes wide. "My bedroom is *so much better* than yours."

I huffed and laughed at the same time. "Wait until I become a second-year. I'm sure the dorm rooms they give me then will be way more impressive."

"Pfft. You wish. Look at that treehouse! I bet a hundred mystical creatures could live there."

"Neighbors are overrated."

Twain twitched his whiskers. "You sound jealous."

I shot him a sideways glance. "I can assure you, I'm not."

The door to the dorm opened. I turned around, my heart already firing up.

There he was! Sorin entered the dorm with a confused expression. He glanced around until he spotted me. Then a smile bloomed across his face.

"Gray!"

I smiled as well. I couldn't help it.

With excited energy, I jogged over to him, eager to see what kind of mystical creature he had bonded with. But where was Sorin's eldrin? No creature walked in with him. In all my excitement, I had forgotten to grab Twain. My little mimic leapt off the sill and chased after me, running like only a kitten could.

Sorin must've known I wanted to figure out what kind of arcanist he was, because the moment I was halfway across the room, he covered his forehead with one of his broad hands. I practically ran into him, gave him a hug, and then glared at the hand on his forehead.

"What're you doing?" I demanded. "This is childish."

Sorin embraced me with one arm, and then playfully pushed me away. "You have to guess!"

"I'm not *guessing*, Sorin." I grabbed for his wrist, but Sorin was still larger than me. He shoved me away and laughed. "C'mon," I said. "Stop this."

"You have to guess. That's the rules."

"Curse the abyssal hells..."

I leapt at him, faster than before, and I tried to drag his hand away from his forehead. Sorin just laughed as he turned his body away from me. I practically climbed onto his back as Sorin circled around, just laughing the entire time.

Even *I* started laughing after a bit. What was wrong with him? Why wouldn't he just tell me! Where was his eldrin, anyway? Why hadn't I seen it? Had he sent it to the treehouse already?

The door to the dorm opened, and another boy spotted us wrestling. He stared for a prolonged moment, and then slowly stepped backward and shut the door.

Embarrassment got the better of me. I slid off my brother and pushed him as hard as I could.

"Enough," I said with a huff. "Did you bond with a griffin?"

"Nope," Sorin said, still smiling and chortling.

"A hippogriff?"

"Guess again."

"A fairy."

"That's not it."

I ground my teeth and glared at him. "*Sorin.* I'm not guessing anymore."

Sorin didn't remove his hand from his forehead. He replied with a wider grin, like he was reveling in what tiny information he had that I didn't.

"Mimic arcanists can sense magics," Twain said to me matter-of-factly. "Since you're a mimic arcanist now—"

"Wait, you're a *mimic* arcanist?" Sorin asked with a gasp. He stared at my arcanist mark. "*That's* what that means? Your empty star is a mimic thing?"

"Yeah," I replied. "It's a *mimic thing*."

Twain licked a paw and rubbed it along his face. "Like I was saying... Mimics can sense magic. As my arcanist, you should have the same ability. Close your eyes and feel the magic. Smell it."

I glanced over at him. "Smell it?"

"Uh, yes. And taste it. And *feel* it."

Sorin kept his hand on his forehead, covering his arcanist mark. When I returned my gaze to him, he just shrugged. But he didn't show me his mark.

After a long exhale, I closed my eyes. I wasn't sure how to feel, taste, or smell magic, but I tried to focus on my surroundings regardless. It took me a minute of thinking to realize that I *did* feel something.

Lots of somethings.

In my mind's eye, it was like grasping at string. I felt *thin lines of string* that led from me to everyone else. From... Twain. To Sorin. Even... to other people. I couldn't locate them—I just knew they were nearby. Arcanists in the common room and around the Academy. Probably Nini, too, though it was difficult to determine which string was hers.

"I feel strings," I said aloud, hoping Twain would help me.

"That's weird," my brother commented.

Twain huffed. "Yes. Strings. That's a good way to describe it. Tug the strings."

Tug?

I focused on a string and tried to mentally pull on it. The connection seemed taut after that. Stable. When I pulled on

Twain's string, nothing happened, but when I pulled on Sorin's... I felt something *dark*. Something odd.

I tugged it a little more... and Twain meowed.

My eyes flew open at the same time Twain transformed. His body molded and bubbled, and then changed to a blackish coloration. My forehead burned as my arcanist mark shifted to accommodate Twain's change.

Chapter 20

Classmates

Twain transformed into a suit of armor.

Not just any suit of armor.

He was empty inside, like the reaper. Just a floating suit of armor with no one wearing it, yet somehow moving as though adorning an invisible man.

Twain was now black plate armor with a shadowy cape. Raven feathers lined the collar of the cape, as well as a belt around the waist, giving him a striking appearance.

The armor wasn't complete, though. It was as if... pieces were missing.

Sections of armor were missing from the legs and arms, leaving holes throughout. Why was that? It seemed odd for armor. Was it damaged? Or just missing bits?

The helmet turned and moved without a head. It was a full helmet, with a slit for eyes. Yet there was still nothing inside. When the helmet "glanced" at me, I froze.

"Are you okay?" Twain asked, his voice now deep and gruff. "You look like you've seen a ghost."

"What are you?" I asked.

"Me?" Twain glanced down to examine his new body.

Sorin removed his hand from his head. "He's a *knightmare*."

The arcanist mark on Sorin's head was a seven-pointed star with a cape and shield. Was that the mark of a knightmare? The cape seemed similar to the suit of armor. That had to be the case. Was the knightmare a variant of a reaper? They seemed similar, yet very different.

The shadow around Sorin's feet flickered and moved on its own. Then another suit of armor—identical to Twain—rose from the darkness. It lifted into the room without much movement, emerging from the shadows as though it were made of liquid void.

The same feathery cape. The same missing pieces.

"This is my eldrin," Sorin said as he patted the shadow armor. "His name is Thurin. He's a knightmare, and he says he's a *philosopher knight*, and I can't believe how well we get along."

The suit of armor bowed at the waist.

"You may call me Thurin," the knightmare said, his voice masculine but rusty. He sounded young. Like me and Sorin. "I lived in the Astra Academy Menagerie for some time. I thought I might never find an arcanist..."

Sorin smiled as he turned to face me. "But *I* passed his Trial of Worth. Thurin said that I was willing to give my life to protect another, and that exemplified what it meant to be a knight."

"Who were you willing to give your life for?" I asked.

My brother half-laughed. "Huh? *You*, of course. That weird spider-puppet almost killed you. When I told the whole story to Piper and the headmaster, Thurin was there to hear everything. He said he wanted me to be his arcanist. Isn't that amazing?"

"Yeah," I muttered. "I wanted to thank you for that, by the way."

"That's what brothers do."

I smiled. "Right." I glanced back at his eldrin.

The knightmare armor was rather imposing. Did it really fit

my brother? Sorin didn't seem like the type to bond with something so...

"Your brother will make an excellent philosopher knight," Thurin said matter-of-factly. "It takes great patience and dedication. Sorin has those qualities in spades."

Sorin smiled at his knightmare eldrin. Then he returned his attention to me.

"Can your mimic turn into anything?" Sorin asked. He walked over to Twain and examined his knightmare body. "He looks *exactly* like Thurin! That's amazing."

"I can transform into almost anything." Twain turned on his heel and allowed his cape to flutter about. "But I—"

His body bubbled and collapsed in on itself. One second, he was a knightmare, and the next, he was back to his kitten form. He fell onto the nearest bed, his orange fur puffed.

The mark on my forehead returned to the empty star.

"But I... can't hold it very long," Twain mumbled into the blankets. Then he picked himself up and smoothed his fur. "Once Gray and I train a bit—and I grow a little older—I'll be able to maintain my new shape for a long time!"

"That's excellent," Sorin said, genuine awe in his voice. He tapped his knuckles on the chest of his knightmare. It clanged like real armor. "I've been trying to think of a poem to mark my bonding with Thurin. Do you want to hear it?"

"Not really," I said.

"Oh, you don't mean that. But I'm not quite finished with it." Sorin rubbed at his chin and stared up at the ceiling. "I need a word that's a mix of *angry* and *sad*."

"*Smad?*" I quipped.

"Disheartened?" Thurin suggested.

Sorin snapped his fingers and smiled. "Yes! Thurin. Perfect." He cleared his throat and said, "*In my darkest hour, disheartened and adrift, I fended off monsters between here and a dream rift.*

My destiny sealed, I turned to a knight. Now that we're together, we have fearsome might."

I wasn't sure how to react. It seemed needlessly silly to make a poem out of everything. On the other hand, it clearly made him happy. I wished he wouldn't—especially not in front of others—but I supposed we were alone.

With a half-hearted clap, I said, "That was good. Stick to poems that rhyme."

"Most of them rhyme."

"Well..." I shrugged. "Sure."

The door to our dorm room opened again, ending our conversation. I recognized the man who stepped inside. It was Knovak Gentz—his pointed-hat immediately gave him away. That and his white cape. And his ruffled shirt. And too-tight pants.

Really, the man's whole wardrobe was so flashy that it reminded me of a circus every time I saw it. Knovak had sandy blond hair and dark brown eyes, but I had to work to even notice those kinds of details.

Knovak strode into the dorm room like he owned the place. His chest was puffed as he gave everyone—and everything—a quick once over. With a frown, he said, "This is *it*?"

And then his eldrin pranced into the dorm.

I *also* recognized it.

Knovak's eldrin was a unicorn. *It was Starling!* The same unicorn from my home island. Starling had been taken away before he had bonded. Had they brought him to the Menagerie? And since mystical creatures didn't age out of childhood until they were bonded, Starling was still a foal, even though Sorin and I had grown.

Starling's white coat glittered in the afternoon light. His beauty was on full display as he trotted over to his arcanist. His spiral horn, deadly sharp yet also regal, seemed polished and sparkling. He was still only three feet at the shoulder, though. Too small to ride. Yet.

Knovak's arcanist mark was the seven-pointed star with a unicorn wrapped around the points.

Starling's dark eyes went wide the moment he spotted me. "Y-You!"

I offered him a quick wave. "Hey."

"You're that *dastard!* The liar! The trickster!"

Knovak grabbed at his pointed hat, his own eyes going wide. "You're a liar?"

"Wait." Sorin held up his hands. "I think we all need to calm down. Gray and I can explain. We're not dastards or tricksters."

"You're charlatans," Starling said as he stomped his silver hooves onto the stone floor. Then he whinnied and swished his tail. After a quick circle, he leapt behind his arcanist, like we would attack him at any second.

Twain tilted his little kitten head. "Eh. Unicorns are so fussy... Me and this one never got along."

Although there were only three arcanists in the dorm, the noise level almost hurt my ears. The unicorn snorted and stomped. Knovak whispered calming words. Thurin—the knightmare—walked away from the situation to stand by the far window, and each of his steps a metallic clatter.

What would this room be like with seven other people?

I almost wanted to live in the treehouse.

Then it struck me. This was why the eldrin had the massive tree to begin with. It would allow them to make all sorts of noise, and it wouldn't interfere with our sleep.

Once Starling had stopped shouting accusatory declarations, Knovak shot me a glare. "So, you lied to this unicorn when you were younger to get it to bond with you?"

I half-shrugged. "I guess that's accurate."

"That's a heinous act."

Sorin held up a finger. "Gray didn't follow through with it, though. We told Starling we were sorry and left before bonding."

That clearly didn't satisfy Knovak. He sneered as he backed away from us. With an expression that basically confirmed he thought we were criminals, Knovak went to the bed farthest from us.

"Hopefully, Starling and I *won't* be in either of your classes," he said. "That way, we won't have to see each other for longer than absolutely necessary."

Starling huffed and then held his nose up in the air as he trotted over to Knovak's bed.

I almost reminded him there was another dorm room, but I didn't actually want to speak to the man. He and his snooty unicorn could do whatever they wanted, so long as they just left me alone.

After a short sigh, Sorin walked over to me. He glanced from one bed to the next. Then he finally spotted my bed at the far back. "You're all the way over there?"

"Yeah." I motioned to a bed near mine. "We'll have more privacy if we're back there."

"You don't want to be near the door? We should be ready at a moment's notice. What if adventure comes calling?"

That was the corniest thing Sorin had ever said.

"We don't have to have beds right next to each other," I said.

Sorin stared at me. For a silent minute, he said nothing. Then he nodded once. "You know what? That's true. I mean, we can't be together forever."

His reply surprised me.

I thought... he would've changed his mind and joined me in the back.

But before I could comment, Sorin stepped close. He lowered his voice and asked, "Uh, but what about your dreams? Do you think you're going to be attacked again?"

"I think I'll be fine," I whispered. "I'm an arcanist now. And I think the person behind the attacks was killed."

"Really?" Sorin asked, his voice much louder than before.

Knovak and Starling glanced over.

I grabbed Sorin's shoulder and pulled him close. "Yeah. *And don't mention it to anyone.* Okay? I don't want people knowing about the dreams."

"What about Professor Helmith?"

The mere mention of her name caused my chest to tighten. I hadn't seen her since we had arrived. That worried me. I pushed my anxiety aside and then shook my head. "I'll speak to Professor Helmith. You just... don't mention the dream puppets. To anyone."

"You have my word, Gray."

I offered my brother a smile. "Thank you." Then I pulled him even closer. "Oh—I wanted to tell you something. The headmaster has an *assassin bodyguard.*"

"Really?" Sorin asked, his tone one of clear disbelief. "The headmaster seemed like a gentle man to me."

"I saw it with my own eyes. The headmaster was being bothered in his office, and then *bam.* Bodyguard out of nowhere. He was invisible and just waiting for a chance to strike."

"I wonder if the headmaster gets attacked often?"

The comment made me pause and think. That would explain the need for a bodyguard...

"This place is full of capable arcanists," I said, repeating the headmaster's words. "I doubt people go around attacking one another."

Sorin nodded. "Yeah. You're probably right."

The door to the dorm opened.

Everyone went silent as we collectively turned our attention to the arrival.

In walked another familiar face. It was the man from the boat ride—the one with the scars on his face. The man who had refused to give us his name because "we didn't know if we'd be arcanists or not."

The man wore the same black cloak and large cap as before. They hid most of his features, but I remembered his suntanned skin and dark eyes from the trek over here. He was someone who had spent a lifetime out in the harsh rays of daylight.

A fox walked in behind him—the same kitsune fox from the Menagerie.

What was the fox's name?

Miko.

She had flames on her feet that burned nothing. Embers wafted from her as she pranced around, her fluffy, red tail swishing behind her. Miko stayed close to the scarred man, flashing everyone else a coy smile.

"What do we have here?" Miko asked. "I see I've found some of my Menagerie friends."

Twain turned away and said nothing.

"Ah, Miko," Thurin said from the back of the room. "I see you've found someone to tolerate you."

The little kitsune puffed her red fur, and her pointed ears stood as straight as they'd go. A little flame burst to life on the tip of her tail. "I'll have you know that I'm *mysterious*. Why do you keep equating that to *being underhanded*?"

"I asked you simple questions, and you refused to answer."

"You're a weird suit of armor! I'm not going to trust someone like you."

"I'm your senior, and the questions were reasonable."

The scarred man stepped in front of his kitsune eldrin. He glowered in Thurin's direction. "Leave my eldrin alone," he stated, his tone cold. "Before I *make* you."

The kitsune peeked around the man's legs with a smug smile. "Yes. We wouldn't want to show you whose magic is superior, would we?"

Everyone was aggressive today, for some reason. Perhaps it was the close quarters. Or perhaps everyone was simply tired after a long couple of days. Either way, it seemed as though there was a lot more yelling and bickering than what I had imagined in the Astra Academy dorms.

"And who are you?" Knovak asked as he stepped forward. His unicorn stood proudly at his side. "I think I remember you from the pier."

The man removed his hat, revealing his dark hair and scarred face. He had obviously been slashed by something. He had a few scars near his hairline, and one on his lip.

"I'm Raaza," the man said.

Miko walked around him, her fox fire glowing a bit brighter. "My lovely arcanist."

"Well, *Raaza*, where I'm from, it's considered proper to introduce yourself with your full name." Knovak tipped the front of his pointed hat. "I'm Knovak Gentz, and this is my unicorn eldrin, Starling."

He said the last part with a haughty tone.

"Feh," Raaza said with a roll of his eyes. "Very well. I'm Raaza *Luin*. And this is my eldrin. Where *I'm* from, they introduce themselves."

"I'm Miko the kitsune." Miko wove her way between Raaza's legs.

I wondered if anyone in the Academy wanted to get along. With a sigh, I reminded myself that they were probably fatigued. I had to chant that in my mind over and over, lest I make a snarky comment and get everyone angry at me in a matter of seconds.

Did I need to introduce myself? Sorin had already introduced us on the ship, when Raaza hadn't been very talkative. That was good enough, wasn't it?

Sorin stepped into the middle of the room. "It's great to

finally know your name, Raaza. It's definitely unique. I like it. It rolls off the tongue well."

"Are you mocking me?" Raaza asked, his words slow, like he was genuinely confused.

I shook my head. "Sorin just likes words. He's not making fun of anyone."

"Hm."

Silence.

Raaza never answered. My brother clearly didn't know how to follow up after that interaction, and Knovak was too busy unpacking a mountain's worth of clothes.

"I'm going to take a nap," I said as I headed for my bed. "Don't wake me unless class is starting, okay?" Whatever they were going to argue about, I didn't want any part of it.

And I could meet everyone else in the dorm later, after they were well rested and in better moods.

CHAPTER 21

THE FIRST CLASS

I awoke in the middle of the night to the shining of a full moon.

With a shiver, I pulled my blankets up over my shoulders. Moonlight streamed into the room through the gigantic window that led to the treehouse. There were curtains beside the window, but I didn't want to get up and deal with them. Not only that, but the window itself acted as a door for everyone's eldrin, so that they could travel to the treehouse. Shutting the curtains seemed rude.

The branches of the paradise tree didn't offer any shade to shield me from the light of the moon, which was unfortunate.

At least I hadn't experienced any more nightmares.

Maybe they were all over now, now that the woman in the Menagerie was dead.

That would be a relief.

The window creaked open. I glanced over just in time to catch sight of a tiny kitten-shaped silhouette. Twain had gone to the treehouse, even though I had wanted him to stay. I suspected he had gotten lonely over there, because he crept over to my bed and silently leapt onto the mattress.

Without a word, I lifted my blankets and allowed him to snuggle up next to me. Then I lowered the blanket and tucked him in. Twain's purring practically rumbled the whole bed.

No one else had entered our dorm. It was just me, Sorin, Knovak, and Raaza. Had all the other boys gone to the second dorm? That seemed odd, but I had a theory.

The four of us were the boys who had bonded to a mystical creature in the Menagerie. We were the "special recipient" arcanists—the ones too poor or lacking in connections to become arcanists on our own. I bet that angered Knovak. His family, the Gentz Merchants, typically considered themselves quite wealthy. Why hadn't Knovak traveled with his family around the islands? That was normally how members of the Gentz family became arcanists.

The rest of the first-year boys had probably become arcanists before arriving at Astra Academy. They probably wanted to avoid the four of us.

The thought swirled around in my mind, getting me angrier the longer I thought about it. Did they think we weren't good enough to mingle with? Or perhaps everyone else already knew each other.

"There are lots of mystical creatures in the treehouse," Twain whispered.

"I bet," I replied, my voice equally quiet.

"There's a dragon here."

"What kind?"

Twain stopped purring. "I don't know. He liked the water, though. He slept in a fountain."

The floorboards groaned. I rolled over, my heart hammering. What if it was another spider-puppet? But I breathed a sigh of relief the moment I spotted Sorin. He tiptoed over to the bed next to mine, but he was so large—and unstealthy—that he wasn't silent about it. Even the bed creaked as he rested on top of it.

The moonlight provided ample illumination for me to see my brother smile.

"Gray?" he whispered.

"Yeah?"

"I can't sleep."

"I can see that," I quipped.

"I'm too excited." Sorin pulled the blankets up around his body. His feet hung off the end of the bed. "Sleep is a luxury for an untroubled mind—a comfort for the confident."

"Hm."

Twain pressed his tiny body up against mine. I gently petted him under my blankets.

"Where's your eldrin?" I asked.

Sorin pointed to the floor. "Knightmares are mystical creatures made of shadows and terror. Apparently, Thurin can make himself into a pool of darkness, and hide in my shadow. Isn't that amazing?"

I turned my attention to the floor. The darkness fluttered at the edges all around Sorin's new bed as though bats were hidden in the shadows and silently flapping their wings. The knightmare, Thurin, seemed both ominous and mystical.

I was almost jealous.

Almost.

Twain could become a knightmare, though. So, in essence, my eldrin was more versatile—more powerful.

"Thurin said that baby knightmares aren't complete suits of armor," Sorin said as he scooted to the edge of his bed, the closest he could get to me. "That's why there are pieces of his armor missing. As he gets older, the missing parts will form."

"Like an old woman slowly knitting clothing."

My brother snorted and shrugged. "I thought you'd be happier, Gray. We're finally here! You've been talking about this for years."

"I'm happy."

Mostly.

"Is it because you haven't spoken to your honeysuckle?" Sorin playfully asked.

"*Don't call her that*," I hissed under my breath. "Professor Helmith is probably twice my age. It's creepy when you call her my honeysuckle."

"But love is a force that shatters all boundaries. Professor Helmith's maturity will deepen your understanding of the world. And yourself."

"Oh, good stars save me... That's even creepier." I ran a hand down my face, hoping that Sorin wouldn't say anything like this in front of anyone else.

My brother rolled onto his back and laced his fingers together under his head. He stared at the ceiling, the moonlight blanketing him as much as the bedding. For a long moment, he seemed lost in thought.

"You don't mind if I take this bed, right?" he whispered.

I shook my head. "I was hoping we'd... ya know. Stick together. At least for a little while longer." I hadn't wanted to admit it, but I figured I should say it now because I might not get another chance.

"Good night, Gray."

"Night, Sorin."

In the morning, I awoke in a groggy haze.

I dressed, washed my face, and brushed my hair back before exiting the dorm and entering the common room. All the other first-years were gathered in front of the fireplace, and just to conform to the others, I lingered around the group. My eyes were heavy. I hadn't slept much.

Twain was small enough—and light enough—that he could

sit on my shoulder without a problem. I petted his head. He, too, wasn't really awake.

Sorin stuck close to me as everyone left the fireplace and headed for the stairs. Our classrooms were on the first floor of the main Academy building, and as I rubbed the sleep crust from my eyes, we arrived at the first classroom.

Piper stood by the door with a stack of papers in her hands.

Today, she wore a black-and-blue robe, similar to the headmaster's during orientation.

"Urg," she groaned as the twenty-seven of us approached her, each with our own eldrin. "Why is it so bright this morning?"

Reevy, her ferret-looking rizzel, sat at her feet. He grabbed the bottom of her robe and then pulled himself onto the hem. He "rode" the train of her robe like a little moving bed. He even curled into a ball and closed his eyes as though this were too early for him to function.

Piper squinted at us. She straightened the paperwork and then counted everyone one by one. "All right," she muttered. "Class One will be made of nine arcanists. These were picked at random. Listen up for your name."

The haze of sleep began to clear.

Would I be in this class?

Piper pinched the bridge of her nose and then focused on the list of names. "Class One is... Nasbit Dodger. Exie Lo...lilan?"

"*Lolian*," a girl in the crowd snapped. With a harsh whisper, she added, "It isn't that difficult."

"Right. Exie Lolian." Piper rustled the paper. "Ashlyn Kross. Nini Wanderlin. Sorin Lexly."

I held my breath, hoping that I'd be placed in the same class as my brother.

"Knovak Gentz. Phila Hon."

When she didn't immediately say my name after Sorin's, my

heart sank. Twain glanced over at me, a slight frown on his kitten face. I didn't say anything.

"Raaza Luin. And lastly... Gray Lexly."

I stifled a laugh. Thank the good stars. I had thought she was going to skip right over me. My brother turned to face me, an odd half-smile on his face. Had he been worried as well? Probably.

So, that was the nine of us.

We separated from the others. Piper motioned to a large oak door. On the front of it was carved the words: CLASS ONE, YEAR ONE.

"This will be your room," Piper stated. "In Astra Academy, the professors are the ones who move from classroom to classroom. Each day of the week, you will have a different professor, for a total of six. The last day of the week is a free day. We encourage you to join a club during that time. That isn't required, it's just highly advised."

Mutters and whispers flew through the group of first-years.

Piper pointed to the door. "Go on, Class One."

I headed for the classroom, along with the other eight arcanists. One at a time, we entered a large room with five long tables, a gigantic chalkboard, nine wooden trunks, and a desk for the professor.

The window at the back of the room had a walkway that led to the redwood treehouse. That meant our eldrin could meet us here in the classroom—they didn't need to enter the dorm and walk with us. That was probably for the best. Some of the mystical creatures, even in my class, were gigantic, and they would only get bigger as they grew older.

Once everyone was in the room, I gave my fellow classmates my full attention.

There was me, obviously. A mimic arcanist.

Sorin—the knightmare arcanist—with Thurin, his shadowy armor eldrin that had exited the shadows and now walked around with him. My brother went to the center of the room and spun around once, getting a good look at everything in one go.

"This is amazing," Sorin said. "This room is huge!"

Nini—the reaper arcanist—kept her massive coat on, even though it was warm in here. She ducked her chin below the collar, half hiding her face. She, too, spun around to take everything in.

"It's so much nicer than anything on my island," she whispered.

Sorin shot her a smile. "Right? What more could we ask for?"

"I agree."

Her reaper floated over to a wooden table. The edge of his cloak lifted and then wiped the surface and bench clean. "Here you are, my arcanist," Waste said, his hollow voice frightening.

Nini hesitantly smiled as she hurried over to the table. "Thank you, Waste."

"My pleasure."

Everyone in our class avoided her and the table that Waste had cleaned. They even walked around the table, giving it plenty of space.

Reapers were bad luck. It didn't surprise me that no one wanted to get close.

Knovak—the unicorn arcanist—wore an outfit of bright red. His pointed hat was tilted back to show off his unicorn arcanist mark. His unicorn, Starling, proudly pranced at his side.

"Now *this* is a proper classroom," Knovak said, smirking.

Raaza—the kitsune arcanist—didn't say a single word as he shuffled across the classroom. The man loved his cloak. He kept his gaze on the floor and immediately took a seat at the back of the room without talking to anyone.

What a friendly chap.

His kitsune leapt onto the table and proudly showed off her red fox fur. "I like it here. So many people and creatures."

The last four arcanists...

They stuck together, away from the rest of us.

Nasbit Dodger—the stone golem arcanist—was shorter and portlier than everyone else. He wore a fine silk shirt, tailored trousers, and a sock-cap that reminded me of sailors at the docks. The sock-cap seemed thick and warm, though. Very comfortable.

His golem was the size of a human kid but made of boulders and large rocks. It was a sandstone golem, really. Bright gold flecks of dirt sparkled throughout it. The golem had no eyes, just stone.

The creature lumbered through the room, each step creating a hefty *thump* sound.

"Over this way," Nasbit said to his golem. "We need to sit at the front of the class if we want to make sure we'll hear everything."

His golem rumbled as it turned around and headed for the front table.

Exie Lolian—never pronounce her last name wrong, apparently—stood with her arms crossed, a scowl marring her otherwise beautiful features. Her curly chestnut hair was so well-cared for and maintained that each little curl had its own bounce and shimmer. It only went to her shoulders, but her hair was still striking.

She wore a dress, which was odd. No one else had chosen such an outfit. The white dress was tight on her and reminded me of the fancy gowns some girls wore when they finally became an adult. It accentuated her darker skin, and also allowed her green eyes to steal the show. They were a pop of bright color.

Exie was, without a doubt, the most gorgeous person in the room.

And she was... an *erlking* arcanist.

Erlkings were the kings of fairies. They grew larger than most fairies and were more powerful. Exie's was a baby erlking, though. He was the size of my fist and fluttered around with tiny peacock-like wings, and because they were also masters of light and illusion, the little fairy left an after-image trail behind wherever he flew. The erlking sped around everywhere, creating half-images of himself in the air.

Exie glanced over at me, then at Sorin, and then finally at Nini.

"Oh," she said, her voice higher pitched and quite loud. "*You three* are the ones who bonded with the bizarre mystical creatures in the Menagerie."

"Bizarre?" Sorin asked.

"I heard that there were three creatures in the Menagerie that hadn't bonded in years," Exie said as she brought her fingers to her chin. "My cousin said it was a knightmare, a reaper, and a mimic. And here you three are."

Nini fidgeted with the sleeves of her jacket. "Um. Yes."

The erlking fluttered about like only fairies could. "Bizarre. Look at you all."

Exie pointed to my arcanist mark. "Your star is empty... That's just plain *weird*."

"Nice to meet you, too," I quipped.

She fluffed her hair and gracefully turned away from me. I wasn't even that mad, really.

The last two arcanists in our class entered the room together, and relatively quietly.

Phila Hon was a woman with red hair down to her waist. It was a strawberry blonde—much lighter than Nini's bloodred hair. Phila wore a gentle expression and a beautiful green shirt that seemed crafted for royalty. It had beads and jewels woven into the fabric. It flowed past her waist like a tunic and highlighted her hair. Her trousers were loose as well. But I barely paid attention to her.

She was the coatl arcanist.

Her serpent eldrin had rainbow wings and colorful feathers around its head. It was the length of a person, but still thin, because it was a hatchling. It seemed just as beautiful as Phila's shirt.

"Astra Academy," Phila said with a slight smile. "I've longed for this day."

The last person in our class...

Ashlyn Kross.

Her blonde hair was pulled back in a tight ponytail, and she wore leather riding pants, a vest, and a shoulder guard as though she expected some sort of combat. Her boots went to her knees, and her outfit reminded me of an old-world adventurer.

Athletic. Confident. Tall.

Very tall.

The tallest of the women in our class, for sure.

And her eldrin...

It was the largest one in the class.

A baby typhoon dragon. They were regal guardians of the sea—dragons who spent their days beneath the waves. Her dragon's scales were every color of blue, from sapphire to aquamarine. He was the size of a desk, and instead of wings, he had fins on his spine, tail, and arms.

The dragon had a serpent-like head, but he had gills along his long neck.

To bond with a dragon... Hadn't Twain said they had deadly Trials of Worth?

Ashlyn turned and caught me staring. Normally, I would glance away, and feign disinterest, but I didn't do that this time. I blatantly stared, wondering how she would react. Ashlyn had blue eyes—not gray-blue, like mine, but dark blue, like the ocean.

She didn't flinch or back down. We stared at each other for a prolonged moment, as though locked in a challenge. Who would glance away first?

I lifted an eyebrow. Ashlyn offered me half a smile.

Our little game seemed more playful than I had been expecting.

Exie walked over to Ashlyn and touched her elbow. "Have you seen our class? It looks like you got exactly what you wanted."

Ashlyn didn't glance away. Instead, she addressed me when she said, "You there. Mimic arcanist. What did the professor say your name was?"

"Gray Lexly," I replied.

Everyone else in class stopped what they were doing and paid attention to our conversation. Did they think we were going to get into a fight? The tension in the air seemed thick.

"And you're Ashlyn Kross," I said. "I paid attention when the professor was calling names."

Her dragon stepped to her side and lifted his head. With his long neck, and the fins on his head, he was already tall enough to stare down at me. Still a baby—and very thin, for a dragon—but still powerful enough to bite me good.

The dragon glared, but said nothing.

"I don't know much about mimics," Ashlyn said, her tone slow, her words precise. "What kind of Trial of Worth do they have?"

Twain dug his tiny claws into my shoulder. This was the moment he had been fearing, apparently.

I didn't answer immediately. Ashlyn must've sensed my hesitation, and for some reason, this amused her. She stepped closer.

"Typhoon dragons require a competition." She patted the brilliant blue scales of her eldrin. "Their Trial of Worth requires hopefuls to gather a special kind of pearl from an abyssal clam.

During my Trial, one boy drowned, and one girl was killed by the abyssal monster."

Her statements sent a chill through the room. No one looked away.

Twain had been right. Dragons always had difficult—and deadly—Trials of Worth.

Ashlyn cut straight to the chase when she said, "I heard you were injured in the Menagerie. Was that from the mimic's Trial of Worth?"

Everyone glanced in my direction.

No one spoke. No one took in a sharp breath. They waited for the answer.

I wondered why.

Twain gripped my shirt tighter, and even *he* was anxious to hear what I would say. We had made a deal, though. I wouldn't reveal his secret.

"It wasn't part of the mimic's Trial," I said with a casual shrug. "What happened in the Menagerie was an attack. Someone tried to kill me."

"Really?" Exie asked, interjecting her way into the conversation. "*You?*"

I nodded once. "That's right. Little 'ol me."

"But why?"

"I'm not sure."

"Okay, then—what was your Trial of Worth?" Ashlyn asked.

She seemed pretty fixated on it, for some reason.

I patted Twain's head and said, "I apologize, but mimics are secretive creatures. The only people who get to know their Trial of Worth are them, and their arcanists."

"It's a secret?" Ashlyn's tone a mix of amusement and irritation. "Is that what you're saying?"

"Sorry." I shrugged a second time. "But no one gets to know unless they're a mimic arcanist. Those're the rules."

"Arg!" The kitsune on the far table fluffed her fur. "That's so mysterious even *I'm* jealous!"

Raaza chuckled as he stroked the fur down on his eldrin. "I think he just doesn't want to say."

Twain held his head high. "Nope. Gray's right. It's a mystery. Deal with it."

The others glanced between each other. A few of them stared at me with renewed interest. My plan to keep it a mystery seemed to be working. Now they would ponder my situation. The air of mystery was a useful tool.

"*Gray* is really your name?" Exie asked, once again interjecting herself into the conversation. "Is it short for *Grayson* or something?"

"No," I stated. "It's just *Gray*."

Sorin stepped close to my side. "Everyone always assumes it's short for something longer. One time, the baker on our isle made Gray a little cake for his birthday, and he wrote *Graywart* in berry slices on the top."

I ran a hand down my face. "Oh. Right. I had *almost* forgotten about that."

"It was hilarious. I called him *Graywart* for like a year. He hated it." Sorin laughed and playfully smacked me on the shoulder.

Exie snickered into the palm of her hand.

Everyone else remained relatively quiet. Someone coughed once. The silence in the room was almost unbearable.

I patted my brother on the arm. "Let's *not* talk about awkward childhood stories, okay, Sorin?"

Then Exie grabbed Ashlyn's elbow and pointed to the classroom door. The door opened, and in walked our first professor.

I recognized her, of course. I almost called out her name the moment I spotted her.

Professor Helmith.

Chapter 22

Professor Helmith

I t felt like a dream made reality.

Professor Helmith walked into the room, and I couldn't breathe. My chest tightened as I strode past all the other students. A few of them shot me odd sideways glances, but I didn't care. I had been waiting to speak to Professor Helmith for what felt like an eternity.

Technically, the last time I had seen her had been month ago.

It felt like a lifetime's worth of events had happened between then and now.

Would she be proud that I had become an arcanist?

"Professor?" I asked as I approached, smiling even though I was trying not to.

She turned to me, her lavender eyes striking. No one else had her color of eyes.

And she wore a sleeveless dress, revealing the blue and pink swirling tattoos flowing across the skin of her shoulders. No one else had those kinds of tattoos. What were they? Why had she gotten them? They were storm clouds, stylized and glittering.

Her inky hair, black as midnight, fell straight and beautiful all the way to her shoulder blades. None of her locks blocked her ethereal whelk arcanist mark. The spiral shell of her eldrin was woven between the seven points of her star.

Her eldrin wasn't around, however.

Still, it was amazing to see her in person.

"I'm so happy to see you," I whispered as I made it to her side.

But the expression she gave me afterward...

Professor Helmith pursed her lips and knitted her eyebrows. "Good morning. Please take your seat."

She spoke as though she were talking to a stranger.

Ice ran through my veins.

Professor Helmith must have sensed my shift in mood. She tilted her head slightly and forced a smile. "Hm? Is something wrong?"

"Professor Helmith..." I found it difficult to speak. "It's me. Gray." When she didn't immediately respond, I continued. "You helped me in my dreams."

Maybe I looked different? Maybe in my dreams, my appearance was altered? Why would she stare at me as though I were insane? This wasn't...

This wasn't how she normally acted.

"Oh!" Professor Helmith placed a hand on her collarbone. "*Gray*. Yes. I've been meaning to discuss your dreams with you. But after class, all right? We're already behind."

"I..."

She reached out and touched my shoulder with a gentle graze of her fingertips. "I'm so sorry. I've been so busy these last few months. I'll explain everything after class."

For a brief moment, I almost believed her.

I wanted to.

By the good stars, I desperately wanted to think this was her.

But in my heart...

I knew this wasn't Professor Helmith.

"Oh, of course," I said as I stepped away. "Sorry. It's just been forever since we spoke. I keep forgetting how busy you are."

She smiled wider. "Excellent. We'll speak afterward. Now, please take a seat." She motioned to one of the tables.

I didn't know how or why, but this woman was an imposter. Even the way she walked to the desk at the front of the room—it wasn't with the fluid grace of a dancer. It wasn't like Professor Helmith.

My head buzzed as I ambled my way over to a table.

"That was your professor?" Twain whispered in my ear. "She barely recognized you. I thought you two were close?"

"Shh," I replied.

Everyone quickly sat down.

Ashlyn, Exie, and Phila sat at one table.

Nasbit sat at his own table at the front.

Sorin and Nini sat at a table in the middle.

And Raaza and Knovak sat at the farthest back table.

There was one empty table remaining, but I didn't want to sit by myself. Instead, I took a seat next to Nini and Sorin. Waste floated around the table like a haunted outfit, and Thurin shifted through the darkness under our feet.

We really were the weirdos in the room.

Although I wanted to just relax, and enjoy my first day of class, I couldn't. My heart hammered against my ribs. My vision tunneled. If this *person* wasn't Professor Helmith, then where was she? And why was someone masquerading as her?

Twain leapt off my shoulder and landed on the table. He licked his orange fur and gave me odd glances from time to time.

The fake Professor Helmith walked to the front of class and stood behind the desk. She smiled wide and held up her arms. "Welcome, class. My name is Professor Helmith. I'll be one of the many professors who will guide you through your first year at the Academy."

"Good morning, Professor Helmith," Nasbit said with a small wave of his hand.

Helmith nervously chuckled before turning her attention to the chalkboard. "First, let me explain something basic. Your first year at the Academy is considered *general studies*." She wrote the words at the top of the chalkboard. "During this year, you'll learn about mystical creatures, how to use basic magical abilities, further your reading, writing, and arithmetic, and even learn core combat techniques and survival lessons."

Professor Helmith then wrote a few more words. The chalkboard read:

FIRST YEAR = GENERAL STUDIES

SPECIALTIES TO CHOOSE FROM:

KNIGHTS
ARTIFICERS
MYSTIC GUARDIANS
CULTIVATORS
VIZIERS

"These are the specialties you'll get to choose from once you enter your second year," Professor Helmith said as she turned back around to face us. "Once you graduate, you'll be offered positions in various nations based on your new skillset."

Arcanists were the driving force in every nation. Their magic could change the tide of battle, reshape the land, even control the weather. Every nation wanted as many as possible, and being appointed to a position of power would be a life-changing career for Sorin and me. Better than being a candlemaker, that was for sure.

Nasbit raised a hand.

"Wait until I'm finished," Helmith stated.

He put his hand down.

She continued. "Knights are arcanist military officers who lead soldiers. Artificers create magical items, and further research on permanent magics. Mystic Guardians are adventurers who explore dangerous territory looking for new mystical creatures. Cultivators use their magic to improve the land, and the quality of life for the people living on it. Lastly, viziers are trained in politics, strategy, and higher forms of education."

"We have to pick one of these?" Exie asked. She hadn't even bothered to raise a hand.

"Yes," Professor Helmith replied. "Just one."

Although Nasbit had raised his hand before, he just blurted out, "Which specialty is a golem arcanist best suited for?"

When Professor Helmith turned to him, she frowned, her expression one of blatant irritation.

Which wasn't like Professor Helmith *at all*.

For nearly two years I had sat with her and discussed mystical creatures. Even on days when I had interrupted her, or I was grumpy, or I was just generally not as well behaved as I should've been... Professor Helmith had never lost her composure. She was calm, patient, and kind beyond compare.

"*You must all raise your hand before you speak,*" the fake Professor Helmith said. She smoothed her long black hair and then smiled again. "That's a rule of the Academy. Wait until you're called upon."

"I apologize," Nasbit said as he ducked down in his seat.

Exie didn't apologize. But she didn't say anything else, either.

Professor Helmith pointed to the nine wooden trunks that lined the back wall. "Each one of you should come get your school supplies. Astra Academy has given you a set of uniform robes, a notebook, pencils, and three books for your general studies."

Everyone got up from the tables and hurried over to the trunks. I went along for the ride, trying not to act suspicious or give away the fact that I knew this Helmith was a fake. My palms were sweaty as I opened my trunk and removed the contents.

The robes were mostly black and blue but lined with silver. They were marked with the same four symbols that were all over the school.

"Professor," Nasbit said, lifting his hand as high as it would go. His golem eldrin also raised its hand.

"Yes?" Professor Helmith asked.

"I see the globe, sundial, star, and upside-down gates on everything within the Academy. What do they mean?"

"The motto of the Academy is, *In Life, Through Time, With Magic, Till Death*. It is part of an oath, one that all of you will make once you graduate."

The others in our classroom exchanged excited glances. Sorin and Nini both turned back to me as though wanting to know how I felt about that. It was difficult to care, though. All I wanted was to mull over the situation with Professor Helmith.

Was the real professor in danger?

Nasbit just kept his hand in the air. His stone golem did the same.

"Yes?" Helmith said, one of her eyebrows raised. "You have *another* question?"

The real Professor Helmith would never be that curt.

Nasbit finally lowered his hand and asked, "Why do we need to wait to take the oath?"

His golem also lowered its massive stone hand.

"Because it's only necessary once you graduate." Professor Helmith gestured to the specialties on the chalkboard. "Each specialist class fills in the last of the oath. The motto of the knights is—*justice will prevail when reason has failed*. So, when

219

you say it all together... *In life, through time, with magic, till death; justice will prevail when reason has failed.*"

"Oh. What's it for artificers?"

"How about I just write them all on the board? Hm?"

"Okay."

Professor Helmith turned and wrote on the chalkboard again. The mottos read:

KNIGHTS—*Justice will prevail when reason has failed.*
ARTIFICERS—*Better living through magic.*
MYSTIC GUARDIANS—*We venture where others won't.*
CULTIVATORS—*Improving the foundation of civilization.*
VIZIERS—*Granting the wisdom to govern.*

Better living through magic... I liked that.

It also made me wonder.

But I didn't dwell long. No matter how interesting the future might be, I still had a real and immediate problem. Professor Helmith was in trouble. I didn't know how or why, but I knew she was. This imposter could fool everyone else, but she couldn't fool me.

"General studies will include a little bit of each of these specialties," Professor Helmith said matter-of-factly. "So you'll all get a taste of each before you need to decide. Don't worry. Most arcanists know which specialty they want once they've gone through a year of study."

I gathered up my notebook and books from the trunk. Then I pulled my robe on over my clothing.

Everyone else did the same. Even Nini, who was already wearing a gigantic coat. She pulled the robes on over everything else as though she couldn't bring herself to remove even a single layer of clothing.

The robes were velvety soft, and I rubbed some of the luxurious fabric across my cheek.

"Very impressive," Knovak said as he patted his new robes. "You can tell by the sheen and depth of color that these were made by a textile craftsman in the south. No one makes velvet silk like they do."

"You've seen a lot of velvet?" Raaza asked as he slipped into his robes. "These are... beyond luxurious."

Exie twirled around in her new robes. "Oh, yes. These are nice. Not as good as the velvet pillows my mother gave me on my last birthday, but still exquisite."

Knovak huffed and rolled his eyes. "Your mother didn't get you pillows better than these. Feel the hem! These robes were made with loops on a weaving rod. There's no higher quality."

"Look at the fabric." Exie grabbed the sleeve of her robe. "The loops have been cut. My mother gave me pillows with uncut loops *and* multicolored threads through the hem and pattern. Trust me, they're far superior."

I had absolutely no idea what they were arguing about.

"Take your seats," the fake Professor Helmith said with a clap of her hands.

Everyone headed back to their tables. Along the way, Sorin smiled at Nini. "That robe looks great on you."

I almost laughed. Nini resembled a pile of laundry more than a human being.

But her cheeks flushed pink as she half-hid in her coat. "Oh. Thank you." As we took our seats at the table, she stared up at me over the rim of her glasses. "You don't think I look silly, right?"

I shook my head. "Of course not. Blue is your color."

Her face grew redder. It made me wonder how often she received compliments.

I set my new supplies down. Then I glanced at the spines of the books. The first one was titled: *A Magical Bestiary*. The second was titled: *World History, Economics, and Famous*

Arcanists. And the last was titled: *Magical Studies, a Guide to Mastering Magic*.

Very generic. No wonder they were required reading for general studies.

"I'm a professor of mystical creatures," Professor Helmith said as she stood by her desk. "I've studied them for years. Please open your bestiary and turn to page ten. We'll start by learning the tiers of mystical creatures."

Once again, she wrote on the chalkboard.

I flipped through my book, my mind half on our studies, and still half focused on the fake Helmith. I almost asked to go to the washroom, but I didn't know what I was going to do after that. Who would I tell? What proof did I have?

I needed time to think.

Page ten of the bestiary was fairly hefty. It read:

TIERS OF MYSTICAL CREATURES

It is a well-known fact that different breeds of mystical creatures have varying levels of magical capability. Although salamanders and sovereign dragons can both breathe flames, sovereign dragons can melt stone with the heat and intensity of their fire, whereas salamanders cannot, no matter how old they become.

How does this translate to the strength of the arcanist bonded to one of these creatures?

An arcanist's maximum power is determined by two factors: the tier of their eldrin, and their own soul.

A person's soul is similar to their blood. Their soul bleeds for their eldrin, empowering the creature with each year they are bonded. A mystical creature only grows by feeding off the soul of a human, and for each year the eldrin grows older, so does the magical power they provide their arcanist.

Just as a human grows older and becomes stronger, so does a mystical creature. However, if an adult human wants to develop their strength, they must rely on exercise and training. A human who doesn't train themselves will stay weak. It is the same with mystical creatures. The soul of their arcanist, coupled with their training, improves them to their maximums.

Training magic was exercise for the soul, huh?

It didn't surprise me. Muscles needed exercise to grow larger. Why wouldn't other parts of our being require that?

The book continued:

There are essentially five tiers of mystical creature. The higher the tier, the more magic the creature can create with its arcanist.

Tier 1

Examples: will-o-wisps, sprites, gnomes

This is the weakest level of creature. They will reach final maturity in a few short years, and their abilities are very limited.

Tier 2

Examples: unicorns, trolls, ghouls

This is a capable creature. They will reach final maturity in a few decades, and their abilities are varied enough for item creation.

Tier 3

Examples: phoenixes, manticores, leviathans

This is an impressive creature. They will reach final

maturity at close to a century of bonding, and their abilities are substantial, both for item creation and auras.

TIER 4

Examples: king basilisks, pyroclastic dragons, sovereign dragons

These creatures are set apart from the rest in most capabilities, and the longer they're bonded, the more power they exude. Some arcanists have gone multiple centuries without finding their plateau.

Nasbit's hand shot into the air.

Both of Helmith's eyebrows drooped down low. "Yes?"

"Are we going to learn about unique creatures? And god-creatures?"

"No. Those are advanced lessons for second-year students and beyond. We're only going to learn the basics."

"But…" Nasbit slowly dropped his hand. "My tutors already taught me the basics. My stone golem is tier three—one of the strongest non-dragon mystical creatures. I was hoping we could delve into more advanced studies."

"My tutors also taught me the basics," Exie chimed in— again, without raising her hand.

Ashlyn, who had been quiet and polite the entire class, nodded in agreement at the statement. She had learned the basics as well?

And while Professor Helmith—the real one—had taught me all about mystical creatures in my dreams, she'd never spoken to me about the tiers of creatures. She had just told me about the lore around the creatures, and what they were known for.

I didn't know the basics.

Neither did Sorin.

"*My* tutors also taught me everything in this book," Knovak said, his volume rather loud. "And then some!"

Something in his voice told me he was lying, though. He hesitated when he lied—he needed that extra moment to pump himself up. But why lie? Did Knovak just want to pretend he *also* had tutors?

Exie glanced over her shoulder and shot Knovak a glower. The two of them sneered at each other before returning their attention to the professor.

"Everyone quiet down," Professor Helmith said. "Just... flip through your books until you find *your* mystical creature. Everyone should know the designation of their eldrin."

Silence blanketed the classroom. The only sounds were the rustling of pages as everyone hurried to find their eldrin. Twain sat by the edge of my book, staring down at the pages with his multi-colored eyes.

"Gray," Nini whispered as she scooted closer to me. "Um. This says tiers one through four, right? I'm not... imagining things?"

I glanced down at the page she showed me.

It read:

REAPER
Tier 1-4 (depending on the amount of arcanists killed)

"Yeah, it seems so," I whispered.

Nini frowned. "Killing..."

Her reaper fluttered around behind her, more ominous than ever. It made me wonder what Sorin had found. He just stared at his book, his expression neutral.

Reapers were creatures of death. Apparently, they only grew stronger so long as their arcanist killed others. Which made me think that Nini would have a difficult time. When would the Academy permit the death of another? Probably never. Right?

When I flipped through the pages to locate the mimic, I was surprised by how many creatures were in here. I flipped by dozens—hundreds—of creatures, some so obscure, I hadn't even known they existed until just now.

But I finally found the entry for the mimic.

It read:

MIMIC
  Tier 1-4 (depending on the shape taken)

I leaned over and showed the page to Nini.

"You're not the only one with an odd tier number," I said.

She fixed her glasses and offered me a genuine smile. "We really are the weirdo table."

I didn't like that term, but I supposed we were stuck with it.

"Has everyone found their eldrin?" Professor Helmith asked. "Normally, no arcanists in my class have a tier-four creature, but this year is different." She waved a hand over to Ashlyn. "We have our very own typhoon dragon. Very impressive. *Very* powerful."

Ashlyn stood from her seat and offered a quick bow of her head. Then she motioned to her dragon eldrin. "His name is Ecrib. I couldn't ask for a finer eldrin."

Her typhoon dragon lifted his head, his fins flared. "We are the rulers of the water," Ecrib stated, his voice deep, even for a baby dragon. "Titans of the seas."

Exie clapped.

The others eventually joined in. Except for me. Instead, when Ashlyn glanced over, I gave her the same half-smile she had given me before. This amused her, for some reason. She lifted an eyebrow as she took her seat.

We already had our own little nonverbal language, apparently.

I could tell she took my lack of clapping as a challenge.

And while that enticed me, my thoughts immediately went back to Helmith. She wrote on the chalkboard, muttering something about other tiers. But I didn't hear much. I focused on the books in front of me, my thoughts jumbled.

What was I going to do?

How was I going to help the real Helmith?

I pretended to study while I dwelled on that problem.

I would speak to this imposter once the class had concluded.

CHAPTER 23

ACADEMY LIFE

The rest of the class was pleasant, though I barely paid attention.

Twain glanced at me a few times, his little eyes narrowed. I patted him, but refused to say anything. The hours went by at a crawl. Apparently, each class day was ten hours, broken up by various breaks.

Two hours of study, then a thirty-minute break.

Two more hours of study, and then an hour break for lunch.

An additional two hours before we took another thirty-minute break in the afternoon.

And then the final two hours before we were released for dinner.

Six days a week.

That kind of schedule was more intense than anything I had experienced on the Isle of Haylin. Which was fine. Astra Academy didn't want us to have too much idle free time, and they probably had a lot to cram into five short years.

During our final hour, Professor Helmith pointed to the chalkboard. She had scribbled down groups of mystical creatures based on similar abilities. Phoenixes and salamanders both dealt with fire, obviously, so they were lumped into a little circle.

"Some arcanists share abilities," she said. "Because their eldrin have similar powers." When she glanced back at the class, she smiled. "My husband's eldrin has powers that involve light, for example. It's the same as mine."

Ethereal whelks were made of light and dreams. That was what the *real* Professor Helmith had told me.

Funny how it seemed to be the exact opposite of my brother's knightmare.

"Wait," Sorin blurted out in the middle of class. "You have a husband?"

Several others in class snorted and stifled laughs. I shot him a glare.

My brother glanced over at me. "I'm so sorry, Gray," he whispered.

That also elicited chuckles. I knew my brother was trying to be quiet, but he wouldn't know quiet if it bit him. And since everyone knew I had "been dreaming about Professor Helmith" because I had admitted as much on the Academy pier, I was certain rumors would fly wild.

The fake Professor Helmith motioned for everyone to quiet themselves. Her ears were slightly red as she rolled her eyes. "The personal lives of the professors are not for any of you to concern yourselves with."

The murmuring didn't stop, though.

Professor Helmith glanced toward the far window. "Ah. Look at the time. Class is dismissed for today. Oh, and tomorrow, you're to go to the training field for your practical magic use lessons."

I turned around and glanced out the far window. How could she tell the time? Then I spotted it—a clock built into the trunk of the treehouse. The time was tracked through rotating cogs. Depending on the positions of the smaller cogs around the larger central cog, one could tell the exact time of day. I hadn't noticed it before, probably because I had been focused on the living accommodations.

The clock on the tree trunk was massive, though. I suspected each tiny cog was larger than a full-grown adult.

Everyone stood from their tables and gathered their materials. While most hurried for the door, Sorin and Nini lingered behind, obviously waiting for me. I motioned them to go.

"I want to speak with the professor," I muttered.

Nini pushed her glasses up her nose. "So, you and Professor Helmith really *do* know each other from before?"

I nodded once.

Sorin patted me on the shoulder. "I really am sorry."

I knocked his hand away. "Stop that. She was never my honeysuckle. That was all in your head."

"Still. You haven't seemed yourself the entire lecture. Ever since she came into the room."

Of course Sorin would notice. I had tried to hide it, but he knew me too well. Regardless, I pointed to the door. "I'll meet you at the dorms, all right?"

He half-shrugged and headed out of the classroom with Nini. His shadow moved with a mind of its own, slithering across the ground with his feet. It was both distracting and creepy.

Not as creepy as Nini's reaper, though. Waste silently floated by her side, his scythe occasionally twirling.

Twain sat on the table. He watched them go, his ears perked straight up. Then he turned to me and frowned. "Want to tell me what's going on?"

"Just wait. I'll tell you after." I scooped him up and placed him on my shoulder. He was so small, and lightweight, that I barely noticed him. "I think there might be a problem, so just stay quiet and follow my lead."

"A problem?" Twain whispered.

I walked over to Professor Helmith's desk, ignoring Twain's confusion. My chest tightened into a knot as I reached her desk. She stood behind it, her fingers on the surface. She wasn't tall, but in my mind, I always imagined her as powerfully mystic.

Not this fake Helmith, though. She had none of the presence the real Helmith did.

Once the last of the other students had exited, I offered her a smile.

"Do you have a moment, Professor Helmith?" I asked, excitement in my voice.

She stayed on the other side of the desk. With a hesitant grin, she replied. "Of course."

"I just wanted to thank you for helping me in my dreams. I said I would meet you at Astra Academy—and here you are."

Professor Helmith nodded along with my words. "Like I said, I've been very busy. I apologize. Astra Academy has been looking to expand, and I've been helping the headmaster with all the preparations."

"It's all right."

She tapped her fingers on the desk. Then she played with her hair, seemingly positioning it just right. Silence seemed her best defense. She clearly didn't want to say anything that would reveal herself as an imposter.

"Well, I should catch up to my brother," I said as I motioned to the door.

"Yes, you have plenty of reading ahead of you." The fake professor smiled wide, all too eager to get me to leave.

"I'll bring you a blueberry tart at some point."

"A blueberry tart?"

"Yeah. I wanted to thank you for helping me, so I figured I would get you one."

She lifted her eyebrows. "Oh. That would be wonderful. The perfect gift."

"They're still your favorite, right? I mean, you helped me in my dream so long ago... I'm not sure if your tastes have changed."

"Definitely still my favorite," she said. "You're very thoughtful."

Her words confirmed everything for me.

I no longer had any doubts. She was a liar and a fake—Helmith's favorite were raspberry tarts. We had discussed that on more than one occasion. This phony had no idea. She clearly wasn't aware of my and Helmith's relationship.

Probably because it only took place inside of dreams.

No one ever saw us together. The only people who knew about it would be the people I told, or the people that Helmith had told.

With a forced smile, I waved to her. "I look forward to your next class!" Then I went straight for the door, trying my hardest not to run out of the room.

"Have a pleasant week, Gray. See you next class."

I didn't glance back.

I sat in the boys' dorm, on the very back bed, flipping through the pages of my bestiary.

But I saw nothing. I didn't read any of the words, I didn't even see the pictures. My mind was focused on the situation. Twain sat next to me, occasionally glancing at the book, and sometimes up at me.

Finally, he asked, "Are you going to tell me what happened?"

The sun set in the distance. The redwood of the treehouse practically glowed crimson. It was a beautiful sight—for anyone paying attention.

I still didn't know what to say. Should I panic and tell

everyone? Again, I wasn't sure what to do with my information. Professor Helmith hadn't visited my dreams in months, but until then, she had seemed normal. Which meant this imposter had only recently assumed Helmith's identity.

Sorin sat on the bed next to me. He, too, flipped through the bestiary, but he was actually reading the thing.

"Did you know that knightmares aren't born like normal creatures?" he asked.

Twain glared at me. He was obviously upset that I hadn't told him what was on my mind.

I half turned to Sorin. "What do you mean?" My voice was devoid of emotion, but that didn't seem to bother him.

"So, babies normally come from a mother and father, but knightmares aren't like that." Sorin poked at a page in the book. "They're born whenever the sole ruler of a nation is assassinated."

"Huh."

"The blood of their body mixes with their shadow, and then *bam*. A baby knightmare is born." Sorin sat up and stared at the floor. "Is that true, Thurin?"

A voice floated out of the shadows. "That is correct."

"How were you born?"

"King Nurith was visiting the Hydra's Gorge with his disgruntled wife. On a night when he had had too much to drink, she pushed him into the gorge. He died when he struck the bottom. The death was painless and quick, but I was born from his shadow, filled with the hurt of that betrayal."

Sorin rested back on his bed. He placed the open book on his chest and just stared at the ceiling. "That's interesting. A spiteful shadow, steeped in sorrow. Suffering. Struggling. Seeking salvation."

On any normal day, I would've found this all fascinating. But as it was, I still couldn't focus. I just nodded along with Sorin's poetics, and then returned to my thoughts.

The door to the dorm burst inward. Knovak stormed into the room, his unicorn clopping behind him. Raaza and his kitsune entered afterward, silent as the dead. Raaza went straight for his bed, but Knovak turned and dogged his every step, shouting the entire time.

"Did you hear them?" Knovak *huffed* and *scoffed*. "They spoke like they knew everything! And that everything here was beneath them."

"Hm," Raaza replied.

He sat on his bed and turned away from Knovak. But Knovak clearly couldn't take the hint. He walked around the entire bed, until he was in front of Raaza. "It's just rude, that's what it is. Perhaps I wasn't born to a noble family, but I've still experienced the finer things the world has to offer."

"Uh-huh," Raaza mumbled.

Starling stomped his hooves and neighed. "That's right! How dare they. Unicorns are among the noblest of mystical creatures. Me and my arcanist deserve respect."

"They think they're better than us." Knovak paced back and forth. "That's what's going on."

"*Us?*" Sorin asked from across the room.

"*Us.* Yes. Everyone who isn't *them.*" Knovak grabbed his velvet robes and pulled them tight across his chest. "Aren't we all students here? We're all equals. We should be, at least."

Sorin muttered disbelief as he went back to his book. Ever since those two had argued on the pier in front of Nini, they hadn't even glanced at each other. Clearly, my brother wanted nothing to do with Knovak.

But then that pompous man came marching down to our end of the dorm. His unicorn held his snout in the air as he walked. He was a beautiful animal—Starling's shimmering coat still impressed me—but I dreaded their approach.

"You're both outraged, aren't you?" Knovak asked once at the foot of Sorin's bed.

"Not really," I muttered.

"You must be! That woman, Ashlyn, called you out before class by demanding to know your Trial of Worth. She was looking down on you, surely."

I shook my head. "No. She was just sizing me up."

"What do you mean?" Twain asked, his ears perking up as he spoke.

"The stronger the mystical creature, the more elaborate and dangerous their Trial of Worth seems to be." I glanced down at the bestiary. "Dragons have difficult Trials, right?"

My eldrin slowly nodded.

"And Ashlyn made a big deal to point that out. She told us about the people who died taking the typhoon dragon's Trial—and then, because she likely knows everyone else's tier and Trial of Worth, she singled me out about my Trial. She wanted to know if it was difficult."

Twain blinked a few times. "Really?"

"I'm pretty sure." With a shrug, I glanced away from Knovak. "Ashlyn wasn't talking down to me. She just wanted to know if my eldrin was strong or not."

Knovak crossed his arms. Then uncrossed them. "I still think you all should be more upset about this."

Sorin rolled onto his side, his nose deep in the book. "Hm."

"I think you should focus more on your magic," Raaza said. He held out his hand, palm up. "We learned *nothing* about practical magic in class today. That upset me more than your petty squabbles."

Knovak frowned. Then he dramatically ripped off his hat and tossed it over to an empty bed. His dirty blond hair was squished over to one side as though he had been sweating heavily under the cap. "My family has a saying. *A man is only as good as his reputation.* We mustn't allow our names to be dragged through the mud."

"I completely agree," his unicorn said with a nod.

"Tsk." Raaza shot Knovak and Starling an icy glower. "Reputation isn't going to save you in combat." Raaza ran a finger down a scar on his face. When he got to his lip, he jerked his hand away. "We need to learn *actual* magic, not all this book nonsense."

Before anyone could comment, Raaza thrust his hand forward. A flash of flame erupted from his palm. It was there, and then gone, in the blink of an eye. Sorin and I both leapt to our feet.

Thurin emerged from the darkness. He was a partial suit of armor rising from the shadows on the floor, forming from the void, and coalescing like an inky specter. His raven-feather cape fluttered behind him.

I held my arm up, and Twain leapt from my bed onto my elbow. Then he clawed his way to my shoulder. We were... still new to this. His little kitten claws dug into my skin, and I grimaced.

Knovak ran back to his bed and grabbed his bags. His sword was tied to the side, and he unfastened it within a split second. Then he brandished the weapon, pointing it at Raaza. Knovak's unicorn stood next to him, his head lowered, his horn pointing forward. If Starling were fully grown, it probably would've been intimidating, but as a little foal, it was more adorable than anything else.

"Don't you dare think you'll get away with using your magic on us," Knovak said in a serious tone.

Raaza frowned. Then he showed us his palm.

There were no flames. Just... gold coins. They glittered in the sunset, sparking like only polished coins could.

The coins were minted and stamped with the picture of a scorpion. Which was odd. The coins used by most islanders were stamped with a leaf and were slightly smaller. Where was Raaza from? I had no idea.

Knovak lowered his sword. "What happened? You made money?"

Raaza closed his hands, and flames puffed out between his fingers. When he opened his hand again, the coins were gone.

"Apparently, my magic allows me to make minor illusions," Raaza stated. "I learned that on my own, while everyone else was reading from the book in class."

"It's called *fox fire*," his kitsune said matter-of-factly. She walked between her arcanist's legs. "We kitsune use fox fire to trick people all the time." Miko lifted her paw. The flames on her feet flickered with power, but not heat. "My fire becomes illusions."

"Can you put the fox fire on things?" I asked, trying to think of all the ways that could be useful.

"I just learned it," Raaza snapped. "I don't know."

"Sorry. I was just asking."

Raaza glanced over at me. Then he shook his head. "No, I should apologize. That was uncalled for. The truth is, I don't know the extent of my magic, and I was frustrated that we didn't practice it with a trained arcanist."

His reasonableness surprised me.

"We'll practice magic tomorrow," I said. "You heard what Professor—" I swallowed her name. "You heard what the professor said. We'll be practicing out on the field tomorrow. I'm sure everyone will be impressed you can use some of your magic already."

Raaza took a seat on his bed. Miko leapt into his lap. He patted his eldrin as he said, "I just... don't want to be weak. It bothers me that we're arcanists, yet we haven't developed any real capabilities yet."

"It was the first day of class," Knovak drawled. He rolled his eyes as he tucked his sword away. "Honestly, learning the foundation of magic, along with mystical creature classification, doesn't seem like a bad place to start."

"I want to learn *magic*. Not history. Not science. Not arithmetic."

"I'm pretty sure we're still going to be learning those," I quipped. "Normal adult arcanists need those skills, too."

Raaza slammed himself down on his bed. "Yes, well, those skills won't save me in a fight. So, until I'm confident with my magic, I don't want to focus on anything else."

At least he had a goal.

Sorin and I both returned to our own beds. I hadn't thought about what magical abilities I would have with Twain. He was a mimic, after all. I could do whatever anyone else could, in theory. It made me wonder if there was anything he could do on his own, though...

I rested back on my pillow, and Twain scurried onto my chest as I positioned myself. Then he lay down on me.

My thoughts immediately returned to the fake Professor Helmith.

Perhaps I could ask the other professors about her. I would gather information. Maybe everyone already knew about this deception. Maybe there was a logical reason.

I just needed to find out before I did anything reckless.

CHAPTER 24

THE MOST POWERFUL STUDENT

The next morning was much like the first. I awoke in a groggy haze.

After dressing, and washing, I stumbled my way out of the dorm and followed the others to the dining hall. Once we ate our fruit slices and milk, we headed straight for the training fields. Sorin and I were the only ones with our eldrin. Twain had slept with me, and apparently Thurin could just hide in darkness. The unicorn and kitsune had gone to the treehouse.

The corridors of Astra Academy were livelier on the second day, and it caught me by surprise.

Second-year students hurried past us, each carrying a brown sack. It occurred to me that their robes were different. They all wore the same four symbols as the rest of us, but they also had a hammer stitched into the blue, black, and silver.

A hammer...

That was probably for the artificer course. Artificers were arcanists who specialized in crafting magical items, after all. A hammer was appropriate to symbolize their studies.

When Sorin, Raaza, Knovak, and I turned down a long hall, I spotted a few taller arcanists standing near the double doors that led outside. One of them was bonded to a river nymph, and all their robes were marked with a tree instead of a hammer.

They were probably cultivators.

Some mystical creatures weren't suited to adventure because their abilities revolved around nature, improvement, or minor abilities that just weren't suited for combat. I had heard that river nymphs could improve the quality of fish in their rivers. It made sense that the nymph's arcanist would want to specialize in cultivation.

"Hey, first-years," one of them called out as we headed outside. "Remember to join the Gardening Club! We actually have a lot of fun."

Raaza scoffed as he marched past them.

I had to admit, *gardening* didn't sound like my idea of a grand time. It didn't offend me like it offended Raaza, though.

When we stepped outside, the morning light flooded into my eyes. I held up a hand, squinted back the bright light, and then glared at the distant clouds. What were they doing? They had *one* job! Hopefully, they had floated over before the afternoon.

I had seen the training field a couple of days ago, and while it had seemed huge from the second-story window, it was much more massive now that I had my boots on the ground. Someone had carved out a chunk of the mountain landscape to create a plateau of flatland. The grass beneath our feet was unnatural. Grass this green *shouldn't* be able to grow on a mountain like this.

Right?

It made me wonder if the emerald green all around us was sustained by magic. Maybe the cultivators and the Gardening Club had something to do with it.

The running track, sparring ring, and weights were interesting sights. I hadn't ever trained my body for hard labor, or for combat. Candlemakers didn't have to fight off bees to get their wax, nor did they have to lift much when pulling the wicks out of the vats.

Captain Leon and his faithful cerberus, Sticks, stood in the middle of the field.

Most of our class was already here. Nini, Ashlyn, Phila, and Nasbit all stood around the field, glancing around at the distant stands. Nasbit seemed focused on the treehouse. From here, the clock in the trunk was easily visible.

Knovak and Raaza spotted their eldrin on the side of the field, both of them sniffing the vibrant grass. They headed over to greet their mystical creatures for the morning.

Nini and her reaper hurried over the moment Sorin and I entered the scene. She smiled as she approached, her breath coming out as visible mist.

"There you are," she said. "I was starting to worry."

"Worry? Why?" Sorin furrowed his brow.

"W-Well, you hadn't shown up... I guess I was just lonely."

"Lonely? There are lots of people here already."

Nini fidgeted with the sleeve of her coat. "That's true. I just..."

But she didn't finish her sentence. Sorin waited with bated breath, remaining quiet, probably so that he wouldn't accidentally interrupt her with an ill-timed question.

I knew what was going on, though.

"The others aren't talking to you much, are they?" I asked, keeping my voice down.

Nini shoved her glasses up onto her nose. She didn't say anything, but she shook her head, confirming my suspicions.

"Really?" Sorin frowned. "What about the other girls in your dorm?"

"No," Nini mumbled into the collar of her coat. She kept her gaze on the ground.

A chill morning wind removed the last of my grogginess. I shivered and pulled my robes tight around my body. Twain leaned against my neck, his tiny body shaking something fierce. The bright sunshine wasn't enough to repel the cold.

The weather didn't seem to bother Waste. The floating cloak just hovered around his arcanist, the hood as empty as ever.

"Don't worry," I said with a shrug. "We're here now, and we like talking to you."

"That's right." Sorin offered her a genuine smile.

Nini tapped her fingertips together. "Thank you."

"In life, through time, with magic, until death—we'll be friends you can count on." Sorin bowed a courtly bow. "That is our oath."

I thought it was mildly embarrassing, but Nini laughed. "You don't even really know me," she said, her voice half-sad, half-chuckles.

"I know you enough."

That answer seemed to please her. She returned Sorin's playful gesture. "It's an oath I'll make for you as well."

The others in our class just stared at us, their eyebrows lifted. I wasn't sure what they were thinking, but I didn't want to deal with it at the moment. It was still early, and I wanted to question Captain Leon about Professor Helmith.

So I wandered away from Sorin and headed straight for the cerberus arcanist.

The man's white hair was as striking as snow, especially in the cold weather. He rubbed his hand through it, and I swear flakes of ice flew off into the wind.

With my voice low, so that the others wouldn't hear, I said, "Good morning, Captain Leon."

"Good morning," he replied.

"Are you the one instructing us on magic use?"

"That's right." He huffed and then shot everyone a scrutinizing glower. "Where is the last one? I count eight of you here…"

Exie was still missing. Had she slept in? On the second day of class? Or maybe she wasn't feeling well. I really had no idea.

"Uh, Captain Leon," I said. "Do you know Professor Helmith?"

"Yes, of course."

"She taught our class yesterday."

"She's an expert on mystical creatures. It makes sense."

"I like Helmith," Sticks said, his voice a deep rumble. Only one head spoke, and the other two stared at me—observing me. Sticks's long tail wagged at a quick pace. "She's a talented arcanist."

I stepped close to Leon and asked, "Do you spend a lot of time with her personally?"

He stroked at his short beard. It was trimmed neat, and just as white as the hair on his head. "Why do you ask?"

"Oh. She seemed under the weather yesterday. I was hoping she was all right."

"Ah, I see. Well, truth be told, I rarely speak with her on a personal level. She's mostly in the basement helping with artifact creation or writing up a paper on a new discovery she made with a mystical creature."

"Perhaps she's friends with Doc Tomas? Maybe he can help her."

Leon shook his head. "Doc Tomas never ventures far from the infirmary or his office. He's a man who operates at his own speed—and it's the speed of a corpse."

All three of Sticks's heads chortled. But then they glanced at me, and then at their arcanist.

"Oh, forget that last part," Leon said, straightening his half-plate armor. "That was just plain unprofessional of me. Doc Tomas does a good job for the Academy. He just does it... at his own pace."

"I won't mention it to anyone," I said.

I didn't care about Doc Tomas's lack of speed. All I cared

about was who had connections to Professor Helmith. And now I knew that Captain Leon and the doctor weren't close friends with her. They wouldn't be able to recognize slight differences in her behavior, or subtle inconsistencies in her speech or statements.

But I knew who *would*.

"Does Professor Helmith's husband teach here at the Academy?" I asked.

Leon quirked an eyebrow. "*Kristof?* Oh, no. No, no. He's off gallivanting around the world, adventuring through deadly magical terrain with fellow mystic guardians. He'll be back in about four months." The captain patted me on the shoulder and then motioned me to join the others. "You needn't worry about Helmith. I'll tell someone to go check up on her."

"All right. Thank you." With my teeth gritted, I ambled my way back to the group.

Professor Helmith's husband wasn't here. If he was, he would've surely spotted the differences in her behavior. But since he wasn't here, I had to find someone else.

As I headed toward my brother, I realized he was engrossed in conversation with Nini. That rarely happened, so I veered away, allowing them to have some time as I mulled over the situation.

"You're really acting weird over this Professor Helmith lady," Twain whispered into my ear. His words were laced with irritation. "Are you going to tell me what's going on or what?"

"I think she's an imposter," I whispered as I headed over to the other students in my class.

"*What?* Really? An imposter?" Twain shivered. "What makes you think that?"

"The way she acts. The things she says. Blueberry tarts aren't her favorite, yet she said they were. Lots of little things."

"And you're hoping to find someone else to verify all your suspicions about her behavior?"

"That's right."

Twain's eyes went huge, and the pupils of his eyes became giant circles. "We're like detectives now."

I chuckled. "Why does that excite you?"

"A year ago, the Menagerie had this pixie who said she had helped solve a crime, and I've thought about it ever since." Twain exhaled and puffed up his fur. "She made it sound so amazing. You just reminded me of her, that's all."

When I arrived at the group of other students, they regarded me with odd glances. Except Ashlyn. She stepped to the side, offering me a place in their little circle. They had been mumbling to themselves this entire time, and I had no clue what they were discussing, but I decided to step into their group regardless.

Phila's long hair—so long it practically tangled with every gust of wind—was half-tied back in a ponytail. She fumbled with it, and then eventually sighed.

"Where's your last classmate?" Captain Leon barked.

"She was sleeping when we left," Phila said, her voice soft but distinct.

"What?" Leon's exhale was one of long suffering. "Can you go get her, please? The sun is already in the sky."

Phila nodded. "Of course." She didn't wait for anyone to say anything else. She headed for the Academy, her coatl slithering along after her.

Nasbit and his golem wandered away after that. They didn't follow Phila—they went for the weights on the other side of the field. Had they left because of me? Or were they just so fixated on everything else that my presence wasn't even a concern to them?

It didn't matter.

That just left me and Ashlyn, and I preferred it this way.

Well, her typhoon dragon was also here. The fierce beast didn't seem to mind the frigid weather. His glittering blue scales were just as icy as our surroundings. His fins flared as he turned his attention to me.

I ignored him.

Ashlyn had a presence about her. Like her eldrin, she didn't seem to mind the cold. She wore her school robes, but she had armor and well-tailored clothes on underneath. She was prepared for anything that might happen today, her blonde hair braided tightly behind her.

"Hey," I said to Ashlyn. "How's your morning going?"

She half-smiled. "Really? That's your opener?"

"Hm? You don't like it when people ask about your day?"

"I just expected something more original."

There was something about her. She was playful, yet aggressive. It intrigued me.

"Everyone asks about your morning, so now it's passé?" I asked, lifting an eyebrow.

Ashlyn crossed her arms, but her smile didn't fade. "I get approached by a lot of men. It just gets tiring hearing the same things over and over again."

"You're so humble," I quipped. "No wonder they approach you."

"I'm just telling you the truth. I'm a dragon arcanist, from a well-to-do family, and I'm not betrothed."

"And that's all a man needs, obviously."

"I'm the most magically powerful one in our class. Probably the most educated." Ashlyn shook her head. "A lot of people think of me like a trophy they need. It gets tiring."

I held up a finger and clicked my tongue in disappointment. "Tsk. I'm gonna have to stop you there. You've already made a mistake."

Ashlyn tilted her head. "What mistake?"

"You're not the most magically powerful one here." I placed my hand on my chest. "I am."

It was her turn to lift an eyebrow. "Oh? Perhaps you weren't paying attention to the professor yesterday. Dragons are the strongest mystical creatures."

Her typhoon dragon growled and flashed his fangs. Again, I ignored him. He was all bark and no bite.

I scoffed and waved away Ashlyn's comment. "Look, I'm happy for you. Really. But I'm *also* a dragon arcanist. *And* a knightmare arcanist. *And* a reaper arcanist." I pointed to the others. "I'm all of them. Which means I'm more magical than everyone here. I hate to say it, because you seem wrapped up in how amazing you are, but I'm just telling you the truth."

Something about Ashlyn changed in that moment. She hardened her expression, even while she maintained her confident smile. "I've never seen a mimic arcanist in action. I'm intrigued. I'll look forward to the magic you demonstrate during training."

"I can't wait to show you."

She chuckled, but our conversation was cut short.

Exie and Phila entered the training field, followed by their eldrin. Now class could finally begin, and while I had been focused on Professor Helmith, I was also determined to make a good impression with my magic.

CHAPTER 25

BASIC MAGIC

Captain Leon motioned us all into the center of the training field. Nasbit had to be called over. His baby golem lumbered around behind him, its heavy steps crushing the vibrant grass. Despite that, the grass sprang back to life whenever the golem moved off it. The crushed blades fixed themselves before my eyes, and the field returned to its pristine form.

I wondered why.

"It's important to start class *on time*," Captain Leon stated with a glare.

Exie's face flushed red. She crossed her arms. "No one woke me up."

Her erlking fairy fluttered around Exie's head. He landed on Exie's shoulder and shrugged. With a higher-pitched voice, he said, "And no one bothered to tell me at all."

"For being late, and for holding up class, I'll be issuing you a demerit," Captain Leon stated. "In the future, consider how your actions will affect the rest of your class."

"*A demerit?*" Exie frowned. "But no one woke me!"

"Waking on time is *your* responsibility. There are clocks around the school, and bells sound near the dorms."

"They're too quiet."

"There are still solutions you could have employed," Leon said through gritted teeth.

"I just don't think it's fair. No one told me we could be issued demerits."

Exie kept her arms crossed tight. Just like yesterday, though, she seemed well put together and beautiful. Her curly hair, lace-up boots, sash belt, and dress with a ribbon tie in the back, probably took her considerable time to adorn. She wore her school robes, but haphazardly, as though they were the last thing she had just thrown on afterward.

"Each dorm has a book with the school history inside," Nasbit said in a matter-of-fact tone. "There are rules inside, as well as a description of the demerit system. After three demerits, you'll be sent to the Academy's counselor, and after five demerits, you'll be sent away for two weeks for *individualized training*, and if you get seven demerits—"

"That's enough," Leon barked. "No one here should be thinking about what happens if you get seven demerits. We should be *focused*." He held up a hand and then pointed to a spot on the field. A small wooden target was set up on the grass. "I'm going to teach you the basic fundamentals of magic use."

Raaza stepped forward, his kitsune eagerly hopping at his feet.

Captain Leon kept his gaze on the target. It was a circle of pine wood thick enough to stand on its own, with red and white circular stripes, positioned a good twenty-five feet away.

"The three most basic uses of your magic are called evocation, manipulation, and augmentation." Captain Leon held up his hand. "Evocation is where you temporarily create something. Watch closely." He waved his hand. "And also keep your distance."

Once everyone was at least ten feet away, an explosion of flame erupted from his palm. It gushed out in a straight line with enough force to wash over the small wood target. The poor piece of pine wood toppled over and caught fire. Once Leon was done with his evocation, the target continued to burn.

He returned his attention to the class. "The second ability—manipulation—allows you to control something already in existence. You all see the target and the fire? My manipulation allows me to control flame. Since the target is on fire, watch this."

He waved his hand.

The fire moved in time with his motion. When he gestured his hand to the left, the fire leapt from the target and struck the ground on the left. When Leon did the same with the right, the exact same thing happened.

It was almost artful.

Phila, a quiet girl from what I had seen, gently clapped her hands. "Impressive."

Captain Leon rubbed at the back of his head. With a chuckle, he continued, "And the last technique we're going to discuss is augmentation. That's when you push your magic into something and alter its properties. Like evocation, this is temporary. However, the more you train, the longer this augmentation can last. For example..." He glanced around the class and then settled on Raaza. "Come here for a minute, boy."

Raaza eagerly stepped forward. He didn't have his hat today, so the scars were plain to see. Most of the class regarded him with quizzical expressions, and I wondered if anyone outside my dorm even knew Raaza's name.

It seemed like Captain Leon didn't.

"Hold out your hand," Captain Leon commanded.

Raaza did as he was told.

Leon grabbed Raaza's hand, and for a long moment, it seemed as though nothing had happened. They just stared at each other. Then Leon released Raaza and pointed to the burning target.

"Go over there and prop the target back up," Leon said.

Raaza frowned. "It's... on fire."

"Yeah, I can see that."

Leon's cerberus wagged his tail. "You won't be hurt," one of the heads said with a pant and lolled tongue. Another head nodded. "Cerberus arcanists' augmentation gives people, and objects, immunity to flames."

Our whole class *oohed* and *ahhed*.

Raaza, after squaring his shoulders, marched over to the smoking target. He knelt, picked up the piece of pine wood, and propped it back up. The embers wafted into the wind, but the grass never seemed to catch flame.

Neither did Raaza. He touched and handled the burning wood without a problem. Some char and ash got on his hands, but his skin never burned.

He stood and turned around, half-smiling. "It worked."

Phila clapped again, this time louder.

Captain Leon chuckled. "Yes, well, I knew it would, because I've practiced my augmentation for years now." He pointed to his armor, and then to the distant target. "I could've used my augmentation on any object."

"But it's only temporary?" Exie asked. No raised hand. No nothing.

Nasbit raised his hand, though.

Captain Leon glanced between them. With a frown, he pointed to Nasbit. "Yes?"

"If you use star shards, you can use *imbuing* to permanently create magical items, correct?"

"That's right."

Nasbit turned to Exie, a smile on his wide face. "If you read your *Magical Studies, a Guide to Mastering Magic*, you would have seen the part about imbuing. It's really fascinating. It's how artificers make magical items. Trinkets are classified as anything with less than—"

"Are *you* the professor, or is Captain Leon?" Exie interjected, her tone haughty.

"Hey, now," Leon said, snapping his fingers. He pointed at Exie and glowered. "I've never given anyone *two* demerits on their first day of class, but you're yanglin' to earn that distinction, young lady."

Yanglin'? It was as if anger caused Leon to slip into some weird dialect I only ever heard from distant foreigners.

Leon coughed, and then said, in a standard speech pattern, "No more discussions. We're not learning about imbuing today. That's for a different class. *Today* we will be focusing primarily on evocation. Everyone here has something *physical* to evoke except for..."

He glanced around, his frown deepening.

"Except you four."

Leon pointed to me, Sorin, Nini, and then Exie. The four of us exchanged puzzled looks.

"You four step over here," Leon said, motioning to the side of the field. "The rest of the class will go first, and then we'll deal with you."

"What?" Exie groaned. In a low voice, she muttered, "I have to be with the weirdos?"

When Leon flashed her a glare, Exie became quiet. Once satisfied she wouldn't say anything else, Leon gestured her away from the others. With a pout, Exie ambled over to Sorin, Nini, and me.

Sorin actually waved to greet her, bless his little heart.

"I'm Sorin Lexly, and this is my knightmare, Thurin. Also, this is my twin brother, Gray, and his mimic, Twain." Sorin turned to Nini. After being yelled at for introducing her, it seemed he was fearful to do it again.

Nini grew stiff. "I'm in your dorm." Her reaper floated close, but didn't say anything.

"I know who you all are," Exie stated. She pointed to her erlking fairy. "This is *Rex*, and he's a beautiful erlking, the strongest of the fairies."

Rex gave a little bow.

Up close, it was apparent that the fairy was wearing a black cape, little shoes, and a long tunic. He seemed child-like in all other ways, with a puffy face, and short arms and legs. He was still tiny—no larger than my fist—so it was difficult to make out *all* the details, but I understood his general appearance.

"We'll have the coatl arcanist go first," Leon said to the main group of our class.

Phila walked up with her coatl. The winged serpent held its head high, proudly displaying its rainbow wings and practically preening. Phila stood where Leon pointed.

"I want you to focus on ejecting the magic from your body." Leon held out his hand. "Most arcanists use their limbs, because it's easier to visualize, but some people can evoke their magic from other places."

Phila nodded. "I see." She held up a delicate hand, her strawberry blonde hair flowing like gentle water in the mountain air. "And what will I evoke?"

"Wind," Leon replied. "Coatls are creatures of weather and wisdom. Fearsome beasts to their enemies, and gentle protectors of their friends and family." He said the last few sentences like he had just memorized them and wanted to recite them.

Phila inhaled and then slowly exhaled. Everyone watched as she kept her hand raised. Her coatl never moved. It remained at her side, steadfast and confident.

"I want you to aim for the target." Leon pointed to the smoking piece of pine.

"All right."

Phila hesitated a moment, but then a burst of wind, like a

slice of precise air, shot forward. It disturbed the grass, and then struck the target with enough force to knock it over. A *whoosh* rumbled throughout the training field.

I smiled, impressed.

Phila clapped for herself. "Oh, excellent."

"That was very good," Leon said. He walked over to the target and propped it back up. The wood had a shallow slash in it. "Coatls are known to be dangerous. I can't wait to see what you can do at your end-of-the-year exams."

Phila returned to the group. Everyone patted her on the shoulder or whispered words of encouragement. Her coatl received a fair number of pettings as well.

"Next up is..." Leon stroked his beard.

Nasbit shot his hand into the air.

"Yes? You want to go?"

"Well, I wanted to start." Nasbit stepped forward. His stone golem stomped up as well. "You see, stone golems have a slight disadvantage when it comes to evocation." He spoke like he was the professor teaching the class. "Stone golems evoke sand and rocks, but it takes considerable effort. Unlike most arcanists, who summon fire or wind in the blink of an eye, golems require extended periods of time to *amass* the *magical mass* of their evocation." Nasbit pantomimed making a sphere.

"That's true," Leon drawled.

"So, I'd like to start mine, while everyone else goes."

"All right."

Nasbit stepped off to the side. He held out his hand, palm up, and focused on the lines in his skin. Even from where I stood, I could see small grains of sand forming in his grasp. It was minor, but it was obviously building up.

"That's it?" Exie asked, loud enough for everyone to hear.

"Stone golems are strong in many ways," Captain Leon stated. "They're almost invulnerable to damage and can't bleed out or starve to death. But they are *slow*. Having an evocation that takes a little time is nothing compared to the many benefits a stone golem offers."

Exie still seemed underwhelmed.

I had to admit, slowly evoking sand—or a single rock—didn't seem impressive, but it was better than me, apparently. What could I evoke? If Twain changed shape, I could pick whatever I wanted, but what if no other mystical creatures or arcanists were around?

Captain Leon pointed to Ashlyn and her typhoon dragon. "All right. Let's see a dragon at work, shall we?"

Ashlyn smiled as she stepped up to the starting position. Her dragon was rather agile on land. He matched her pace, and remained at her side, as a faithful companion. Ashlyn patted his head before turning her attention to the distant target.

Leon was still standing next to it. When Ashlyn lifted her hand, he frantically leapt away.

A bolt of lightning shot out of Ashlyn's palm. She hadn't needed any preparation. It was like she had already practiced, and now she was just showing off for the class.

The bolt of lightning, while impressive, wasn't super powerful. It struck the target—which fell over, and there was now a black divot in the middle of it.

All young mystical creatures were weak. They'd only get stronger with time and training. So, while her dragon had the strongest capability of our whole group, it wasn't yet so outrageously powerful that it overshadowed everyone else.

Phila clapped, and so did Exie.

"Ashlyn is so amazing," Exie said to us. "So talented."

Nini said nothing.

But my brother was always down for celebrations. He clapped as well and nodded along with Exie's words. "Yeah, that was amazing."

As Ashlyn left the field, she glanced over at me. I offered her a sarcastic salute. That made her smile. She replied with a lifted eyebrow, and I gave her a confident nod.

We were still speaking our own little language.

Exie must've caught me, because she glanced between me and Ashlyn and frowned. Her erlking even fluttered his way into my sight, blocking my view.

Before Captain Leon could call someone up to the stand, Raaza walked forward. His kitsune pranced along at his feet. He took his position and inhaled.

"So, kitsune arcanists evoke fox fire," Leon said, more to everyone else than Raaza. "It's a form of illusion. However, it's a *special* illusion. Fox fire can form tangible objects. An illusionary ball will bounce and interact with the environment. If you threw a fox fire ball at a stack of cups, you could knock them down and break them."

Everyone in class whispered curious musings. Leon set the target back up, though it appeared like it was ready for the grave.

I had to admit, I hadn't known that about fox fire. A kitsune's illusions were a little more impressive to me now.

Raaza seemed to know that already. He held out his hand, and a burst of his fox fire *whooshed* into existence. He created three gold coins, just like he had the other night. Then he threw them at the target.

The three coins struck the smoking wood. The target, once again, fell over. The coins really were tangible.

Then they puffed out of existence with a poof of smoke.

"All right," Knovak said, drawing everyone's attention. He fixed his large-brimmed hat and stepped out in front of everyone. His unicorn held his head high, his bone-horn glittering in the daylight. For a brief moment, he seemed like an old hero or knight from the storybooks. Knovak even placed his hands on his hips as he strode forward.

"It's my turn," he said as he dramatically swished out his

robes. He turned to face the target with a quick pivot on his heel. "I'm ready to test my evocation."

"Unicorn arcanists evoke *force*." Leon bent over, positioned the poor target back in place, and then stood straight. "Not wind. Think of it more like telekinesis... But without any of the finesse. It's a *shove* away from the arcanist, and that's all."

Knovak's lips curled down at the corners into a slight frown. "What do you mean, *that's all*?"

"I'm saying that's all that really happens. There's no... developing it further."

Nasbit raised his hand. Leon hesitantly pointed to the man.

"Unicorns are a *tier-two* creature," Nasbit said in his same professor voice. "The tier designations indicate the total potential for the creature. The higher the tier, the more they can potentially do. Since unicorns are weaker, their evocation isn't very powerful, and won't ever reach the maximum power or the versatility of other higher tier creatures.

The statement swirled around everyone in class. We had already learned that, but now that we were seeing it in practice, it hit harder.

Exie turned to Sorin, Nini, and me. "That Knovak is such a pretender." She rolled her beautiful green eyes. "He thinks he's *so* wealthy, but he isn't really. Now he thinks he should be *so* powerful, and we all know that isn't true. It makes me cringe thinking about it, really."

"Unicorns are amazing," Sorin said.

That surprised me.

Sorin didn't like Knovak, but here he was defending him.

"Unicorns are weak," Exie stated.

The whispering and muttering must've bothered Knovak. He stayed frozen in place, not moving or attempting to use his magic. Starling stepped close to him, and even poked Knovak in the arm with his unicorn horn.

"He's the only tier two," Exie mumbled under her breath.

It hadn't occurred to me until then. Everyone in class had a tier three or higher creature—except Nini and me, but ours were variables. We *could* have a powerful eldrin.

But not Knovak.

He *was* the weakest one here in terms of long-term potential. It seemed to weigh on him.

"Enough chatting," Leon said. He made sure the target was ready for the next evocation. "Let's go ahead and do this."

Knovak swallowed, and then forced himself to stand straight. He held out his hand, like everyone else, and then closed his eyes. After a few silent moments, a blast of force rushed from his hand and struck the target. The piece of wood hit the ground and cracked in half, finally dead.

It had done its duty admirably.

Leon smiled. "Perfect." Then he reached into the pocket of his trousers. "Now I have something a little special. A test. I have here a moving target. Whoever hits it first gets a special little prize at the end of class."

"What kind of prize?" Nasbit asked.

Leon pulled his hand out of his pocket, his fingers curled around an object, hiding it from view. "You'll see. Are you all ready?"

The five students who had practiced their evocation all nodded.

"Good. Because here it is."

CHAPTER 26

IMP TARGET

Captain Leon opened his hand.

He held... a bizarre toy?

It was a teacup saucer. With a face drawn on one side. Not a smiley face or something pleasant—a snide expression, like the saucer was mocking whoever had the misfortune of gazing upon it.

And the saucer had little ornamental wings. They reminded me of a dragonfly's in basic shape, but clearly magical. They fluttered around as soon as Leon released them.

I suspected the saucer would've taken off into the sky, had it not been for the fact that a string was tied to a hole in the bottom of the toy. Leon kept hold of the string, and the saucer fluttered around in the air, spinning in a limited circle. With a grunt, Leon knelt and then fixed the string to the ground. He used his fist to hammer in a small pin he withdrew from his other pocket.

Now that the saucer couldn't take off to the mountaintops, it just struggled against its minor restraint. The face on the saucer taunted us with a look of condescension.

"What is that?" Exie asked.

"It's *target practice*." Leon smiled as he stood. "You all will love this. I used this all the time when I trained as an arcanist. This is a trinket made with imp magic. Imps are known for their mischievous spirit, and this target fits the bill."

Mischievous?

Leon walked back over to the group. He clapped his hands together, rubbing dirt off his palms. "Who wants to go first? Whoever can hit the imp target will get the special prize at the end of class."

Everyone exchanged glances.

Sorin raised his hand. "Wait, but... What about *us?*" He motioned to Nini, Exie, and me. "We didn't get to practice."

"This will just be a moment," Leon said with a chuckle. "This will keep the *other* group busy while I teach you four all about your special evocation."

"Oh. Okay."

My brother crossed his arms and sighed. I felt his frustration. I wanted to practice my magic as well.

Phila was the first to step up. Her wind had been effective last time. When she held up her hand, she took a moment to breathe before releasing a gust of fearsome wind.

I thought she was going to hit the target, but at the *last moment*, the saucer with the face dodged out of the way. The tiny dragonfly wings whizzed into hyperactivity, and despite the string, it swirled around the wind.

The face...

It seemed smugger than before. Curse the abyssal hells—was that even possible?

Phila's eyes went wide. "It... dodged?"

Leon chuckled. He didn't reply, though. He just stroked his beard and watched from the sidelines. His cerberus also observed everything, though one head looked like he wanted to run over and eat the saucer. The head just panted and drooled.

Raaza evoked his fox fire, created a coin, and then threw it.

Way too slow. Much slower than the wind. The tricksy saucer easily dodged.

Nasbit, who had finally created a single palm-sized rock through his slow evocation, stepped forward. He was a large guy —more pillow than brick, but still—and he threw the rock as hard as he could. He was slower than even Raaza. His rock never got anywhere close to the saucer.

Then Knovak tried.

His blast of force missed as well.

He didn't say much as he walked away from the target. His unicorn circled close. "We'll get it next time!"

But Knovak didn't respond.

When it came time for Ashlyn, she strode over with confidence. The rest of the class paid close attention, everyone eager to see the destructive force of the dragon remove this little imp saucer from existence.

That was my hope, at least.

Ashlyn held up her hand, but instead of aiming for the saucer, like everyone else had, she aimed for the *string*. Brilliance. It was exactly what *I* would have done.

A bolt of lightning shot from her palm, crackling through the air. It was almost too fast to watch it travel through the air. Yet, somehow, Ashlyn *still* missed. The imp target had slammed itself onto the ground, ducking under her attack.

Everyone in our class gasped.

Then silence settled over us. The saucer flew back into the air, buzzing around with the same mischievous smile. Undamaged. Unlike Ashlyn's pride.

"You'll get it next time, Ashlyn!" Exie called out.

It surprised me. Ashlyn stood staring at the saucer, like the whole event had taken her by surprise as well. She clenched her jaw and then evoked her bolt of lightning a second time, this time aiming for the ground, where the saucer had ducked last time.

Her lightning scorched the grass and left a small crater. Ashlyn almost unrooted the pin holding the tiny saucer in place, but she had obviously avoided that.

She didn't hit the saucer. It didn't even fly close to the ground as though it knew what she had been planning.

"I think that target is cheating," Phila stated.

Captain Leon just chortled. He stroked his beard as though he were an amused villain in a stage play. This was clearly his intent—to frustrate us.

Ashlyn shot a third time—it almost hit the saucer—but the tricksy saucer nimbly moved aside, its little face appearing happier than before, though I couldn't prove that.

Ashlyn lowered her hand, clearly disgusted with the assignment. She narrowed her eyes, and somehow, I knew she was mulling over the situation, trying to formulate a plan of attack.

"You got this," I shouted, trying to be encouraging.

Twain snorted. "I don't know about that."

Ashlyn glanced over at me. She lifted an eyebrow. "Why haven't *you* taken a turn? You're the mighty mimic arcanist, after all. What was that you told me? You're the most magically powerful one in the class? Right?"

I hadn't meant to provoke her. Apparently, she thought my encouragement had been sarcastic.

What was *I* going to do? If no one else in class could hit the target, I wasn't about to out-aim them.

"Oh, no," I said with a nervous chuckle. "I'm over here. With the weirdos. Never mind me."

"I think you should try and show us all how it's done."

Everyone in class turned to face me. The mounting pressure to perform drove me to sweat, despite the cool mountain air. I tugged at my robes, stalling for some time while I thought about the situation. "I still haven't received any lessons."

Leon held up a hand, saving me. "I need to teach Gray how

his transformations work."

"Oh, he knows," Ashlyn stated. "Or are you saying you can't do it, Gray? You're all talk, is that it?"

Curse the abyssal hells. Now I had to do it. I couldn't let her statements stand. After a deep sigh, I headed for Ashlyn. What was I going to do? Have Twain transform into a dragon and miss just like she did?

Captain Leon snorted. "Oh, well, if Gray knows how to transform his mimic, he can try hitting the target. You can all try to your hearts' content."

He clearly thought we would never do it.

Which didn't bode well for my odds.

Everyone kept their gaze on me. My brother, Nini, Raaza, Nasbit, Exie, Ashlyn, Phila—even their eldrin. The only ones who *didn't* seem that interested were Knovak and his unicorn. They stood at the side of the field, away from the others. Knovak's shoulders were slumped, and he focused most of his attention on the ground.

"You can do it, Gray," Sorin shouted.

Twain clung to my shoulder. "Uh, what should I transform into? Everyone else failed already. You think you're a better aim than those people?"

"No."

"So... what's the plan?"

"I'm a mimic arcanist," I whispered. "I'm not limited to one evocation. I'll use that to my advantage. Somehow."

"Spoiler alert: shooting lightning *and* then wind isn't going to do much."

"I'll think of something."

"We're already out of time!" Twain hissed into my ear as I reached Ashlyn's side.

Ashlyn looked me up and down, and then turned to face the distant target. "Well, I can't wait to see you in action."

"That's what everyone says," I said as I rotated my shoulders.

That got her chuckling to herself. Then Ashlyn hardened her expression and faced me. "What're you planning?"

"You'll see. It's a surprise." I had no idea what I was doing.

Ashlyn's dragon flashed his fangs. "I'm betting he fails."

"You're just jealous you didn't bond with Gray first," Twain said with a hiss at the end of his words.

"I have no use for overconfident tricksters."

Ashlyn held up a hand. "Let's not judge him too quickly, Ecrib."

"Thank you," I said.

"We'll just judge you *after* you miss," she replied sweetly. Then she strode back over to the rest of the class, leaving me to my challenge.

Twain shuddered. Then he narrowed his eyes at me, his ears flat back. "We better not miss now. It'll be so embarrassing if we do... We might as well bury ourselves in a fresh grave."

"It's fine. We've got this."

My eldrin growled, his voice tiny and cute, even if he was trying to express doubt. I patted him and scratched behind his ears. Then I closed my eyes and tried to focus on the magic. The threads—like I had felt last time—were so numerous. Twain could transform into a great many things.

The typhoon dragon.

The cerberus.

None of those would work, though. When I scrunched my eyes, I almost felt like I felt the imp magic in the saucer... Would that help me? Probably not. I needed something else. Something to outsmart the target.

But what?

Then I felt a string. Something faint. Something distant. Who did it belong to? Someone familiar. Someone I had met in the headmaster's office.

That gave me a brilliant idea.

I mentally tugged on that string of magic.

Twain leapt off my shoulder. I gritted my teeth as my forehead burned with his transformation. Which thread had I pulled? The *ice*. The assassin who protected the headmaster had used ice. He had frozen everything in the study.

That was the skill I needed in this situation.

Twain bubbled and shifted, his whole body growing larger in a mere second's time. I didn't know what he was going to change into. I didn't even know what the assassin's eldrin had been—I just felt his distant magic.

Twain transformed into a wolf.

Well, an emaciated wolf. His fur was patchy and black, practically sickly. His ribs were visible, and his tail rough. And his face was covered with a skull mask.

It was a wendigo—a creature of death and frost.

The whole class gasped. Even Captain Leon's mouth fell open. No one had been expecting me to use a mystical creature from somewhere else in the Academy.

But I didn't have much time. Twain couldn't remain transformed for long.

I held out my hand and smirked. "Let's hit us a target."

I did as Leon had instructed. I imagined pushing magic out of my body.

Ice erupted from my person. It coursed through my veins and washed over the grass. The frost and rime shot all the way over to the imp target. Then the ice traveled up the string holding the saucer. The saucer tried to fly away, its dragonfly wings buzzing with all its might. But it wasn't enough. The frost caught it midflight.

And then the thing fell to the ground with a *thunk*.

The power of the wendigo...

I hadn't realized it would be so vast. I couldn't handle it.

It was like trying to lift something well outside my physical capabilities. Or trying to shove a watermelon through a keyhole. My muscles hurt, my chest twisted in agony, and my heart fluttered as though it were being squeezed. The moment I *could* release the string of magic, I did.

I gasped for air as Twain transformed back into his mimic body. But I wasn't done. I had frozen the target, but my class could still argue that I hadn't struck it. So, with what little strength and time I had left, I tugged on the string for the typhoon dragon.

Twain transformed a second time.

His body morphed—growing scales, and fins, and large fangs—until he appeared identical to Ecrib, Ashlyn's typhoon dragon.

With her stolen magic, I held up my hand. Then I unleashed a bolt of lightning and hit the imp target. It was still frozen on the ground, after all. Sure, the ice was melting, since I had lost my wendigo powers, but it happened slow enough for me to hit it with my lightning.

The typhoon dragon was a hatchling. Its magic hadn't burned me like the wendigo. This was more my speed, but the damage had already been done from the blast of ice. Everything hurt as I turned around.

The whole class remained quiet, their eyes wide.

I sarcastically bowed, but that was a mistake. I almost didn't have the strength to stand straight afterward. No one did or said anything, though. It made me worry.

Twain shifted back into his cat form. He huffed and puffed, and I felt the same way. I was exhausted. The wendigo had been too much. Its magic was more than I could handle, but I didn't want to appear weak. Even though my legs ached, I bent over, scooped Twain up into my arms, and then forced myself to amble over to my brother.

That was when Phila clapped. "Wow! Impressive!"

The others clapped afterward, even Ashlyn and Knovak.

I hurt way too much to acknowledge their applause. I gritted my teeth to prevent myself from groaning in agony. It was as if I had run fifty miles and never once stopped to rest. My muscles practically seized up on me.

No one seemed to notice my internal struggle.

Except for Sorin. He jogged to my side, his eyes wide.

"Are you okay?" he whispered.

I forced myself to nod. But under my breath, I said, "I feel like I'm dying. Don't let anyone know."

Sorin nervously laughed. He walked with me over to Nini, Exie, and Leon, his arm around my shoulder, tight enough that he carried some of my weight.

"That was amazing," Sorin said. "A dazzling demonstration defining your dashing and debonair demeanor!"

"Me, too," Twain grumbled in my arms. "I'm dashing..."

"Definitely." Sorin patted his head.

"I agree," the shadow around Sorin's feet said. It was Thurin. "And excellent use of powers. It shows your versatility, which is important for mimic arcanists."

Captain Leon cleared his throat as I approached. Then he clapped his hands together once and motioned to the rest of the class. "The imp target will be back up and running in a few moments. Everyone else, practice your aim. I have to help these three."

"Not four?" Exie asked.

"Clearly I don't need to teach Gray the basics," Leon stated. "But you three... Let's go over your powers together."

"Wait," I said. "Didn't you say I'd get a prize? Or something?"

Leon frowned. "Er. I made that up. I didn't think anyone would actually hit the target today." He rubbed the back of his neck. "Sorry about that. I'll make it up to you. You have my word as a knight."

"Uh-huh. In the meantime, can I go sit down?" I struggled not to double over. "Just for a moment."

"Of course. Sit on the side of the field until I call you over."

CHAPTER 27

A MULTITUDE OF CLASSES

I rested on the side of the field, watching the others go about their practice. When the ice faded, the imp saucer went back to buzzing around through the sky, evading attacks left and right.

Captain Leon motioned for Exie to step forward. She and her little fairy king were pointed away from the rest of the class.

"Erlkings evoke light," Leon said to her. "Powerful light. They also *manipulate* light, which is how they create their illusions. Unlike fox fire, which creates something tangible—physical—your illusions will be visual only."

Exie held up her hand. After a full minute of hesitation, she eventually evoked light. It was small, the illumination of a single candle with a thin wick. Nothing special. When she got more powerful, though...

"Practice over here," Leon said.

Then the captain took Nini and Sorin away from Exie. He grouped them together, the shadows flickering around their feet from my brother's knightmare.

"You two evoke *terror*," Leon stated, his tone somber. "You force people to see their fears—experience them. It's not visible, but the people you affect will see things, I guarantee."

"Terror?" Nini said, glancing down at her hands. Then she turned to her reaper.

The floating cloak and scythe nodded its empty hood.

Sorin motioned to his shadow. His knightmare, Thurin, lifted out of the darkness, forming into a hollow suit of armor with missing pieces. Thurin's feather cape waved in the wind. He had a gallant demeanor.

"You create terrors?" Sorin asked.

"Indeed," Thurin replied. "It's a form of poetic punishment. Those who face me will face their actual nightmares."

Waste turned his empty hood to face Thurin. "Terror and fear are the songs of death. As a reaper, I sing my opponents to sleep."

Nini's eyes went wide. She said nothing, but she stared at the hood of her reaper for a thoughtful moment.

I didn't pay much attention after that. With an exhausted sigh, I lied back on the grass and closed my eyes. Twain curled up on my chest. Within a few moments, his breathing was even. The cold mountain air didn't seem as troubling as before. The freshness didn't compare to the salt of the ocean, but it had its own allure.

The stomp of a large creature pulled me out of my musings.

I opened my eyes.

Sticks, the cerberus, loomed over me, his three heads panting. I stared at him, too tired to sit up straight. Would he drool on me? I hoped not.

"Yes?" I asked.

"My arcanist asked me to make sure you knew of your powers," Sticks said with all three heads at the same time. They spoke in relative harmony. "A mimic is a shapeshifting eldrin. Shapeshifters are rare. And while some shapeshifters can transform into a great many things, mimics can only become mystical creatures and items."

"Items?" I asked.

I *had* been able to sense the magic of the imp target.

"Transforming into an item is difficult," Twain said with a yawn. "I don't like doing it. I say we stick to eldrin."

"At least for now," I muttered.

Someday, when we were powerful and had mastered our abilities, I'd want to branch out and make sure Twain could transform into all sorts of things. That would be helpful.

"You seem tired," Sticks stated.

I closed my eyes again. "Yeah."

"You're still a new arcanist. If you want to improve yourself, you need to stand and use your magic more."

He was right. I wouldn't get better if I just sat here. After a long exhale, I forced myself to my feet. Twain tumbled off my chest, but I caught him before he hit the ground. Then I lifted him up to my shoulder.

Then I glanced around. Ashlyn was opposite the imp saucer, trying to hit it once again. She held her hand out, studying her target. When she unleashed her bolt of lightning, it wasn't a straight shot, like before. Her lightning arced—it practically curved around and hit the imp saucer from the side.

The mischievous little target hadn't been expecting that. It was fried by the lightning, and collapsed to the ground.

"What the?" Leon shouted. He jogged over to his item. "Dang it all. Students just keep gettin' better and better every year... Took the last class weeks before they hit my little target."

I mostly ignored him. Instead, I glanced over at Ashlyn. She had her eyes on me, smiling a coy, yet confident, smile.

I mouthed, "*It took you several tries.*"

"*But at least I didn't cheat,*" she mouthed back.

Yet another silent conversation between us.

I hadn't cheated, though. My mimic abilities were perfectly

legal. What else was I supposed to do? She was just jealous, obviously.

The others in our class applauded and cheered for Ashlyn. They ran over to her and then patted her on the shoulder, telling her what an amazing job she had done. It was impressive—arcing her evocation was a clever move—but it wasn't *that* impressive. My demonstration had been grander.

I thought.

Exie clapped the loudest. "You're amazing, Ashlyn! That was marvelous!"

It didn't really matter. I had other, more pressing, problems.

The next day was history class.

We entered our classroom, and everyone took their usual seats. Today, our professor was none other than Piper. She was already here when we arrived.

Piper sat at the desk, her elbows on top, her posture slumped. Her rizzel eldrin sat on top of the desk with a large mug held between his paws. When I walked by the desk, I caught a whiff of the contents.

It wasn't coffee or water.

It was hard liquor. Definitely. It burned my nostrils slightly when I inhaled it.

I gave the rizzel an odd glance. "Should you really be drinking during class?"

Reevy sipped from the side of the mug. "What? *I'm* not the professor."

I didn't have a comeback for that.

Bemused, I took a seat at the table with Sorin and Nini. Her reaper hovered close to the table, and Sorin's knightmare shifted through the shadows, creating enough haunting ambience for a graveyard.

"Gray," Sorin whispered as I sat next to him. "I think Knovak isn't feeling well."

"Why's that?"

"He just doesn't look himself."

I glanced over my shoulder. Knovak sat at the back of the room, at a table all his own, with only his unicorn for company. He didn't wear any of his ostentatious clothing, nor did he seem energetic. Without his flair, Knovak really was a plain guy. Dirty-blond hair. Slightly tanned skin. No tattoos, no scars, no real distinguishing features. He was lean, but not impressive. Just... average.

Almost forgettable.

Everyone else in class seemed content to ignore him. Even *I* had been. Only Sorin seemed aware of the change. Or perhaps he was the only one who cared.

"He does look off," I muttered.

"Will you talk to him?" Sorin asked.

I narrowed my eyes and shot my brother a glower. "Why?"

"Knovak and I don't get along."

"So why do you care about him?"

"I just don't like that he's so upset. He didn't say a word last night when we all went to bed. He just curled up in his blankets and remained quiet all night."

I had been too exhausted to notice. With a sigh, I replied, "Fine. I'll speak to him."

My brother offered me a pleased grin, but I ignored it. What was with him? Knovak had been the bully on the dock, yet Sorin was concerned about his mental wellbeing.

"Attention, class," Piper said as she slowly got to her feet. "My name is Professor Piper Jenkins, but you can just call me Professor Piper. I'm not too fond of my last name nowadays." She pinched the bridge of her nose and then turned to face the chalkboard. With slow and shaky movements, she wrote her name out for us all to see.

Reevy sipped his liquor and nodded along as though he approved of this message.

"I'm your history professor," Piper said. She returned to her desk. "Everyone open to page three and read the first chapter."

The rustle of books filled the classroom as everyone did as they were instructed. The first chapter was titled: THE TRIUMVIRATE OF ARCANISTS IN ANCIENT TIMES.

It was... ancient history. About one of the first massive cities ever built by arcanists. It was in a time before arcanists could imbue magic—before they could make magical items—back when they were constantly warring with each other.

That was a long time ago, when the world was more barbaric, and people killed each other in brutal and often public ways. Not my favorite subject. It had always given Sorin nightmares when we were kids.

Nasbit raised his hand.

For a long time, Piper didn't notice. She rubbed at her temples, mumbling something to herself. Reevy leaned over and tapped her shoulder. Then he pointed to Nasbit.

Piper straightened her posture. "Yes?"

"I was hoping we could talk about the God-Arcanists War," Nasbit said. "I read about the attack on Thronehold, and the arcane plague, and I was hoping to learn more about that."

"That's not until later in the year. Right now, we're going to learn about the building of Kurthage, and how that city shaped a nation."

"But I wanted to know about how the plague and—"

"We'll get to it eventually," Piper said, holding up a finger. "Trust me. It's very interesting. But first we need some context." She pointed at Nasbit's book. "Go ahead and read that first chapter."

Nasbit flipped through the pages. "It's a hundred and eight pages..."

"Exactly. It should take you most of the class."

A round of groans circled the room. Piper didn't seem to notice. Or perhaps she didn't care. She pulled a small book out from the drawer of her desk and leaned over it. Reevy sipped his drink, never moving from his spot. He curled his white tail around the mug and practically hugged it.

Everyone went to their silent reading.

But before we got too deep into our studies, I quietly stood and walked over to Piper's desk. The others in class regarded me with odd glances, but then they returned to their books or whispered conversations.

When I reached the professor's desk, I said, "Good morning."

Piper lifted an eyebrow. Her silky black hair was tangled slightly. She swept it to the side to get a better look at me. "Is it?"

"Do you mind if I ask you something really quick? It's important."

"All right." She leaned forward. "What is it?"

"Are you good friends with Professor Helmith? She taught our class the other day, and she seemed sick."

"Sick?"

"Yeah. She was pale. Said a few random things."

Piper waved away my concerns. "Professor Helmith sticks to herself. She's always in the basement, helping with the trinket and artifact creation."

Reevy sipped his booze. "She doesn't mingle with us much." Then he hiccupped.

"So, you're not good friends with her?" I asked.

Piper shook her head. "No. But we're good associates, if anyone asks."

That was an odd answer. And not the one I was looking for. I *needed* to find someone who was close to Professor Helmith so that I could ask them about her strange behavior. I wanted to figure out what was happening. I had so many things I wanted to speak with her about.

"Who else works in the basement?" I asked.

Piper ran a hand down her face. "Hm? I dunno. Professor Zahn? He's another one I barely interact with."

I had heard his name before. The woman in the laundry room had mentioned his name. He was a recluse, I supposed. So far, I had yet to meet him.

He was the one I needed to speak with.

"Thank you," I said as I tapped my knuckles on Piper's desk. "Really appreciate it."

She just waved me away.

After I returned to my seat, I flipped open my history book and scanned the sentences. When I glanced over at Nasbit, I caught him just reading ahead. He had turned to a later chapter of the book and was clearly reading about the God-Arcanists War. I appreciated his boldness. Clearly, Piper didn't care, she just didn't want to be bothered with it.

I didn't feel like studying history at the moment.

I set Twain on the table. "We should practice our magic," I whispered to him. "I need to get used to identifying magic. When I close my eyes, and feel the threads of magic, sometimes it's difficult to know who's who."

Twain smiled and nodded. "That's a good idea."

And I could do it without making a scene. My ability to sense magic wasn't flashy. And when I closed my eyes to focus, it wasn't like Piper would care about that either. She clearly had her own problems to focus on.

CHAPTER 28

BIRTHRIGHT OR MENTALITY

The dining hall was a great place to socialize.

Everyone gathered around large tables with individual firepits. The food at the center table was always hot, fresh, and delicious. There was such a variety, it made me wonder where the Academy got its supplies from.

Tonight, they served us dozens of types of bread with meat and vegetables on the side. I made a plate for Twain and then went to sit at a table with Sorin and Nini. As I walked through the dining hall, I took note of everyone else. Humans were creatures of habit, it seemed. Everyone sat at the same table they always did, since the first day they arrived.

A large group of girls gathered near a table in the corner. It wasn't just first-years—girls from every year of the Academy congregated there.

I recognized Ashlyn and her typhoon dragon. Exie sat there as well. They laughed and giggled and made enough noise for a small platoon of soldiers.

There was a table at the front of the room for professors and staff. Piper and a woman I had never met were eating in relative quiet. The other woman—probably a professor, given her robes —read from a book while she ate.

Did *she* know Professor Helmith? Perhaps I should speak to her.

I set my plate—and Twain's plate—down at my table. It was relatively small, but warm. Sorin and Nini were the only others who sat with me. That was fine. I enjoyed their company.

"I'll be back in a moment," I muttered, my gaze locked on the mystery professor.

"Wait," Sorin said, holding up a hand.

I turned around, my eyebrow lifted. "Hm?"

"You said you'd speak with Knovak."

"Right now?"

Sorin pointed to the corner opposite the girls. There was a single table—one of the smaller ones—where Knovak ate his food with his unicorn. It was a sad sight. Everyone else avoided the table as though there was an active rain cloud over it.

"All right," I muttered. "I'll go speak with him."

Sorin flashed me an earnest smile.

Twain stayed on my shoulder as I headed through the dining hall. People got up and down from their seats constantly in order to get seconds or thirds of their food. It encouraged a lot of mingling. People had impromptu conversations throughout the room, which I appreciated. A few people even waved as I walked by, though I didn't recognize them.

I *did* spot Ramona, the black pegasus, as she flew overhead. A pixie was chasing her as they zoomed through the air playing tag. The younger mystical creatures were adorable. They'd soon grow older, though.

Then I took a seat at Knovak's table, right on the bench beside him.

His unicorn, Starling, stomped his hooves and snorted. "Why are *you* here?"

"Calm down, ya prancy pony," Twain said with a cute little growl.

"Hmpf!"

Knovak glanced over. Without his unique clothing, he was tragically plain. "Can I help you?"

"Is there a reason you're moping?" I asked. "You're really being a downer."

There was a long second of silence between us. I figured he wasn't going to answer, but then Knovak went to poking at his food with a spoon. "Everyone in our class hates me or thinks I'm a pretentious loser."

"Who cares?" I shot off—it was my gut response, and I couldn't hold back. "Just prove them wrong."

Knovak whirled on me as though I had slapped him in the face. "Have you *seen* our class? It's a who's who of important nobility and influential people! I'm rubbing elbows with the elites, and they want nothing to do with me."

"Elites?" I didn't know much about our classmates other than their names and eldrin.

"Yes. Of course. Exie Lolian comes from a long line of dukes and duchesses. Her mother is a famous mystical creature breeder, and her father governs an entire trade port. And don't even get me started on Nasbit *Dodger*. That whole family created a trinket-crafting empire after the God-Arcanists War. They sell at every major trading hub!"

"They do?" I asked, honestly not aware of any of this.

Knovak shook his head at me. "Both Exie and Nasbit come from families with so much wealth it puts mine to shame. And the Gentz House is very well off, mind you."

"Yeah, I got it." I leaned in closer to him. "What about Ashlyn? What do you know about her?"

"She's from the *Kross* family." Knovak said that like I should know something. When I was silent, he continued, "Her paternal grandfather was the Marshall of the Southern Seas, and her maternal grandmother was Queen of the Jade Isles. Her father is an archduke, and her mother is the Grand Artificer at the Elliot Library."

"That's... impressive."

I was the son of a candlemaker.

And that was about it.

Knovak slowly nodded like he couldn't believe my ignorance. Even his unicorn nodded. My irritation was quickly eclipsing my embarrassment.

"Even Phila Hon comes from a powerful magical society that often secludes themselves from the rest of the world," Knovak stated. He returned to glaring at his food. "She grew up in a palace. Even *she* wants nothing to do with me. You want to know why?"

I didn't, but I was already neck-deep in this conversation. "Why?"

"Because I'm *new money*. I'm not descended from royalty or nobility or some famous arcanist." Knovak crushed some of his food with his spoon. Then he stopped halfway through, and frowned.

He was silent.

His unicorn nudged him. "It'll be okay, my arcanist."

Knovak jerked away from Starling's touch. "No. It won't. My father told me to make friends while I was here. I'm supposed to be networking—helping the Gentz family by making allies." He motioned to himself. "But look at me. No one will even sit at my table." He sighed. "They all see right through me. I'm just... some kid from the islands. No real money. No real influence. Even my eldrin is... the weakest one here."

"Your father wants you to make friends?" I asked.

"It's a privilege to attend Astra Academy. So many arcanists get turned down every year. My father did, when he was younger." Knovak sighed even harder as he leaned half his body onto the table. "I'm the first in my family to attend."

I didn't know tons of people were rejected every year. It made what Headmaster Venrover did for us all the more special. I never properly thanked him...

"You're not a pretender," Starling muttered. "You're trying your hardest."

Knovak shook his head. "No. They're all right. I'm not... I'm not really one of them."

I grabbed the man's shoulder. Knovak stared at me in surprise. I just glared at him. "Listen—there are only two options. Either *nobility* is a birthright or it's a mentality. If it's a birthright then, it's an immutable quality that you either have or you don't. And you don't, so you don't have to worry about it any longer. But if it's a mentality..."

"What do you mean?" Knovak asked as he sat up straighter.

"Hundreds of years ago, the nobles were just the arcanists who cared for the land and their people. They were in charge of protecting everyone from bandits or warlords, and making roads, and collecting taxes, and using their magic to make life easier."

"Yes. Okay. And?"

"The role of a noble was leadership and self-sacrifice. They led troops into battle. They used their magic for everyone else's sake. But kids born into wealthy families don't do any of that anymore. They haven't earned their wealth and status—they just have it because of their parents."

"Well, okay. And?"

"Those kids aren't dedicated to using their power and influence to help others—*they're* the pretenders. A real noble would dedicate himself to improving the land, the people, and the nation."

Knovak knitted his eyebrows together. "I don't quite understand what you're saying."

"I'm saying the heart of nobility is to hold yourself to a higher standard." I playfully smacked Knovak on the chest. He flinched, but I continued regardless. "You need to hold yourself to a higher standard of duty, personal accountability, self-sacrifice—even a higher standard of life. That's the mentality of nobility. And if you do that, people will notice."

"You make it sound so... noble." His eyes widened a bit as though the meaning of the word had just dawned on him.

Starling clopped his hooves on the floor. Then he held his snout up. "Well, as an arcanist, Knovak is already among the ruling class, but I do see what you're saying about this mentality. Too bad *you* don't follow your own advice."

I chuckled. "I never said I wanted to make friends with our classmates."

"Still."

"And you think that doing this will earn their admiration?" Knovak asked.

"I think it'll earn a lot of people's admiration." I shrugged. "And it couldn't hurt, right? That's what you want? To make your dad proud by making lots of friends?"

Knovak narrowed his eyes. "Are you making fun of me?"

I stood from the table. Clearly, Knovak was feeling better. "Well, you look chipper. I'm going to go back to my table. Try not to get too depressed in the future."

My odd statement obviously left him baffled. I didn't care. As long as he didn't get too depressed, Sorin wouldn't ask me to handle the situation, and I could focus on the things that really mattered.

Like Professor Helmith.

I turned to the professors' table, but I was already too late. Piper sat by herself, her rizzel eldrin the only other occupant of the table. The other professor had left.

With a sigh, I headed back to my table.

"Do you believe all that?" Twain asked into my ear. "Everything you just said to Knovak?"

"No."

"N-No?" Twain poked his kitten nose into my cheek. "*Then why did you say it?*"

"Because I knew it would make Knovak feel better." I shrugged. "I can't really tell Sorin *no*, so I just have to handle this problem as quickly as possible, and if that means making up a little speech about how anyone can be noble, then so be it."

Twain grumbled something and then huffed.

When I sat back down, I realized my brother was at the food table, piling another helping onto his plate. His knightmare swirled around his feet, never emerging from the shadows. Did knightmares need to eat? Did they even have a stomach?

Nini's reaper didn't eat anything, either. It just watched as she picked at her bread.

"Did you speak with Knovak?" Nini asked me. She fixed her glasses as she nibbled on the crisp crust.

"Yeah, I cheered him up," I said as I pulled my plate closer.

Nini glanced over at the large table with all the girls. "I wish I could just go over there and speak with them."

"Why?" Twain asked. "They're so loud."

"I wanted to make friends with *someone* in my dorm. But none of them will speak to me."

Being a reaper arcanist was really taking its toll. I understood —Waste was creepy—but surely everyone realized it wasn't *that* bad.

"Maybe have your reaper hang out in the treehouse while you speak to them," I said.

Nini shook her head. "No. That won't help. They just don't like me."

"Try striking up a casual conversation. I'm sure you'll be surprised." I motioned to the dining hall. "And do it in a public area. Everyone is so worried about appearances—no one will make a scene. It'll be fine."

"Maybe."

Sorin returned to the table with a plate overflowing with meat and bread. He had grabbed four personal rolls—enough for a whole family—and at least a pound of braised beef. Some spilled onto the table as he set the plate down.

"We should practice evoking our terrors more," Sorin said to Nini.

"Yeah," she mumbled into her bread.

"We don't want to disappoint Captain Leon when we see him next."

"Hm."

After that, the conversation died as we focused on our food.

CHAPTER 29

PROFESSOR ZAHN

In the middle of the night, I awoke feeling cold.

The window was closed, and somehow, though I wasn't sure why, the floors were warm. I wrapped myself in my blankets, threw my legs off the side, and pressed my bare feet onto the wood. The heat spread from my toes to my knees to my shoulders, and finally through my frigid ears. It was wonderful.

The dorm was dark, though.

It reminded me of my dreams.

I had been sitting on a black rock—one that appeared wet and shiny—waiting for Professor Helmith. But she never came. I was just alone, without Twain or Sorin or anyone else. It seemed haunting, now that I thought back on it.

Sorin rolled over on his bed. The moon provided enough light for me to see he was awake. He didn't say anything—he just pulled his blankets up to his broad shoulders and tried to position himself as comfortably as possible.

"Sorin," I whispered, trying not to wake Raaza or Knovak. "Do you think the other students in our class are avoiding us? The ones from high families."

"Definitely," Sorin whispered back.

I hadn't been expecting that answer. I thought he would've said something more pleasant, or given them the benefit of the doubt.

"What makes you say that?"

Sorin shrugged. "The four of us are the only ones in this dorm. The other ten boys all went to the other room. And they all seem to avoid us. No one's talking about how you hit that target, either, even though it was impressive. It's like they want to forget it even happened."

"Because admitting I did it so easily makes them look bad," I muttered.

"Yeah. But it also means they're definitely avoiding us."

Although I wanted to shrug off the situation, and not care, it still stung. I wanted to make friends with my arcanist peers, after all. I wasn't like Knovak, who seemed on a mission to make friends for business reasons. This was more personal. This was the first time I was interacting with peers outside my island, and their rejection seemed unfair somehow.

What was I to do?

Nothing. I'd just have to show them they were making a mistake.

"I think you should get some sleep," Sorin whispered. "You've seemed extra tired lately."

"Yeah..."

I had been practicing my magic with Twain whenever I could. I would sense threads of magic and attempt to identify them. Thinking about it reminded me that Twain was asleep at the foot of my bed. I glanced over and found his little orange body snuggled in the blankets. He hadn't gone to the treehouse, even though Starling and Miko had.

Thurin was still here—the second shadow that never left my brother's side.

I rested back on my bed. "Good night, Sorin."

"Night, Gray."

The next day, we all gathered in our classroom after breakfast.

Everyone took their usual seats, whispering excited conversation between each other. Today we would meet a new professor. I had hoped they would be here before us, but that wasn't the case. The room had been empty.

Knovak was back to his colorful clothing. His robes covered most of his outfit, but his large hat, and red shirt, were still visible. He seemed a little more confident, though he still sat away from most people.

Which was good, I supposed.

While everyone gossiped, and the mystical creatures wandered around, Raaza got up from his table and walked over to Sorin, Nini, and me. His hair was slicked back, and the claw scars on his face were more visible than before.

He had four scars in total. One on his cheek, one on his chin, one near his hairline, and one on his lip. Like a claw had swiped him, but not too deeply. They were white, and obvious, but I tried not to stare.

Raaza set his books down and took a seat at our table.

"Hey," Sorin said with a wave. "Good morning."

"Hello." Raaza turned his attention to his bestiary. He read through a couple of lines and then turned the page.

Nini gave me a questioning look. I just shrugged. Raaza didn't seem too bad. Although, he wasn't very likeable, either.

Before I could question the man about his decision, the door opened. Our new professor walked into the room, his robes billowing behind him as he walked.

He was wiry and walked with confidence. His muddy brown hair went to his shoulders, some of which was tied back to prevent any hair from getting in his eyes. He wore glasses—like Nini—though his were small, like he only needed them for reading.

The arcanist mark on his forehead...

It had a rizzel twisted through the seven-points of the star, the little ferret body flexible but distinct. He was a rizzel arcanist, just like Piper.

But that wasn't the detail that fascinated me the most. This professor had tattoos similar to Professor Helmith. Glowing tattoos of pink, blue, and gray were wrapped around his hands, running the length of his knuckles and on his palms. They practically sparkled, but it was faint enough that it didn't distract.

The tattoos disappeared under the sleeves of his robes, and it made me wonder how many he had.

And why.

The man took a seat at a desk at the front of the room. He placed a couple of books down, and then a rizzel popped into existence with a puff of silvery glitter. It stood on the desk, its nose twitching as the professor patted its head.

Everyone quieted down as the professor readied himself.

But...

The professor seemed distracted. He mumbled things to himself as he spread out papers and flipped through pages of his books. At one point, he turned around and wrote: PROFES on the chalkboard, like he was about to write his name, but then he got distracted and returned to his paperwork.

The quiet stretched on.

Then Exie started whispering to Ashlyn and Phila. Their mumbled conversation grew louder and louder.

I figured the professor's rizzel would say something, but the little creature never did. When I glanced over at it, I was surprised to find it staring at me. Its blue eyes were practically drilling a hole through my head, that was how intense the gaze seemed.

But then it turned away.

The professor cleared his throat. He turned back around to the chalkboard and finished writing his name. PROFESSOR ZAHN.

"Hello, everyone," he said as he faced the class. "I'm Professor Zahn, just in case you can't read the board. I do several things here at the Academy. Mostly trinket and artifact creation."

Nasbit raised his hand.

This clearly confused Professor Zahn. He stared for a prolonged moment, a half-smile on his face. "A question already? All right..."

"Do you work in the basement?" Nasbit asked.

"Well, Astra Academy doesn't really have a *basement* per se. The term *basement* is more slang than reality. The rooms below this floor are mostly subterranean, but some of them exit lower on the mountain, you see. I like to refer to them as the foundation floors."

"And you work there?"

"Yes. All trinket and artifact creation are done on the foundation floors."

"Is it haunted?"

A few hushed giggles circled the room. Nasbit turned a bit pink, his cheeks changing color first, but he still seemed interested in knowing the answer. His stone golem stomped around the table and stood directly by his side.

This subject matter interested me, mostly because of how it related to Professor Helmith.

She worked in the basement. And supposedly, Professor Zahn was her friend.

I needed to find a time to question him.

"The foundation floors aren't haunted," Professor Zahn

stated. Then he hemmed and hawed, and added, "But there are mystical creatures that show up from time to time. They can be described as ghost-like, but that's not entirely correct."

"So it *is* haunted?" Exie asked.

"There are plenty of mystical creatures who some call *undead*, but the correct term is *arisen*. Things like ghouls, zombies, and the bake-kujira are all creatures with a different existence than from our own."

Nasbit scooted forward on his seat. "My older brother said that the basement of the Academy was haunted because he saw souls there. Not mystical creatures. The souls of people."

Professor Zahn nervously laughed. Then he shook his head. "Well, that's strange, to say the least. While every arcanist has a soul, most never see anything related to it. It's more a magical concept. People have souls that create raw magic. That magic is given form through bonding with a mystical creature. The soul then feeds the creature, and ages it —causes it grow."

"I know," Nasbit said. He flipped through one of his books. "It's all written out here in the bestiary. But I was wondering, since you work in the basement, what does—"

"Foundation floors."

"—since you work in the foundation floors, what does a soul look like?"

Professor Zahn tugged at the collar of his black-and-blue robes.

He hadn't even told us what kind of class he was teaching. This entire conversation had spiraled out of control because Nasbit had a bunch of wild questions he wanted answered.

That didn't seem to bother Professor Zahn. He just kept diving deeper into this random discussion about whether the basement was haunted, like he had no control over the situation —or perhaps because he liked to answer questions.

"They say you can't see a soul," Professor Zahn stated. "Well, that's not entirely accurate. You can only see them in the abyssal hells—the realm of the dead."

"Is it a real place?" Nasbit's eyes grew large. Then he whispered, "Is it possible the abyssal hells are in the basement?"

"Foundation floors," Zahn corrected. Then he held up a finger. "And I'm glad you asked that because I'm your professor for *magical fundamentals*. In my class, we will discuss the origins of magic, the limits of magic, and even the theories surrounding magic."

He turned to the chalkboard and drew a circle.

The entire time, his rizzel remained still and quiet. It just sat at the edge of the desk, observing the class with its bright blue eyes.

Not a word.

It seemed strange. Reevy, Piper's rizzel, was talkative, even when hungover.

Professor Zahn pointed to the circle. "Let's pretend this is our world, Vardin. At the center of the world is its heart. Its core. Most magical theories say souls originated from this location."

Nasbit opened his notebook and grabbed his charcoal pencil. He wrote notes, including drawing the exact same diagram that the professor was drawing. He was the only one doing that, though. Everyone else paid attention, engrossed by the information.

"They say life and magic first entered the world when there was an earthquake," Professor Zahn said. He drew a crack on the world. "And souls were freed. During this time, the sun and moon hung in the sky at the same time. Mystical creatures were born, and the first arcanists came into existence. Whenever someone died, they returned to the center of the world, but only after passing through the crack."

"There's a physical canyon?" Exie asked, her wide eyes on the drawing.

Professor Zahn nervously chuckled. "Well, uh, that's up for

debate. You see, this pathway to the center of the world is what we call the *abyssal hells*. Which means the abyssal hells can't be in the basement of Astra Academy. Sorry."

"Foundation floors," Nasbit corrected.

The professor cursed at himself under his breath. "The kids have me doing it now," he mumbled. Then he shook his head. "Listen, the reason *abyssal* is in the name is because the word *abyssal* refers to the darkest depths of the ocean. According to magical theory, this crack—or *fissure*—that leads to the center of our magical world, is far below the ocean waves and impossible to get to for the living."

The classroom buzzed with excitement.

"I thought the abyssal hells weren't real," Exie said.

Nasbit turned to face her. "It's real. It has to be real."

"Why? It sounds fake to me. It's a place you can't even get to. It's like... an old sailors' tale or something."

"There is some debate about whether the abyssal hells exist," Professor Zahn stated. Then he drew an upside-down gate on the crack of his world drawing. "Some say it's a myth, but others have offered evidence of its existence. You see, several ancient documents talk about the sun and moon in the sky at the same time, and the creation of the upside-down gates. Why would anyone write about that if it weren't true?"

"Aren't there Death Lords in the abyssal hells?" Nasbit asked.

The classroom fell silent.

Professor Zahn stopped drawing. For a short moment, it seemed as though everyone held their breath.

What were the Death Lords? I didn't know this one. They sounded like something my father would hate to discuss. Talking about them would be a bad omen.

"The Death Lords are supposedly arcanists who rule over the abyssal hells," Professor Zahn said as he turned around. He fixed his glasses and sighed. "They're all bonded to abyssal dragons, and each has a specific role in the *land of the dead*. The abyssal hells are made up of several layers, and the Death Lords fight for control over them. But their existence is more grounded in myths than anything else. We're not sure if such arcanists exist."

Once again, everyone muttered things between each other. Most of this was fantastical news. Death Lords? Souls? Magical gates? Sounded preposterous. Like an old adventure story for children.

"Do they exist?" Nasbit said, his voice low. "What do you think, Professor?"

"I think there's as much evidence for their existence as the abyssal hells themselves," Professor Zahn diplomatically replied. "According to old documents, the Death Lords used to travel from the abyssal hells up to the surface to gather souls, but once the gates were crafted, the Death Lords were forever locked away from the land of the living. Tales of fighting abyssal dragons are numerous, but no one has seen one in over a millennium."

More whispers. More gossip.

It was fun to think about weird death arcanists living in a realm of magic and souls. But it felt like something for children. Weren't we all adults here?

Nini tugged on the sleeve of my robes. I glanced over, my brow furrowed.

"Yeah?" I whispered.

"Waste talked about the Death Lords," she said under her breath.

"Oh?"

"Waste said that reapers and grim reapers are meant to send souls to the Death Lords, and that they're supposed to judge them. If they're good, they get to go home. But if they're bad, they're grafted to the abyssal dragons, forever increasing their might."

That also sounded fantastical, but who was I to argue?

"Sounds interesting," I whispered.

"Quiet down," the rizzel said, his voice raspy.

The professor turned and faced me. "I don't want to issue demerits, but sometimes it's required to maintain order. What's your name, young man?"

Exie turned and giggled into her hand. Everyone else in class gave me sideways glances. Except for Nini, who whispered a quiet apology.

The fact that *I* was chosen to make an example of ate at me. I hadn't been the only one speaking, but it was hardly worth arguing.

"I'm Gray Lexly," I said.

"Wait. Lexly? As in, one of the twins?"

I lifted an eyebrow. "Yeah."

Professor Zahn smiled—the first time the entire class. "Oh, it's *this* class that I have you. The headmaster told me about you and your brother. I was fascinated because I also have a twin."

CHAPTER 30

NIGHT CLASS

"Really?" I asked. "You have a twin?"

"My brother," Professor Zahn said as he set down his chalk and walked around the desk. "I haven't seen him in ages, but we were always very close." Zahn smiled wider and even laughed to himself. "He was the big one in the family. Always getting into fights. I was more of a reader, you see. We didn't look alike."

Sorin leaned onto the table, grinning ear to ear. "That's just like me and Gray! People are always surprised when we tell them we're twins since Gray is so much smaller than me."

"I'm not *that* much smaller," I snapped, trying to keep my voice low.

"Well, compared to me," Sorin mumbled.

Professor Zahn chuckled knowingly, like he had lived through all our stories himself. He had probably had a similar childhood, from the sounds of it.

"Well, I'm glad you're here with us, Gray, Sorin," the professor said. Then he walked back to the chalkboard, having completely forgotten about that demerit he was going to issue.

I preferred it that way.

"Where was I..." Professor Zahn muttered. He tapped his chalk on the board. "Oh! That's right. I don't know how we got into such a deep discussion on the abyssal hells, because that's something we typically learn a little later... First, I like to teach everyone about *star shards*."

The professor drew little stars all around our world.

"I like to teach this as our first lesson because it comes with a field trip." Professor Zahn turned back around and motioned to the door. "I'm going to dismiss class early, but tonight, instead of heading to your dorms, you need to meet me at North Peak, just beyond the training field. And please be there before sunset."

"What?" Exie asked. "Won't it be cold?"

"Very. Make sure to wear warm clothing."

A few grumbles answered him, but nothing substantial. That was when Professor Zahn turned his attention to his books.

"You're all dismissed," he said as he took a seat. "I know it's early, but I have some things I need to read up about."

The rest of the class stood from their tables and headed for the door. I lingered behind, taking my time gathering my notebook, books, and charcoal pencils. Sorin and Nini headed out, with Raaza close behind them. His little kitsune gave me an odd look before hurrying after her arcanist.

Once most everyone had left, I walked over to Professor Zahn's desk.

His rizzel glared at me.

Twain flashed his kitten fangs and puffed his fur. "What're you lookin' at?"

The rizzel said nothing.

Professor Zahn glanced up and smiled. "Ah. Gray. Is there something else you wished to ask me?"

"Well, sort of," I said, half-shrugging. "I was told you worked alongside Professor Helmith."

"That's right. She's rather talented."

"Uh. Yeah. I was wondering... Did she ever mention me?"

Zahn thought for a moment, his gaze falling to the desk. Then he shook his head. "I can't say that she has."

My chest twisted in silent pain. She had *never* mentioned me to anyone? "That's understandable. I've only had her as a professor for one class, after all."

"We don't talk much outside of our work," Zahn said in an apologetic tone. "I can get single-minded, and Rylee is always there to keep me on track. Without her, I doubt I would've made as many trinkets for Astra Academy as I have."

Rylee.

I never used Professor Helmith's first name when I spoke to her, but I knew it well.

"Has she... been feeling well?" I asked. With a forced chuckle, I added, "She seemed sick when we had class. Like, she was pale and not acting herself."

Professor Zahn mulled over my words. "Well, now that you mention it... she's been a lot less focused recently."

I caught my breath, hoping I wasn't giving too much away. "*Recently?* How recently?"

"In the last few weeks. Normally, Rylee comes to talk to me in the evenings, but lately she's been turning in to sleep much earlier than normal. Perhaps she *isn't* feeling well."

More proof.

Someone who knew Professor Helmith was seeing it, too. She wasn't acting right. Something was wrong.

My heart pounded with a renewed sense of purpose. This wasn't all in my head.

"Maybe you should tell the headmaster," I said. "About Professor Helmith."

"I'm sure she'll be fine." Zahn dismissively waved away my comment. "Or Doc Tomas will see her soon. Either way, she's a fully grown woman. I'm sure she can handle it."

"Right." I smiled and headed for the door. "Thank you for speaking with me. I'll see you later tonight."

"Remember. It's at the training field. We'll be heading to North Peak."

"Okay. Until then."

Getting out of class early revealed some facts to me.

Not every student had lunch at the same time. I strolled the halls of Astra Academy, admiring the various paintings, and keeping my eyes open for the fake Professor Helmith. When I passed the dining hall, I found it filled with arcanists. Their eldrin were larger and older. One griffin was the size of a cart, and someone else had a fully grown pegasus with a brown coat and hawk-like wings.

Twain purred on my shoulders as we walked.

I patted his head occasionally.

Sorin and Nini wandered the halls with me, each pointing out places of interest.

"There's a telescope out on North Peak," Nini said as she pointed out a window. "One of the girls in my dorm said it's used for seeing far away things as though they're nearby."

"Like a spyglass?" I asked.

"She said it saw things even *farther* away. Beyond the clouds. To the stars in the sky."

Sorin thought for a moment. "That seems impossible. How does it work?"

Nini shrugged. "I don't know. I've never seen a telescope before."

"We'll probably see it later tonight," I said. "Maybe we can ask Professor Zahn about it."

"I like that professor," Sorin said, grinning. "He's my favorite so far."

"Mine, too."

Twain frowned. "I don't like his eldrin. What a weird rizzel... He bothers me."

Zahn's eldrin had been strange. I didn't know much about rizzels other than their sarcastic nature. Apparently, they were often used as lures for other creatures, because their smell was distinct. Professor Helmith had said rizzels became the most elusive mystical creatures ever because so many other creatures hunted them.

I had always found that story interesting. A mystical creature developed its magic to evade people because it was being hunted? How? Through generations of evolution? Or was their magic changed somehow?

Professor Helmith had said origin myths were her favorite to study. I understood why.

Astra Academy was too big to walk around in one day. We hadn't even seen the locomotive yet. Apparently, we'd have to take it to get to other compounds. I couldn't wait.

Once we were done wandering, Sorin, Nini, and I returned to the dining hall for our own lunch. The volume was louder than normal. The table with all the girls seemed lively.

"Do you think today is a good day?" Nini asked as she eyed the table.

"For what?" I asked.

"To go speak with them."

Sorin smiled. "Yeah. They look like they're having fun."

"You two won't mind?" Nini asked. "If I skip lunch with you today?"

"Of course not."

Nini smiled genuinely, her growing confidence on display. "Oh, excellent. I think today is a good day. I have this feeling."

Sorin gave her a thumbs up. "You can do it."

She pulled her giant coat tight around her body, her smile growing a tiny bit at the edges. Nini would've been the picture of adorable if it weren't for the reaper looming behind her. It was like a death shadow—a mythical executioner ready to strike at any moment. It gave her an air of deadliness, even in the sweetest of moments.

Nini headed to the serving table in the middle of the room. Sorin and I followed behind, but she quickly loaded her plate up with anything and everything before heading straight for the loudest table in the room.

"Did you read the chapter about star shards?" Sorin asked as he gathered his food.

I shook my head. "I haven't been reading anything."

"You seem really distracted. You didn't even wish Nini good luck."

"Hm."

Why hadn't I told anyone about my theories? Twain was the only one I had said anything to. I now had proof—more than just my own perceptions—but it wasn't enough. If I was going to expose the fake Helmith for what she was, I needed something tangible.

And perhaps a motive.

Why was someone impersonating her?

It still baffled me.

I wanted to be the one to help her. She had helped me for so long—*for years*—fighting the nightmares that were trying to kill me. How could I best help her here? If I just said someone was impersonating her, they'd never believe me. Even with Zahn's testimony, it wasn't enough.

Sorin looked me up and down. "Have you thought about any of the clubs?"

"No."

"Want to join the Boating Club?" Sorin asked, smiling wide.

"We'd be naturals. We could show everyone here a thing or three."

I rolled my eyes as we took our plates and then headed over to our usual table. "I don't want to go *boating*, Sorin. We escaped our island life, remember? Sailing a boat around the mountain lakes doesn't sound appealing to me."

"Why not? We'd be so good at it."

"We should do something we've never done before."

When we reached the table, I hesitated. Raaza was already sitting there with his little kitsune. The fox creature had a tiny plate of shrimp. She ate them one at a time, occasionally batting a small one around the edge of the plate.

Raaza slowly ate his rice and curry, taking his time while he read a passage from one of his schoolbooks. He didn't even glance up as Sorin and I took our seats.

"Oh, hey," Sorin said, offering him a wave.

Twain leapt off my shoulder and landed on the table. He was smaller than Miko—she was a kit fox, but her tail was mighty puffy—and when he walked over, he stood on his tiptoes as if trying to appear larger.

"And what're you two doing here?" Twain asked.

"Eating," Miko replied. "I thought it obvious."

"Yeah, well, this is *our* table."

Miko's tall ears twitched. With a frown, she said, "I think it's big enough for all of us. Plus, you definitely want to be friends with me and my arcanist." Miko swished her fox tail in front of her face, hiding everything but her eyes. "We're powerful in ways you can't even yet comprehend."

"Hmpf!" Twain turned away from her. "Anything you can do, I can do better."

I grabbed Twain, dragged him back over to my seat at the table, and kept my hand over his face. "Never mind him. He's just grumpy because he hasn't eaten yet."

My eldrin flailed around under my hand. When he finally

freed himself, he gave me a glare and then moved his plate a good foot away from mine. Then he sat down and ate his beef tips with a frown. Twain's grumpiness slowly melted away as he ate, which I found adorable.

Sorin and I exchanged questioning glances. My brother just shrugged, and I figured it wasn't worth arguing with Raaza. If he wanted to sit with us, that was fine.

A crash filled the dining hall. Someone had smashed a plate on the stone tile floor.

Both Sorin and I stood from our seats. Twain leapt back to my shoulder, his fur on end.

At the far corner of the hall—near the table with all the girls —was a shattered plate. Food had splattered across the boots of several students. Exie was at the center of attention, food on her blue and black robes.

Nini stood over the mess, her face hardened by anger I had never seen from her.

"*You think you're special?*" Nini yelled, her voice shaky, her hands clenched into fists. "You think you're *unique?* You're not the first one to treat me like a freak."

She turned and stormed out of the dining hall so fast that no one had a chance to say anything. When a girl stood—perhaps to give chase—Waste slammed his scythe down on the wood table. The rusty blade cut through a section and rattled all the plates on top of it.

A girl screamed and leapt away from the reaper.

Another girl practically fainted.

Exie's erlking flew in front of her, his little arms raised. "I'll mess you up, *monster!*"

But Waste didn't respond. He pulled his scythe from the table and quietly floated away from the group of panicking girls. Silence followed him as he made his way to the door. Once Waste exited, however, the whole dining hall erupted into conversation.

"Did that reaper arcanist attack another student?" someone shouted.

"Someone get the professors!" a boy yelled from the back of the hall.

"What if that reaper arcanist killed somebody? That would be crazy."

Sorin and I shoved our way through the groups of anxious arcanists. I didn't care what they thought about the situation. I had never seen Nini angry. She was practically a different person. I didn't even know she could yell that loud.

"We have to go talk to her, Gray," Sorin said as he grabbed my upper arm and practically dragged me toward the door.

"Yeah, I'm coming," I said through gritted teeth.

"We shouldn't let her be alone too long."

"I'm sure we won't..."

CHAPTER 31

REAPERS AND KNIGHTMARES

Sorin yanked me into the hallway.

He stopped and glanced around, his brow furrowed. Nini wasn't anywhere nearby. At first, Sorin just stepped back and forth, torn between turning left or right, but then I pointed to a window slightly ajar. It was one of the many windows with a pathway attached to the treehouse.

Nini must've wanted to leave the Academy as fast as possible. It made me wonder what had transpired between her and Exie.

"C'mon," Sorin said as he jogged over to the window.

This time, I grabbed his arm and held him back. He stopped and turned to face me.

"Are you sure you want to get involved?" I asked now that we were away from the other arcanists.

"Why would you even ask that?"

"Because Nini *did* kill someone. We both know that for a fact."

Sorin clenched his hands into fists. "*I* also killed someone, according to the reaper. I don't think it's fair to judge her."

"I'm confident Nini's situation isn't like yours. Are you sure you want to associate with someone like that?"

"We don't know what happened," Sorin stated. Then he mulled over everything for a moment, and added, "A person isn't one deed or event. You may know the outcome, but you don't know the story."

The shadows around Sorin's feet fluttered. "A knight strives to withhold premature judgment."

With a sigh, I motioned to the window. "All right. But let's just be cautious, okay?"

Sorin smiled. Without any hesitation, he threw the window wide open.

The walkway to the treehouse was a wooden path carved straight out of a massive branch. The wood had been polished and smoothed, making it easier to walk on. Whenever it angled upward or downward, steps had been carefully crafted into the branch, and both sides of the walkway were lined with wrought iron railings.

Sorin leapt onto the tree branch. I followed afterward, surprised by how wide it was. Two horses could walk side by side on this thing.

It made me feel like I was the size of an ant.

Twain jumped down to my feet. He walked on the wooden path alongside me as though he was proud to be here. "This is my turf. I'll show you around here."

"It's just a walkway," I quipped.

"I-It's still basically my dorm!" Twain huffed and walked with his nose high. "This is a place for mystical creatures. Lots of places to hide and get comfortable. You wouldn't understand. Humans just don't get it."

With a chuckle, I patted his back. He smiled and purred, despite his anger moments ago.

We hurried along the branch walkway, and I was shocked to see how far it went. The treehouse was on the eastern side of the Academy. The door we had exited faced north. In order to get to the treehouse, we would have to walk around one full side of Astra Academy—a fact I hadn't realized until just then.

The giant tree was even larger than I had imagined.

Glancing over the railing caused my heart to leap into my throat. We had to be ten stories up from the ground. I quickly turned away, already dizzy from a half second of staring.

There weren't a lot of heights around my home isle... We had a single mountain. I had never visited it.

This was a new experience.

Chill winds whipped over us as we traveled along the walkway. Occasionally, few small paths branched from our walkway to other windows around the Academy, and I glanced through the clear glass to see inside. None of the other arcanists seemed to notice us.

It didn't take long before I heard soft sobbing carried along by the wind.

We weren't even to the eastern side of the Academy—I had yet to spot the treehouse—and I wasn't sure where Nini could be hiding. I grabbed Sorin's arms, stopped him, and then glanced around.

"Allow me, my arcanist," Thurin said, his disembodied voice emanating from the darkness.

Sorin nodded to the shadows. "If you can find her..."

The darkness moved on its own. An extra shadow darted away from my brother's feet and slithered across the walkway. It moved and operated like any good shadow—it clung to every surface, unhindered by gravity. The shadow went under the walkway it searched everywhere.

When I lost sight of it, I just waited with Sorin.

Before a full minute went by, the knightmare returned to us.

"She is on the smaller branches," Thurin said.

"Show us," Sorin commanded.

The pool of darkness guided us along the path until we came

to an area with giant leaves. Small twigs were growing off the side of the walkway, providing shade for whoever walked here.

The gigantic tree had leaves that resembled pine needle clusters, but since the tree was gargantuan, the individual needles were the size of swords. I loved their appearance. I hadn't seen anything like it before. With slow and hesitant movements, I reached out and touched some of the leaves, surprised by how rough they were to the touch.

Sorin didn't bother with anything. He headed straight for Nini. Once I broke out of my momentary trance, I ran after him. He actually left the main path, leapt down to a smaller branch, and headed down that way, always following his shadow eldrin.

The smaller branch wasn't carved or shaped. It was a tree branch. And it wobbled a bit as Sorin ran along it.

With a sigh, I got down onto it and followed.

I refused to look down.

Twain chased after me, his ears erect.

Then I finally spotted Nini. She was seated at the very end of the small branch, her reaper floating nearby. The branch was so thin, it barely supported her weight. Sorin had stopped a good twenty feet away, his steps disturbing everything, even the leaves.

"Nini?" Sorin asked.

I walked up behind him, my heart pounding, even though I hadn't looked down. A fall from this height...

Nini quietly sobbed inside her coat. She used it like a blanket, covering her head. Only a small bit of red hair poked up beyond the collar.

Sorin slowly inched closer to her, but the branch creaked in protest. He quickly backed away, his breath held. "Uh, Nini? I don't think it's safe to sit out that far."

She was half his size. I suspected the branch wouldn't break with her on it, but it might if we were all out as far as she was.

I placed an unsteady hand on Sorin's shoulder—half to support me, and half to calm him.

"Nini," I called out. "Look, I think we should go back inside."

"L-Leave me alone," she said from within her coat, her voice muffled.

I turned to Sorin. "Welp. We tried. Let's go."

He shot me a glare. "We can't leave her here," he growled under his breath. "What's wrong with you?"

My confidence was as shaky as my balance. I hadn't realized how much heights would bother me. But with a forced smile, I returned my attention to Nini. "What happened? You can tell us."

The wind howled as it swept by, taunting me with its power. Sorin didn't flinch. He held my arm, never once succumbing to the terror of our perilous situation. His knightmare didn't seem concerned, either. But Twain was. My eldrin dug his little claws into the wood as the wind rushed by. Once it was over, Twain leapt onto my leg, shredding my trousers and my flesh and he scrambled up.

"Everyone hates me," Nini muttered from within her coat, her sobbing less than before.

"We don't hate you," Sorin stated.

"*You don't even know me.*" Nini brought her arms up over her head. She was buried in her clothing and limbs, her voice almost inaudible. "I just get... so sad... It's like, all my sadness builds up... And then I just yell."

"Sad about what?" I asked.

"The other girls... kept making fun of me."

Sorin shook his head. "Not all of them. I don't think."

What a smooth line. My brother. A real master at comforting people.

"I... I was getting along with them." Nini grabbed the collar of her coat and pulled it down. Her glasses were smudged with fingerprints and tearstains. Her puffy red eyes matched her disheveled hair. "I was talking to them at the dining table... They

307

laughed at my joke. I had practiced it all morning. Everything was going better than I had imagined. But then Exie told them."

Waste hovered close. His cloak wrapped around her in a protective bundle.

"Told them what?" Sorin asked.

But I already knew.

Nini scrunched her eyes shut. "Exie told them about a reaper's Trial of Worth. *Right in front of all the girls.*" She sucked in air and shivered. "Now everyone knows I lied about it. The Trial wasn't killing animals... It was..." Through gritted teeth, she whispered, "They'll hate me forever now."

Sorin and I remained silent.

Finally, I said, "Sorin and I have always known the reaper's Trial of Worth."

Nini glanced up and turned to face me. Her lip quavered. "R-Really?"

I nodded once. "Yeah. You're not the only one here who could've been a reaper arcanist. Sorin could've bonded with Waste. Our mother died during his birth. Waste offered to bond with him."

Sorin didn't say a word. He just half-smiled, putting on a brave face for Nini.

The reaper...

It slid more onto Nini. The hood fell over her head, and the cloak settled around her shoulders. She was *wearing* her eldrin. The fabric of the creature seemed to secure itself in place around her—but Nini didn't seem concerned. She gripped the edge of the cloak and pulled it tight.

"I killed my brother."

When Nini spoke, she had two voices. Her voice, and Waste's voice. They had blended together to form the words.

Waste's hollow tone added a sad and haunting echo to Nini's whisper.

The way they spoke... I shivered. So did Twain.

I didn't know people could wear their eldrin—I didn't know they could merge with them.

Before Sorin and I could answer Nini's statement, she quickly added, "*It was an accident.*" Her double-voice was just as ominous, even when she was upset. She almost sounded murderous now. More confident. Her sobbing had ended. "I didn't want to hurt him. I didn't mean for it to happen."

Sorin slowly turned to face me.

Could we believe her claim?

Probably. I doubted Nini was a master liar—or a bloodthirsty villain. If it had been an accident, that would explain why she wasn't locked away or in the stocks. It had probably happened when she was young. No one would jail a small child over a terrible accident.

"I'll understand if you two want to leave me as well," Nini and Waste said as one.

It was like they were a single person now.

With her face obscured by the cowl, and the scythe in her hand, Nini was the image of the lady of death. A terrifying omen given physical form.

I could already hear my father's advice. He wouldn't want us to associate with Nini.

That was when the shadows moved around my brother's feet. At first, I thought his knightmare was just rising out of the darkness to join us.

But that wasn't the case.

Thurin lifted around my brother, the black armor forming around Sorin's body. It hardened and pieced itself together, merging with my brother like a suit of armor built specifically for him. I released his shoulder and stepped away. The feathery cape formed on Sorin's back and fluttered with the wind. It wasn't a complete suit of armor—some of the pieces were still missing—but it was enough to be impressive.

Sorin and Thurin had *also* merged.

"Nini, I think you and I have a lot in common," Sorin said, his voice intertwined with Thurin's. "Let's navigate the Academy together."

I stared with wide eyes, shocked by how the knightmare and the reaper interacted with their arcanists. They were rarer creatures—at least, according to our bestiary book—and I wondered how long Sorin had known his eldrin could do this.

Was there a benefit to merging?

Twain climbed up my clothes and then clung to my shoulder. He must've known exactly what I was thinking, because he whispered into my ear, "Knightmares and reapers merge to become one being. They live and die together—and when together, they're much stronger."

"How do you know that?" I whispered.

"Waste told me all about it in the Menagerie. We were there a long time... Only so many things to talk about after a while."

Sorin's display had an effect on Nini.

She stood from her spot on the edge of the thin branch, her new cloak caught by the winds and swirling behind her. With her scythe held close, she leapt forward. She moved as though lighter than before—like her reaper was helping her basically float through the air. She landed on the branch without disturbing anything.

Then Nini walked the last of the distance to Sorin.

"Everyone on my island avoided me," Nini and Waste said as one. "They said bad luck must follow me. And they also said that because of the accident, I shouldn't be an arcanist. So I ran away."

Her confession shook me.

I glanced around, worried someone else might hear, but no one was nearby. If Exie wanted to make Nini feel unwelcome, this was more information that could be used against her.

Sorin didn't reply.

Nini grabbed her reaper's cloak. "With Waste, I feel

powerful." Their combined voice was stronger than before. "Like I can change anything. Even fate."

"That's how I feel with Thurin." Sorin touched his knightmare, his merged voice more regal than Nini's. "Our destiny is ours to decide. And we don't have to do it alone."

Sorin lifted his arm.

It was like Darkness was offering Death its hand.

Nini hesitated. Then she finally placed her palm on top of Sorin's. For a short while, they stood there, cloak and cape fluttering in the wind. Then Nini let Sorin's hand slip through her fingers. The moment blew away with the wind over the mountain peaks, but the memory remained.

Nini took a deep breath, and then exhaled. Her reaper untied himself from Nini's shoulders. The hood floated off her, and the scythe left her hand. Nini patted down her disheveled hair, and then wiped away the tears from the edge of her eyes.

"I don't want to talk about this anymore," she whispered, her gaze on the branch. She fixed her smeared glasses. "Let's just... go back to the dorms. Even if everyone else knows now... I think I'll be fine. I had to deal with this before, after all."

CHAPTER 32

STAR SHARD SHOWER & THE NIMBUS SEA

We returned to the dorms, and Nini disappeared into hers as soon as she could.

Sorin and I waited in our dorm until dusk. We didn't speak much. He read through his bestiary, focusing on knightmares and reapers, and occasionally glancing up to tell me tidbits about those mystical creatures.

I had to admit, I was intrigued.

The thought of merging with my eldrin seemed both interesting and terrifying. What was it like, I wondered? Whenever I glanced at Twain, he seemed to know what I was thinking. He narrowed his little kitten eyes at me, like it was a silly idea to test out the powers of the reaper or knightmare just for the fun of it.

Once the sun began to set, Sorin and I exited the dorms and headed outside. North Peak, according to everyone else, wasn't too far from the training field. The cold of night made things uncomfortable, though. I wore my robes, but they weren't enough.

I hadn't packed much—I didn't *have* much—and while I had a coat, it wasn't thick enough to protect me from the mountain climate. With Twain tucked away inside my coat, I shivered the entire walk out of the Academy.

Sorin didn't appear cold. He strode forward, half-smiling the entire time.

The sunset wasn't like on the islands. It set behind the mountains, tucked away by clouds, creating a dark purple hue across the sky before finally setting. It seemed gloomier than the sunsets I was used to.

Sorin and I spotted the other arcanists of our class heading north. Nini was among them.

Well, she wasn't *with* them. She followed along at a distance —at least twenty feet behind the others. Sorin and I joined her as we headed for the stone brick trail to North Peak.

The trail led to a long stairway up to the top of a small mountain. The most interesting detail was the presence of thick clouds swirling around the peak. They were a solid white, and even at night, seemed fluffy and vibrant. They weren't black and stormy, and they didn't travel with the winds, like normal clouds.

What were they?

Our class climbed the stairs up toward the cloudy peak.

Raaza and his kitsune were the first to rush upward. Phila and her coatl were just as excited. The snake with wings actually flew up most of the steps, its rainbow feathers practically glittering.

Knovak and his unicorn hurried after them, his unicorn complaining the entire way. "We're creatures of speed," Starling was saying. "We shouldn't be last! Or even in the middle!"

Exie and her erlking fairy went up with ease. She seemed quieter than before, and occasionally glared daggers at whoever spoke to her. It was obvious she had changed her clothing after lunch—she wore her robes open, despite the cold as though she couldn't stand the thought of hiding her beautiful silvery dress.

Ashlyn and her typhoon dragon went up next. The dragon

was massive, and he moved slowly up the stairs, but he was clearly determined. The dragon huffed as he climbed, but he never complained.

"Just a little farther," Ashlyn said, her tone encouraging. "We're almost there."

Typhoon dragons were creatures of the water. It didn't surprise me that her eldrin hated the long walk up a hundred stairs to the top of a random mountain.

Sorin, Nini, and I all went up without any issues, mostly because I didn't look down at any point. Twain rode on my shoulder, Thurin traveled through the darkness, and Nini's reaper floated along as though carried by the air.

The last person up the steps was Nasbit.

His stone golem wasn't having a fun time. It thumped up each step, its stubby child-sized legs unsuited to long travel. It didn't breathe—could stone golems even talk?—but it had to take careful steps.

Nasbit wasn't enjoying the trek, either.

"You'll be okay," Nasbit said through deep breaths. Was he talking to himself or his eldrin? I wasn't sure. "The star shards... will be worth it... You'll see..."

After a couple hundred steps, we reached the clouds. Literally. I suspected magic brought them close to the peak, but I didn't know why.

It was like walking into a fluffy ceiling. We stepped up, higher and higher, and walked through a layer of white clouds. It felt like thick mist, and I was wet by the time I managed to get all the way through.

And once I made it past the cloud line...

I caught my breath.

It was like I stood in the night sky itself. The clouds shrouded everything beneath me, stretching out as far as I could see. Illuminated by the moon, it was like I was standing in a sea of silver smoke. I couldn't see the ground below—or the Academy—just rolling hills of pillowy clouds.

"Wow," Twain said, drawing out the word.

The stairs led up to a platform large enough for thirty people. In the center was an odd device. It was a gigantic spyglass —a telescope, I supposed. It was pointed at the sky.

Professor Zahn and his rizzel stood next to the telescope, his hands behind his back. He fidgeted with his glasses as he said, "Welcome, students. The show is just about to begin." He swept his arm out to gesture toward the sky. "Make sure you have a good view. Whether you stand or sit, it matters not. This is the Nimbus Sea, a place where we can use the telescope without fear of the weather interrupting our observations."

"How are the clouds so low?" Exie asked as she rubbed at her arms.

"A nimbus dragon arcanist helped create this peak specifically so we could better observe the night sky."

The tattoos on Zahn's hands glowed in the dark. They were all manner of colors, and seemingly pulsed with power. They reminded me of Professor Helmith. Her beautiful tattoos also glowed in the dark.

Once all nine students from our class were on the platform, Professor Zahn pointed to the Nimbus Sea. We turned to look.

The stars seemed larger than normal. They twinkled, and some practically spun.

"We're about to witness a *star shard shower*," Zahn said with a smile. "A few dozen star shards will rain down around us. The shards are no bigger than my thumb, but they're packed with magical power."

Nasbit took deep breaths before saying, "How do... you know... they'll be falling tonight?"

"Astra Academy was built on this mountaintop because of the prevalence of star shard showers. The headmaster's eldrin can sense when they're about to fall."

Exie threw back some of her curly hair. "Why are star shards so important? This seems like... a lot of effort."

Professor Zahn patted his rizzel eldrin. "Well, you see, we need star shards to imbue our magic into objects. Star shards are raw magic, and they act as an adhesive. Similar to glue, they hold magic in place. Without the star shards, we wouldn't be able to make permanent magical items."

When Zahn pointed to the sky, everyone held their breath.

As if rehearsed, the star shard shower began.

Dozens of "stars" fell from the sky, streaking overhead with white and silvery lights. Everyone gasped as the shards pierced the clouds like meteors. They left craters in the fluffy white waves, but the clouds quickly mended themselves afterward.

The Nimbus Sea was magical to watch.

Another round of star shards shot down around us, disturbing the clouds for only a few moments.

One even headed straight for the platform. Everyone tensed and pointed. Would it smash into us and break our telescope? Would it hurt if it struck someone?

But as soon as the star shard neared the platform, it slowed its descent and gently fell onto the stone bricks, disturbing nothing. The tiny thumb-sized crystal twinkled with inner power.

There it was.

A star shard.

Everyone pointed at it, but no one dared to approach.

Professor Zahn walked over and plucked the shard from the ground. "Some of you might be wondering where the star shards come from." He held the shard with his pointer finger and thumb, displaying it for everyone to see.

Nasbit raised a hand and then said, "I thought all magic came from inside our world."

Zahn forced a tight smile. "Yes, well, according to myth and theory, corrupted magic sometimes seeps out into the world from the core. Star shards were once corrupted, but later cleansed by god-arcanists so that we can use them for item making."

"Oh. So they seep out from the abyssal hells or something?"

"In a sense, yes. Some say, that's where corruption comes from. Others say it's the purest magic—where all life begins and ends." Professor Zahn held up a finger. "However, since we have no way to go there, most of this is just speculation."

When I returned my attention to the sky, I realized the star shard shower had ended.

"That didn't seem like a lot," I said.

"Most star shard showers only yield a small amount," Professor Zahn stated. "But that's fine. You all have a wonderful assignment. You will break into teams of three and search the surrounding area for the star shards. Then you'll bring them back to me. They should be easy to find at night. They glow quite brightly."

Excited whispers filled the platform.

"Wow," Sorin said as he nudged me with his elbow. "This is a *very* important task. Star shards are super valuable."

Nasbit and his stone golem turned to us. His puffy cheeks were still red. "An individual star shard is worth *two years'* worth of income from a small family-owned shop. Which means that, *yes*, star shards are very valuable."

"Why would you say it like that?" I asked. "In terms of a family's earnings?"

"Oh, that's how all my uncles talk about it." Nasbit inhaled and exhaled. Then he patted his chest. "They always phrase things in terms of yearly earnings."

"Really bizarre." My father always referred to things in terms of coin.

"My uncles deal with appraising magical items all the time.

They buy and sell so many trinkets and artifacts, they have books full of receipts."

Professor Zahn clapped his hands. Then he made a circle motion with his finger. "Gather round. I'm going to split you into groups of three. Let's see..." He glanced at us all, his eyes narrowed. "Um. Yes. Well. You there."

He pointed at Exie.

She smiled sweetly. "Yes, Professor?"

"Er, what's your name again?"

Her smile instantly turned into a deep and hateful frown. Even her little fairy eldrin frowned. "*Exie Lolian*. I'm the erlking arcanist!"

"Right. Uh, you can be with..." Zahn pointed to Raaza. "That one. You're... *Ricky*?"

"Raaza," he replied, deadpan.

"Whatever. And your last group member will be Sorin Lexly." Professor Zahn pointed to my brother. "You can watch over them, right?"

Sorin gave Nini a quick glance before nodding. "Uh, sure."

"All right... Then we'll have *you*—" he pointed to Nini, "—and *you*—" he gestured to Phila and her coatl, "—and *you*." His last choice was Knovak.

The three of them awkwardly clumped together. The unicorn gave the winged coatl an odd glance. But no one turned to face the reaper. It just hovered behind them

"Gray," the professor said as he turned to me. "You can lead your group, all right? With, uh, the other two?" He motioned to Nasbit and Ashlyn as though he couldn't remember their names, either.

I glanced over my shoulder and noticed Ashlyn's frown. I offered her a playful shrug. "Welp, looks like I'm in charge."

She smiled as she rolled her eyes. "Whenever you and your kitten get scared, me and my dragon will be there to protect you."

"Pfft," Twain said with a swipe of his paw. "I'm not a scaredy cat. I'm a big mean *jungle cat*." He flexed his tiny claws. It was adorable, and not at all intimidating.

Nasbit snorted back a laugh.

Professor Zahn whispered something to his rizzel eldrin. The cute ferret-like creature wore the same scowl it had during class earlier in the day. It nodded once and then teleported away in a flash of glitter and a pop of air.

"My eldrin will help you all find the star shards," Zahn said. "It shouldn't take you more than an hour to gather them all. Bring everything you find back to this platform. I'll be here to take inventory."

"Is it dangerous?" Exie asked.

Zahn shook his head. "No. There aren't any mystical creatures on these mountains, and many pathways have been built throughout the woods. I'm certain you'll be fine."

"But wasn't there an attack in the Menagerie? I mean, what if someone attacks us tonight?"

I hadn't thought about that. *Would* someone come for me? I wanted to doubt it.

"You're all arcanists," Zahn said with a nervous chuckle. "I heard you learned to evoke your magic already. That means most of you should have a way to drive back thieves and scoundrels. Although, I think the cold will kill them before long."

A few others from my class laughed.

But everyone's voice was filled with uncertainty.

"It'll be fine," Sorin said as he stood tall. "We can handle this."

Raaza smiled. "That's right. This will be the perfect test of our new might."

"W-Well..." Zahn shook his head. "No one should need to test anything."

Raaza's kitsune circled her arcanist and smiled. "A beautiful test..."

"No one is listening to me." Zahn pointed to the cloud sea. "There's a set of stairs on all four sides of the platform. If you need light, there should be a glowstone lamp at the bottom of each staircase. Try to get back here in a reasonable amount of time."

CHAPTER 33

SURPRISE

Nasbit's golem held our glowstone lamp as we made our way west, beyond North Peak and further away from the Academy. The surrounding woods reminded me of a funeral. Everything wore black, even the tree trunks.

That made it easier to find the star shards, though. The sparkle of their inner power pierced the gloom. They were like fireflies in the distance—twinkling and beckoning us to retrieve them.

It amused me that the star shards hadn't caused damage when they landed. They sat on the ground, tucked between leaves or on the soft dirt, like someone had just gently placed them there.

When I knelt to pick up the fifth shard we had found, I also marveled at how warm it was.

"Why don't these leave little craters on the ground?" Twain asked as he stared at the shard.

Nasbit smiled, eagerness in his voice as he answered. "Long ago, when the star shards were corrupted, they *smashed* into the ground and caused problems for everybody! But now that they're cleansed, they don't disturb nature. Magic and nature are deeply intertwined, you see. That's what it says in all the books."

His golem nodded its stone head along with the words. It was a walking example of the nature of magic.

"That's great," I muttered, only half paying attention as I brought the star shard close to my eyes. The magic inside the shard moved around... swirling.

Twain leaned over on my shoulder. With his eyes wide, and his pupils dilated into huge circles, he batted at the shard, patting it several times with his paw.

Nasbit turned to Ashlyn. "Also, some people believe star shards are actually souls that escaped the abyssal hells, and they're trying to find people they once knew in life."

"That's... depressing," Ashlyn said. She tied her blonde hair back in a tight ponytail, her stance stiff. She turned and stared at the far darkness between trees.

"It's not *too* depressing, actually. I heard that the Death Lords are sometimes mean to people caught in the abyssal hells, so—if you think about it—the people here are happier and—"

Ashlyn held up a hand, cutting Nasbit off. "Shh!"

We all went still and quiet. I glanced around, but the woods were too dark to see anything. The glow of our lamp extended ten feet at the max. And Ashlyn's dragon was large enough that it blocked some of my sight.

After several strained seconds, Ashlyn lowered her hand. Her typhoon dragon flashed his fangs and stepped closer.

"I keep getting this feeling like we're being watched," Ashlyn whispered.

Nasbit grabbed the arm of his baby stone golem. "Oh. You're not afraid, right, Brak?"

The stone golem shook its head. The beast didn't *say* anything, it just always indicated its answer through motion. Nasbit didn't release his grip. If anything, he tightened it.

"We're fine," I said with a shrug. "Let's keep going." I

pointed to the tree line. "Look. That's the end of the creepy woods. Let's go get star shards over there."

As a group, we slowly made our way out of the woods. The walk was pleasant, but the dragon and golem made plenty of noise as we moved. If anyone *was* following us, it wouldn't be difficult.

Ashlyn strode closer to me. "How's Nini?" she asked.

"Hm? Why?" I lifted an eyebrow.

"She seemed quite upset in the dining hall. I didn't know she could yell like that."

"Oh. Yeah. Sorin and I spoke to her. She's feeling better."

Ashlyn relaxed her shoulders. "That's good to hear."

Once out of the woods, we found a rocky slope.

We were on the side of a mountain, that much was certain. Fortunately, the side of the mountain wasn't *too* slanted—we could walk around—but I imagined if anyone slipped, we would tumble for a good five hundred feet until we hit the trees at the base of our little mountainside.

Several granite boulders jutted up from the ground all around us, some as large as houses, some as small as a bowl. Loose pebbles covered the ground. Little tripping hazards.

Thin grass grew over the rocky terrain. This was the most overachieving grass of all time. I almost felt bad for stepping on it.

"Look," I said as I pointed to the base of a large boulder. "Another star shard."

It twinkled with enough inner light that it wasn't difficult to spot.

Nasbit, Ashlyn, and I walked out onto the sloped mountainside. The dragon and stone golem stayed behind, near the trees. They were heavy enough that they'd likely cause a landslide.

I went to great lengths to be careful. I didn't step on any loose pebbles, and I stayed within arm's reach of a boulder at all times. Nasbit did the same. Ashlyn went ahead, though, her confidence on full display as she half-slid over some of the terrain to make it to the star shard first.

Ashlyn knelt and picked up the thumb-sized crystal. The illumination from the stone lit up her heart-shaped face.

She was rather beautiful.

When Ashlyn turned to face me, I immediately looked away and pointed to another shard. "There's one more."

Ashlyn offered a coy little smile as she tucked the shard into the pocket of her trousers. Then she walked over and scooped up the second one. "Are you afraid of falling, Gray?"

"What?" I balked. "Of course not." I removed my hand from the nearby boulder and crossed my arms. "I'm just aware of my surroundings."

"You're not as quick to grab the shards anymore."

"I'm just letting everyone else have a chance to pick them up." I lightly smacked Nasbit on the shoulder. "It's your turn now, buddy."

Nasbit rubbed at his arm as he lifted an eyebrow. "Um. No, thank you. We're on the side of a mountain. What if I fell?" He grabbed at his substantial gut and jiggled his stomach around. "Do I look like a man who enjoys scrabbling up a mountainside? If I fall, I'm going *all* the way to the bottom. And then I'll splatter."

Splatter.

Curse the abyssal hells, did Nasbit really have to use that word? I didn't want to think about it. We were pretty high up. A five-hundred-foot fall down a rocky mountainside would be the end of me.

Sweat dappled my forehead. I wiped it away before Ashlyn could notice.

"*Nasbit* is afraid," I said with a forced laugh and huff. "But not me. I've done way crazier stuff than this before."

Ashlyn pointed to a third shard. It was by another large

boulder, but further down the slope. "There's another one. Why don't you get that one? Unless you're afraid, that is. If you are, I can do it."

Was she challenging me? It awakened all the competitiveness in my spirit.

Her dragon chuckled. "Maybe he should send his kitten to do it."

"Uh, no way in the abyssal hells," Twain said as he dug his claws into the shoulder of my robes. "Gray and I go together. Always. Even if that means we fall off the side of the mountain."

I shot him a glare.

Twain smiled, showing his little kitten fangs.

"Just admit you're scared, and I'll handle it," Ashlyn said.

For a long moment, I just stared at the distant star shard. It *was* on a part of the mountain that was more slanted. And there were loose rocks everywhere. If I slipped, I'd look like a fool. But if I didn't go and get it, I'd look like a coward.

I couldn't have any of that.

When I gave Twain another look, he just frowned.

"What're you thinking?" he whispered.

"Better living through magic," I quipped.

I just needed some sort of magic to help me in this situation. I was a mimic arcanist, after all. Twain could transform into something that could help me.

But what mystical creature had I seen with an ability to help in this situation? Obviously, there was a rizzel nearby—and they could teleport. But if I teleported over to the star shard, there was still a chance that I'd slip and fall. And since Twain couldn't remain transformed for long, I probably wouldn't have time to teleport back.

Wait...

The head of housekeeping...

She had telekinesis. She had moved the laundry around without ever touching it. Her eldrin—the engkanto—was known for its powerful telekinesis. If I used that, I could grab the shard without needing to walk over to it.

"Stand back," I said. "I'm going to handle this."

Nasbit narrowed his eyes. "Are you sure about this?"

Ashlyn returned to her dragon near the trees, leaving Nasbit and me by the boulders. Then she gave me a sarcastic salute. "Go ahead. I can't wait to see what you do this time, *Captain Surprises*."

Ah. Look at that. We already had cute nicknames. This was going great. I just needed to make sure I followed through and actually retrieved the star shard.

Nasbit faced me with a frown. In a harsh whisper, he said, "My uncle said the number one way that men die is trying to impress a woman."

"I'm not trying to impress anyone," I snapped back, keeping my tone low. I glowered at him. "I'm just looking for ways to practice my magic."

"She's not worth it," Nasbit whispered.

"Shh. I got this."

I closed my eyes. The threads of magic—the string that led back to each magical person and creature—were so numerous. I scrunched my eyes, closing them tighter than before. A string for the dragon, for the golem, for the many others in our class...

The students in all the other classes...

The professors...

Maybe more...

Then I found a thread of magic that felt familiar. The laundry room. The head of housekeeping...

I tugged on the thread. Then I opened my eyes. Twain carefully leapt off my shoulder and then bubbled as he transformed into an engkanto elf. It was the same woman elf the housekeeper had—a mystical humanoid elf with silvery hair. The elf even came clothed, which was comfortably modest, and made me wonder if engkanto created clothes for themselves from magic.

Nasbit stared at the engkanto.

"Oh, my," he muttered.

Ashlyn just watched from the tree line, her face twisted in confusion.

I held up my hand and then hesitated. I had learned how to evoke magic—but nothing else yet. Was telekinesis an evocation? Or was it manipulation? Or maybe augmentation? I didn't know.

"Twain," I whispered. "Do you know how to use the telekinesis?"

He shook his elf head. "Nope. I can... try?"

"It's okay. I got this."

"I'm getting the feeling that you might *not* got this."

"It worked out for us last time."

Twain had nothing to say after that.

After a deep breath, I tried pushing my magic out of me, but in a slow way.

It hurt. Just like the ice of the wendigo, it coursed through my body at a quick and powerful rate. I wasn't used to it, and the engkanto was *powerful*. With my teeth gritted, I tried to imagine grabbing the star shard and floating it over to my hand. It was right at the base of a medium-sized boulder. It should be easy to float over.

Instead, I blasted the boulder—and the shard—off the side of the mountain.

They just flew off. A hundred feet sideways.

The rumble and *boom* of my magic left me momentarily stunned. I almost lost my footing from the quaking.

Ashlyn and Nasbit watched with unblinking eyes as the boulder angled down, twirling as it went, and fell all the way to the trees below. It crashed into the woods at the base of the mountain, leaving a mess of shattered trees and a slight crater.

The star shard was long gone. It was in the hands of the Death Lords now.

My whole shoulder burned.

Twain transformed back into a kitten as I fell to one knee.

With a forced chuckle, I said, "Yeah, well, we didn't need one star shard, right?"

"It's worth *two years'* worth of someone's income," Nasbit whispered, reminding me of their extreme value. He pointed to the new crater out in the distant woods. "And it could've been someone's *soul*."

"*It's not someone's soul*," I hissed. "What's wrong with you?"

"We can't be sure of that... and now it's lost forever."

Damn. Why did Nasbit have to make it sound like the worst situation possible?

Ashlyn ran a hand down her face. "Oh, no. Do you think anyone will find out about this?"

I half-shrugged. "It was an accident."

"It doesn't matter! If anyone finds out, I'm sure we'll all be issued demerits for losing a star shard." Ashlyn brought her knuckles to her lower lip. She bit on one of her fingers, her eyes practically staring a hole into the ground. "This isn't good..."

I glanced over at Nasbit. "Is Ashlyn having a panic attack?"

He nodded once. "Probably. Ashlyn's father wants her to do better than her brother. He never received any demerits while attending Astra Academy."

Ashlyn flashed Nasbit a glare that could kill. "Keep that to yourself, Naz."

"Her father and my uncles go boating every summer," Nasbit whispered to me, despite Ashlyn's constant glowering. "If Ashlyn gets in trouble, her father is going to hit the ceiling. He's expecting her to be top of the class."

I hadn't known that.

"What're we going to tell Professor Zahn?" Ashlyn asked as

she turned and petted her typhoon dragon. Her eldrin wrapped his finned tail around her feet.

"That we found seven shards," I quipped. "Why would we tell him anything else?"

Ashlyn's dragon chuckled. She turned to me with narrowed eyes. "And that's it? Because I don't want anyone to think—"

Another rumble cut Ashlyn short.

The ground shook harder than before. I grabbed the nearby boulder, and so did Nasbit. The trees rocked back and forth, their pine needles falling off in disturbing amounts. The pebbles on the mountain slope slid down all around us.

"What's happening?" Ashlyn asked as she turned to face the forest behind her. "Gray? Is this because you disturbed the mountain?"

"Uh, I doubt it," I said.

Nasbit gulped down a swallow.

Another *boom* rang out across the mountainside. It sounded like the telekinetic blast I had just used, only it came from the forest.

A tree—*a whole fully-grown pine tree*—smashed out of the woods, shattering the trunks of other trees in its path. It sailed straight for me. My heart hammered, and I didn't have enough time to react.

Thankfully, Ashlyn was quick on her feet. She thrust her hand out and blasted the tree with her lightning evocation. It struck the trunk and the tree swerved off course. It almost slammed into me, but due to the lightning strike, it just barely missed and sailed off the side of the mountain.

A few stray splinters had cut my face, but nothing bad.

The tree fell all the way to the base of the mountain, and then crashed into the forest below.

Nasbit and I scrambled behind our boulder, just in case another tree came our way.

"Are you okay?" Ashlyn called out.

Blood wept from a cut on my lip and chin, but I wiped it away. "I'm fine."

"What's going on?" Nasbit asked as he glanced around the boulder and stared at the ruined forest.

"I don't know," Ashlyn shouted back.

Her typhoon dragon flared his fins and stood protectively near her. "Someone is attacking us!"

Nasbit's golem held the lantern up high, but the light wasn't enough to illuminate the whole forest. Who had attacked?

Another rumble disturbed the mountainside.

Whoever was out there—they were definitely aiming for me.

CHAPTER 34

HOW LONG DO ARCANISTS LIVE?

I knew it.

The lady in the Menagerie—the one trying to kill me —wasn't dead. Piper's eldrin hadn't disintegrated her with the rizzel's white flames. *My attacker was out here in the woods, trying to finish the deed.*

"Ashlyn, Nasbit, run!" I yelled.

Ashlyn turned, her eyes narrowed, but she didn't run off. She remained tensed and ready to evoke her lightning. Even her typhoon dragon widened his stance, his fangs bared.

Nasbit also didn't move. He stayed next to me, his brow furrowed in confusion. His golem didn't move, either. It held the lantern higher as though that would help.

Whoever was out in the woods wasn't after them. If they just ran, they would be safe, I was certain.

Twain twitched his long ears. "Gray... What're we going to do?"

My arm still hurt from the botched attempt at using telekinesis. What kind of magic could I use in this situation? When the woods rumbled and another *boom* sounded across the mountainside, my heart practically stopped.

Another tree flew out of the woods, breaking several other pine trees in its path. Once again, Ashlyn evoked her lightning. Her dragon did, too. The bolts of raw power split the tree into two large chunks. The tree bits slammed down the side of the mountain, missing Nasbit and me again.

But Ashlyn lost her footing from all the quaking.

Her baby dragon roared as Ashlyn slid down the slope. Thankfully, she managed to grab ahold of a boulder before tumbling too far. Her clothes were scuffed, and her palms were bleeding from a few scrapes, but overall, she seemed fine.

"I'm okay," she called out.

Despite his size, Ecrib slid down the slope to be closer to his arcanist. He used his finned tail to control his descent. Then he stopped his sliding by digging his clawed hands into the boulder nearest Ashlyn. She patted his side and whispered something to him.

Nasbit's golem also slid down the slope toward us.

"Wait!" Nasbit called out.

But it was too late.

The golem practically rolled into us. Nasbit and I had to grab the golem's arms to make sure it didn't go flying off the side of the mountain. The beast was heavy! Both Nasbit and I grunted as we yanked the golem into a standing position. It was only a baby, about the height of a preteen, but it had to weigh hundreds of pounds.

The lantern in the golem's hand swung back and forth.

Another rumble in the woods brought my thoughts back to our reality.

"Twain, turn into a rizzel," I said. "We have to teleport."

His eyes grew wide. "But we haven't learned that yet! It's just been evocation!"

"It's the only way!"

Twain closed his eyes, and then a second later, his body bubbled and transformed into a cute little white-and-silver rizzel.

It was Piper's rizzel, Reevy! Or Professor Zahn's rizzel. I didn't know his name. They looked identical, actually. Perhaps all rizzels did.

Quaking disturbed everything around us. The pine needles in the trees rustled. Was my attacker preparing to throw another? They were obviously using powerful telekinesis to rip a tree out of the ground and then shoot it through the air, all from the safety of the shadows.

What a coward.

"If you weren't such a craven, you'd come out to fight me!" I shouted. Then I snapped my fingers and turned to Twain. "Okay. Let's do this."

The shaking of the mountainside caused more pebbles to cascade down the long slope. Ashlyn's dragon protectively wrapped his tail and one arm around her.

"What're you planning?" Nasbit asked me with a frown.

I grabbed his arm. Then I waved Ashlyn and her dragon over. She took a deep breath and then hurried over to my boulder, her typhoon dragon close behind. She stared at Twain in his new ferret form and immediately understood what I was planning.

"Don't accidentally send us off the side of the mountain," Ashlyn said as she grabbed my shoulder. "You're better than that."

I was better than that?

Well, I couldn't disappoint her now.

The typhoon dragon and the golem gathered around, both touching their arcanists. Hopefully, we would all go at once. Hopefully.

Before another tree could be thrown, I closed my eyes. I didn't push the magic outward this time. What could I do? Augmentation altered. I was *altering* our position in space. I was changing something internal and intrinsic. And I remembered the feeling I had when Piper teleported us, so...

With my teeth gritted, my insides swirled.

I almost vomited.

But that was the moment I felt a terrible tugging sensation. We teleported with a pop of air and a splash of glitter.

The magic...

I didn't have control of it.

We appeared a few feet above the forest. Then we all fell screaming into the pine trees. The stone golem crashed through several branches, snapping everything in its path. My arm felt useless as I collided with a tree and then tumbled down onto another one.

Ashlyn and her dragon managed to cling to a branch, but it was too dark for me to see much, and I felt like I was spinning. It quickly became impossible for me to understand what was up and what was down.

Twain screeched like a cat as his rizzel form faded.

I hit another branch before finally smacking into the ground. In that moment, I would've preferred if my attacker had just killed me. Everything hurt. My vision spun. I wanted to vomit.

With a grunt, I slowly fluttered my eyes open. I had landed... on the brick stone path back to North Peak and the Nimbus Sea.

The wind had been completely knocked out of me. It took a second to cough and wheeze. I slowly managed to stand, but it took a significant amount of effort.

Teleporting was dangerous business. I wouldn't be doing that again anytime soon.

Our glowstone lantern had smashed on the ground, but the magically infused rocks still illuminated the area. The baby stone golem stood—I was surprised it hadn't cracked—and then, though it had no eyes, it "glanced" at the damaged lantern.

With careful movements, the golem swept up the glass and tried to collect all the glowing stones. It didn't have any fingers, though. The creature did everything with fist-sized rocks for hands. Whenever it picked something up, it had to do so gently or risk smashing it.

Twain staggered out from a nearby pile of dead pine needles.

"I landed on my feet," he said with a cough.

"Of course you did."

Ashlyn and her dragon slowly descended from a nearby tree. Then she withdrew a star shard from her pocket. The inner sparkle gave us more light by which to see by. She took several deep breaths and then felt the arcanist mark on her forehead.

She turned to her dragon. Ecrib wagged the tip of his tail. Then he stretched out his long neck and poked Ashlyn's cheek with his reptile nose. She smiled and hugged his head. They both looked as though they had taken a beating.

"We need to get out of here," Ashlyn said as she stepped away from her dragon. "Before we all get killed. Either from thrown trees or Gray's botched teleportation."

"Don't worry, that lunatic isn't after you." I walked forward, trembling as I went. "They're after me." Rizzel magic was difficult to use because of my inexperience, and Twain's age. Older mystical creatures were more powerful, and arcanists who had practiced for many years could use their abilities with greater control and might.

We had none of that. Like an amateur blacksmith trying to lift the forge hammer on the first day, I just didn't have the muscles.

I needed to rest—no more magic use for just a little bit.

Nasbit stumbled as he got to his feet. Then he held on to a tree to straighten himself. "Gray, you're the target of a murderer? Oh my. What kind of heinous crimes did you commit on your island?" He frowned. "Is that why you're friends with the reaper arcanist? You're both murderers and criminals?"

Ashlyn smacked his shoulder. Nasbit flinched and rubbed at the spot where she had struck him.

"Are you serious?" Ashlyn asked me. "Someone is really trying to kill you?"

"That's why I was attacked in the Menagerie. Before that..." I'd had all those nightmares. Someone had been trying to kill me for a long time.

This had to be the same person.

Where was Professor Helmith? I needed to speak to her. *I needed to find her*. With my jaw clenched, I closed my eyes, trying to focus my thoughts.

What had I learned about Helmith's disappearance so far? Someone was impersonating her. They looked exactly like her. How? Obviously through magic, but I wasn't sure what kind. And why? I didn't know. Was it to get to me?

Why me?

"But why you?" Ashlyn asked, mirroring my thoughts. "Why would anyone want to kill you?"

I shook my head. "I don't know." I had never known. Not even Professor Helmith had known.

Even now, it all seemed preposterous.

I was just... the son of a candlemaker.

Ashlyn frowned—more in anger than disappointment. "You have no clue? Someone is just ripping up the woods to end you, but you don't even have a guess as to why?"

I stood straight and glared. "For the past few years, I've had monsters in my nightmares trying to kill me. One of them attacked me in the Menagerie. There. Now you're caught up. You literally know as much as I do!"

Twain took several deep breaths. He hurried to my leg and pawed at it. After a long sigh, I leaned down, scooped him up, and held him in my arms.

Everyone was quiet. I didn't know what else to say. Either they would believe me or they wouldn't, but I had already stopped caring.

Ashlyn crossed her arms. Her dragon offered me a cold glare.

"You need to speak to Professor Helmith," Nasbit said matter-of-factly. "Her ethereal whelk can manipulate dreams."

"Yeah. I know." I petted Twain, and he purred in my arms. At least he wasn't too hurt.

"But if someone was trying to kill you in dreams, why are they trying to kill you in the woods now?"

I shot Nasbit a sideways glance. "I already told you—you know as much as I do. Maybe my attacker thinks forests double as awesome graveyards. Stop being a bagel and don't ask stupid questions."

Nasbit shook his head. "It just doesn't make sense. If someone had the ability to kill you in your dreams, it's the perfect crime. Barely anyone would have the capability to catch them. And a murderer out in the woods would leave evidence. Like the broken trees and leaving Ashlyn and me as witnesses." Nasbit tapped at the side of his head. "But killing people in their dreams is ingenious. Murdering you in the woods is not. Now, maybe I'm a *bagel*, but my doughy bread-brain says something doesn't add up."

I glanced around, hoping my attacker wasn't heading for us. The woods were quiet. No movement. It seemed as though we were alone.

"What're you trying to say?" I asked.

Nasbit sighed. "I'm not sure. Just that... we're missing a lot of information. Maybe we should tell Professor Zahn."

"Yeah," I muttered. "That's probably for the best."

If I asked Zahn to go to the headmaster, maybe they could catch the fake Helmith, and we could finally get to the bottom of this. On the other hand, what if...

What if the other professors were in on this somehow? I still didn't have any tangible evidence about the fake Helmith. And all the professors except for Zahn had feigned ignorance when it came to noticing changes in her behavior.

I needed more time. I didn't want to show my hand unless I knew it would result in Helmith being saved.

I didn't know who to trust. While Astra Academy was famous, I knew no one here. Not even the headmaster. What if *the staff* had hurt Helmith?

"No, I've changed my mind," I said. In a hushed voice, I added, "I think Professor Helmith might be—"

Nasbit's eyes grew wide. "*The murderer?*"

"No! I just... I don't want anyone to know that I know something is wrong. So I have longer to figure things out."

Ashlyn knitted her eyebrows together as she narrowed her eyes. "Why?"

"Because. I think other professors might be in on this."

Professor Helmith. She was in danger. And I didn't know why or how. Something told me this was all related.

Nasbit rubbed at his chin while he studied me.

Ashlyn pointed to the path. "Let's head back to Professor Zahn. We've gathered enough."

All of us turned to the brick road. Even Nasbit's golem, but now the creature was cradling a broken lantern in its arms as though it were a member of its family that had tragically passed away.

"We shouldn't say anything to anyone," Ashlyn said as we walked, her voice hushed.

Nasbit quickly glanced over. "Are you serious? Someone tried to kill us!"

"Gray. They tried to kill Gray." She sighed. "Not us."

"And you don't want to say anything? Is it because your father will be angry? I don't think that's a good enough reason to hide things from one of the Academy professors."

Ashlyn shrugged. Then she motioned to me. "It's Gray's problem. Do you want to tell Professor Zahn, Gray?"

I shook my head. "I'd rather not."

Nasbit just glanced between us like we were insane. His look of utter disbelief—his mouth half-open, his eyebrows raised—was the most shocked I had ever seen him.

"But... someone is in the woods! *Right now*." He waved one of his arms at the darkness all around us. "You don't want them to get caught?"

"Well, yeah," I muttered.

"Then we should tell someone. It's simple logic! What's wrong with you two?"

Ashlyn and I said nothing. We were clearly in unspoken agreement. She didn't want to admit anything that might cast us in a negative light, and I didn't want to alert anyone to the fact I knew something sinister was going on.

For the rest of the walk, we remained silent. Not even our eldrin spoke. Thankfully, the mountain woods were just as quiet as we were. The animals had likely fled after the incident with the trees.

Though there were only so many people who could use powerful telekinesis.

Surely, the housekeeper wasn't the one after me.

Was she?

I rubbed at the side of my face. Perhaps the panic and attack had been too much, because I found it difficult to come up with a plausible explanation.

Ashlyn, Nasbit, and I trekked through the woods and then up the stone steps until we reached the platform above the clouds. The chill wind and beautiful Nimbus Sea helped me relax, but it didn't fully remove my anxiety over the situation.

Twain slept in my arms, obviously tired.

Most of our class was already waiting for us. They were gathered around the telescope, some even taking turns using it.

Despite the fact that Ashlyn's robes were scuffed and dirty, and my arm was stiff by my side, no one commented. They were too busy giggling and chatting about all the star shards they had found.

Only Sorin seemed to notice my agony.

He kept glancing over and mouthing questions.

"*What happened?*"

But I just shook my head and indicated I would tell him later.

"Has everyone returned?" Professor Zahn asked. His rizzel leapt onto his shoulder, still as grumpy as ever. Maybe even grumpier.

"Professor!" Nasbit called out. He hurried over, as fast as he could, though that wasn't saying much. "Professor! Uh, *I* was attacked in the woods!"

"Attacked?" Zahn asked.

Ashlyn rolled her eyes. I held back a groan.

Damn, Nasbit. We had talked about this!

Everyone stopped their conversations and glanced over, their eyes wide. That was when Sorin ran to my side. He looked me up and down and then patted my shoulders. I pushed him away, irritated he would coddle me in front of everyone else. We were adults now! I didn't want to look like a child.

Professor Zahn adjusted his glasses. "What happened?"

"Someone in the woods used telekinesis to throw trees at me and Brak." Nasbit grabbed his golem. "They smashed our lantern." His golem dropped the ruined piece of equipment on the ground, the metal clattering against the stone.

Phila gasped.

"Are you harmed?" Professor Zahn walked over and gave all three of us the once-over. "You look... roughed up."

"We ran away. Gray saved me." Nasbit smiled.

"Who was this person attacking you?"

"We never saw them."

An explosion of whispers and excited chatter flew around the telescope platform. I had never known something so morbid could be so fascinating.

Nasbit kept hold of his golem. "I don't know why anyone would attack me, but that's what happened."

Nasbit had made it seem like *he* had been the target. Was that because he didn't want to anger Ashlyn or me? I supposed it would work, although Ashlyn didn't look happy about this development.

Zahn stared at Nasbit for a long while. Then he glanced over to me. "Perhaps... it's because you all had star shards. There may be thieves out in these mountains."

"That was probably it," Nasbit said.

"The headmaster will need to be informed *at once*."

Professor Zahn snapped his fingers, and his rizzel teleported away in an instant. I suspected the little creature would go straight to Headmaster Venrover to tell the tale.

"Gray, can you stay with Nicholas and make sure he's safe?" Zahn asked.

Nasbit frowned. "My name is Nasbit Dodger."

"Er, right. *Nasbit*. Yes."

I walked over and nodded. "I can watch him."

"Good. Well, since we're all back, and since there might also be someone dangerous out in the mountains, I want everyone to gather up around me. We're going to take our star shards to the Academy. I'm just going to teleport us there."

When I turned to Nasbit, I noticed he was shaking. Was it from the cold? It didn't seem like it. Was he still shaken by the attack? Probably.

I leaned in close and whispered, "They were after me, remember? You don't need to worry."

Nasbit forced a nod but said nothing.

Once everyone had gathered near, we all grabbed each

other's hands to form a circle. This was just like with Piper, only I suspected Zahn wasn't going to forget one of us.

"Now, everyone, hold tight." Professor Zahn half-smiled. "We're going to the foundational floors, where the Academy creates magical items. Very exciting."

A few people seemed genuinely interested, but others looked ready for bed.

My heart was still racing from the attempted murder. I didn't want to see magical items, though. I wanted to see Helmith. The *real* Helmith. I needed her guidance more than ever.

The teleportation rocked my insides a second time. Everyone else remained standing once we had arrived, but I fell to one knee, my chest knotted in agony.

I grabbed my shirt and twisted my fingers into the fabric.

"Gray!"

Sorin ran to my side. This time, his knightmare was with him. The shadowy suit of armor stood by me with a protective stance. Then my brother placed a heavy hand on my shoulder.

"Are you okay?" He knelt and grabbed my arm. When I tried to jerk free of his grip, he just held tighter.

I pushed myself to my feet, Sorin helping me the whole way, even after my protests. "I'm fine. I just hate teleporting. It's like seasickness, only ten times worse."

A few people laughed at my comment.

Professor Zahn watched me with intense focus. When I offered a chuckle and a shrug, he seemed to relax a bit and then motioned for me to pay attention to the nearby door.

"Enough goofing off," Zahn said. "This is our creation room. We're technically two stories under the dining hall, just as reference."

We were definitely underground. There were no windows, and the ceiling was lower here than in most parts of the

Academy. The place had the smell of stagnant air. It reminded me of a cave.

"Wow," Exie said. While everyone else had muddy boots or dirt on their robes from a long night of star shard hunting, Exie's clothes weren't dirty at all. It made me wonder if she had even gathered any star shards. "You can teleport *so far*, Professor. You're amazing."

"It takes years of practice," Zahn said with a slight smile. "I'm a master arcanist, after all." He stood a little taller and even fixed his glasses properly in place.

"How long does it take to achieve the title of *master*?"

"Depends on the arcanist, but through careful study, perhaps five to seven years."

Nasbit continued to shudder. I wondered if it was from leftover anxiety over the incident in the woods. Despite his fear, he couldn't resist asking questions.

He raised his hand, and the moment Zahn sighed and pointed to him, Nasbit blurted out, "How long do arcanists live? When I asked my uncles, they said *forever*."

"In theory," Professor Zahn said as he approached the door to the creation room. "Arcanists can die from disease or accident or murder, but they never grow old and perish."

"So, an arcanist who fought in the God-Arcanists War could still be alive?"

"Yes."

Nasbit's eyes grew wider. "So that means an arcanist could be old enough to have seen the abyssal hells when the gates were open?"

The rest of our class gave each other odd glances. Nasbit came up with crazy questions sometimes. Made me think he needed to stop reading ahead and just learn everything along with the rest of us. His overachieving was giving him nightmares.

Professor Zahn nervously chuckled as he pushed open the

door. "Oh, probably no arcanist is *that* old. That's just silly. Now, come, everyone. Bring your star shards. There's something you all should see."

I walked close to Nasbit—Sorin close to me the entire time —and I just jabbed him in the side with my elbow. "What's wrong with you?" I asked. "You're acting super weird."

"I thought of something while we were walking." Nasbit kept his voice low so that no one would hear. "What if someone is trying to kill you because of an ancient grudge? What if you're being haunted, by, like, something from the abyssal hells? And now that I've helped you, *I'm* going to be haunted, too?"

Where was Nasbit even getting this stuff from?

"I'm not haunted. You're not haunted. *The Academy isn't haunted.*" I glowered at him. "Stop it. You're literally growing your own anxieties in a fear farm you keep in your head."

"I'll try..."

I shook my head and just allowed him to walk ahead of me. Sorin and Nini stayed with me as everyone else funneled through the door and entered the workroom. Once we were the only ones in the long, cave-like hallway, they gathered around me, even their eldrin.

"I'm glad you're okay," Nini said.

I nodded once and smiled. "So am I."

CHAPTER 35

THE BASEMENT

"What's really going on, Gray?" Sorin asked, no mirth in his tone. "Nasbit wasn't the focus of the attack, was he? It was you."

I nodded.

"Were you attacked the same way as in the Menagerie? Did you fall asleep? Were there puppet monsters?"

I shook my head and held Twain close. "It wasn't like that at all. It was almost... random. We were gathering star shards, and then someone attacked from the darkness of the forest. They clearly didn't want to be spotted, because they never got close."

Nini brought both her hands up to her mouth. With her eyebrows raised, she asked, "What did you do?"

I held up my sleeping eldrin. Twain's ear twitched, but otherwise, he didn't move. "Twain transformed into the professor's rizzel, and then we teleported to safety."

"You didn't fight the attacker?"

"I didn't even know who they were." I stared at the stone floor, an odd chill creeping into my body. "And their telekinesis was powerful... If they had gotten close, I probably would've been killed, but they kept their distance. They really didn't want to be caught."

Sorin folded his arms over his large chest. He pressed his lips tightly together as he mulled over the situation.

"I have to tell you something," I said as I turned to my brother.

I also glanced over at Nini, hesitating to include her. I barely knew her. However, after her confession about her brother—and how she trusted Sorin and me—I felt like I could trust her with *my* secret.

"The Professor Helmith here at the Academy is an imposter," I whispered.

Sorin stared at me with the same gray-blue eyes I had. Then a smile crept into the corner of his lips. "I knew it," he said.

"You... did?"

"Of course! You've been talking about meeting Helmith *for years*. I thought, once we made it to the Academy, you would never leave her side. The two of you practically have your own little twin secret language. But since we've gotten here... you've avoided her. Barely talked about her. You stare at the wall more than you daydream about Helmith."

My cheeks grew hot. I rubbed away the heat and shook my head. "Regardless, it's true. She isn't here. And I think whoever tried to kill me in the woods is probably related to her disappearance. I think I stumbled onto... some kind of conspiracy. Or something."

"Have you told the headmaster?" Nini asked.

Waste floated behind her, looming like a deadly shadow. "Let me guess. You aren't sure if the headmaster can be trusted?"

"I don't know who to trust," I said in a harsh whisper. "The headmaster said my attacker in the Menagerie died, but that's probably not true. What if the headmaster was making up a story to get me to stop worrying about it? What if Helmith is being held somewhere here?"

"What're we going to do?" Sorin asked. He squared his shoulders. "I'm ready to help you, Gray. We'll save your honeysuckle."

I glared at him. "Professor Helmith isn't my honeysuckle. *Just focus.* I want to—"

"Is there a reason you all are still in the corridor?" Professor Zahn called out.

He stood in the doorway to his magical item workshop, a curious expression on his face. He glanced at me, then Sorin, and then Nini.

"Sorry, Professor." Sorin walked over to the door. "We were talking to Gray about what happened in the woods."

Zahn offered us a split second of a smile. "Ah. Well. You don't need to worry about that. The headmaster and the guardians around Astra Academy will handle everything."

We all nodded along with his words. Then we headed into the workshop, walking by Zahn as we went. The man stared at us through his glasses, one eyebrow lifted. He examined me the longest, probably because I looked a mess. Pine needles were tangled in my hair, and my pants were covered in dirt.

We entered a gigantic room.

It took me by surprise, actually.

The room was larger than anything else in the entire Academy, even the ballroom. There were long, stone pillars positioned by the walls to help support the roof, which was nearly forty feet above us.

I had thought we were deep underground, but a colossal window had been built into the far wall. It had clearly been built into the side of the mountain. There was no ground outside the window, just a sheer drop—more than a thousand feet—all the way to the vast forest below.

The Nimbus Sea, swirling around North Peak, was visible when I walked up to the window and stared up at the far mountain peaks, but the moonlit night was too dark for me to identify anything else.

"Is that a Gate of Crossing?" Exie asked, drawing my attention back to the workroom.

Leaning against one wall, and nearly forty feet tall itself, was a massive, silver ring. It was carved with the same rizzel designs, but part of the ring was cracked open. The inside of the ring was being filled with... things?

Professor Zahn walked over to the Gate of Crossing and held up his arms. "Yes! Professor Helmith, Professor Jenkins, and I, all helped in the creation of those fabulous gates. We needed a way to transport people to the Academy in a quick and efficient manner. Airships weren't reliable because of the amount of time they take, and the many crashes that occurred due to storms. Headmaster Venrover is adamant that we not risk anyone's life getting them to these mountains."

"Because star shards rain down on these mountains frequently?" Nasbit asked. "So the Academy couldn't be built anywhere else?"

Zahn nodded. "Exactly." Then he pointed to the top of the circular gate. "But in order to use the *old* Gates of Crossing, a star shard must be used every time."

"Because the boats are so big! They need the magic on their end!"

Zahn held his words for a moment. Then he continued, "This *new* gate won't require any of that. It'll be open permanently. The gate will cost more to make, but it will save magical resources over the long run. Headmaster Venrover was *also* very adamant that traveling to the Academy should be as affordable as possible. A noble goal, I think."

Then our professor pointed to a long table.

Hundreds of star shards were stacked on top, each glittering and shining with their own inner magic. Professor Zahn went to the table and ran his fingers over the glorious crystals. "Everyone, please place your star shards here. We need these for the creation of our new gate."

Everyone in our class walked over to the table to marvel at the raw magical power. I even shook Twain awake just to show him. He blinked his little kitten eyes open and then stared at the shards with his mouth hanging half-open.

"Wow!" he said, twitching his whiskers. "That's so many."

The table also had other objects.

Weird objects.

Metal wires twisted into the shape of a bug. Jewelry of a nonmagical nature. A few staffs. A rug that had blue and purple designs woven across the sides. It reminded me of an eclectic marketplace. Was Zahn going to hold a street sale of stuff he didn't need from his home anymore?

And everything was ancient. The metal was rusted, the rug frayed. When I touched them, everything felt stiff or on the verge of crumbling. I suspected that magic had been used to preserve them—that was how old they were.

The professor must've noticed my confusion because he walked over and chuckled.

"Ah, Gray. I can see the cogs of your mind turning." He motioned to the jewelry. "These are used in magical item creation. We apply the star shards to the items, and then we imbue our magic into the objects. The star shards make everything permanent. The more shards used—and the stronger the arcanist—the more powerful the item."

"*Trinket* is the term for anything with less than ten shards used," Nasbit blurted out, excitement in his tone. "*Artifact* is the term used when more than ten shards have been used. My tutors taught me all about the basics."

Half the class groaned or whispered in irritation. Although, at this point, Nasbit's nonstop commentary was just part of the Astra Academy experience.

"Can you put any magical ability into an item?" I asked as I picked up a diamond necklace, honestly curious.

Zahn nodded. "In theory. The better a crafter, the easier it is to get exactly what you want out of the item."

I turned my attention to the odd wire bug. "What is this? For another item?"

Professor Zahn shook his head. He opened his mouth as though he were about to answer, but that was when Nasbit blurted out his own reply.

"The Gates of Crossing need objects tied to the destination," Nasbit said as he pointed to the crack in the gate. The inside of the silvery circle had already been packed full of objects. Everything was wrapped in cloth, though. I couldn't tell what was inside. "Rizzel arcanists have to picture where they're teleporting to, so for the Gates of Crossing to work properly, they need to be filled with objects relating to their ultimate destination."

Nasbit smiled widely, his earlier fear clearly gone now that he was back in his natural habitat, doing his favorite thing— pretending to be one of the professors.

"Those rugs and decorations are probably cultural objects," Nasbit added matter-of-factly. "I'm not sure where they're from, though..."

Professor Zahn patted Nasbit on the shoulder. "Good job, Nathan. But that's enough."

"*Nasbit*. My name is Nasbit."

"Mm-hmm. Interesting." Zahn led him away from the table. "But I'd rather you focus your attention on the gate. You see, we're using hundreds of shards to construct this because it has to teleport people vast distances."

Nasbit grew quiet, and I wondered if that was because he had been told to, or because he was admiring the giant magical marvel.

"Gray, you should come look at this, too." Zahn gestured for me to follow.

I walked over, Twain fully awake in my arms, his two-colored eyes taking everything in with the curiosity of a child. He hopped up and down as much as he could in my grip. Sorin and Nini followed along with me as though they were afraid to get too far away.

This Gate of Crossing seemed even larger now that I was close to it.

The gate was just so... massive.

Only three people had made this?

"What's inside of it?" Nasbit asked, his focus on the innards of the device. "I mean, where do the artifacts come from? Where will the gate go?"

Zahn took a deep breath, then exhaled. His patience had dried up. "The Amber Dunes. Now, if you look at the etchings here, you'll see—"

"Those cultural objects on the table don't look like they're from the Amber Dunes." Nasbit pointed to the wire bug. "My uncles summered in the Amber Dunes twice now. I went with them once. That insect is clearly not from the region."

Knovak placed a hand on the gate and scoffed. "I've been to the Amber Dunes as well. It isn't that luxurious of a place to spend one's summer."

"The heat is dreadful for my hair," Exie added with a roll of her eyes. "I prefer to summer in the snowy north."

Somehow, this had become a competition of who'd had the best summer vacation.

Professor Zahn pinched the bridge of his nose. I wondered if he regretted bringing us here. "If I say it goes to the Amber Dunes, then it goes to the Amber Dunes."

Knovak leaned into the gate, glancing around the inside and poking at the artifacts within. He even lifted up a blanket. Golden glittering crystals were underneath. "Wow," he said, drawing everyone's attention. "What're these? More star shards? They're beautiful. They must be expensive."

"*Get away from there*," Zahn snapped.

Knovak leapt away from the gate.

After another sigh, Zahn said, "You shouldn't disturb anything. Crafting an incredible artifact requires precision and—"

"But what about—" Nasbit started.

"*No more questions*." Zahn clapped his hands. "Actually, no more class. I think you've all had an eventful evening. Yes? You've learned a lot? I think so. Everyone, head out of the work room, go straight down the corridor, and climb the spiral staircase until you reach the ground floors of the Academy. You'll be able to find your dorms from there."

No one protested.

Everyone seemed exhausted from the evening's events. Even Ashlyn, who had leaned on her dragon for most of the tour, seemed ready to get back to the dorm.

I was tired as well.

And I needed to think about what I was going to do to keep myself safe.

The next day passed in a sleepy haze.

Our next class had to do with math and writing. The professor, to my surprise, wasn't an arcanist. He was a scholar who had come for the year to teach us the fundamentals of academy research, as well as advanced mathematical formulas.

I didn't pay much attention, though.

It wasn't until I returned to my dorm that I got excited to *do* something. Sorin pulled me aside, his overactive shadow fluttering around his feet.

"Gray," he said. "What're we going to do about Professor Helmith? I know you want to help her. You weren't even paying attention in class—you were just daydreaming."

The way he had worded his sentence...

It gave me an idea.

"Sorin, go get Nini. Let's meet on the walkway to the treehouse." I pointed to the window, to the branch pathway. "I want to try something."

Chapter 36

Practice

The sun set in the distance, giving us a sad amount of lighting.

Sorin, Nini, and I stood on the long, wooden pathway, away from the windows, and out near some of the enormous needle leaves. We were hidden here—out of sight, hopefully out of mind.

Nini wore her large coat and her robes, giving her a blob-like silhouette. Sorin, for whatever reason, had taken off his robes and stood with us in just a tunic and trousers. The cold wind was relentless this evening, but Sorin never shivered or complained. It was like his muscular build insulated him from winter.

"What're we going to do?" Nini asked as she cleaned her glasses on the bottom of her shirt.

"Professor Helmith used to visit me every night in my dreams," I said. "Her ethereal whelk eldrin allowed her to dreamwalk."

Sorin's eyebrows shot to his hairline. "Oh! I get it. You're going to do the same thing!"

I half-smiled. "Exactly. If *I* can walk into people's dreams, maybe I can find Professor Helmith. Maybe she's here."

Nini's eyes went wide. "Really? You think you can find her?"

"Well, hopefully," I said as I ran a hand through my hair. "I'm not the greatest at magic yet. That's why I need to practice. I don't know if I need to be asleep to dreamwalk, or if I can do it awake... And since Twain is young, and I'm inexperienced, my mimic eldrin can't stay transformed as something else for long. I need to fix that."

"What do you want to do out here, then?" Sorin asked.

"I was hoping to have Twain transform and just focus on holding the shape. Maybe I could use my magic... And you two could play lookout. Maybe use your own abilities as well."

Nini nodded and softly clapped her hands. "Okay. I like that." Her mirth died quickly as she added, "I really don't want to be in my dorm... Anything to stay out of there is fine by me."

Waste used the edge of his cloak to pat her on the shoulder.

"I like this," Sorin said. His shadows swirled, and out rose his knightmare. "Thurin and I will master our evocation! Or maybe even our *darkness powers*." He said that last part like he was on a theater stage. Then he motioned to the shadows all around us.

Sorin could have a great time in the middle of a hurricane. My brother just had a wellspring of never-ending optimism.

I set Twain down on the branch. "All right. Transform into an ethereal whelk, and we'll try to hold the shape for a full minute."

Twain wiggled his whiskers. "*We'll* hold the shape? No. This is all *me*, thank you very much. *I'll* hold the shape—you just try to learn as much as you can about ethereal whelks through magic use, got it?"

I petted his little orange head. "Yup. I got you."

With a huff, Twain transformed into the floating sea snail— the mystical ethereal whelk. His shell, the size of my head, was a spiral of iridescent colors. Tiny tentacles hung from his underside as he hovered in the air, and his whole body was almost translucent.

Professor Helmith's eldrin...

"Okay, Gray," Twain said, his voice now bubbly and otherworldly. "I'm gonna hold this... You just practice." There was a strain to his words.

I hoped this wasn't hurting him.

"Thank you," I said as I turned my attention to the small branches growing off the pathway. "What kind of evocation do ethereal whelks have?" It was a rhetorical question. I already knew the answer.

When I shoved magic through my body and visualized Professor Helmith, it was easy to evoke light. A blast of sunshine lit up the whole pathway, illuminating everything as though it were the middle of a bright summer day.

It still hurt. I had to shake out my hand afterward. The magic... it was so advanced. How could I overcome that?

I'd just have to keep practicing.

We practiced well into the night.

Fatigue was a terrible mistress. She clawed at me, draining my attention and desire to do anything. Only my thoughts of Professor Helmith kept me focused.

At first, Twain could only stay transformed for thirty seconds. He was an ethereal whelk several times, but eventually, I asked him to transform into a coatl. Evoking light would draw someone's attention sooner or later, but evoking wind wouldn't.

Additionally, the baby coatl's magic was more my speed. The wind didn't burn, and I was able to evoke it several times in a row without any problems. By the end of the fifth hour, I understood what evocation should feel like when I was doing it correctly.

I enjoyed the feeling.

The magic coursing through me...

And Twain had managed to keep his coatl form for nearly two solid minutes, which was amazing. The progress really invigorated me.

"Gray," Sorin called out.

I stopped my magical practice and turned around.

It was dark. The night had aggressively settled over us. The dark sky barely had any stars, and even the moon had taken a rest. The lights inside the Academy shone out to the walkway, but barely. The dim illumination made it difficult to see much, but that was okay. I saw their silhouettes just fine.

"What is it?" I asked.

Sorin stepped away from Nini and then motioned at himself. "Watch! I learned something new." After a short moment—as if making sure I was paying attention—Sorin stepped forward.

And then sank into the shadows.

It was exactly the same as how his knightmare disappeared into the darkness. Sorin "fell" into the void of shadows, moved a short distance through a line of darkness, and then stepped out at a new location.

He gasped for air as he emerged, reminding me of a child who had gone swimming underwater for the first time.

Sorin rubbed at his face and held out his arms. "See? Wasn't that amazing? Knightmare arcanists can shadow-step places!"

I softly clapped for him. "Bravo."

"C'mon, Gray. It was amazing. Don't be like that."

"No, I mean it. That was amazing." I needed to remember that trick for the future. Moving as a shadow would be very useful in certain situations.

Sorin gave me a little bow. Then he motioned over to Nini.

"You should see her abilities, too. Actually, would you mind helping her? Her evocation isn't effective on me."

"Why not?" I narrowed my eyes. "And don't the two of you evoke *terrors*?"

Twain, in his winged snake form, flicked out his tongue. "I don't like the sound of this," he said in a hissy voice.

"Knightmares are naturally resistant to fear-inducing magics," Sorin said. "Isn't that right, Thurin?"

His shadowy partner fluttered throughout the darkness around us. "Correct."

With a sigh, I walked over to Nini and Sorin. Experiencing terrors wasn't my idea of a good time, but I supposed helping wouldn't hurt. "Very well. Hit me."

Nini fidgeted with the cuffs of her coat. "Are you sure?"

"Yeah. Do it."

It was night. I was tired. We didn't need any more discussion on the matter.

Waste hung in the air close to his arcanist. Nini held up her hand and pointed it in my direction. I held my breath, prepared for *something*, though I didn't know what. Hopefully, it wouldn't be too bad.

For a long while, nothing happened.

I almost asked if she was even using her magic, but then it struck me.

An icy feeling twisted in my gut. My heart beat rapidly. My vision spun. I stepped backward, but stopped myself when I remembered we were on a branch at least forty feet off the ground. For some reason, my eyes blurred, and everything melted away.

Then my vision cleared.

I was back in my nightmares. The black stones, wet in appearance, were underfoot. Professor Helmith's voice rang out in the distance. She was calling for help. In my panic, I tried to run over the rocks, but I tripped. Helmith's voice became more distraught.

And then I heard the click-clack of wood on stone. The puppets...

They were here.

I tried to stand, but my arms were too weak, and my legs unbalanced.

"*Stop!*" I cried out.

The terrible scenario ended in an instant. I collapsed onto the wooden walkway, my breathing ragged. The night sky and the cold evening wind, were here to greet me.

Sorin and Nini knelt on either side of me.

"Are you okay?" Nini asked.

My brother patted my clothing. "It wasn't too bad, right?"

I rubbed sweat off my face. "That all happened fast."

"Sorry," Nini whispered. She hid half her face behind her coat's collar. "Do you think it would distract you in a fight?"

"Definitely," I said, trying to forget the phantom thoughts.

"I read in our bestiary that reapers evoke terrors, but... they also manipulate *blood*. I'm not sure how to do that."

"I won't be your practice dummy for that one," I quipped.

Nini giggled inside her clothing. With a smile, she pulled down her coat. "I just wonder how I should use it. Everything a reaper does is rather frightening."

Waste spun his scythe around. "We are the masters of death. You shouldn't fear your own magics."

Sorin stood and slapped his hands together to clear them of dirt. Then he glanced around. "It's getting late. I think we've practiced enough."

I jumped to my feet just as Twain lost control of his shape. He fought against the reversion, trying his hardest to remain a feathered snake. It just wasn't working. A cat leg popped out of the snake body, and then a wing molted away into a patch of orange fur.

The slow de-transformation was almost spookier than the terrors Nini created.

Finally, Twain gave up and just shifted back into his kitten form. He collapsed to the walkway, panting hard. The mark on my forehead changed back to a blank star.

"Someday you'll be able to hold it for hours at a time," I said as I scooped him into my arms.

"Days at a time." Twain chuckled. "*Months at a time! There's no stopping me. I'll be the best mimic ever.*"

I walked over to Sorin. Then we glanced over at Nini. She sighed.

"I'm going to return to my dorm now."

She spoke every word like she was marching to her own funeral.

"Everyone will be asleep," Sorin said with a smile. "And then we'll see each other tomorrow."

She offered a hesitant nod in response. Then she walked off toward the girls' dorm, leaving Sorin and me alone on the wooden walkway.

"Let's go," I said to my brother. "I need to get back to the dorm."

"Why's that?" Sorin crossed his arms.

"I want to attempt dreamwalking."

Twain grumbled something in my arms. He rolled around, half-limp, and even stretched out his claws. "I can't. I'm weak. *Too weak.*"

"It'll just be for a short while," I said as I turned my attention to the sky. "Everyone will be asleep. Professor Helmith... I might be able to reach her."

Sorin shrugged. "All right. That's a good plan. Maybe you can talk to her, and she can tell you where she's at."

"Let's hope so."

CHAPTER 37

THE DREAMSCAPE

The dorms were quiet when we returned.

Sorin and I snuck in through the window, and once we were inside, Sorin shadow-stepped into the darkness and slid over to my bed in complete silence. Then he exited the shadows and motioned me over. I was already jealous of that ability. I carefully made my way over to him.

Raaza and Knovak were fast asleep, their heavy breathing echoing throughout the half-empty dorm.

I brought Twain with me as I slid under my blankets. Sorin fluffed my pillow and made sure I was tucked in—like an infant —and I was ready to yell at him, but he just knelt next to my mattress and said, "I'll be here, just in case."

"In case of what?" I whispered.

"In case the monsters try to attack. I'll wake you up."

"I'll have ethereal whelk powers. You don't have to worry about me."

Sorin didn't leave the side of my bed. He placed a hand on the edge of the mattress. "Then just in case someone tries to get you while you're sleeping. In life, through time, with magic, until death... I've got your back."

For some reason, his words really resonated with me in that moment. He had said the same thing to Nini, but this time, it sounded... different. Sorin was always there for me. Always.

"Thank you," I said, my throat tight. "I couldn't ask for a better brother."

"I sometimes wonder why we were born twins, but I think it's because we have to look out for each other." Sorin leaned onto the mattress. "You know. Destiny. I'll watch over you, and you'll watch over me. I'd like to think that also makes Mom happy."

I gripped the blankets. "Don't talk like that. We don't need to talk about her."

"Nasbit keeps talking about the abyssal hells and whether the Academy is haunted..." Sorin hardened his expression, his gaze distant. "It makes me think about her more."

"Do not drown in the miseries of the past, my arcanist." Thurin's dark voice rang out from the shadows.

Sorin said nothing.

I rested on the bed. Then I petted Twain, and my eldrin stared at me with large eyes. What would Professor Helmith have done in this situation?

"You're right," I said to Sorin. "She would have been happy."

My brother perked up.

I poked Twain in the side. "Now let's go slip into some people's dreams and save Professor Helmith. We don't have much time."

Twain sighed. With a twitch of his ear, he said, "All right. But I'm tired. After this, I'm sleeping for three days straight."

He bubbled and shifted, and after a few short seconds, he transformed into the beautiful and mysterious ethereal whelk. The shine of his shell brightened our dorm with an iridescent glow. Despite that, Raaza and Knovak still didn't stir. Lucky us.

I exhaled and closed my eyes, wondering how I would dreamwalk.

Ethereal whelk arcanists could manipulate dreams...

Was it similar to my mimic magic? Could I feel the strings of dreams? I tried sensing Raaza and Knovak, both of whom snored loud enough to announce their arrival in a parade. It didn't take me long to sense the threads of their slumber.

With my breath held, I tugged on their dreams.

Knovak dreamt of...

Unicorns.

And Raaza dreamt of...

Men wearing masks.

I didn't stay long. Now that I knew how to search, I decided to tug on every thread I could sense. In quick succession, I went through a multitude of dreams. Images flashed through my mind, like flipping pages through a book with such speed that I couldn't read the words, but I could still see the pictures.

Dreams of necklaces, snow, clowns, festivals, oceans, broken bones, love, mountains, star shards, frogs, and hair tangling in someone's mouth all flooded my thoughts. It was difficult to sort through them, and for a brief moment, I panicked.

I'd never find Helmith.

But the cold comfort of a small tentacle touched the side of my face. Twain was trying to communicate with me, even while I surfed the dreams of others. He was comforting me.

Twain...

My mimic eldrin.

His presence gave me a little more focus.

Dream after dream, I searched. The images became more bizarre and distorted. One dream involved a sun and a moon in the sky at the same time. One involved someone scratching off their own skin. Another was a nightmarish situation where someone was being chased, but they just couldn't run fast enough to avoid the danger.

"Professor Helmith," I muttered aloud.

That called one of the strings to me. Something about it... felt familiar.

I tugged, and the image of a peaceful field filled my mind. The same field Helmith had created for me.

She was here.

"Professor Helmith?" I called out, my voice drifting into the dreamscape.

"Hello?" her beautiful voice called back, as if lost in the infinite void of everyone's collective dreams. "Is someone there?"

"*Professor?*" I shouted, louder than before.

There was a short period of silence.

The dreamscape was bizarre and abstract. Professor Helmith could manipulate it, but I didn't know how. It felt like swimming through a river of thoughts, unable to control what splashed against me. I wanted to see Helmith, but I couldn't pierce the fog. She was nearby, but I couldn't see her.

But finally, Helmith replied, "Gray? Is that you?"

"Where are you? Professor—I'm trying to find you!"

A rush of excitement and joy filled me. It felt like an eternity since I had spoken with Helmith. Hearing her voice again... talking to her... I had so much I wanted to say.

"Gray, listen closely. I'm in the basement of Astra Academy. *Don't come here.* And don't act rashly. Send the others."

Don't go?

"Professor, what's wrong?" I yelled.

But it was too late. My magic unraveled.

I snapped my eyes open as Twain transformed back into his kitten form. He wheezed and panted, his little body unable to handle another round of transformations. I sat up and held him close to my chest, my heart practically battering its way out of my ribs.

Professor Helmith...

Sorin stood, his body stiff. "Are you okay?" he asked.

I inhaled and exhaled. Then I replied, "Yes. Helmith is in the basement. She needs help."

Sorin glanced around. "Right now?"

"Well..." I shook my head. "She told me not to go. That I should send the others."

"Others *who*?"

"I don't know. I need to go back." I shook Twain, but he swiped at me with his little kitten claws. Although he caused my hand to bleed, I didn't release him.

"I can't!" he said. "I'm too tired." He sounded on the verge of tears.

We had been training for a long time. Even now, I felt exhausted. But the thought of leaving Helmith somewhere in the basement filled me with equal amounts of anger and shame. But at the same time, she didn't want me to go to the basement? I had *just* been there. Nothing had been wrong.

"Gray?" Sorin knelt next to me again. "What do you want to do?"

"I don't know."

"What, exactly, did Helmith say?"

"She said she was in the basement, and that I shouldn't go. She also said I shouldn't act rashly. I should send the others." I ran my hand over my face, rubbing at my skin enough to hurt. "What do you think she meant?"

"Maybe to tell the professors?" Sorin glanced around the dark room. "Or maybe the other students?"

That didn't make sense. Fatigue was stealing my logic. But at least I knew where she was. Maybe tomorrow, I could try the dreamwalking again, and I could ask for the specifics.

Why would I act rashly?

Did she mean I shouldn't panic? I didn't know.

"We should rest," I said.

Twain relaxed in my hands, and Sorin let out a long exhale. Everyone was exhausted. This was the best course of action.

"All right," Sorin said. "Tomorrow. We'll talk it over tomorrow."

I awoke the next morning in a foggy haze.

Again, I shuffled through class with little concern for my surroundings. Today was the study of combat arts. Apparently, we were expected to strengthen our bodies, as well as our magic and minds.

Our instructor—someone named Professor Jijo—hadn't yet returned to the Academy, so Captain Leon was here instead.

We arrived at the training field in order to discuss the many combat arts throughout history.

I didn't pay attention. I set Twain down on the grass and just stood near the edge of the field. Twain fell asleep instantly. He was still exhausted.

Sticks walked among our class, his three cerberus heads sniffing all the students, but I just shooed him away when he approached. One of the heads frowned and stared at me with sad eyes—Sticks was a good boy who didn't deserve to be shooed—but I had too much on my mind to be distracted.

Professor Helmith, and my attacker, were here in the Academy.

The class couldn't happen fast enough. So, while the others picked up practice weapons off a rack, I lingered at the back, trying not to draw attention to myself.

Captain Leon's white hair resembled a flurry of snow when caught in the cold winds. He tried to tame it by patting it flat, but it wasn't working. With a frown, he pointed to the various wooden weapons. "Combat arts are more than just defeating your opponent. They're about honing your body, adhering to discipline, and strengthening your resolve. Professor Jijo has a whole speech about *spirit* and *dedication*, but I can't remember much of it, to be frank."

Leon stroked his beard.

Sticks wagged his tail. "He mentioned respecting the opponent."

"Right," Leon muttered. But then he shrugged and just motioned to the equipment. "For now, just familiarize yourself with these. In a few minutes, I'll run you through a few drills. The same ones I put the knights through. That'll toughen you up."

Most everyone groaned.

Except Raaza. I had never seen the man so excited. He grabbed two wooden practice weapons from the racks—a training sword and a bo staff—and then took a minute with each to see how they felt. His kitsune leapt around his feet, clearly excited with him, but not for the weapons. She laughed and smiled, and her fox-fire went everywhere.

Ashlyn bumped me with her shoulder as she walked by. Then she turned to face me, offering half a smile. "You look lost, Gray. Are you paying attention?"

"Yeah, yeah." I shivered as I crossed my arms. "Spirit. Dedication. One with your weapon. Or something. I get the general gist of it."

"If you ask nicely, I'll protect you from your mysterious attacker," Ashlyn said, keeping her voice low.

I lifted an eyebrow. "Why would I do that?"

Ashlyn held a wooden bo staff in both her hands. With a quick twirl, she circled around me.

"Someone was willing to rip the whole forest apart to get to you," Ashlyn said. "I've been thinking about it for the last two days."

"Oh?"

"If it hadn't been for me, you would've been crushed by a pine tree." She snapped her fingers and a tiny spark of lightning crackled across her knuckles. "You never thanked me for saving you, by the way."

"I'm a little preoccupied at the moment. I'll deal with everything later." Including thanking Ashlyn. She *had* helped me, I just wasn't in the right state of mind to properly show my appreciation.

Ashlyn huffed a laugh. "I think you should probably do something about the person in the woods."

"I've got more important things to handle first."

"What's more important than someone trying to harm you?"

"Someone trying to harm someone I care about," I shot back, almost without thinking.

Ashlyn tensed as she stared deep into my eyes. All playfulness was gone when she asked, "Who's in trouble?"

I wanted to answer her truthfully, but I hesitated. Professor Helmith needed help. I doubted Ashlyn and her hatchling dragon were the ones for the job.

"I need time to think," I finally said. "Just leave me alone for a bit, okay? If you need a sparring partner, talk to Raaza."

Ashlyn obviously didn't like that answer. She hardened her expression and then turned away from me. "Fine." Without another word, she strode off toward the others. Her gait, stiff shoulders, and straight posture all told me she was angry.

I didn't want her mad with me.

But I really did have bigger problems to mull over. Perhaps I could make everything up to her afterward.

That night, I went straight back to the dorms with Sorin at my side. We were the first ones to turn in for the evening, which meant we had the room to ourselves.

"Nasbit kept asking about you during class," Sorin said as he leaned against the door. Anyone trying to get in would have to really push to move my large brother.

"Asking what?" I took a seat on a nearby bed. It belonged to no one.

Sorin shrugged. "He asked about everything, really. If you were okay. If you were feeling stressed."

"Hm."

I carefully set Twain down on the mattress. My cute little mimic eldrin curled up into a loaf shape and immediately closed his eyes. He was still tired. I had pushed him too far yesterday. Twain needed another day of rest. Would Professor Helmith be okay? I hoped she could wait a bit longer.

Sorin stared at me. "Gray? What do you want to do? Should we go to the headmaster and tell him what's going on?"

"I'm more tempted to go to Professor Zahn," I said.

"Why?"

"He was the only one who realized something was wrong with fake Professor Helmith. Everyone else barely talks to her, apparently. And Zahn works in the basement."

Sorin frowned. "If Helmith is in the basement, how come Zahn hasn't found her? Maybe he's the one keeping her there."

"He's busy with his massive project," I said as I mulled over the situation. "And the basement is gigantic. She's probably just somewhere he doesn't go. I doubt Zahn would admit the imposter's behavior was suspicious if he were the one holding her somewhere."

"Okay. Fair enough. But then why is someone impersonating Helmith?"

"So that no one knows she's missing."

"Why, though?"

"Because..." I rubbed at the side of my head. "The only logical answer is... they need time." I sat up straighter. "Here's what I think happened. *Someone* in the Academy is trying to do something."

"Like kill you?" Sorin quipped.

I nodded once. "Yeah. Like kill a student." I held up a finger. "Professor Helmith probably stumbled upon their plan. In order to keep her quiet, they *captured* Helmith and locked her away in the basement. They also did this because they need more time—"

"To kill you," Sorin casually added.

"—so they disguised themselves as the professor so to not raise suspicions. That way, they could keep working on their plan—"

"Of murder."

"—without interruption."

Sorin scratched at his chin. "Huh. Why not kill her, then?"

"I don't know..." I glanced over at Twain. "Maybe they need her for some reason?"

The mystery baffled me. Too many pieces were missing. All I knew was that our opponents were making mistakes. Their sloppiness implied they were desperate. Were they running out of time?

"Tomorrow," I said as I petted Twain. His little sleeping form was one of the most adorable things I had ever seen. "I'll walk through dreams again, and I'll get to the bottom of this."

"Okay." Sorin pushed away from the door. "But not until night, right?"

I shot him a sideways glance. "Yeah. We have to wait until people are asleep. That's the only time I can enter their dreams."

"Until then... we can do whatever we want?"

"Sure."

A smile slowly crept across Sorin's face. "Tomorrow is the day we're supposed to visit clubs so we can pick one to participate in."

"Ugh." With a roll of my eyes, I said, "I'll just sleep in."

"Wait!" Sorin took a seat on the bed next to me. "Let's join the boating club, okay? I really miss the water. Remember all those years we went swimming?"

"It's a *boating* club, Sorin. Not a *swimming* club."

"You know we'll go swimming if we're out on the water." Sorin smacked my shoulder. It hurt, but I shrugged it off. "C'mon. There's something poetic—and majestic—about the water."

With a loud sigh, I shook my head. I was about to deny his request when I remembered what Nasbit had told me. Ashlyn's father went boating on a frequent basis, which meant she probably did, too.

"Okay," I muttered.

"Really?" Sorin scooted closer to me.

"Yeah." I pushed him away. "We'll join the dumb boating club."

Sorin threw his arms around me in a tight hug. I exhaled and then couldn't inhale. Thankfully, the embrace didn't last long. Sorin released me, still smiling.

"Thank you, Gray!" He leapt off the bed. "It's going to be amazing. You'll see. We'll save Helmith, and then we'll get to show her all our boating skills we learned from the islands. Imagine the picturesque adventure we'll have, sailing across the lake."

He was so optimistic. Wasn't it tiring being that joyful?

I half-shrugged. "Sure. I'm looking forward to it."

CHAPTER 38

THE BOATING CLUB

I was *not* looking forward to boating.

We woke at the crack of dawn—a time reserved for try-hards and overachievers. When I woke, my first thoughts were of Helmith, and whether or not she was in danger. It irritated me when Sorin yanked me out of bed and rushed me through changing so we could get out to the lake. Knovak and Raaza were still asleep when Sorin and I exited the dorm.

We traveled the halls of the Academy in relative silence. Other arcanists walked by us in the halls, all of them older. I suspected they were second- and third-years, all heading to their clubs of choice.

Some offered me a wave. I barely managed a wave back.

Twain slept on my shoulder. When I turned down a new hall, he almost rolled off, but I managed to keep him on.

"Isn't your knightmare tired?" I asked Sorin as we walked.

"Thurin doesn't sleep." Sorin smiled brighter than the sun. "He watches over me while I sleep! Like the moon watches the world... A silent protector against the darkness." His grandiose tone bothered me more than normal.

I frowned but said nothing.

We exited the front of the Academy and I almost gasped at the regal grandeur. We hadn't entered the Academy from the front doors before. We had been teleported into the Menagerie, and I had later awoken in the infirmary. The front doors were new for me.

They were massive double doors as tall as a two-story house. One door was etched with a star, and the other door was etched with a globe. The dark wood and silver etchings made for a beautiful sight.

The front staircase to the Academy led down the mountainside. Hundreds of steps, multiple platforms, each decorated with fountains and benches. It was so perfect in its execution, I suspected magic had been heavily used in its construction.

Sorin and I headed down the steps.

Everything was made of black stone.

I touched the rails along the staircase, marveling at the cold beauty.

Normally, Sorin was the one focused on frivolous things, but this morning, he only had eyes for the distant lake. He took the steps two at a time, smiling the whole way. I followed after, my sleepy eldrin now in my arms. The steps bothered Twain too much for him to stay on my shoulder.

It felt like it took forever to reach the bottom of the steps, but in reality, it was only a few minutes. Once down, we headed along the path toward the pier. Sorin walked by my side, even as I dragged my feet.

"You okay?" he asked.

I nodded once. "I just want to bury myself in a shallow grave, that's all."

He punched my shoulder. I shot him a glare.

"We should've gotten breakfast," Sorin muttered. "You'd be less grumpy, then."

"Where's Nini?" I asked.

Sorin's smile waned. "Oh. She didn't want to go boating. She didn't want to join any club, actually. I didn't push the issue."

I didn't ask any further questions. I didn't want to bother him.

His knightmare fluttered through the darkness around his feet. "I'm certain Nini will change her mind in the future. We must respect her decision until an opportunity arises to show her the joys of group activities."

"That's right, Thurin." Sorin's smile returned in full force. "Maybe we can find a club she would really like."

We reached the pier a few minutes later.

I had forgotten how rundown and sad the paths near the lake were. They were nothing but dirt and worn-down signs. Astra Academy didn't much care for this area, obviously.

A single cargo ship, and ten smaller sailing boats, were all tied to the pier. The smaller vessels were for one or two people. They each had a single sail, and space enough for some supplies, but that was it.

Those smaller boats—they called them *windfruit*—were luxurious crafts made for families and arcanists who lived near calm and beautiful lakes. Windfruit didn't sail well in rough weather. As a matter of fact, a sharp breeze could blow them over. They were *only* good for sunny days and picnics.

"Wait," I said, staring at the small boats. "*This* is the boating club?"

Sorin crossed his arms, glaring at the tiny vessels. "Oh. We're not going to sail a *real* boat..."

The arcanists gathered around the windfruit were all chortling and preparing themselves little lunches and drinks. This was clearly a leisurely activity—not something I would consider a useful skill.

"Wait here," Sorin said, patting me on the shoulder. "I'm

gonna speak with the ship captain. Maybe he's also part of the boating club? We can sail with him."

"Sure," I grumbled.

Sorin headed off down the pier, leaving me on land.

The windfruit enthusiasts prepared their sails and polished the boats. One of them had a ghost koi eldrin—a semi-transparent fish with gold and black scales. It was the size of a dog and swam around the smaller boats, occasionally hoping out of the water and splashing around. The ghost koi weren't really ghosts, according to Professor Helmith. They were actually mostly water, and their control over the waves was quite precise. Apparently, ghost koi enjoyed calm waters, and could quell troublesome storms.

The ghost koi arcanist must've seen me staring. She was a small girl with black, windswept hair that was almost as short as mine. It seemed athletic and stylish, which matched her tight-fitting outfit. She didn't have her school robe, but she proudly wore a necklace with the school symbols hanging from the chain.

The ghost koi was clear in her arcanist mark—the fish was wrapped around the seven-pointed star.

She walked over, smiling widely, her suntanned skin even darker than mine.

"Hello!" she said. "I'm Helva. I'm with the boating club. Have you ever sailed on a windfruit before? They're *super* fast little boats. And so fun."

Helva spoke in a dreamy fashion, like the windfruit was a concept that should completely take me by surprise.

"Hello," I said, unable to muster enthusiasm.

"Would you like to join me?"

"No, thank you. I'm... stretching. Can't swim without stretching."

Helva glanced at the blank star on my forehead. "Oh, wow. Are you a mimic arcanist? Super rare."

Super.

She liked that word.

"Yes," I said. I held up my sleeping kitten. "I'm extremely powerful." Twain snorted and kicked his foot once.

Helva slowly nodded. "Oh. Okay. Well, if you change your mind, come join me. I'd love to teach you a few things." She turned and headed down the pier to the rest of the boating club. They all gave me odd glances, but I didn't have the brain power to dwell on it.

"Oh, hello, Gray."

I turned at the sound of the familiar voice.

Phila came down the dirt path, her coatl close behind. The feathered snake slid along the ground, its wings slightly spread. The rainbow feathers practically sparkled in the morning light.

Phila's long, strawberry-blonde hair fluttered freely in the wind. She wore her school robes over a yellow dress. Something about her always seemed bright, from her clothing to her expression.

"You're here to join the boating club?" I asked.

Phila smiled. "Oh, yes. I was never allowed near the water when I younger. When I heard that we could learn to swim and sail while at Astra Academy, I couldn't pass up the opportunity."

"You weren't allowed near the water?" I lifted an eyebrow, baffled.

Phila slowly nodded. "The nursemaids said I might drown. My mother said the same thing."

Nursemaids?

I didn't know what to say. I half-shrugged. "It's not difficult. I'm sure you'll be fine."

Her coatl hissed. I flinched, startled by its reaction.

"Phila should take this seriously," the coatl said, its voice *hissy* but also masculine in tone. "Until I'm large enough to pull her from a violent undertow, we shouldn't risk anything."

"There aren't any *violent undertows* in a small mountain lake," I said, trying to keep any sarcasm out of my voice.

Phila patted her eldrin. "Tenoch is just protective. Aren't you, Tenoch?"

Her coatl—Tenoch—tucked his wings close to his thin, snake body. "I will protect you, my arcanist. That is one of my sacred duties."

Before I could say anything, Phila returned her attention to me. "You're an islander, yes? You swim? And... you're confident in the water?"

"Yes, to all of those." Again, I was *trying* not to be sarcastic, but she was testing the limits of my self-restraint.

"Would you accompany me onto the ship? I would like to look around."

Sorin was already on the ship. Phila should've gone with him, but instead, it was now *my* sacred duty to escort her around, apparently. Knovak had said Phila had grown up in a palace—perhaps he was right. Phila seemed sheltered.

"I'll show you around," I said with a slight groan.

I walked forward until I reached the pier. Then I stopped and turned around. Phila hadn't moved. Neither had her coatl. I stared for a long moment.

"Well?" I asked.

Phila slowly made her way over. She was rather thin and pale. When she glanced at the water, her complexion grew wan. With a hesitant smile, she grabbed my elbow.

"Thank you for taking me," she said. "I've heard such good things about you. I'm happy to know they're true."

"Good things?" I half-smiled as we strode down the pier together. "From Ashlyn, I assume?"

"From Nini," Phila said, her eyes wide, her attention squarely on the gentle rolls of the water.

"Oh. I see." That probably made more sense.

We walked up the gangplank together, and Phila clung to my

arm much tighter than before. Her coatl flapped his wings and landed on her head. Then he slowly snaked his body around her neck, like a bizarre scarf, and clung to her.

Was the coatl afraid as well? Or was it protecting her?

Phila giggled as we made it to the deck of the ship.

"That was amazing," she whispered to me. "I love this."

"You *love* it?" She was practically strangling my arm. "I couldn't tell..."

"Oh, yes. I love experiencing new things."

"How did you get here?" I asked. "Didn't you take a ship to get to the Academy?"

"I took an airship. We flew through one of the Gates of Crossing and ended up here. I've never been on an old-fashioned sailing ship before."

Old-fashioned? Since when were sailing ships old-fashioned?

Phila must've seen my expression. She smiled. "Steamboats are the talk of the town where I'm from. Everyone wants to ride one down the rivers. The tickets are sold out for months. *They'll kill sail boats*, is what my mother said at breakfast once."

Steamboats?

Once again, I felt like an island bumkin. What was a *steamboat*?

I held Twain close. He snored in my arms.

We stood on the deck of the ship. It was smaller—only two masts—but Phila glanced around as though this were a massive vessel that we would surely lose our way on. I wanted to make a joke, but I held back.

I glanced around.

The sailors worked on the rigging and swabbed the deck like any good crew should. But then I noticed their dour expressions. Each had a frown, and a terrible look in their eyes. This was a gloomy ship of sadness.

When one man walked by, sweeping the deck clear of dirt, I held out my hand.

"Excuse me," I said. "Are you part of the boating club?"

The sailor wore a long coat, a tricorn cap, and a long frown. "Aye."

"Are you taking the ship out to sail?"

"Nope. Not today. We're in mournin'."

"Mourning?" Phila asked, her eyebrows knitted.

The man sighed. "The helmsman died two days ago. A sad day. We'll be drinkin' with his brother most of the night, so we're not takin' the ship out, ya see."

Phila nodded once. Then she returned her attention to the lake, her curiosity apparent. Even her coatl, who was still coiled around her neck, seemed mesmerized by the small body of water.

But the death interested me more.

My father had said deaths at sea were worse than those on land. Something about falling into the abyssal hells. I had never much paid attention, but now that I knew the abyssal hells were under the ocean, maybe there was some truth to his old tales.

I followed the sailor as he headed for the quarterdeck. The man turned around and squinted at me, obviously confused.

"Uh, do you mind if I ask about the sailor who died?" I motioned to the ship. "You don't look like you were attacked by pirates recently. Did he fall overboard?"

The sailor's frown deepened. "The helmsman died in his sleep, lad. Strange thing. Woke with all manner of injuries, like he had been cut. No one aboard would've—or could've—done it, though. It's a mystery. The ship might be cursed."

My heart almost stopped.

The man had died... in his dreams?

Professor Helmith had said there were several people getting attacked. And if she was being held somewhere, there was no one chasing away the nightmarish monsters.

It was still happening. Someone was *still* killing people through their dreams.

"Can I speak to the helmsman's brother?" I asked, my throat

dry. "I've had similar dreams where I woke with injuries. I'd like to know more."

The sailor shook his head. "I'd like to help ya, lad, but I don't think it'd be right." The man gripped the handle of the broom tightly. "Boro is really torn up. They weren't just brothers. They were twins. Looked identical—down to the last beard hair. They did everything together. Boro hasn't been talkin' to anyone since it happened."

This time, my heart did stop. Just for a second.

My thoughts became a buzz.

This was the detail I had been searching for. A piece of the puzzle that connected to so many others.

"Is Boro the older or younger twin?" I asked, my voice barely above a whisper.

I stared at the sailor, but I didn't really see him. My mind was elsewhere as he answered, "The younger, I think. They made jokes at times. I might be wrong."

No. He was right.

Because if Boro was the younger twin, that meant the older one had been killed. *I* was the older twin between Sorin and me. Sorin never had the strange nightmares, but *I* did. And in the forest, Sorin's group hadn't been targeted.

It had been mine.

Someone was killing the eldest twins. I had no idea why, but now I had more information. *New* information.

This seemed more important than everything else I had learned.

"Are ya okay?" the sailor asked.

I turned away from him, barely aware of his presence. "I'm fine." I hurried across the deck of the ship, glancing around for Sorin. I needed to speak with him. Immediately.

Fortunately, my brother was an easy target. He stood taller than most—sometimes by a foot—and I ran to his location at the stern of the ship. When I approached, he smiled, but the moment he realized I was distressed, his mirth vanished.

"Gray?" he said as he ran to meet me. "What's wrong?"

I grabbed his arm. "We need to go. I know I said I needed more time before I told people about what I've learned, but I'm done now. We need to go see the headmaster."

"Why? What changed?"

I pulled him closer and lowered my voice. "Someone is killing the older sibling in sets of twins. One of the sailors died in his dreams. An older twin."

"When?" Sorin asked.

"Two days ago."

And although I still didn't have physical evidence, or even a motive, I felt like I couldn't dwell on this problem any longer. I needed help. *Helmith* needed help. I had to take everything I knew to someone who could do something substantial with it— and I hoped I wasn't making a mistake by trusting them.

Sorin turned toward the gangplank with a grim expression. "Okay. Let's go."

I walked with him off the ship, passing Phila as we went. I thought she tried to speak with me, but I didn't even pay attention. Nothing else mattered.

"We'll go straight to the headmaster," Sorin stated.

"And then to Professor Zahn," I said as we headed down the pier.

"Why Zahn?"

"Don't you remember? He's a twin, too. Either he or his brother could be targeted as well. Maybe his brother is already dead... Zahn said he hadn't heard from his brother in a long time."

"You think lots of twins have died?" Sorin's voice was so low, I almost couldn't hear it.

"I do," I stated. "Hopefully we can put a stop to this before it's too late."

"I don't think you should go to sleep again," Sorin said as we strode forward. "I have a bad feeling, Gray. Like... bad omen feeling."

We headed straight for the path back up to the Academy.

I just hoped the headmaster was someone I could trust.

CHAPTER 39

TWINS

We pushed open the gigantic doors of the Academy and went straight for the courtyard. No one stopped us. A few people waved, and a couple of professors called out, but Sorin and I didn't slow for any reason.

"Maybe you should have Twain transform into a rizzel so we can teleport," Sorin said.

Twain—who had curled up comfortably against my chest—was still asleep. I could wake him, but I figured he should regain his strength first.

"I'm terrible at teleporting," I said. "Unless you want to risk tumbling down the side of the mountain, I recommend we just walk."

"Oh. Right. Okay."

We strode across the vast courtyard and then entered the faculty portion of Astra Academy. Then we went for the stairs and traveled up to the next floor. Pure anxiety coursed through me. I felt nothing. I probably could've walked a hundred miles without feeling anything.

Sorin's knightmare shifted between shadows, moving as

silently as darkness. I liked having Thurin nearby. It felt like we had a hidden ally who could strike at any moment, and most people wouldn't even see him coming.

The Academy was just waking up. Mystical creatures were emerging from the treehouse as other arcanists were getting up and starting their day. It seemed most of them had clubs in the afternoon or evening—like sane people—but I didn't dwell on that information long.

Instead, Sorin and I climbed the last of the stairs to the headmaster's room.

When we approached, the muffled sound of angry voices blared from within.

Sorin and I stopped at the solid wooden door.

"*Piper*, your behavior has been completely unacceptable. How could you show up to class late? You live here in the Academy. Your room is mere minutes from the classroom! *And you can teleport.* There's no reason for any of this!"

I recognized Captain Leon's voice, despite his angry tone.

Sorin was about to knock, but I held up a hand. He waited, though he kept his hand up, like he was prepared to knock at a moment's notice.

"It was a rough morning," Piper shouted back. "And it's not like the artificer students *needed* me there. We always practice crafting items near the end of class. They were reading when I showed up."

"How many rough mornings are you going to have? We're on rough morning number two hundred!"

"*Hey*," Reevy's cute little rizzel voice cut in. "Why don't you watch your wife elope with someone else, and then we'll see how *you* handle it, huh?"

Leon's sigh was loud enough to be heard from the courtyard. "Look, I've never been married—"

"And everyone can see why," Reevy quipped.

"—*but no matter what happened, this kind of behavior is inexcusable!*"

Twain's ears twitched, and he slowly awoke in my arms.

I nudged Sorin. This wasn't a conversation we needed to hear, and it was also something that could wait until later. The murders were more important.

Sorin slammed his knuckles on the door, knocking far louder than necessary. The arguing in the room ended. Someone stomped over and threw the door open.

Captain Leon.

He was red in the face, his lips pursed.

"Yes?" he barked.

"I need to see Headmaster Venrover," I stated.

"He's not here. Come back in a few days."

This couldn't wait.

Leon was about to close the door, but I shoved my foot between it and the doorframe. When he realized I was preventing him from shutting the door, he opened it back up. I stepped into the headmaster's office, practically pushing Leon out of the way, but the headmaster really wasn't in today.

Sticks stood next to the headmaster's desk, his tail wagging in a circular motion the moment all three heads laid eyes on me.

Piper sat in one chair with Reevy on her lap.

Professor Zahn sat in another, his rizzel on his shoulder and a cup of tea in one hand.

Doc Tomas sat on the couch while his golden stag stood nearby. They looked like the oldest things in the room. More so than even the antique furniture.

The *fake* Professor Helmith was also here. Her violet eyes went straight to me. She didn't smile, though. She just stared. Did she know something was wrong? She tensed in her chair.

Zahn and Helmith were the only ones with sparkling tattoos that practically glowed with inner power. The tattoos were beautiful and striking and stole my attention for a fraction of a second.

The professors, and Leon, had all been having some sort of conference. Or perhaps a group therapy session.

I didn't want to tell them all what I knew. Not when the imposter was in the room.

I turned to Leon, shaky. "I need to speak with you," I whispered. He was in charge of protecting the Academy, wasn't he? He was the Guardian Captain.

And someone was better than no one.

Leon opened his mouth to say something, but he stopped himself. With narrowed eyes, he studied me. Then he sighed. "I'll be right back," he said to everyone in the room. Then he ushered me out into the hall. Once we were out—and he had closed the door—Leon glared. "What is it, boy? I'm in the middle of something."

"Someone's trying to kill Gray," my brother blurted out. "They've been after him for years. They attack him through his dreams. That's what happened in the Menagerie."

He spoke so quickly, Leon didn't have time to get a word in.

"Gray was attacked a couple days ago after the star shard shower. We also heard from the sailors down at the lake that one of them died recently from nightmares as well." Sorin grabbed Leon's bicep. "The sailor was a twin! We think it's all connected. We need to speak to Headmaster Venrover right away."

Leon soaked that in as well as a rock soaked up water. He stared for a long moment and then ran a blistered hand down his face. "Wait. So... Someone is killing people in dreams, and they're targeting *twins*?"

Sorin and I both nodded.

"Professor Zahn is a twin." Leon furrowed his brow.

"We wanted to warn him, too." I stepped closer. "But I have something even more important to say."

"What is it?"

I kept my voice low as I said, "Professor Helmith—the one in the headmaster's room—isn't who she appears to be. She's an imposter."

"What?" Leon almost chuckled.

I hardened my expression. "*It's true.* Ask Zahn. Even he said that Helmith's been acting abnormally lately. I *know* Professor Helmith. That woman in the other room *isn't her.*"

I said everything as clearly and sincerely as possible. Twain nodded along with my words. I doubted he even knew what was going on, since he was so groggy, but he backed me up regardless.

Leon stopped his chortling. "You're serious?"

"Yes. Definitely. We need to do something right now because I'm pretty sure these two things are connected."

"Why?" Leon asked, now completely engrossed in the conversation.

"Because ethereal whelk arcanists can manipulate dreams. The real Helmith was protecting people—preventing them from dying—so *I think* the fake Helmith took her out of the equation. Helmith is being held somewhere here at the Academy. I know because I went into her dreams and spoke to her! Well, briefly."

Leon's eyebrows slowly migrated upward. "You used your mimic to transform into her ethereal whelk? And you spoke to her?"

"I probably should've led with that," I muttered. "Look, she said she was in the basement, and that I shouldn't go there."

Leon placed his hand on my shoulder. Then he squeezed his fingers. "You've done a good thing by coming to me. As the Guardian Captain of Astra Academy, I will handle this."

I wanted to believe him. "You need to warn Zahn," I said. "Please. His brother might be in trouble."

"I'll tell him."

That sent some relief through my body, easing my anxiety.

Leon grabbed Sorin's shoulder as well. "I want the both of you to head to your dorm and stay there. Don't go anywhere until I come to get you, all right? Sticks and I will handle everything. Cerberuses have a keen sense of smell. We'll investigate the basement."

"What're you going to do about the imposter Helmith?" Sorin whispered.

"You just leave that to me and the rest of the faculty, understand?" Leon patted our arms. "Now head to the dorms. I'll come talk to you before nightfall."

I didn't like being left out of the loop.

What was happening? Had they locked up the fake Helmith? Had they found the real one?

I paced up and down our dorm room. Twain leapt from one bed to the next, trying to match my pace. He was clearly feeling rested. More than rested. He had excess energy as he bounded from one pillow to the next.

"Do you think Helmith is asleep?" Twain asked. "Maybe we should try going into Helmith's dreams again."

I glanced over at the bright sunshine streaming into the room. "I doubt she's sleeping."

Sorin stood at the back of the room, far from the window. He faced the shadowy corner, his knightmare by his side. Since we had been banished to the dorm, Sorin had lingered near the door, as if guarding me. At the same time, he seemed obsessed with the darkness.

I stopped my pacing and turned to him. "Sorin, are you okay?"

"Oh, yeah. Definitely."

"What're you doing?"

Sorin glanced over his shoulder, grinning. "Look at this, Gray! Knightmare arcanists evoke terrors... and manipulate *shadows*."

He waved his hands around. The darkness answered his summons. The shadows around the room bent and turned, heading toward him at unnatural angles. Some of the darkness lifted off the floor, coalescing into something hard and tangible.

"Are you seeing this?" Sorin asked, a laugh at the end of his words. "I can make *solid objects* out of darkness. I'm manipulating it so well right now, too." He waved his arms again, and the shadows danced around. "I'm a natural. Maybe I was destined to be a knightmare arcanist, ya know?"

Sorin jerked his hand to the left, and the shadows lifted off the floor and then shot in the same direction, like little ropes or strings, stretching to hit the wall. The darkness dissipated after a moment. Sorin was still a new arcanist—his manipulation was still in its infancy.

I turned to Twain. He stared at me with giant, kitten eyes.

"What?" he finally asked. "Do you want me to transform into a knightmare?"

"No."

I glanced down at my hands. Mimic arcanists really couldn't evoke or manipulate or augment anything unless their eldrin were transformed. It made me feel both powerful and weak. What if no other arcanists were around? What if I was alone in the woods and some thugs surrounded me?

What magic would I have then?

I shook the thought away.

Someone knocked on the door.

Both Sorin and I jumped to answer it. We practically fought each other to grab the handle. Eventually, Sorin won, because he was bigger—and maybe stronger, but I would never admit that.

Sorin opened the door. Then he glanced down.

Nini stood in front of him. She fixed her glasses as she tilted her head back to meet his gaze. "Um. Sorin? I heard you were in your dorm, so I came to see you. I thought you were joining the boating club?"

"Gray and I told Captain Leon about everything, including the attack in the forest," Sorin stated. "And then Leon told us to wait here."

Sorin motioned for Nini to enter. She and Waste joined us in the boys' dorm, even though I thought that might have been against the rules.

Sorin smiled. "Oh! Watch this."

He waved his hands around again, creating shadowy tendrils to lift out of the darkness.

Nini softly clapped as she watched his short demonstration. Then she frowned. "You're just waiting in here? All alone?"

"Yeah."

"Is it okay if I wait with you?"

"Sure. I'd like that."

Again, I wondered if this was against the rules, but I didn't really care. What were we going to do? Practice magic together? That was the extent of anything happening in the dorm while we waited for Leon.

"I, uh, practiced with my manipulation as well," Nini murmured into the collar of her coat. She took a seat on the edge of an unclaimed bed. Pulling her coat sleeve up, she revealed her entire left hand. "I had to poke my fingers to get blood, though."

She had a bunch of tiny scabs on her fingers and palm. I suspected she had used a sewing needle to draw little droplets.

"You hurt yourself?" Sorin walked over, knelt in front of her, and then examined her damaged hand. With a frown, he said, "You shouldn't do that."

Nini pulled her hand away and hid it in her coat once again. "Arcanists heal faster than mortals. And Doc Tomas can heal these kinds of injuries really quickly, if I need them to go away faster. I wanted to practice my magic, too."

"But hurting yourself..." Sorin turned to Waste. "You thought that was a good idea?"

Waste floated close to his arcanist. "I did not. I told Nini she should practice her ability to manipulate blood with someone else's. Preferably Exie's."

"Waste!" Nini said. "We can't do that. It's not right."

"Exie has too much blood as it is."

"She has too much?" I asked.

"She's conscious, isn't she?"

Sorin quickly stood. He glared at the reaper and then frowned at Nini. "You shouldn't hurt yourself." He took a deep breath and added, "You are what you think about most. And if you think about pain and suffering, that's all you'll have. Please, Nini. Gray and I sometimes helped the butcher slaughter animals back on our home island. Maybe they have something like that here at the Academy. You can use *that* to practice."

After fidgeting with the sleeves of her coat, Nini nodded. "Okay. Sorry. I just wanted to test out my magic without bothering anyone."

"Don't worry about it." Sorin's smile returned in full force. "We'll just keep each other company while we wait to hear something."

Nini stood and returned his grin.

I resumed my pacing, uninterested in anything else.

The day was the slowest of my life. The sun crept its way across the sky and then down behind the mountain peaks. Sorin and Nini practiced their magic—nothing intensive, but I wasn't paying too much attention.

The moment it was even slightly dark outside, I went to my bed and sat down.

"Twain," I said. "Let's try again. Maybe I can speak with Helmith and ask her what's going on."

My mimic eldrin leapt onto my bed with me. "I'm hungry."

"We'll eat afterward."

His kitten tummy rumbled. I patted his head as I rested back on my pillow. Twain stepped onto my chest and stared down at me.

I closed my eyes. "Afterward. I promise."

As soon as Helmith was okay, and my attacker was apprehended, I could finally start enjoying my stay at Astra Academy. That was what I wanted. Desperately.

Another knock came at the door. Much harder than the one before. I opened my eyes and glanced at Sorin. We exchanged a hopeful look.

Then I leapt off my bed—making sure to take Twain with me—and ran to the door. Sorin made it there before me.

CHAPTER 40

THE BEAUTY OF WORDS

S orin threw the door open to reveal Captain Leon and
Sticks.

The captain wore his plate armor, the chest etched
with the four symbols of Astra Academy. He had an
authoritative stance and presence. Sticks stood with all three
heads held high, his body tense. He looked ready for anything.

"Thank you for waiting, boys." Leon's attention
immediately went to Nini. "Wait, this isn't your dorm."

"I'm sorry," she whispered, her gaze falling to the floor. "I
didn't join a club, and I wanted to keep them company."

"Ah. I see." Leon stroked his white beard. "That's fine. The
three of you, and your eldrin, come along with me. I'll explain
everything once we reach the headmaster's office." He ushered
us out of the dorm.

I eagerly leapt to his side. Sorin and Nini were close behind,
but neither of them was as excited as I was to finally see Professor
Helmith. What had happened to her? Was she okay? I had to
know.

Twain snuggled against my chest as I walked. He seemed to
share my enthusiasm.

"Is Helmith okay?" I asked Leon as he headed for the stairs.

"She is, indeed."

We walked the long corridors, my heart beating quicker than before. Sticks was a large cerberus dog, and when he got close, I patted his side. His rippling muscles were just barely contained by his black-and-rust coat of short fur.

"Will I get to see her?" I asked.

"Of course. She's eager to see you, too."

That eased some of my anxiety. The real Helmith would be happy to see me. Of course.

We went down a set of stairs and then headed for the faculty section of the Academy. The entire time we traveled, Sorin and Nini had short, whispered conversations. I couldn't hear their words, but their tone wasn't one of panic, so I didn't pay them much attention.

When we finally reached the headmaster's office, I couldn't stop smiling. Leon opened the door. I stepped inside.

But no one was there. Even Twain was disappointed. His ears drooped.

"Helmith isn't here yet," Leon said with a chuckle. "You, your brother, and Nini—all of you just wait here. I'll go get her."

Sorin and Nini walked into the office to join me. Sorin sighed. "We have to wait *again*?"

"Just a little longer. I didn't know how much Gray wanted to see Helmith." Leon chuckled again as he shut the door to the headmaster's office.

The desk was cold and cleared of all objects. The chairs were scattered around the room from the previous meeting with Piper. The door leading to the balcony was closed, and the curtains were drawn. It was a boring room. I supposed it was better than waiting in the dorms, but not by much. I took a seat on the couch under the clock and placed Twain in my lap.

Nini ambled around the room, her reaper by her side. "I've

never been in here before... It's weird to be here without the headmaster. Or anyone else, for that matter."

Sorin placed his hands on his hips and glanced around. His attention went to the clock. Then to the rug on the floor.

He grew quiet and stiff.

"Gray?" my brother whispered.

"Yeah?"

"Something's wrong."

"Hm? What do you mean?" I examined our surroundings. Everything looked as it should have. It was quiet, though. "What is it?"

Sorin whirled around on his heel. "*Thurin.*"

His knightmare rose out of the shadows, forming from solidified darkness. The cape formed last, each feather a flutter of the void. "Yes, my arcanist?" Thurin asked.

"Vigilant and virtuous. A philosopher king strives to..." Sorin glared at his knightmare. "To do what?"

"Give me a moment." Thurin brought a gauntlet up to his empty helmet as if to think. "I will finish with something lyrical."

Sorin stepped away from his knightmare and then quickly returned his attention to me. "Gray. *We're in a dream.* Hurry! Use your mimic magic to get us out of here!"

I stood up, Twain stiff in my arms, his eyes wide. "We're in a dream?" Twain asked.

Nini ran over from the corner of the room to be with us. "How do you know we're in a dream? How is that even possible? I never went to sleep."

"I know we're dreaming because Thurin can't sleep," Sorin said as he shot a glare at the fake knightmare. "Thurin and I came up with a series of words to say to one another to make sure we were who we said we were. This isn't Thurin—*he's just a dream figment of Thurin.* The real Thurin should've answered that a philosopher king is steadfast and stalwart."

The fake knightmare stopped moving. It "stared" at us with its hollow helmet, its feathery cape now sinister and haunting.

The room grew colder and darker than before, like the shadows themselves were swelling in the corners. I stepped close to my brother, my heart hammering.

"When did we go to sleep?" I asked, never taking my eyes off the empty suit of armor. Had it been while we had been waiting in the dorm? Had we fallen asleep without even knowing it?

"I don't know. I just figured if it could happen in the Menagerie, it could happen anywhere. That's why I made a plan with Thurin."

"Waste doesn't sleep, either," Nini murmured, her hands shaking.

We all slowly turned to watch as the fake Waste lifted his deadly scythe.

"Interesting," Waste said, his voice just as hollow and eerie as before. "I thought I could keep you calm if I wove a dream so realistic, you couldn't see through it. I didn't realize you brothers were so good at overcoming this kind of ruse."

"Who are you?" I demanded.

This wasn't Waste. *This was my attacker.* The person after my life. They were speaking through the dream they had woven —finally addressing me.

"It doesn't matter who I am," the fake Waste said.

"So, you're craven. Even now." I scoffed, disappointed. I had expected more from the person trying to take my life. "Where's Professor Helmith? *What have you done with her?*" I supposed I should've been afraid, but I was too angry to register the fear.

The imposter Waste moved closer, floating through the air with a creepy silence. "Your concern for her is misplaced. I've kept her asleep to prevent her from meddling in my affairs. But you won't be as lucky."

Twain didn't wait for my command. He transformed into an ethereal whelk while I still held him in my arms. His body bubbled and shifted and then transformed into the giant, mystical sea snail. My forehead burned as my mark changed. I now had a star with a spiral shell woven throughout.

The fake reaper fell to the floor, its cloak spreading out. When it rose again, it was just a blanket covering something else. A wooden spider-puppet—the same dreadful monster from my previous dreams—emerged from the darkness, like my brother's knightmare.

The puppet brought its spider legs up one at a time. A human hand was on the end of each, and the fingers scratched across the floor of the headmaster's office as it stood to its full height before me. I had to look up to stare at its masked face. The blank expression seemed more menacing than ever before.

Fear crept into my thoughts, but my anger remained.

The puppet-spider lifted a leg, and knives sprouted from the fingers of its human hand. The monster swung at my eldrin, like it wanted to slice Twain into pieces in a single slash. Before the creature's claws could connect, Nini pushed me out of the way. The blades cut her from her shoulder all the way down to her elbow.

She screamed as she hunched over and grabbed her arm.

"Nini!" Sorin pulled her close, away from the puppet-spider.

Once I had regained my wits, I held out a hand. I didn't know how to manipulate dreams, but I had seen Twain and Helmith do it. I just *imagined* the ceiling crashing down on the puppet, the rubble so intense that it would shatter the wood frame of the monster.

My magic surged throughout my body.

It felt like it mixed with both my fear and anger. I envisioned one thing, but another thing happened instead.

The floor lifted as the ceiling came down. The headmaster's office had become a mouth, and the stone bricks were jagged teeth. The room crunched the puppet, gnawing it down to splinters.

"Oh, nice," Twain said with a giggle. "Take that!"

Once the puppet was destroyed, our surroundings *felt* like a dream. Everything melted away. The floor, the desk, the clock, the colors... Everything shifted to darkness, and then I was able to open my eyes.

I was lying on a cold, stone floor, my side hurting. How long had I been asleep? I fluttered my eyes open, trying to absorb the details of my surroundings as quickly as possible.

The basement.

I was in the basement.

I recognized the gigantic workroom and the tables where we had set our star shards. The Gate of Crossing was still leaning on the far wall, and the window opposite showed me the same view as before—the mountains at night, and the Nimbus Sea circling North Peak.

With a groan, I forced myself to sit up. Twain was next to me. He had transformed back into a mimic. He got to his feet and shook his head, his large ears twitching.

Professor Zahn stood at the base of the massive Gate of Crossing. To my surprise—and horror—the puppet-spider stood next to him. It was taller than Zahn, at least seven feet, and its wooden body just as disturbing as in my dreams. Its face mask stared at me, the mouth and eyes unmoving.

And Zahn's arcanist mark...

He didn't have a rizzel laced within the star. The spider-puppet was woven between the seven points.

It took me a moment to realize Professor Helmith stood at Zahn's side.

I pushed myself to my feet. "What's going on?" I stared at the freakish puppet. "*What is that?*"

Zahn motioned to the creature. "This is a *soul catcher*. A beautiful mystical creature that was more prevalent thousands of years ago. Sadly, they're mostly extinct." With an amused smile, Zahn patted the wooden beast. "They weave webs to catch dreams—and to steal the souls of people who are sleeping."

A soul catcher? I had never heard of one. Zahn spoke with fascination in his voice, though. I suspected he was telling the truth.

But why? Why did he have it?

"I don't understand," I said.

Zahn frowned, his expression bordering on apologetic. "It's nothing personal. You just have something I need, Gray. And you never would've given it to me willingly."

I turned my attention to Helmith and took a step forward. Then I stopped. The look in her violet eyes wasn't one I recognized. I hardened my gaze as I took three steps backward. "You're not Helmith. You're that imposter."

The fake Helmith scoffed, her expression twisting into one of irritation. "Damn this kid. Everyone but him was fooled." She spoke with Helmith's voice, but that wasn't her tone or mannerisms.

"I told you that Gray was on to you," Zahn snapped.

"It wasn't my fault! I didn't know Rylee went traipsing around other people's dreams, making friends along the way and telling no one."

Zahn shoved his glasses up his nose. "She's always been a secretive one. It doesn't matter. It's all over now. Drop this farce, and let's complete our mission."

As I watched, Helmith's body shimmered and shifted. Her black hair disappeared, her purple eyes dulled, and the glittering tattoos faded away. Her clothes didn't change—the robes and dress barely even moved during the transformation. But now it wasn't Helmith who stood next to Zahn. It was another woman. She had short, brown hair, barely over her ears, and squinted green eyes in the middle of her narrow face.

The mark on her forehead was different.

It was a seven-pointed star with a *person* interwoven through the points. I stared at it, baffled. What mystical creature looked like a person?

"What?" the new woman asked with a smirk. "You've never seen a doppelgänger arcanist before, kid?" She touched the mark on her forehead.

A doppelgänger? I remembered Helmith mentioning them in passing. She hadn't known much about shapeshifting mystical creatures, so we hadn't spoken about them for long. She had only said that doppelgängers were creatures who enjoyed impersonating others.

"Gray!" Twain pointed with his paw. "Look!"

I glanced away from Zahn and the doppelgänger arcanist and followed Twain's gaze. Sorin and Nini were here in the basement as well. They were sprawled out on the floor, both asleep. Thurin and Waste were also here, but they were battered and ragged, like someone had shredded them. The hem of Waste's cloak was frayed and ripped more than ever before. Thurin's black feathers were all over the floor, like a chicken that had been plucked.

They were both covered in translucent webbing.

"Sorin!"

I ran to my brother and knelt at his side. My hands shook as I examined him. Sorin took in breaths—even and steady. He wasn't injured.

Nini wasn't as lucky, though. Her arm was slashed, just like in the dream. Besides that, she was whole and healthy.

"Gray!" Twain pointed again.

Leon and Piper, along with Sticks, were also asleep in the basement. Where was Piper's eldrin, Reevy? Leon and Piper were propped against the wall near the large double doors, Piper leaning on Leon's shoulder, Sticks slobbering all over Leon's leg. None of them were injured. They almost seemed peaceful in their slumber.

"What're you doing?" I asked, heat in my voice as I shot a glare at Zahn.

He motioned for me to calm down with a wave of his hand. "If you hadn't gotten Leon involved, I wouldn't have had to drag everyone down here. He put the staff on high alert. Astra Academy is filled with too many arcanists. I had to move you all into the basement before the students returned from their extracurricular activities and discovered your sleeping bodies."

I stood between Zahn and my brother. "Where's Helmith?"

"Rylee is unharmed. She and her eldrin are being held someplace safe. I never wanted to harm her—she just kept getting in the way."

"What're you planning? Are you really the one who has been trying to kill me this whole time?"

"Listen," Zahn said, holding up a finger. "I'm nearly finished with everything I need. And guess what? Because of your *bumbling*, you're the last soul on the list. Which means I no longer need to kill you. I just need you over here. Close to the gate." Zahn pointed to a place by his side. "As long as you cooperate, I won't hurt anyone else."

"You can drown in the abyssal hells for all I care." I wasn't helping Zahn do a single thing.

"Ironic you should say that," Zahn replied with an amused tone.

The doppelgänger arcanist chuckled.

Then Zahn's soul catcher scuttled forward a few feet, its wooden body clacking on the floor with each step. Within a split second, the puppet-spider bubbled and transformed. It turned into a beautiful elf with silver hair and a dress—the engkanto. The telekinesis elf that the housekeeper had.

My eyes went wide as I realized that Zahn was *also* a mimic arcanist.

The star on his forehead shifted to reflect that he was now an engkanto arcanist.

Zahn waved his hand in a circular motion. His new telekinesis allowed him to turn the Gate of Crossing. He spun it all the way around, the metal scraping across the stone floor and wall, the screech of the movement echoing throughout the workroom.

Zahn turned the whole gate upside down.

"The abyssal hells are *exactly* where I'm going," Zahn said, staring up at the gate like it was his honeysuckle.

One look at Zahn's face told me he meant it. Terror swept through my thoughts as I recalled every story I had ever heard about the abyssal hells.

I grabbed Sorin and shook him as hard as I could. The moment his eyes opened, I jumped to Nini and did the same thing. "Wake up," I yelled. "*Get up!* We have to get out of here!"

Then I ran to Piper and Leon, practically slapping them in my rush to get them all on their feet. Piper jerked awake, her eyes wide, her expression one of baffled confusion.

Sticks and Leon were quick to get to their feet. Leon pulled a short sword from a scabbard on his belt. He still had his armor—he looked like a man who could handle a paper-pusher like Zahn. Even confused and somewhat groggy, Leon held his weapon with a firm grip.

"Zahn?" Leon asked. He rubbed his eyes with the base of his palm. "What's going on?"

"He's going to kill us," I shouted. "He's going to send us all to the abyssal hells!"

"*What?*" Leon turned his attention to the upside-down Gate of Crossing, his confused expression fading to horrified understanding.

"I already told you," Zahn drawled. "If you'd just *cooperate*, I can finish this. I'll be merciful. I'll let you go then."

Zahn flicked his wrist. His telekinesis took hold of my body, and I was jerked forward. Without moving my legs, I flew across the workroom and nearly slammed into the silver ring of the Gate of Crossing.

"Just stay there," Zahn stated.

His telekinesis practically crushed me around the ribs. It felt like a giant was curling its fingers around my body, holding me tighter and tighter. I cried out through clenched teeth.

"Gray!" Twain called out. He didn't run for me, but that was probably a smart move. He stayed next to my brother.

Sorin jumped to his feet. His injured knightmare managed to stand, but just barely. The webbing was gone, likely because Zahn's mimic had transformed. But the hollow suit of armor was still shredded at all ends. Despite that, Thurin merged with my brother, the darkness sliding over Sorin's body until they were one and the same.

"Get away from my brother," Sorin and Thurin said together, forceful and intimidating.

Nini stumbled into a standing position. Her reaper fluttered up and then onto her shoulders. The hood slid over her head as the scythe floated into her hands.

"Reaper arcanists grow more powerful with each kill," Nini and Waste said. "That'll be your only warning." Their calm tone and choice of words mixed together into a chilling threat.

Sticks's three heads barked, and then the cerberus growled. Leon and Piper readied themselves for a fight, even though they both exchanged concerned glances.

I couldn't believe it. We were about to have a war in the basement of Astra Academy.

CHAPTER 41

BROTHERLY BOND

I tried to pull myself off the Gate of Crossing, but Zahn's telekinesis was too much. The side of the gate still had a crack in it, allowing me to peer inside. The old artifacts—including the wire bug—were stuffed inside, along with sparkling golden crystals. They weren't star shards... They were something else.

The glitter within took shapes. Little faces, twisted in agony.

And they were all held together with spider webs. Was this the work of the soul catcher?

A shiver ran down my spine as I stared at the web-covered crystals.

Zahn turned to the doppelgänger arcanist. "Seven, handle this."

The doppelgänger arcanist—her name was Seven, like the number?—turned and replied with half a smile.

Sorin and Nini stepped forward, but Leon leapt between them and Seven. He held one arm out as if trying to shield them. "Stand back. I'll handle this." He glared at both Zahn and Seven. "You fiends are in for a surprise," Leon growled, his gruff voice more forceful than I had ever heard it before.

He swept his hand out in an arc and blasted the basement with a torrent of flame so hot, it hurt my eyes to even look at it. The orange-and-red fire rushed over the stone floor and crisped the books and small boxes around the edge of the room.

Zahn motioned with his wrist, and a nearby table flew in front of him and Seven, acting as a shield. The fire smashed against the underside of the table, charring the wood and burning the legs.

Once the fire had dissipated, leaving nothing but embers and smoke in its wake, Seven leapt over the charred table without even touching it.

Cerberus arcanists could evoke fire.

What could doppelgänger arcanists evoke?

Seven held up her hand, and my question was answered. My head hurt, and my temples pounded as my eyesight blurred. Everything became so confusing. I could barely understand my surroundings.

She was evoking confusion—just like how Sorin and Nini could evoke terrors. Nini was disoriented by the attack, but Sorin seemed resistant. He jumped to her side, trying to help her as she grabbed at her head.

The confusion made it difficult for me to sense magic. I wanted Twain to shapeshift into *something*, but what? An engkanto, like Zahn? No. I wasn't good at using the telekinesis.

I needed to think of something!

Despite the evocation causing muddled thoughts, Leon readied himself. He wasn't easily incapacitated. Leon grabbed the blade of his sword, his fingers on the flat sides, and then dragged his hand down, lighting the weapon on fire. His cerberus manipulation allowed him to keep the flame alive and healthy.

Then Leon hefted his weapon, the metal superheating—practically glowing from the intensity of his magic.

The doppelgänger arcanist just smiled. She continued to

evoke her confusion. My head pounded. But what would she do next?

What did doppelgängers manipulate? Hopefully, nothing too useful...

Piper walked over to Leon.

She hadn't been doing anything—I had forgotten she was even in the room—but when she reached for Leon, to touch him on the back, I knew something was wrong. That wasn't Piper. She was entirely too sober, and her mouth too twisted in a sadistic grin, to ever be Piper.

Sticks must have realized that as well because the three-headed dog rushed her before she could touch Leon. All three heads bit down on her arm. One on her wrist, one on her bicep, and one on her shoulder, the fangs of the cerberus digging deep. But no blood wept from the injuries.

The fake Piper chuckled.

Then her whole body transformed into something horrific. She was nothing more than a human-shaped monster. A scarecrow made of skin and hay. The *thing* wore Piper's clothes, but nothing else remained the same.

Hay stuck out from all its joints—the elbows, the fingers, the shoulders, the feet—some of the hay golden, some of the hay blackened with blood.

The monster's face...

It didn't have one. It had a mouth—the skin over the head was cut open and held together with thread that had been stitched at the edges—but even that was almost too disgusting to call a proper mouth.

That was Seven's eldrin.

A doppelgänger.

It could take the form of anyone it wanted.

All three of Sticks's heads released the beast and then exhaled flames over the doppelgänger. The bright explosion of fire and heat filled the basement once again. The roil of flame washed over Sticks and Leon, but neither of them were affected by the destruction. Leon was a cerberus arcanist—he stood in the ocean of fire, his expression so serious and menacing, he looked like a completely different individual from the man I knew.

The Gate of Crossing lit up.

I hadn't realized it until that moment, but Zahn wasn't fighting. The entire time everyone else had been engaged in the scuffle, he had been busy with the giant ring, slowly activating it now that I was here.

He had said he needed my soul?

I struggled to pull myself away from the gate, but nothing worked.

The doppelgänger didn't bleed, but it sure did catch fire. The freakish monster screamed as it leapt away from Sticks. Then it collapsed to the ground and rolled, trying to extinguish itself. Then it stopped moving, burned but not yet dead. Perhaps unconscious.

Sticks ran to end the monster, but Zahn's mimic, still in the form of the engkanto elf, intervened with its telekinesis. The mimic grabbed the doppelgänger and hauled it to safety. With a howl and burst of flames, Sticks tried to chase after, but he was too slow.

Leon charged for Zahn. He sliced through the wooden table with his flaming sword, effortlessly cleaving his way toward the professor.

Seven finally stopped evoking her confusion and instead ran straight for Leon. She sprinted far faster than any normal person could. Were doppelgänger arcanists stronger and more agile than the average person?

When she neared Leon, Seven reached out to touch him.

Leon leaned away, his combat prowess on display. When he slashed with this sword, he caught Seven's robes across the stomach, cutting them open and catching them on fire.

She jumped away, but that was a mistake.

Leon manipulated the flames on her clothing. He lifted his hand, and the fire went straight for the woman's face—specifically, her eyes. He was trying to incapacitate her.

Zahn had never stopped his work with the gate.

But then the shadows around his feet fluttered and moved on their own. Zahn glanced down just as dark tendrils grabbed his ankles. Zahn jerked his feet free—the tendrils weren't very strong, nor were they powerful—but that was when he was struck in the back by *something*.

Zahn cried out as he stumbled forward and slammed into the silvery ring of the gate.

His back had been cut up.

I turned my head slightly, as much as I was able, and spotted Nini. Her arm was still bleeding, but she seemed to be using that to her advantage. She waved her arm and then manipulated the blood as it flew off her body.

She *threw* splatters of blood. They hardened into darts—made lethal through her magic—and then pierced into Zahn.

It wasn't the strongest attack, as Nini was still a novice arcanist, but it was definitely enough to distract the man from his work.

Zahn gritted his teeth, his patience clearly running dry. His elf mimic, still protecting the doppelgänger from Sticks, turned her attention to my brother and Nini. It held up a hand. Nini was hit by a telekinetic blast and sent flying into the wall.

Sorin managed to step into the darkness and avoid the attack altogether. With more cleverness than I had ever seen from him, he shifted through the darkness and emerged next to Zahn and his eldrin. Then Sorin held up his hand and evoked his terrors.

He also hit me with the attack, but that was fine.

Another hallucination filled my mind, this time of all of us dying, but I couldn't do anything about it. I tried to think of something positive as dread filled me.

But Zahn and his mimic weren't as affected. They shuddered

and shook their heads, clearly disturbed by the terrors that haunted their thoughts, but it wasn't enough to stop them. Zahn waved his hand, and Sorin was slammed backward.

His terrors ended.

"If you all would just *listen*," Zahn growled through gritted teeth. "*This would be over sooner.*"

The tattoos on Zahn's arms and knuckles grew brighter. They glowed with a magical intensity I hadn't felt before. He held up his hand, and telekinetic force grabbed Sticks and held the cerberus in place.

Then Seven and Leon—who had been dancing around each other—finally ended their little duel. Seven managed to touch Leon's neck. At first, I thought she had paralyzed him, because Leon stiffened and stood straight, but that wasn't the case.

With jerking motions, like Leon was fighting against his own legs, he walked over to his eldrin. Each step, he grunted. Each step, he shook his head. His cerberus couldn't move, his giant canine body shaking with Zahn's telekinetic grasp.

Then Leon lifted his sword and slowly stabbed it into Sticks. The tip of the blade slid between the ribs of the cerberus, blood weeping from the injury as Leon moved it up and down, mangling his own eldrin.

The fearsome dog barked and snarled, but he couldn't seem to do anything.

Why was Leon stabbing his eldrin?

The whole scene played out like a terrible nightmare.

Seven cackled in delight, her laughter echoing throughout the ruined basement. "Weren't expecting that, were you, *Captain Leon*?" Her face was blackened from smoke, and her clothes were half-charred from the fight, but she hadn't been blinded or rendered helpless, like Leon had been aiming for.

How was she controlling Leon?

"Doppelgängers manipulate *people*," Sorin and Thurin said

together as they got to their feet. "You fiends... Such a tactic is unforgivable!"

"I didn't want this." Zahn turned his glare on Seven. "If they surrender, let them live. But if they continue to fight... End this."

Seven frowned. Then she shot Zahn a glower. "*This would be easier if you hurried up.* The longer we're here, the higher the chance someone comes into the basement looking for the students."

Nini and Waste barely managed to get to their feet. Nini still bled from her arm, her scythe in hand.

Sorin and Thurin were breathing deeply. Their armor had protected them more than Nini's cloak had protected her, but they still looked beat up.

Leon was being manipulated by the doppelgänger arcanist, and Sticks was held in place, just like I was. Only Sticks was bleeding to death.

The telekinesis seemed to cost Zahn, though. The man bled from the back, his forehead dappled with sweat and his glasses cracked. Nothing about him looked right, and his hands shook as he touched the Gate of Crossing.

Using his telekinesis required a lot of effort.

Zahn was a powerful arcanist, that much I was certain of, but everyone had their limits. The strongest man in the world would eventually grow tired, and it was obvious Zahn wasn't going to hold out much longer.

Twain was the only one in the room who hadn't been injured. And I didn't know where he was. In all the commotion, he had disappeared from my sight. There were boxes, tables, and magical supplies all around us. Was Twain hiding? Or had he run away, leaving me to my fate?

I hoped he was somewhere nearby.

"Stop this!" I shouted.

The Gate of Crossing flared to life. The center of it sparkled and shimmered, much like rizzel magic whenever someone teleported.

"I can't do that," Zahn muttered. "I've waited too long for this moment."

"What're you even doing? Who wants to go to the abyssal hells? It's like opening a portal to a lake of lava! It makes no sense!"

The center of the gate pulsated with magical power.

Zahn clenched his jaw. "I'm not doing it because I want to go there. I'm doing it for my brother." He smiled, though it was weary and tired. "I figured you and Sorin would understand. It's been forever since I've seen my twin. I'm opening this gate for him."

"For your twin?" I balked.

"That's why I needed all those souls. I had to attune the gate to his location. I needed his personal belongings. I needed the souls of older twins—because he was born before me. Now that the gate has all those things, it'll open *right where he is*. Don't you understand?" Zahn shook his head. "You probably don't. You're all too young to grasp anything happening here."

"Have you lost your mind?" I shouted. "You're trying to see your brother? That's... *That's insane!* If he's dead, just let him stay dead! He wouldn't want this!"

Zahn actually laughed at that comment. "My brother isn't *dead.*"

The Gate of Crossing finally stabilized.

It opened to a strange and bizarre world. The sky was red and thick with fog. A vast body of water stretched on in all directions, deep and roiling. Hundreds of creatures were below the surface.

It was a portal straight to the abyssal hells.

Bloody water rushed into the basement from the Gate of Crossing. Bones floated in the crimson liquid. Skulls. Femurs. Hands. Ribs. Shreds of clothing and disgusting mats of fur from animals joined in the fun. The basement filled with the smell of rot and disease.

My trousers were soaked up to the knees.

The water just kept gushing in.

The faint sound of moans, screams, and screeches wafted out of the gate. It all mixed together to create a symphony of suffering.

The silhouette of a dragon formed in the center of the portal, its body obscured by the scarlet fog.

"My twin brother is *Death Lord Deimos*," Professor Zahn said as he backed away from his creation. With a genuine smile, he added, "And now... he can finally return to *my* world."

CHAPTER 42

REUNITED

The dragon stepped through the fog.

It was unlike anything I had seen before. My eyes couldn't get wide enough.

It was a dragon that walked on four legs, its body rotting, its white scales sloughing off at a disturbing rate. Its tail was a coil of tentacles. Clear mucus covered everything, dripping off the creature as though it had just been birthed from slime. The beast's wings were a cobweb of transparent faces. They reminded me of a foggy window that someone had smooshed their face against. The mouths of the faces were open, their eyes nothing but circles.

The faces in the transparent wings moaned in agony, some whispering their fears between cries.

The dragon's head was reptilian, but its horns were spiral in shape, much like a ram's. It had six eyes, three on each side. Each one moved independently of the others—they blinked at random times, they stared in all directions—but they were all sickly white with a single black slit as a pupil.

This was a beast made of foul nightmares and terror.

This was an abyssal dragon.

The man riding on the creature's shoulders resembled Professor Zahn. He had an intelligent gaze, and his black hair was swept back. Unlike Zahn, this man didn't wear glasses and was quite muscular. He wielded a long spear—the kind used by riders on mounts. It had a shaft long enough to reach someone at the foot of his mighty dragon.

Wait. The tip of the spear had three prongs.

A trident.

And the man—Death Lord Deimos—wore full plate armor crafted from white bone and steel. The material was woven together to create star shapes throughout.

The abyssal dragon grabbed the edge of the Gate of Crossing and pulled itself forward, struggling to make it across. The moment its head entered our side, the sky beyond the window changed.

Rays of sunlight trickled into the basement. It wasn't day, but it seemed as though the sun were now in the sky, hanging close to the moon, creating a scarlet sunrise.

"*Finally!*" Seven shouted, her eyes wide as she stared out the window. "So beautiful. This is what *real* magic looks like."

"You're both insane," Sorin and Thurin said together as they turned their attention to the celestial phenomenon.

Zahn held up his arms. "You're all too young to understand. The Death Lords used to roam the lands! They were locked away in the abyssal hells. But no more. I'll help my brother return the world to how it should've been. He'll conquer the oceans, and the lands, and then all the levels of the abyssal hells."

Sorin shook his head. "No good will come of this!"

"You're wrong! Now that he's here, we'll rule it all *together!* Just as we were meant to."

More blood-laced water rushed into the basement.

"Brother," Death Lord Deimos said, his voice *far* different than Zahn's. It was as if he spoke with an echo—a haunting set of voices whispered his every word. "I never doubted your dedication. We will share everything from the womb to victorious conquest."

"As it should be," Zahn said, rubbing at the corner of his eye.

Then Seven screamed.

I whipped my head around and caught sight of the doppelgänger arcanist.

While most everyone had been watching the abyssal dragon and its nightmarish arcanist enter our world, Nini had moved closer to Seven and struck. Her scythe was buried in the back of the arcanist, deep enough that she couldn't seem to pull it free. It seemed as though the reaper gave Nini strength—much more than a girl her size should have had.

Seven's lungs must've been punctured, because when she tried to speak, her words were gurgled, and blood dribbled from her lips.

Her magical manipulation of Leon ended.

Without hesitation, Leon threw his flaming sword with all his might. It made a *woosh, woosh* sound as it spun twice and then slammed into Zahn's engkanto. The mimic screeched and then untransformed.

The elf woman bubbled and shifted until it took the shape of a cat. The creature had soft pink fur, one gray eye, and one orange-tan eye. Normally, it would've been sleek and beautiful, but Leon's attack had left it with a giant gash down its chest. The mimic collapsed into the bloody water, practically drowning as bones and lumps of flesh swirled all around it.

"*No!*" Zahn roared.

His arcanist mark became a blank star. He no longer had telekinesis.

His hold on me ended.

"*Twain,*" I called out.

My mimic leapt out of a nearby box of star shards and then leapt into the water to get to me. "I'm coming!" he shouted. "I'd never abandon you, Gray! I'm here!"

I felt the many threads of magic all around me. But Twain couldn't hold a form for long. As the abyssal dragon and Death Lord Deimos slid into the basement, half the dragon's body on our side, half the dragon's body in the abyssal hells, I knew I didn't have the power to defeat him in a straight fight.

I wasn't powerful enough yet. Twain could only stay transformed for a short period of time. It wasn't enough for a fight. It was barely enough for a parlor trick.

But there was something I *could* defeat.

I sensed the thread of magic I needed and tugged.

Twain, mid-swim, bubbled and transformed. His orange fur became rotting, white scales. His paws changed into gruesome claws. His large ears shifted into transparent wings filled with human faces. And his head morphed into the dreadful form of a dragon's head.

And Twain grew. His back legs crashed into the wall as his entire body expanded to fill most of the room. He was colossal.

My mark on my forehead seared my skin as I became an abyssal dragon arcanist.

And then agony ravaged my insides. The dragon's power utterly eclipsed my current capability. It was breaking me— killing me. But that didn't matter.

I held my hand up.

Death Lord Deimos turned and readied his trident, a smirk on his smooth face. "You would challenge *me*, boy? I've outlived gods and endured millennia in the abyss. You will die like all the others."

Two of his dragon's six eyes turned to focus on me.

But I didn't aim for Deimos. I pushed my magic outward, trying to evoke whatever abyssal dragons evoked, and set my sights on the Gate of Crossing. I hoped it would do the trick.

Sorin shifted through the darkness and rose up next to the abyssal dragon. He had no weapon. He was just merged to Thurin.

Death Lord Deimos lifted his trident to throw it.

That was when Sorin evoked his terrors. He was weak enough that it didn't cause the dragon or its rider to stop, but it did bother them enough to flinch. When Deimos threw his weapon, his aim was just *slightly* off. Sorin always had my back.

The trident still hit me.

Of course it did. I was just unlucky like that.

Of the trident's three prongs, one caught me in the side of the gut, slicing me open. But I pushed my magic out regardless, even as I cried out.

A blast of raw magic, so forceful and bright that it reminded me of the afternoon sun, shot forth in a straight line. Twain opened his dragon maw and unleashed the same type of raw blast. Both our evocations struck the Gate of Crossing. The abyssal dragon's evocation was so powerful, it *sliced* through the gate. When I moved my hand down, the beam of raw magic went with it.

It also sliced through the far wall and part of the floor, practically disintegrating anything it touched.

And then my vision tunneled. I staggered backward, sloshing through the blood and gore, my legs shaking. My own blood mixed into the pool of abyssal waters.

"*What have you done?*" Zahn screamed.

The Gate of Crossing grew bright. Brighter than my evocation.

The abyssal dragon turned its head around to get a better look. Death Lord Deimos held up his hand, like he was going to do something, but then...

The Gate of Crossing exploded.

Fragments of the silver ring went in all directions. They shattered out the window. They smashed through the stone wall.

A few slammed through the floor. And they just kept going, sailing down the side of the mountain or off into the horizon.

One even clipped me across my right shoulder, digging deep enough that it scraped against bone. I fell backward, splashing into the red water, my body weak, my vision blurry.

Someone dragged me out of the depths. It was Captain Leon. He said something, but I couldn't understand a damn word. His voice drifted in and out of my awareness.

The portal that Zahn had created shimmered as it disappeared. Death Lord Deimos and his dragon were sucked into it, but the dragon fought to stay on our side. Its claws dug into the floor. The beast ripped up several stone bricks as the magic repelled it, pushing the dragon back into the abyssal hells, where it belonged.

The monster managed to keep one clawed hand in the basement, even as the portal shut. It was a determined beast, all right.

Unfortunately, that just meant it lost a hand. The dragon's clawed hand was severed from its body, leaving a bloody stump in the middle of the basement. It was larger than a horse, and its white scales were the size of plates, but there it was.

In my groggy and delirious state, all I could think was that Death Lord Deimos would really hate us for that.

The sun vanished from the night sky, returning control to the glorious moon. It was dark again. As it should have been.

One piece of the Gate of Crossing remained. It was by the far wall, just a sliver of silver. But it glowed with power. A shimmer of the abyssal hells appeared around it. The tiny fragment of the gate was still operating—*still trying to remain open*. I saw flickers of red waters and white bones.

Despite bleeding from between his ribs, Sticks ran over and blasted the silver fragment with his fire. The sliver of the gate burned and died out. The portal closed as the piece charred.

"Gray?" Leon's voice cut into my perception. "Gray? Can you hear me?"

I tried to respond. But then I glanced down at my stomach and saw my intestines, and that was all I thought about as my vision went black.

CHAPTER 43

PROFESSOR HELMITH'S ARRIVAL

"Wake up, Gray."

Though it took most of my energy, I opened my eyes. A bright blue sky dappled with fluffy white clouds greeted me. The warmth of a breezy summer day filled my body. The scent of flowers reminded me of simpler times.

Once I had managed to turn my head, I realized I was near Honeysuckle Meadow. This was the Isle of Haylin. Or at least, it *looked* like my home.

I was on my back, staring at the sky, my head resting on someone's lap. When I tilted my head back to get a better look, I smiled.

Professor Helmith.

Her violet eyes stared down at me, her black hair cascading over her shoulders, inky and beautiful in the sunshine. She had a gentle smile that told me this was no doppelgänger.

"I'm glad you're awake," Helmith said.

"Am I really, though?"

Helmith laughed once. "Oh, well. You're right. You're not

awake—you're just well enough to be coherent. Which I'm glad for."

This was a dream she had woven for me. That was nice of her. Although I had thought I hated my home, I realized my memories of it brought a bit of comfort with them. The Isle of Haylin would always be a special place to me.

"What happened?" I asked, desperately needing clarification.

"Zahn created a Gate of Crossing that opened into the abyssal hells." Helmith leaned down a little closer to me, her inky hair spilling around my face. "He stole the souls of one hundred and six individuals, gathered relics from his old hometown, and even slew mystical creatures in order to accomplish his goals."

"One hundred and six twins?"

"All of the *eldest* twins in a set." Helmith sighed. "I'm sorry, Gray. It took me too long to figure out that Zahn was behind this. I was too fixated on the soul catcher. If I had realized Zahn was a mimic arcanist sooner, this wouldn't have gone as far as it did."

I shook my head. "It's all right. I'm sorry it took me so long to figure everything out. I... I wanted to save you. Like you saved me."

Professor Helmith's genuine smile made my stomach flutter, and my chest tighten. "You have nothing to apologize for. You managed to destroy Zahn's gate. That's all that matters."

"Is it... over? It broke apart and went everywhere."

Helmith brushed some of her hair back behind one ear. She mulled over the question for a long while before answering, "Let's just say that the immediate threat is dealt with. We'll hunt down the fragments as soon as we're able."

"And Professor Zahn?" I asked, my throat tightening. "Did you catch him? Is he going to pay for what he did to those one hundred and six people?"

"He teleported away before Leon could apprehend him."

That bit of news brought me down more than anything else. What would he do out there in the world? Zahn didn't seem like the most stable individual I had ever met. He didn't seem like a psychopath, either, but that didn't mean he should get away. The man had haunted my dreams for years. He'd probably hurt others.

"The souls of twins allowed the gate to open to his brother?" I asked.

"There are several Death Lords and several layers to the abyssal hells. Zahn wanted to make sure the gate opened to Death Lord Deimos, and *only* Deimos. By ensuring that the rizzel magic was homed in on the eldest twin, Zahn made it so that the gate only went to his brother."

There were legends of Death Lords fighting each other... It made me wonder if Zahn wanted to help his brother with that.

"Thank you for saving me," I said, staring up at Helmith.

"Thank your eldrin," she whispered. "Twain transformed into a golden stag to heal you long before anyone could get you to Doc Tomas."

"R-Really?"

Helmith nodded.

"Is my brother okay?" I asked. "He wasn't hurt too badly, was he?"

Helmith ran her hand through my hair. "Sorin, Nini, and Leon will all live. They were hurt when the Gate of Crossing exploded, but they will survive."

"What about Seven, that weirdo doppelgänger arcanist?"

"She died, along with her eldrin."

That news didn't disturb me. Between her and Zahn, she had seemed more willing to just end everyone so that she could get what she wanted. But... what *had* she wanted?

Professor Helmith shook her head. In my dreams, she always seemed to know what I was thinking. "There is a small group of arcanists who believe that the world is incomplete until the gates of the abyssal hells are ripped open. They're cult-like in thinking and behavior. I believe Seven belonged to this group. She probably thought she was doing the world a service by helping Zahn."

Seven *had* been elated to see the sun and moon in the sky at the same time.

A sign of sheer lunacy.

"So Zahn is old?"

"Ancient," Helmith said with a giggle. Then her gaze hardened. "He has bonded to several creatures over the years, it seems... His mimic was his latest eldrin."

Some arcanists killed their eldrin to bond with another, but it was considered a heinous act. Some nations even deemed it a crime punishable by death. It made me wonder what Zahn had been thinking. Why go through all the effort?

"I was attacked in the Menagerie," I said. "The soul catcher must've put us to sleep. But then there was a woman who attacked when I woke up. Had that been Seven?"

Helmith furrowed her brow. "I don't know. If I had to guess, I would say she was probably there to ensure you died. Or perhaps to hide the body."

Zahn really had been desperate. After he failed to kill me, he replaced Helmith and attacked me at several points, all to collect my soul with his creepy eldrin. But in order to transform into the soul catcher, one had to be nearby, didn't it? Perhaps I would need to be prepared to fight it again, even in my dreams.

"Oh." Helmith sat straight. "I never got to introduce you to *my* eldrin. Meet Ushi, the ethereal whelk."

I turned my head and watched as a bubble of light glistened in midair. Beads of light grouped together and then merged into a circular shell the size of my head. Although I had never met Ushi, I knew exactly what she looked like. From her little tentacles to her slightly transparent body and iridescent sheen.

Twain had transformed into her several times.

Helmith held out her hand. Ushi wiggled her tentacles and touched Helmith's fingertips.

"A soul catcher is the exact opposite of an ethereal whelk," Helmith muttered. "They hunt for people in their dreams and use their spider silk to wrap up the souls of their victims." Helmith sighed, her expression shifting to something woebegone. "When you sleep, they say you're close to death itself. Your heart beats slower. You breathe less. Dreams are your soul touching the gate of the abyssal hells."

"You make me afraid to ever sleep," I quipped.

Helmith smiled again. "Don't worry. I know what to do when I find a soul catcher now. Zahn will never create another gate like he did before."

I closed my eyes and just enjoyed the warmth of a perfect summer day. Helmith touched my hair a second time, and I wondered how long she'd allow me to stay this way.

Then someone shook me. At first, I thought it was Helmith, but her hands weren't as large or forceful. My brother's voice broke my tranquility.

"Gray! Gray? Can you hear me?"

Sorin shook and shook, jostling me out of my perfect dream and dumping me into reality. I opened my eyes, only to see the stone ceiling inside the infirmary. I had only been here once before, and already I hated it.

My brother stood next to my infirmary bed, his black hair slicked back, his blue-gray eyes staring down at mine. For a short moment, neither of us said anything.

Then Sorin half-smiled. "I knew you were okay."

I ran a hand down my face, clearing away the oil and sweat from a long night's worth of sleep. With a groan, I shoved the blankets down to my waist. I wore a long tunic and nothing else.

Which became awkward the moment I realized how many other people were in the infirmary.

I grabbed my blankets and hastily pulled them back up, as

424

my entire class stood around the room, most of them with their eyes on me. "What're you all doing here?" I blurted out.

"Rude," Exie said with a huff.

"We were ordered by the professors to come see you," Ashlyn stated. "As moral support."

Nasbit held up a finger. "Also, we were afraid you were dead. Some of us wanted to make sure you were okay with our own eyes."

Sorin remained on one side of my bed while the other arcanists from my class crowded around on the other side, each trying to get to me. They silently decided to take turns, but even that was done with a few glares.

Nini was the first to walk over. She handed me something wrapped in white cloth stained with oil and crumbs. "Good morning, Gray. I thought you might be hungry, so Waste and I snuck you a pastry."

Her reaper hovered around behind her. He had a chain dangling from his red cloak. Before, it'd had two links—barely a chain, really—but now it had three. The third link caught my attention only because it looked like it was made of gold.

The word SEVEN was etched into the side.

"I hope you slept well," Waste said, his voice hollow and emotionless.

"Thanks," I muttered as I unwrapped the pastry. It was still warm.

Before Nini moved aside to let someone else see me, she leaned down and threw her arms around my neck. I hadn't felt any pain until that moment. Her embrace reminded me that I wasn't well. My shoulders hurt, my neck hurt—even my earlobes hurt, which was bizarre because when were *those* exposed to anything painful?

But I didn't say anything about that.

I returned to her hug.

It lasted longer than I would've expected, but that wasn't a big deal to me. I had to stay in the infirmary regardless of what the others did.

When Nini released me, she smiled. "I'm really glad you're okay, Gray. Thank you for saving us all. I thought it was really courageous."

With a nervous chuckle, I shrugged. "Don't mention it."

"You blew up part of the Academy, though..." Nini fixed her glasses and frowned. "They're in the middle of repairing it right now."

"It's really bad," Sorin interjected with a nervous laugh. "They called in arcanists to come fix it before some walls collapsed."

"I'm sure it'll be fine." Nini offered me a half-smile before stepping aside and letting someone else come see me. Waste moved aside as well, his new chain clinking.

Nasbit and his golem both lumbered over. At first, I thought they weren't going to say anything, but Nasbit leaned onto the mattress and whispered, "Is it true you saw one of the layers of the abyssal hells?"

I nodded once as I took a bite of my food. It was a flaky pastry filled with raspberries. So delicious. My eyes almost fluttered closed in delight.

Nasbit didn't care that I was eating. He asked, "And is it true you were face-to-face with a Death Lord?"

Again, I nodded.

Nasbit straightened his posture and then patted his stone golem on the shoulder. "Did you hear that, Brak?" Nasbit shot me a smile. "When you're well, we'll need to talk. I have so many questions."

I half-shrugged. That was all Nasbit had needed. He didn't even ask if I was okay or if I needed anything. He just... lumbered away. Probably daydreaming about the future, when I would finally tell him all the gory details.

Phila and her coatl walked over. She handed me a flower. I

took it and placed it on the blanket in front of me. It was a lavender flower, its petals healthy.

"This is for good luck," she said with a smile. "That's what my nursemaids said. They filled my room almost every morning with these whenever I was bedridden."

"Thank you," I said. "I appreciate it."

Her coatl nodded for her, and the pair moved away.

Raaza and his kitsune hurried over. He didn't have any treats or flowers for me. He kept his hands in his pockets as he gave me a skeptical glance. "You were pretty beaten up."

"Yeah," I muttered between bites. "It happens."

"Nini said you fought one of the professors. And won."

"I did. Kinda."

Raaza slowly smiled, the scars on his face not as noticeable when he was happy. "That's impressive. You'll have to teach me a few moves sometime."

His kitsune leapt onto my mattress, the flames on her feet flashing with each step. They burned nothing, though. "We have some new tricks to show you as well."

"I look forward to it," I said after swallowing.

Raaza didn't even get a chance to leave. Knovak shoved his way close to the bed and then shooed the kitsune off the mattress. His unicorn, Starling, pranced over as well, his horn pointed high.

"Can I help you?" I asked.

Knovak straightened his pointed cap, then smoothed his school robes. He leaned in close. "Everyone has been talking about you."

"Lucky me."

"Even some of the second-years and third-years."

"It's all according to my master plan," I quipped.

Knovak narrowed his eyes into a glare. His unicorn did the same damn thing. He didn't say anything else, though. It made me wonder. Was he upset that I had gotten all this recognition? Probably. It wasn't like I had asked for it, though.

When he finally moved, Exie was the next to approach. She wore a black dress, like she was in mourning, and then walked over with a sway. Her erlking fairy fluttered around her, creating bits of illusionary stars.

"We were all forced to be here," Exie said. "Apparently, Doc Tomas knew you'd be waking up soon, and said it would be good for you to have company.

I finished the last of my pastry. "That's nice of him." I would've preferred to spend more time with Professor Helmith, but I wasn't going to mention that part. They already thought I was a strange one for having dreams with her in them.

"I don't like the infirmary." Exie fluffed some of the tight curls of her beautiful hair. "I'm not happy that we're missing class."

"I'll try not to get kidnapped in the future," I said, unable to hold back my sarcasm.

Exie didn't pick up on it. "If you could, that would be great. We have a lot of material to get through."

I wondered if she even knew why I was here.

Exie wandered off without another word. Just what I had always wanted. A casual berating.

Ashlyn was the last to see me. She and her typhoon dragon took up the most space in the room—even more than the stone golem had. The scaled dragon *almost* reminded me of the abyssal dragon.

Almost.

"Are you okay?" Ashlyn asked, giving me the once over.

I lifted the blankets and then tugged down my tunic. My heart dropped into the pit of my stomach. I had a large scar over my stomach, a bizarre black scar on my shoulder, and several small white scars around my body. Although I was only fifteen, it looked like I had served in thirty wars during that time.

My face drained of color as I lowered the blankets back into place. "I've been better," I finally managed to say.

"You really shouldn't gallivant off on your own." Ashlyn crossed her arms. "If *I* had been there, you wouldn't look like this."

Her dragon snorted and laughed at the same time.

Their playfulness did lift my spirits a little. But only a little. The many scars on my body weren't normal. Arcanists could heal, after all. That typically meant they never scarred. Had my injuries been that bad? Or just that strange?

Sorin placed a hand on my shoulder. "Don't worry. Once you feel better, you'll get right back into the swing of things. Classes. Studying. *Boat club and poetry.*"

I held back a groan.

"You joined the boat club?" Ashlyn asked, her eyebrow lifted.

"Well... I was there for a grand total of five minutes."

"If you join, I'll join as well."

I nodded as I held back a smile. "All right. I'll show you how it's done." I placed a hand on my chest. "I'm an expert, after all."

Ashlyn sarcastically glanced over at her typhoon dragon. She rubbed her chin like she was both confused and curious. "Huh. *What's this?* I'm bonded to a creature who has control of the water? You don't say!" She turned back to me with a sardonic expression, her eyes half-lidded. "I think *I'm* the expert in this arena, thank you."

I shrugged. "We'll see about that."

Before we could get into another round of one-upping each other, the far door opened. I expected to spot Doc Tomas wandering in, but instead, it was none other than Professor Helmith. The real one.

She walked with a graceful stride, her bare feet barely touching the floor. Her long flowing dress matched the blue of her robes. The glowing tattoos on her shoulders occasionally glittered in the light whenever her robes moved slightly off her collarbone.

Helmith carried my eldrin in her arms. Twain was fast asleep, curled up in a little orange ball.

When she approached the bed, Sorin stepped away, giving us plenty of space. Then he shot me a private smile. I didn't return it. What was wrong with him?

Professor Helmith placed Twain next me on the bed. "Here you are, Gray. Your eldrin is perfectly healthy. I cared for him myself."

I nodded once, my throat tight. "Thank you."

"I expect you'll be healthy in just a few short days. Just in time for my first class." She smiled as she added, "I've been looking forward to having you in my classroom. I can't wait to see all the magic you've learned while... while I've been away."

My brother—along with half my class—chuckled to themselves at the comment. I was certain my brother would joke for months about how my *honeysuckle* wanted to see me use magic, but I didn't care. All that mattered was that Helmith was safe, the nightmares were over, and I would *finally* be able to study at Astra Academy in peace.

THE END

BLOOPER SCENE

The situation was dire. Zahn had me trapped, Leon had stabbed his eldrin, and Sorin and Nini weren't fully trained arcanists. Seven, the crazed doppelgänger arcanist, seemed far too powerful to handle.

"Doppelgängers manipulate *people*," Sorin and Thurin said together as they got to their feet. "You fiends... Such a tactic is unforgivable!"

"I didn't want this." Zahn turned his glare on Seven. "If they surrender, let them live. But if they continue to fight... End this."

Seven frowned. Then she shot Zahn a glower. "*This would be easier if you hurried up.* The longer we're here, the higher the chance someone comes into the basement looking for the students."

"Foundational floors," Zahn hissed. "Not *the basement*. These are the *foundational floors*."

"Are you serious? At a time like this, you're hung up on semantics?"

Zahn's glare grew icier. "Yes. It isn't that hard, dammit. If the students can remember, then you can as well."

"Literally no one cares." Seven huffed out a laugh. "Especially not me."

"*I* care! Just call them the foundational floors."

They stared at each other, a silent chill filling the basement. Er, I mean the *foundational floors.*

Their little argument was all we needed. Leon managed to shake away Seven's control. He held up his hand and unleashed a powerful torrent of flames. It washed over Zahn, his mimic, and the doppelgänger arcanist all in one amazing blast.

"Curses!" Zahn yelled as he crumpled to the floor. "My love of technically accurate descriptions was my undoing! I never saw it coming!"

THANK YOU SO MUCH FOR READING!
Please consider leaving a review—any and all feedback is much appreciated!

Gray's story continues in Mimic Arcanist!

To find out more about Shami Stovall and Astra Academy, take a look at her website:
https://sastovallauthor.com/newsletter/

To help Shami Stovall (and see advanced chapters ahead of time) take a look at her Patreon:
https://www.patreon.com/shamistovall

Want more arcanist novels? Good news! The Frith Chronicles is where is all started! Join Volke and the Frith Guild as they travel the world.

Knightmare Arcanist (Frith Chronicles Book 1)

ABOUT THE AUTHOR

Shami Stovall is a multi-award-winning author of fantasy and science fiction. Before that, she taught history and criminal law at the college level and loved every second. When she's not reading fascinating articles and books about ancient China or the Byzantine Empire, Stovall can be found playing way too many video games, especially RPGs and tactics simulators.

Shami loves John, reading, video games, and writing about herself in the third person.

If you want to contact her, you can do so at the following locations:

Website: https://sastovallauthor.com
Email: s.adelle.s@gmail.com

 facebook.com/SAStovall
twitter.com/GameOverStation